SHORTCOMINGS

Darryl Stephens

This is a work of fiction. Names, characters, places and incidents are products of the author's imagination and are used fictitiously. Any resemblance to actual events, locales or persons, living or dead, is entirely coincidental.

SHORTCOMINGS

© 2011 by Darryl Stephens.

All Rights Reserved.

978-1-257-12799-3

Dedicated to all the parents, teachers and community leaders who have the strength and patience to inspire young people with love.

o o o

The sugar rushes up his arm, tingling like specks of electricity in his shoulder and then into his back like a wave of bright light. Just as swiftly, it slips back down, sending magic through the tips of his fingers…

He closes his eyes and fills his lungs with as much air as he can swallow...and the sick in his stomach completely disappears. His entire body is engorged with the quiet, discordant hum of rapture mingled with calm.

That voice, the one that wakes him up in a four a.m. panic, taunting him with unuttered apologies to friends he's lost and lists all the mistakes he prays to forget, whispers to him: "Savor this moment. Wallow in this quiet. Drink in the love that God is pouring down all over…"

Then another voice hisses, "Because it won't feel this good for long."

He opens his eyes and the voices go silent.

Lights from noisy Alvarado Street flash red against the wall of the tiny studio apartment, smearing the dingy, eggshell paint like a giant lipstick smudge.

The hair on the back of his neck bristles, but in a good way.

He pushes off his Adidas to wriggle his toes. It feels perfect. How does something so small make his entire body feel so right? So at ease. So easy. It's so easy…

He closes his eyes and thinks about the amazing healing properties of black tar. Black sugar. The sweet blackness. Black is beautiful. Vida is beautiful. Sweet Vida...

She'll come back. He knows she will. She loves him. And in his way, he loves her. The things she doesn't understand about him are so beautiful and complex and deep and intricate, his secrets ground up so fine and vaporous, they cover his insides like a diaphanous cape. All blues and grays with splashes of silver. No one will ever know how deeply, how profoundly and completely he has loved. He has loved without ever speaking the word. But that's all over now. Everything changed after that summer…

His head falls back in slow motion, plunging through the soft, cool air like a party balloon at dawn. The back of his skull grazes the floor, his wavy black hair standing straight out… And for a moment, he hears the ocean. He can smell the salt water...and he can feel the creamy white sun block sticky between his fingers.

Suddenly, he sees giant squids beached on the sandy dreamscape in front of him and he opens his eyes, remembers where he is and tries to shake the image of the monsters.

He reaches for a bath towel on the floor a few feet away and clutches it to his chest like a baby...

Seconds of life melt off the stained ceiling above his head and drip into a puddle of wasted minutes, coagulating around his stiff body into a sheet of deep sleep...

His right leg slides out from under him and tenses for an instant before going limp again.

His left hand floats an inch above the floor, suspended in some delicate liquid, swirling with amber-tinted memories of his best friend holding him close. If only. But it was never sexual. Never base.

He opens his eyes and sees the grimy base of the toilet bowl sliding toward him. The dingy tile glows pink reflecting the red lights from outside the window. How is any of this real…? Then another wave of bright light washes over his body. He closes his eyes again…

His heartbeat echoes in his ear and slowly grows faint like a marching band drummer wandering away in a wide open field under a clear blue sky...

Silence.

Silence.

Silence.

"Fernando! Fernando, can you hear me? Wake up!" Wobbling in her Steve Madden wooden platform mules after dragging her baby brother into the tiny shower, she twists the knob with the scraped blue letters. He opens his eyes and looks up at her calmly, hardly responding to the cold water splashing against his emaciated frame. Then, suddenly alert, he jumps up, hands sliding against the tile walls, legs kicking at the mildewed shower curtain. She grabs his track marked arm to hold him steady.

He screws his eyes shut to open them wider and finally realizes what he is seeing: his beautiful sister's swooping, jet-black hair and her full, plum-glossed lips, tensed with determination.

"Bianca? What...? What are you doing here? How did you...find me?"

"Nando, get your stuff. I'm taking you home."

PART ONE

1

o o o

Someone accidentally snapped a photo of Colin and Danny just minutes after their high school graduation. They were sitting alone under a lopsided elm tree near the quad, still in their blue caps and gowns, sweating profusely, giggling like ninnies. The woman who took the picture wasn't familiar with her daughter's new digital camera and while trying to figure out how to activate the view screen, pushed every visible button, unwittingly capturing the two boys, candid and crazed, just before pressing 'power' and turning off the contraption altogether.

Neither of the boys would later recall sitting under the tree that afternoon because they'd been so high on magic mushrooms. Colin's older brother Garrett had made a special trip down from Berkeley to deliver the shrooms for them to do at Grad Nite two weeks prior, but they'd gotten so stoned that day, weed-induced paranoia about getting arrested by Disneyland park security compelled them to skip the event altogether.

So the morning of graduation day, with Colin's parents out of town visiting his stepfather's sick mother and Danny's father 'stuck at a meeting,' they decided to get the last laugh on the school that had written them off as a joke. Colin came up with a ploy that Danny agreed was, 'like, totally fucking inspired.' They decided to pose as one another during commencement. It was Danny who concluded that the success of their ruse hinged on them exchanging their identical graduation caps. "Oh my God, *now* you look just like me!" Never mind that Danny was slim and olive-toned, with half his face hidden behind floppy skater hair...and that beefy Colin's 'high yellow' face was splattered with freckles and his curly brown hair was buzzed to a tight fade.

Danny wiggled up to Principal Dunbar like James Brown to pick up Colin's diploma and Colin tucked and rolled down the ramp at the edge of the stage, tangling Danny's diploma somewhere in the robe of the unamused girl in front of him.

Jefferson High had dismissed them as burn-outs long before they started smoking weed together behind the Math/Sciences Building in tenth grade. So not only did no one notice their stealthy switch-a-roo or that they were shrooming out of their brains during the hallowed ceremony--most people didn't notice them at all.

They both got by with grades that were barely passing. Their teachers and guidance counselors didn't see enough potential to encourage them to try harder. Their parents were too preoccupied with their own lives to care either way. Personal ambition, by way of extracurricular activities or social climbing, was completely foreign to the boys. In their minds, they'd never be so desperate to 'work that hard at being popular.' They weren't very good at anything anyway.

It's not that they were stupid, either. They just smoked too much weed to say anything intelligent in the company of other people. Socially, they were held in the same regard (or disregard) as any typical high school outcasts. They just couldn't be bothered with holding grudges or acting out against their would-be tormentors. They couldn't be bothered to do much of anything. Best friends since eighth grade, Colin and Danny had no girlfriends, no life goals and not a whole lot going for them.

While they also shared a complete lack of interest in sports, they both managed to stay in surprisingly good physical shape. Danny, like all the men in his family, was so lean and well-proportioned, he could have easily passed for an athlete--or, based on his bouncy walk, a dancer. Colin had been the scrawnier of the two, but had really bulked up by the end of junior year when he started lifting Garrett's weights in the garage. Danny chalked up the transformation to Colin's crush on Amber Dorsey, noting that when she started dating Josh Koontz, he started working out even harder. It was like he was convinced he'd eventually get big enough to demand her attention--even if it just meant kicking Josh's ass and dragging her away kicking and screaming.

The fact that they were both unemployed with no plans for college wasn't even necessarily about them being lazy. Danny had only recently lost his register job at Dairy Queen, after his manager caught him reeking of marijuana with bloodshot eyes, devouring an ice cream cake behind the store. Colin, who could never make it past the urine test of any job application, did yard work and chores around the house to earn his modest allowance. They may not have understood much, but they knew weed wasn't going to pay for itself.

Unfortunately, with no real ambition beyond *staying stoned,* they hardly noticed that most relationships and opportunities crumbled around them like kind buds into rolling papers. They were going nowhere fast and still somehow managing to take their time getting there. As that chronic haze clouded their futures and kept them oblivious to the cause of their perpetual predicaments, they remained confident that no matter what happened, they could always count on one another.

Garrett was several years older and had warned Colin and Danny long before they graduated to *ride it out* with the parents as long as they could. "The charm of being responsible for yourself wears off real fuckin' quick. Writing checks to the Department of Water and Power sucks balls." But while Colin shared all the general misgivings about paying rent and pouring quarters into laundry machines, Danny was the one feeling real pressure to step up and move out.

His father had finally remarried in May. The new wife was much younger than her husband--actually closer in age to Dan Junior than Dan Senior. During the eight months of his father's expensive courtship, Danny had always seen Maggie as *cool.* She liked his favorite band Bloc Party, she laughed with him at Andy Samberg's SNL skits and she agreed that, "Smoking an occasional joint is better than getting drunk every night." While she could have easily been making a dig at his alcoholic mother, Danny chose not to see it that way. "Maggie's just a cool chick."

But ever since his graduation, he had started to suspect that his father's already tepid affection had grown further strained by some suggestion that Danny needed to move out and 'do something with his life.' His dad may not have been considered *cool*, but he'd always seemed generally amenable to the notion that a child should just stay in his room, mind his own business and find a place when and if it was convenient. (Parents on the Mexican side of the family usually let their kids live at home until they got married.) Whether he enjoyed Danny's company or not, he understood his role as the parent was to provide food and shelter. Danny's mildly autistic fifteen year old sister Monica was more likely to eat the family out of house and home anyway.

By the end of June, the shift in Danny's relationship with his father was palpable.

One particularly hot night, *the family* was waiting for a table at El Torito. Maggie wasn't much of a cook, so on the nights they bothered to dine together, they often ended up at one of the shopping center restaurants in town. Danny had smoked too much that afternoon, but hadn't realized he was still stoned until he screamed like a girl when he backed into a waiter and knocked over a tray of margaritas.

Monica, normally huffy and sardonic, came to Danny's defense, pointing out that the waiter hadn't been watching where he was walking. But his father used the incident to launch into another lecture on 'being a man and taking responsibility,' the third or fourth speech on the topic since graduation. "It doesn't matter if he was watching where he was going, because at least he's accountable for his own livelihood." Danny was hardly able to hold back a laugh at that logic.

When the hostess interrupted Dan Senior to seat them, Danny thought he was off the hook. But when they got to the table, his father grunted, "You really need to be thinking about getting a job and finding your own place soon."

Danny turned to Maggie to interject in his defense, but she averted her eyes and got all skittish. That's when he knew: she was the one starting all the shit. From that point on, Danny hated her... *That two-faced bitch.*

He woke up every day a little more stressed about his living situation. Without even talking to his best friend about what was happening, he quieted the nagging in his brain by smoking a bowl and telling himself that he could eventually just find another job and *get that place with Colin.* He'd close his eyes and replay all the THC-charged conversations they'd had about getting out of Sylmar together. He'd sometimes even fantasize about moving into Garrett's old room. Colin's parents seemed to like him better anyway. But that was all fantasy...and the reality, that adulthood was closing in and Danny wasn't ready to face it, made it virtually impossible for him to make it through the day without getting high.

Then one Thursday afternoon, their pitiable little world cracked wide open.

Colin was mowing his parents' front lawn, shirtless in gym shorts and a fitted baseball cap. He had gone to the back to get trash bags and when he stepped out of the garage, he saw an SUV had pulled into the foot of the driveway. He didn't recognize the car, so he assumed who ever it was would just back out and continue down the street. But by the time he'd reached the lawn mower, the car still hadn't moved.

The headlights flashed and an arm reached out, beckoning him. As he approached, he noticed that the pearl white BMW X5 was immaculately detailed. He peered into the window and a red-haired guy with freckles, about thirty, was grinning back at him. Colin squinted without saying a word, skeptical that the guy was someone he didn't recognize from his mother's estranged side of the family coming around to start more shit.

"Um, hi. Do you live around here?" The guy's voice was nasal and...well, effeminate. His toothy grin seemed inappropriately familiar and he didn't even bother trying to hide that he was ogling Colin's body.

"Do I know you?" He could see the guy was gay and sizing up his naked torso and while there was no doubt he was strictly heterosexual himself, Colin tightened his abs and flexed his pecs ever so subtly. It was his automatic response to anyone showing appreciation for the one thing he had managed to accomplish.

"Oh, sorry. My name is Jeff. I was just driving by and I saw you pushing that lawn mower and I wonder if you've ever thought about a career in *modeling*..." He spoke by rote, as if reciting a script he wasn't quite comfortable with yet, and he placed an inflection on the word 'modeling' that gave it extra meaning...

Colin thought of himself as kind of cute--but he knew he wasn't *model* cute. His coarse hair was buzzed unevenly and too short and the skin along his neck was a little rough from razor bumps; he was boy-next-door meets prison-trade cute. "What kind of modeling?" Colin placed his hand on top of the side mirror so he could flex his biceps.

"Well, I have this friend who is a photographer. He lives in San Diego, actually. I sometimes do scouting for him, you know, looking for young men in really good shape. If he likes your look, you could literally make thousands of dollars for just a few hours work and I have a feeling he would like your look." The guy glanced all the way down to Colin's shorts that time.

Colin pictured himself on the cover of a men's fitness magazine...and then on television, sitting on the Solo-Flex machine, smiling at the camera, lying about how easy it was to have 'this amazing body.' He looked up at the guy, not sure he understood. "So...you mean, like fitness modeling, right?"

Jeff just grinned and reached back into the console for a business card and handed it to Colin. "My friend's name is Anderson. Give him a call if you're interested. He'll give you all the details. It's a lot of money and I think you'd be great."

Colin read the card, "Anderson Bates, Office." It had a phone number with a 619 area code. The guy smiled again and shifted the X5 into reverse. Colin nodded, 'thank you' and watched the car back out of the driveway. He slipped the card into the waistband of his shorts and stood there for a moment, thinking about Amber seeing him on the cover of Men's Fitness. Then he went inside to make himself a protein shake and smoke a bowl before he finished the yard.

A week later, Danny and Colin got really high and went to see a preview screening of "G.I. Joe: Rise Of Cobra." While they were trashing the film in the parking lot, Colin overheard Josh What's-His-Name barking at Amber from about two lanes away. He couldn't make out what they were saying, but he could see Amber shaking her head 'no' and Josh waving his scrawny arms around like an asshole.

Colin, all fired up after the testosterone-amped movie, strutted over with balled fists, ready to be a hero. Amber and Josh were getting into the car, a Mercedes CLK-Class, by the time he reached them. Amber's door was still open and the complicated convertible top was folding and stacking like a Decepticon when Colin stepped up. "Is everything all right over here?"

Amber and Josh looked up, shocked that someone else was suddenly in their conversation. Josh scoffed, " Yeah dude, move along. Nothing to see here." Amber looked away, embarrassed. Danny pulled around and waited a few cars back, prepared to jump in if something went down, but praying under his breath that nothing would. Colin cleared his throat, hoping to get Amber to turn around and see how handsome he looked coming to her defense. She never did. Josh finally hopped out of the car and noticed Danny standing outside his car twenty feet back.

"How about you get back into your boyfriend's little car and we all go back to minding our own fucking business, eh?" Josh sat back down and Amber closed her door, still not bothering to look at Colin. When they pulled out of the spot, she turned to glance back at Danny's banged up '99 Sentra. Colin could see she was laughing and shaking her head as they pulled away.

Suddenly resentful of Danny's soft eyes and slim, effeminate wrists, Colin got into the crap car and they rode home without a word.

Resolved to put that stuck-up bitch Amber out of his mind for good, he sank into the seat, relieved she hadn't seen them drive away in his own '95 Volvo station wagon. His mom had given his brother that car after she'd bought the new Lexus and Garrett had handed it down to Colin when he went away to college. That beat-up Volvo was becoming the symbol of his family's commiseration with his own unfounded complacency. Colin knew he had to make some changes in his life and that those changes involved making some money. Some *real* money...

o o o

"Hello, this is Anderson." Colin couldn't speak for a few seconds after he heard the man's voice. Something about his singsongy timbre made it impossible for Colin to deny that he knew exactly what he was getting himself into. It had nothing to do with Solo-Flex or fitness magazines. *This is some gay shit.* As sure as he was that he had absolutely no problem with gay people--didn't care if they got married and raised families or spent their whole lives fucking in bus station bathroom stalls--he couldn't get his head around the idea that he was about to take a step into the gay world himself. The voice on the other end of the phone sang out again. "Hello?"

"Hey. Um... A friend of mine...er, of *yours* gave me your card. Said you were a photographer. And..." Colin sat up in his bed, suddenly panicked, but unable to put down the phone.

"Great. Sounds like you spoke to one of my talent scouts. Do you remember who gave you my card?"

"I think...his name was...Jeff?" Colin's mouth was so dry, he hissed like leaky tire.

"Jeff. Great. And what's your name?"

Heart beat. Heart beat. Heart beat.

"Colin?"

"Hi Colin. Do you have any recent photos of yourself you could email me?" The guy's new no-nonsense, straight-down-to-business tone helped put Colin at ease. It wasn't like he was responding to a personal ad. He wasn't doing anything gay, per se. He was just looking for a job.

"Sure. Just my face? Or..." Colin's dick twitched awake...

"Well, a body shot, shirtless, and a close-up of your face would be great. If you have Skype, you could just instant message me and I can get a look at you right now. Whatever works for you." Without even thinking about it, Colin stood up and clicked on his computer. He threw the blanket over his unmade bed, straightening up for the webcam. He locked his bedroom door and pulled his shirt off over his head. He was moving like he was in a trance...until to his surprise, he felt a full-on chub in his nether regions. He froze. *What the hell is that about?*

"Are you still there? Colin? Whichever works best for you is fine." The voice was getting less singsongy and more perfunctory. Mindless reflex. It was as if the voice knew exactly what Colin was thinking, had seen this scene played out a thousand times and was already bored with the process. Colin grabbed his swelling crotch and sat down in front of the computer. He signed on to Skype.

"Yeah, I'm here. What's your screen name?"

There was a pause... "Batesboy74," and he spelled it out.

Colin typed in the screen name and hit the green 'call' button. Anderson accepted the call and Colin clicked 'video.' The webcam window popped up on the screen. Colin put down the phone, stood up and flexed his beefy arms for the camera...

"Very nice ;)" popped up in the chat window. "Ur in amazing shape."

When Colin read that, his dick throbbed at full-mast against his sweatpants. Right away, he understood that his sexual arousal was directly connected to the ego-trip of someone looking at and lusting after his body. He didn't have to be sexually attracted to--or even *see* the viewer to be turned on by the adulation. And that's how it all started...

Danny was in a wake-n-bake coma when the phone rang. It was just after eleven a.m. and he had already been up smoking for an hour and a half. He'd had another fight with his dad about 'adult responsibilities' the night before and he was hiding out in his room until everyone was out of the house. A *How I Met Your Mother* repeat was playing on mute in front of him and Vampire Weekend was blasting from his iPod dock. He squinted to read "Incoming Call: Colin." Colin always gave him shit for his 'faggy college rock' taste in music, so Danny kicked the dock plug out of the wall before he growled into the phone. "'Sup, dude?"

"What's goin' on, home skillet?" Colin was uncharacteristically upbeat.

Danny grunted something that was meant to convey boredom, but nothing intelligible made it to the other end.

"Hey, you think you could drive me down to San Diego this weekend? I got us a hotel and I can get you gas money and stuff. My piece of shit car is still making that rattling noise and I don't know if it'll make it all the way down the 5 without blowing up."

Danny got distracted by a glob of lotion in between the keys on the remote control and fell silent...

"Bro? Do you need to call me back when you're done jacking off?"

"Already took care of that. Twice." Danny considered jacking off one more time, just to really get his day started.

"So can you drive? We can get high and go to the beach and just chill and shit."

"What's in San Diego?" He figured the trip would be another hopeless pussy quest for Colin... Another trek chasing some girl who couldn't care less all the way down the coast so she could tell him to his face that he didn't have a chance in hell.

Danny had always had slightly better luck with girls in school--probably because they saw his politely oblivious demeanor as a sharp contrast to the brutish single-mindedness of other boys their age. He'd been sort of a wimpy kid, but getting picked on as a boy imbued him with humility and sensitivity that young women would later find disarming. (It probably didn't hurt that his huge hands and feet, his wiry build and his Mediterranean features also screamed 'big dick.') His preference for smoking with Colin over suffering the drone of female neediness just made him appear shy and that gentle ambivalence only proved more mysterious and appealing to women... Colin, on the other hand, had desperation written all over him. Sure, his muscles looked good in the right T-shirt, but they also gave the impression that he was overcompensating for something. Danny knew that money wasted chasing hard-to-get girls was better spent buying weed to smoke, but he was already too high to put any of those concerns into words. Then, after what seemed like too long a pause, Colin finally answered his question.

"I'm gonna... I got a job down there."

He's gonna he got a job? Something in Colin's voice made him think there was more to the story, but Danny didn't really care. He was already excited about getting out of the house and from under the judgmental gaze of his father and whore-stepmother for a while. And getting stoned and chilling on the beach sounded really nice...

2

o o o

With Danny snoring like a rusty chainsaw inside, Colin quietly closed the hotel room door. He stood holding his breath in the hallway for a moment to confirm Danny was still asleep. Once assured, he turned and walked briskly down the hall to meet his ride in the lobby.

His heart was beating so fast in the elevator, he seriously considered stopping on one of the lower floors and running back up to the room. *Fuck it, we'll just drive back!* But Anderson had already paid for the room. Did Colin have some legal obligation to at least show up to the studio? Was sleeping in a hotel room legally binding?

Even though he felt terrible when he'd twice lied to Danny that it was a fitness modeling job, he was more convinced than ever that his body was *his body* and he could do whatever the fuck he wanted with it. The problem was that he was better at telling himself he had 'the right to choose' than he was at convincing himself that it was a choice he wanted to make.

He stepped out of the elevator foyer into the main lobby and a skinny Asian dude with Zac Efron bangs stood up from an oversized armchair to greet him. He introduced himself as Sky and extended a limp, cool hand to shake. Colin took for granted the guy was gay...but when Sky wasn't especially friendly and hardly seemed to notice Colin's body at all, he considered the possibility that maybe he wasn't.

Colin always got nervous around girls, but he'd learned to feel more confidence around men through his body building. He believed that most guys coveted his physique, so any time he was feeling insecure, he would make his muscles impossible to ignore. Every jock who asked him how much he benched and every gay dude who slowed down in his car to check him out helped affirm his worth. When Sky didn't give any indication that he was impressed with his body--already fit to be consumed in a black 2(x)ist tank-top--or his freshly shaven baby face, Colin was at a loss. He puffed up his chest and widened his gait, because sometimes slowing his walk helped people notice how thick his thighs were...

As they headed out of the lobby toward the street, Sky waved goodbye to the dude behind the front desk, who then nodded at Colin. Just to be safe, Colin left enough distance between them so that anybody paying attention wouldn't necessarily assume they were together. He wasn't being homophobic; just professionally discreet. Noting the bright turquoise Calvin Klein briefs peeking out from under Sky's sagging Abercrombie cargo shorts, Colin decided to stick with his first assumption. He was obviously gay and just uncomfortable around Colin's far superior physique. Or maybe he wasn't into black guys. Not even black guys who sometimes passed for white.

On the way to the studio, Sky absentmindedly skipped through songs on his iPod shuffle, eventually settling on a Mariah Carey dance remix. Colin barely repressed a snort. Sky skipped to the next track: that SugarTank song that Danny liked, but this version had disco strings and horns--*so gay*. He skipped again to the Dave Holdredge remix of Big Pun's "Still Not a Player." Colin was almost impressed, bobbing his head to the hard rock hip-hop beat...until he realized, hearing it in that context, that there was something kind of gay about that song too. He made a mental note to review all the songs on his own iPod for possible gay subtext when he got back to Sylmar.

The studio turned out to be a huge, one-story, mid-century house with a roundabout driveway and geometrically shaped hedges. The pearl white X5 was parked next to a black Range Rover. Sky seemed to warm up by the time they got inside, finally making eye-contact and small talk as they walked past the huge living room, through the Crate & Barrel catalog-inspired dining room into the immaculate kitchen.

Sky twisted open a bottle of Smart Water and placed it on the kitchen island countertop right next to an open manila folder with contracts, model releases and tax forms, each showing Colin's full name typed in all-caps. He asked for Colin's drivers license to photocopy, handed him a pen and told him to take his time filling out the papers. Then he was gone.

Colin skimmed through the pages and pages of unintelligible legalese. After reading the words "hereby release all rights" in three different places, he closed the envelope to think for a moment. *Is this really about to happen?*

He sipped his Smart Water and glanced out the window above the sink, noticing a guy in khakis holding a camera over by the pool. He was facing a guy who was lying naked on a chaise lounge. The naked guy had black hair and dark Latin features, but he seemed too scrawny to do porn. Colin walked over to the sink to get a better look and he saw the guy's selling point. His erection was the size of a rolling pin.

Colin had seen his fair share of straight porn and had obviously seen dicks larger than his own--which, for the record, was comfortably above average. But seeing such an inordinately long and thick one--and seeing its magnitude from that distance, suddenly made him feel deficient in a way he hadn't anticipated. He'd never been in a situation where other guys' erections would be directly compared to his own. Someone cleared his throat right behind him and Colin whipped around, busted.

Sky stood there smirking and holding a bagel smeared with cream cheese, his pinky finger extended, cementing for Colin which team the kid played for. "That's Anderson. And I think that model is going by 'Escobar,' although I'm not sure we're going to use that name for the site. Sounds a little sinister. Have you thought of what you want your name to be? He told you models don't use their real names, right? Makes it a little harder for people to Google you..." Colin just shook his head no, noticing the food spread--fruit, pastries, yogurt, juice--on the table in the breakfast nook behind Sky.

He continued, "You can really think of it as, you know, like, playing a character, which adds to the whole fantasy element of it for the audience." The word 'audience' made Colin's dick twitch.

Sky opened the manila envelope on the counter, noting that nothing except the Social Security Number had been filled in, and he paperclipped the drivers license to the top of the papers. He looked up at Colin, whose hands were braced against the sink behind him, shamelessly flexing his triceps with nervous, shifty eyes. "Anyway, you should fill all this out ASAP. I'll be in the office if you have any questions." Without a smile or a nod, he disappeared down the hallway.

Colin walked back over to the envelope and signed his name on all the blank lines. He put his license back in his wallet and turned to the table with the food. He picked up a banana, thinking he could use the potassium for energy. When he realized his stomach was too tight with nerves to eat, he put the banana back and settled for a glass of orange juice instead.

He glanced toward the hallway as he stepped quietly back over to the window to see what was going on outside. The flashing had stopped. He didn't see any sign of Anderson or Escobar. He stood on his toes, stretching his neck to see back past the pool, toward the lawn and the hillside littered with cactus plants at the edge of the yard. Nothing. When he heard a patio door slide open and shut in the dining room, he knew right away that neither of the approaching voices belonged to Sky.

Anderson walked in first. He was probably forty, brownish hair, with a slight sunburn on his alabaster cheeks and an open, midwestern smile that held a mouth full of perfect teeth. He was holding the huge camera that he carefully placed on the island before he spoke. "Colin! Welcome to San Diego. I'm Anderson." He walked over and shook Colin's hand firmly, smiling right into his eyes. He excused himself and quickly disappeared with the camera in the direction of the office. Watching him walk away, Colin's first thought was that, in person, he would never have assumed Anderson was gay. He wasn't particularly good-looking or well-put together. He wasn't effeminate or hyper-masculine. He looked like a young dad or an accountant.

Then Escobar strolled in looking over his shoulder at Anderson in the hallway. He was Colin's height, lanky, wearing just a pair of floral board shorts, his skin slick with something oily, his wavy black hair greased back. "I'm starvin', yo. Did homeboy make waffles today? Last time y'all had blueberry waffles." He turned and glanced up at Colin looking back at him, uptight. "Ay, wassup dawg?" His smile sparkled with a charisma that read as ominous from where Colin was standing...

"Hey, man. Colin." He felt his pecs tighten and his neck get thick as he reached for Escobar's hand to shake. Colin immediately recognized the self-assured swagger that had always put him on edge with the 'cool kids' at school. Their relaxed nature always felt like a direct affront to his ever-shrinking sense of self. It was one of the reasons he smoked so much weed and worked out so hard. He hated feeling small. He hated feeling anything...

The model's grip was firm. "Nando." Colin watched him saunter like a panther back towards the table and snatch up a couple of fat strawberries. He turned back around with red juice running down his chin and said, "So this must be your first time, huh?"

Colin shrugged, *I guess so*.

Nando leaned up against the countertop, resting on his elbows, biting greedily into his strawberry and watching Colin from across the island. "Relax, man. It's just jacking off. Ain't nothin' different from what you be doin' everyday anyway, right? Just watch the porno and ignore ol' boy with the camera."

Colin, clearly unnerved, nodded as if to say, *good thinking*. Then, fearing his silence might read as weakness, he grunted, "Right." When his voice fell flat, he realized silence might have been the stronger choice.

Nando strolled right over to the sink where he was standing and Colin, mistaking Nando's advance for some macho challenge, stood his ground at the sink, the throbbing veins in his neck the only indication of his defensiveness. Nando slid behind him, oblivious, turned on the faucet and rinsed the strawberry juice off his fingers. When Colin realized he wasn't being tested, he stepped out of the way.

Nando finished washing his hands and wiped the water on his shorts. "Damn, son, you be hittin' them weights pretty hard, huh? All cock-diesel for the ladies... Lookin' like the Barnum and Bailey strongman and shit." With a mischievous glint in his eye, Nando picked up Colin's bottle of Smart Water and drank it down.

Slightly more at ease after Nando's recognition of his physical superiority, Colin forced a chuckle and strutted over to the table to grab the banana. *Cock-diesel for the ladies*. On one hand, he was relieved that his heterosexuality was so apparent. On the other hand, he found it ironic that two straight guys were affirming their sexual appeal to women in a conversation that was only taking place because they were both performing sex acts for men. And in Colin's case, the ladies couldn't be *less* interested. He wondered if Nando shared in his misfortune with the delicate sex and was overcompensating for both of them, or if he actually imagined Colin to be a ladies' man. He glanced down at the banana and flashed an image of Nando's rolling pin by the pool... Then Anderson walked back in.

He whinnied and nodded at the very large banana in Colin's hand and said, "Looks like you're eager to get started. Shall we get to work?"

Colin's mouth went dry. He looked over at the empty bottle of Smart Water and Nando winked back at him encouragingly. His stomach tight with nerves again, Colin put the banana back down and followed Anderson into the long hallway.

As he watched his sneakers move in slow motion across the plush beige carpet, he heard Nando chuckle from the sink, "Do that shit, Bailey!"

o o o

Danny leaned with his arm extended to brace himself against the wall above the tank and aimed his erection down toward the toilet bowl. When he was finally able to release the stream, a fart slipped out with a blissful sigh. He'd been holding his bladder for a few hours, drifting in and out of sleep, putting off getting out of bed to pee for as long as he could. He was always too anxious in his father's house to sleep-in, so he was intent on taking advantage of being away from home. He finished pissing, stepped out of his tighty-whities and into the glass-encased shower.

The soft water from the huge golden shower-head cascaded onto his face like a rippling sheet of hot wax. His erection was still standing straight out in front of him and when he wiped the water from his eyes, it was all he could see. The pink tip peeking out from under the smooth sheath of cocoa foreskin was practically winking at him, whispering his name. He squirted the tiny bottle of orange ginger shower gel into his hand, grabbed his meat and lathered himself up. He started off slow and steady, just warming up. He pictured painted pouty lips lapping at his cock. He tightened his grip and intensified his stroke. For an instant, he confronted the question that taunted him everyday, at least twice a day... "Am I addicted to my own dick?" But that fleeting disquiet eventually trickled down his leg along with a trail of suds and disappeared into the drain...and that twinge of shame completely dissipated when he finally shuddered and shot his creamy euphoric vindication onto the golden faucet knob in front of him.

Clean. Refreshed. Ready to face another day.

He dried off, pulled on some shorts and smoked a bowl in the dark with the TV blaring a *Making the Band* marathon. With all the curtains closed, he talked out loud to himself about how all the girls in the band reminded him of the skanky Jefferson High cheerleaders with their excessive make-up and fake hair and all the guys in the band looked like the thugs he used to buy weed from two blocks from campus. He considered that there was something inherently racist about the way MTV was pimping these (mostly colored) kids, showcasing their supposed talent, but then allowing them to look like gutter trash at the same time. For a second he worried that maybe he was just seeing it all through his own racist gaze. Could a half Mexican-American, half Italian-American with a half African-American, half Irish-American best friend even be a racist? That white girl was just as slutty looking as that black girl, but the Latin looking girl wasn't quite as trashy. *Oh my God! Am I a racist?*

There was a machine gun-like rap at the door. He yelped and jumped up, running in circles between the two beds, waving his arms around to hide the smoke, trying to figure out where to stash the pipe. Finally, he heard the woman's thick accent repeat, "Housekeeping?"

Oh. *Housekeeping.*

"NO! No thanks. Not right now?" He stood frozen, listening for her cart to get pulled down the hall. Then he scurried into the bathroom, locking the door behind him and finished off the bowl sitting on the toilet, with the TV still blaring from the other room.

o o o

It was almost two o'clock when Colin snuck back into the pitch black room. In the swath of light beaming through the doorframe from the hall, he could see Danny passed out on the far bed, surrounded by candy wrappers and empty Sun Chips bags. He wasn't snoring, but he appeared to be sound asleep. Colin quietly closed the door behind him and made his way to the bathroom in the dark.

He ran the shower so hot that steam clouded his reflection in the mirror above the sink, but he still faced the shower wall the whole time. He wasn't ready to see himself yet. Wasn't ready to process whatever had just broken inside him and see it reflected back in his tired brown eyes. He didn't even mind that the water almost scalded his skin...

Somehow, he had been less freaked out about the job while it was happening. Once he'd taken off his clothes, the ego trip of it all had helped relax his nerves, simplifying the task at hand. On the ride back from the studio, however, the depth of his transgression really hit him. Sky had gone back to being cold and distant and his music selection was so banal it didn't serve as anything but a bland backdrop to Colin's own racing thoughts.

The ways this could come back to bite him in the ass were suddenly all too clear. Where before, being found out seemed a distant possibility, obscured by the unlikelihood of the required random coincidences all playing out just so, his brain was suddenly flooded with very simple scenarios that made disclosure obvious and imminent.

For example, his brother Garrett's best friend in high school went away to college and came out as gay. What if they both happened to be in Sylmar for the holidays, got to talking and Kevin mentioned to Garrett that he had come across someone who looked just like his little brother jacking off on a gay porn site?

What if some gay guy in his mother's office recognized him from the family photo she had framed on her desk? "Your younger son looks just like..."

What if in two years he was on a date with the girl he planned to marry (*no, not that Amber Dorsey bitch*) and some gay waiter wasn't satisfied with his tip?

What if Danny, who watched more porn than anyone, was on Fucktube and Colin's gay video got mixed in with the straight videos? What would he think? Of course, Fucktube was cluttered with videos of guys jacking off for free in their own bedrooms. Would Danny really fault him for making a hefty wad of money doing something that most saps did for free?

Gradually, all the 'what ifs' piled up into a steaming heap of, 'who cares?' He wasn't the first man to jack off for a porn site...and the Earth was still turning. He exhaled sharply and tried to let it go. *What's done is done. Life goes on.*

He turned off the shower and was surprised to hear Danny's voice coming from inside the bathroom. He pushed opened the glass door and found him facing the toilet, in the middle of a long piss and a story about someone calling the room and asking for Bailey.

"...said he met someone named Bailey at 'the house.' But then the guy he described was definitely you. Anyway, he's in room 416. He tried to get moved into 420, but the front desk guy didn't smoke herb so he couldn't authorize moving him into a room with two beds or something. I figured he was probably more stoned than me, cuz dude would not shut up."

Danny flushed the toilet and turned around to find Colin naked and dripping wet, staring back at him. He realized it had been a long time since he'd really looked at Colin's body. He was built like a superhero with muscles in places Danny had never even noticed on his own body. Colin's skin was all pink from the hot water and steam was emanating from his beefy shoulders. His rock-hard stomach was indented with what looked like an eight-pack and all his pubic hair was shaved off. Danny didn't look directly at the penis, but he could see in the periphery that it was circumcised and that it wasn't as small as he'd always expected, given how much time he spent working out. *His biological father didn't let him down after all.*

"Could you hand me a towel?" Colin's face was stiff with an almost sad resignation. Danny considered asking if everything was all right, but then figured he was probably just stoned. He turned around to the rack of fresh white towels to the left of the toilet, grabbed the last big one and handed it to Colin, noticing the floor was covered with wet towels. Colin grunted, "Thanks," as Danny stepped past him into the main room without closing the door behind him.

Colin dried himself off right in front of the open door and Danny, for the first time, suffered the odd sense of fighting the urge to look. They were best friends and there was obviously nothing sexual between them, but Danny was strangely fascinated by the splendor of Colin's new body. He imagined creating a physique like that for himself. *If Colin can do it...* He glanced back and let his eyes drift down to Colin's meaty ass and thighs, the paler skin there accentuating the bulging curves. It wasn't until he felt that stirring in his stomach, that tingle in his groin that always preceded the surge of meatiness to his member, that Danny clicked on the television and flopped over onto his stomach to watch a rerun of *Battlestar* on Sci-Fi with his head at the foot of his bed.

Suddenly uneasy, Danny recalled being a little boy and *having a thing* for Korben Dallas--Bruce Willis' character in *The Fifth Element*...and even more so for Will Smith's character in *Independence Day*. They were both so macho and debonair with their big guns and their sleeveless shirts. They felt like crushes, but he was only six or seven years old at the time. Sexuality was hardly a consideration then and he'd always chalked up his infatuation to hero worship. *But what if it was something else...?*

Without looking back in the direction of the bathroom, Danny yelled out, "Anyway, that dude invited us to go with him to some strip club tonight. Said, 'After today, you'd probably need it.' Oh yeah, I need to see if your charger fits my phone. I forgot mine at home."

Colin pushed the door closed with an exhausted sigh, suddenly annoyed with the sound of Danny's voice. He wiped the mirror clean with one of the wet towels off the floor, stood there with his hands braced against the sink and looked closely at his face. It looked like the same face. Same flat, freckled nose. Same full, chapped pink lips. Same cleft in his chin from his mother's side. Same deep-set brown eyes. But something inside was changed forever...

o o o

Danny's tolerance for THC had gotten so high by that summer that Colin would have passed out before matching him puff for puff, but Colin was still more likely to be clocked as a pot-head in public. He either got goofy and loud or skittish and emotional...and as his physical form continued to expand, he became increasingly hard to ignore, if only for his size. Danny normally managed to stay even-keeled and easy-going and only too happy to use the weed to assist in embracing his own invisibility.

That night in the hotel, however, Danny was in rare form. Perhaps being out of his father's house had provided some emotional release which caused his body to process the drug at an accelerated rate. His mind was so disconnected from his body, Colin had to hold out the sleeve and wait for him to figure out how to get his arm into his button-down shirt. (Considering they'd packed expecting to spend the whole weekend on the beach, it was dumb luck that Danny even had that shirt in his bag, as they wouldn't have been allowed into the strip club wearing T-shirts.)

Colin had resolved to tell him the truth about his fitness modeling before Nando got there, just so he didn't have to worry about something slipping in conversation at the club. But as he and Danny sat quietly on their respective beds, already dressed for the evening, puffing on the last of the weed and getting wrapped up in a really good episode of *Friday Night Lights,* he was having trouble finding the right time to bring it up. It seemed like it should have been such a small thing...

He knew Danny totally had his back. It wasn't like he expected him to get angry. The whole situation just felt like it was in direct conflict with the way they saw themselves. They had always been the outcasts, the loners, uncool but too cool to care--*together*. They stayed sane all those years of being invisible because they could always see one another. Would their shared view from the outside suddenly be fractured by Colin's new job? He had stepped outside their universe into something that was totally foreign to everything that was *them*. What if they were never able to go back? What if he lost his best friend?

Without even looking over at him, Colin could hear Danny getting choked up, breathing deep to fight back tears about something Matt Saracen's grandmother had just said on *FNL*. Maybe Danny was too fragile for all this. Maybe they should just go home, find an apartment in Sherman Oaks and get jobs they wouldn't have to lie about. Instead of using the money as a down payment on another shitty car, he could move the two of them out of Sylmar.

Or maybe...maybe he could do one more job. Anderson had assured him he wouldn't have to do anything but sit back, watch a porno and let someone *take care of him*. Blow job, hand job, side-by-side jack off, whatever. Maybe he could do a couple more jobs. Get the car *and* the new place. There was no turning back at that point anyway. Any further work would involve another dude, but he knew he was straight; nothing was going to change that. Why not make as much money as he could while he was at his physical peak and then really get on with his life?

Danny quietly unrolled one of his shirtsleeves to dab at the tears on his face and Colin knew he couldn't keep lying to his friend. It was better for him to tell the truth a few hours after the fact than to have him find out from someone else. His teeth chattered as he started putting together the words...and just as he went to open his mouth, there was a knock at the door. *Fuck!*

The knock was so elaborate, it sounded like a secret code. Danny popped up and disappeared into the bathroom. Colin lumbered over and opened the door to find Nando reeking of Diddy's Unforgivable cologne, his wavy hair fluffed out and feral and his fuzzy chest exposed and dripping with gold and crucifixes. Nando threw up his hand for the hood handshake with the bro-hug and the double back pat. ""S'crackin' Bailey? Looks like you got through today all right."

"Hey, dude." Half way out of the hug, Colin whispered, "I haven't told my homie the whole story about that job, so do me a favor and..." Nando cut him short with nod and a wink, already ahead of him.

"No sweat, son. Y'all finished off the trees?" Nando, his nose wide open, eyed the ashy upturned pipe on the nightstand and pimp strolled across the room, bobbing his head, putting on a real 'ghetto show.' He sat down at the small table in the corner of the room, clicked on the lamp and pulled a small plastic bag out of his pocket.

Danny bounced out of the bathroom, his hair damp and freshly combed, and saw Nando fingering something on the table. "Hey man, how's it going? I'm Danny." He walked across the room, very stoned, with his hand extended. Nando smiled and stood up to shake his hand, but did so in a way that made Danny feel like an asshole for being so formal. Danny zeroed in on the pills and the baggie. "Whatcha got there?" His voice cracked. Something about Nando's slick demeanor made him feel like such a square...like just another white guy trying to look hip next to the cool-breeze Latin dude.

Nando looked up at Danny, stiff in his wrinkled shirt, and back at Colin, practically paralyzed with dread. He shook his head, "Well, the club we're going to doesn't serve alcohol, cuz the girls are butt-naked. So I came prepared to keep the night interesting. I mean, even in a strip club you wanna be a *little* twisted, right?" His eyes blazed with some manic exhilaration that other two didn't even notice...

"Twisted?" Every time Danny spoke, he bristled at the sound of his father's judgment seeping out of his own mouth. "What is it? Cuz, I mean, we already smoked some herb." Even 'herb' sounded panicked and hysterical.

"Calm down, son. It's just ecstasy." Nando pulled a small jar of Lip Medix out of his pocket and slathered it on his lips while he continued. "You don't have to take it. I was just tryin' to be a gracious host. Y'all got any water up in here?"

Colin picked up a bottle of water and walked over to Nando. He knew how wary Danny was of synthetic drugs. The two of them were strict pot smokers who occasionally did shrooms, but never anything harder than that. Thanks to Danny's drunk mother, they rarely even touched alcohol. But that night, with his secret looming and the unpredictable new addition to the duo, Colin felt he needed to be a little out of his mind. He held out his hand and Nando picked up a pill and dropped it into his palm. Colin looked back at Danny, whose eyes were wide with incredulity, popped the pill into his mouth and took a swig from the water bottle.

Nando popped his pill, tossed back most of what remained of the water and then looked to Danny. "If you ain't gonna do yours, me and Bailey could split it later."

Danny turned to Colin, his eyes demanding, *Who is this guy and what is this Bailey shit?* He turned back to Nando. "If I take mine, who's gonna drive us to and from the club?"

Nando smiled, wistful. Danny's cautious concern had conjured memories of his childhood best friend, Paul. They had drifted in the last couple years and things had gotten kind of weird between them after Paul went to college... But Paul had always been the responsible one. Nando realized how much he missed having someone around who actually bothered with the details. "The club is like six blocks from here. We walkin'."

His jaw tight with skepticism, Danny glanced back at Colin, whose eyes were already sparkling with energy he didn't recognize. Danny popped the last pill into his mouth, drank the rest of the water and tossed the empty bottle in the corner behind the table, like he was the cool-breeze in the room. "Fuck it then, let's go!"

3

o o o

Colin grumbled about how badly he needed to pee for the whole forty-five minute walk. 'Six blocks' turned out to be more like twenty-six after Nando decided to cut through a park, got turned around and had them wandering through a fog of cologne and sleeveless shirts in some part of town called Hillcrest. When Colin tried to stroll into a crowded bar called Rich's to pee, the doorman--humorless with a 70s porno mustache--called him "Sweetie" and asked to see some ID. Colin's face was beet red when he insisted through gritted teeth that he'd "just pee at the titty bar..."

The Dollhouse looked like a tweaked-out toy store from the outside; all neon pink lights with gaudy yellow and turquoise pillars and stair rails. But inside, it was dark and sinister with blood red lampshades, cracked black pleather upholstery and a carpet so dingy and stained with DNA, you could practically hear the stifled cries of unborn babies with every step toward the mirrored stage.

Once they each managed to come up with the ten dollars required for admission, Colin disappeared to the bathroom. Nando, still steeped in his city-boy swagger, threw an arm around Danny's shoulder and started yelling over the booty music about his first time in a strip club. The story had something to do with looking for his sister, who was working there or used to work there or wanted to work there. Then something about lesbians, broken Lucite heels and zebra print thongs. Danny was having a hard time focusing on the details because his ecstasy was kicking in and Nando's breath was tickling his ear.

He'd had a vague idea of what to expect, but nothing he'd heard about an ecstasy high had prepared him for the rush of sexual energy suddenly zipping through every nerve in his body. He leaned his head to the right, hoping Nando's lips might graze his cheek, not once considering that he was seeking physical contact from another man for what was essentially a sexual sensation. He didn't even realize how tightly his arm was wrapped around Nando's narrow waist until they got to the bar and Nando had to untangle himself to pay for the three bottles of water...

Colin was standing at the urinal, uncooperative instrument in hand, trying to catch his breath for what felt like days. No matter how much air he would try to take in, the invisible weight on his chest and the tingling around his neck had him convinced he couldn't get enough oxygen...and his preoccupation with breathing made it impossible for his body to relax enough to pee. The pressure, closing in from all sides like giant pillows, was really the drug exacerbating his anxiety about being discovered. He was more emotionally dependent than his strongman body knew how to support. He had to tell Danny the truth or risk suffocating from the lie.

Two overweight frat boys with bad skin in white ball caps, probably drunk from a previous location, were waving dollar bills in the air and barking at one of the girls from the edge of the stage. Her breasts protruded so rigidly off her frail chest that they looked more like upside down cereal bowls than anything that could occur naturally on a human body. But her ass was round and smooth and she moved with a slow, seductive grace.

Danny and Nando slid up near enough to the stage to get a good look at her, but far away enough to avoid feeling any direct pressure to hand her money. When he noticed Nando's eyes fixed on the girl's firm ass and smooth snatch, Danny glanced up at her face. Even though her over-wrought makeup effectively shaped her undeniably average face into a sexy pout, her expression was completely deadpan. There was a vacancy, a hardness in her eyes that immediately struck Danny as depressing. She never made eye contact with any of the men around the stage, keeping her eyes fixed just above their heads.

Danny looked around the dark room and noticed, with each flash of pink light from the stage, how pathetic the men looked. Each set of soulless eyes glued to her hairless vagina reaffirmed the sad state of humanity that would allow such a place to exist. The hours and hours of porn he'd watched hadn't prepared him for the dismal reality of an up-close human being stuck in that world. Like the gross old men in that room, he too had wasted days focused on sex organs, never bothering to consider the personal pain that had brought those women to that place. How had none of this occurred to him before?

In an instant, his ecstasy swept back up, crashing against his body like a wave. He stopped paying attention to the dingy room and the sad girl and the cruel world. He was suddenly standing in a warm beam of golden light and a swarm of soft lips were planting kisses all over his body with swirling hot tongues... His fingers were tingling and he was oozing electric orgasms from every pore. A gush of cool air from a ceiling vent tickled the tiny hairs on the back of his neck and he let his head drop, his chin to his chest, to soak in the sensation.

Brrrrrrrrrrrrrrrrrrrrrrrrrrrr...

He'd been standing there longer than he realized, because when he finally lifted his head and opened his eyes again, he was facing away from the stage and Colin was standing a few feet to his left. Nando was nowhere in sight.

Colin's eyes were fixed on the stage, but Danny sensed that his *energy* was actually directed at him. There was a stoniness about his gaze that made his whole face seem tight and withdrawn. Danny walked over and handed him a water bottle.

"Here. Nando said we need to stay hydrated." Colin took the bottle and sipped it without speaking or looking at Danny. *Is he mad at me?* Danny thought back to the weird moment in the bathroom. Had Colin sensed Danny noticing his body? Was he mad at him for allowing his mind to wander into vaguely bisexual scenarios? Nothing had changed. He was still Danny. It was a fleeting moment of curiosity that never needed to be mentioned or acknowledged at all. Danny was just as surprised by it as anybody--

Then another wave of synthetic titillation washed up into his chest and fluttered against his lungs like sparkling hummingbird wings. Danny slowly turned back to the stage, his entire body tight with chemically charged sexual urgency.

The skinny white girl at the edge of the stage had transformed into a slinky bombshell with milk chocolate skin. She had full, natural tits and a firm ass that was round like an upside down Valentine's Day heart. Her face was vaguely masculine, but maybe her makeup was just contoured liked a drag queen's. She had long wavy hair and she moved with a nubile ferocity that accelerated Danny's breathing. He wanted to kiss her...

A fat man with a greasy comb-over was staring at him from a stool about ten feet to the right of the stage. At first Danny thought maybe the guy was an undercover security guard, scoping the room, trying to weed out all the illicit drug-users mixed in with the perverts. But then the guy snarled his lip and nodded at him in a way that seemed oddly furtive. *Does this fat dude think he's flirting?* Danny fixed his mouth to spit on the ground (a trick he'd learned watching older kids in his neighborhood: *if another dude is checking you out too hard, spit on the ground in his direction*) but then he remembered he was indoors and that the carpet was already dirty enough. He just shook his head...*so not interested.*

He glanced back at the stage and saw Nando yelling up at the chocolate girl from the spot where the frat boys had been. His shirt was unbuttoned and Danny could see his bony ribs every time he lifted his hand to wave money at her. He was much skinnier than Danny had imagined--but then he remembered holding him around his waist and how there was something almost feminine about how slim Nando's waist felt next to his.

Suddenly, a sensory overload, complete with the sound and feel of static electricity, curled Danny's lips into a euphoric smile and his upper teeth rubbed against his lower teeth like they were all horny for each other. His eye lids flickered with jolts of jubilation as he stumbled backwards and his whole brain went fuzzy, overcharged with the escalating pulse of synthetic pleasure flooding his synapses.

Colin grabbed his arm just before Danny landed on the floor. He lifted him to his feet and walked him over to a booth toward the back of the room. Colin was beginning to feel his ecstasy too, and it was feeling good, but it wasn't hitting him like Danny's. The way he was grinning with his eyes closed had Colin worried that maybe Danny was overdosing.

He placed his hand on the side of Danny's face to pull open his eye with his thumb and check his pupils. All he could see in the dark was that his eyes were fluttering and rolling backwards. Then his hand floated up and landed on top of Colin's against his face. Colin relaxed his thumb and Danny's eyes slowly opened to look up at him. He smiled and asked, "Why are we touching my face?"

"I was checking your eyes! I thought you were dying." Colin slid his hand out from under Danny's while Danny continued to caress his own face. Colin's eyes glistened with genuine alarm. "Are you okay?"

Danny sat up quickly, eager to make sure he wasn't dead, and he laughed, "I'm great. Are you okay?" Colin's heart surged with a brotherly love that made it hard for him to speak. The two of them just sat wide-eyed, facing one another in the booth.

Nando appeared like a ghost, standing between their booth and the stage... "Damn, Bailey. You takin' your work home witchu, son?" The slip flashed like a traffic camera across his face before he continued. "Lap dances are mad expensive here. I'm a go out back and talk to that girl Cristål for a minute while she's on her smoke break. She's tryin' to party tonight, so I'll prolly' just get into that. If you guys leave, text me and I'll hit y'all up tomorrow. Cool?"

Colin nodded brusquely. Nando smiled with wild eyes, twisted his body around in a vaguely Fosse-like jazz twirl...and pimp-strolled away to the beat of Kanye's "Love Lockdown," pumping from the stage.

A scantily clad waitress with plumped lips slithered up to the booth. "Drinks?"

Colin turned back to Danny. "I'm not really feelin' it here. Think I might head back to the hotel. What do you wanna do?" The waitress rolled her eyes and wandered off.

Danny was facing the stage with googly eyes, his hair damp with sweat and slick against his forehead, when his lips puckered to blow out a stream of cool air... When he turned to face Colin, his entire expression shifted to an eery calm. "I think I wanna talk about what we're really doing in San Diego. Bailey."

o o o

Their walk back to the hotel was completely silent. Danny was still swimming in his ecstasy and working hard to not be overcome by the flood of physical sensations. His gait was clipped with a concentrated focus that betrayed his fear of ending up writhing naked in the grass if he didn't keep his mind on his stride and his destination. Holding it together required all of his focus so he moved with a pinched determination. He looked like he was rushing to get to a toilet...

Colin's ecstasy was taking him on a far more cerebral journey now that they were outside. Every mental image was tinged with glimmering whooshes of fantastical excess. Like a waking dream... He pictured Danny's delicate features, sparkling gold with tiny jewels under a bright white beam of light, smiling and nodding with an understanding that was borne of years of mutual trust and love. They were closer than best friends--more like brothers. They'd have a long, loud, echoey laugh about Colin's little video transgression and then thunderous applause would peal out from a million faceless audience members cheering on the impenetrable strength of their brotherly bond from somewhere outside their hotel room window...

Already relieved about things going back to normal, Colin exhaled and ran his hand up and down the back of his head, imagining the velvety swirl he was creating was helping his mind stay focused. Focused on what? He had no idea...

Before he'd even conjured the presence of mind to wonder if they knew the way back, Colin heard the hiss of sliding doors and looked up to find the back of Danny's wrinkled button-down shirt glowing in the bright light of the hotel lobby. Watching his shoes trod along the yellowish marble walkway lined with gold trim and dark red carpet on the left, he glanced to the right to see a horrified desk clerk looking back at him...and realized his feet were still moving. But turning his head had made walking suddenly seem far more complicated than it had been before; a virtually unmanageable task. Was he really responsible for choreographing the entire movement of every step he took? What would happen if he was in charge of all the details required of breathing...or digesting food? Could he manage all of it on his own?

The elevator door opened with a ding and mysteriously, his feet carried him inside. *Who's doing that?* There must have been tiny technicians in his brain manning all the inner workings of his body...like Oompa Loompas tending to every function of the Chocolate Factory.

The doors closed and the elevator jerked awake. He looked over at Danny, who was gripping tightly onto the gold rail on the back wall and staring up at the small screen listing the ascending floor numbers with an expression that could have easily been mistaken for terror. If a photo had been snapped in that instant, one might assume the elevator had been plummeting to the ground floor and that Danny was falling to his death. But in the next instant, his face had shifted to a childlike smile. He turned to Colin, shook his head in slow motion and mouthed without sound, "This is fucking bananas," as he stumbled forward with his arms spread wide for a hug. Then the door dinged open and he fell right past Colin out into the hall. The door had started to close when Colin remembered it was his responsibility to move his feet out of the elevator. The technicians must have been getting sleepy...

Colin watched the carpet pattern carefully as he walked, expecting it to flit and swirl around his feet like it would have if he'd been on mushrooms, but it didn't move at all. The carpet must have been getting sleepy too. He looked up at Danny floating clumsily with his arms extended like Jesus, his fingers brushing against the wall on the left side of the hall. They got to room 707 and Colin stood staring at the door handle, confused.

Danny reached into his wallet, pulled out the keycard and swiped the door unlocked. He gently pushed open the door and then waited for Colin to walk in. That moment perfectly exemplified their roles and their relationship dynamic: Danny, the polite pragmatist and Colin, the modest, if somewhat cavalier frontman. At least, that's how Colin saw it at the time...

The room was a lemon meringue-colored disaster. Scattered clothes and empty food wrappers on every surface made it look like the two beds had been ransacked by a sounder of wild boar. Danny slid gracefully out of his shirt and started carefully picking clothes up off the floor, maybe straightening up, maybe looking for something more comfortable to wear.

Colin slipped into the bathroom. Had he ever peed back at the club? He couldn't remember... He stood in front of the toilet, but didn't bother to unbutton his pants. The drug made his dick look smaller and he didn't want to see it again if he didn't have to.

Danny walked in behind him. "Do you think we should go back out and get some bottled water? I only have one and I think we killed yours before we left." Colin didn't turn around, telling himself he had to really focus if he was ever going to pee again. When he heard the sink cut on, he knew Danny was fixing his hair and not refilling a water bottle.

Colin had been in the bathroom for a good five minutes by the time Danny realized he could use the room's alarm clock as a dock for his iPod. His ecstasy was telling him to play something soothing and melodic, but after mistaking the silence in the bathroom for residual weirdness about the naked moment that afternoon, he considered adjusting his selection to appease Colin's taste. He looked though his hip-hop instead...

After some exhaustive deliberation, he settled on Mos Def, figuring a few of the more soulful songs on *New Danger* could work as a compromise. He toiled over selecting music that would put them both at ease, but didn't think twice about how anyone would react to him swooping and slithering like that Chocolate Valentine. He raised his arms and swirled his torso, popping his hips in opposition with the bass drum... If he took some inspiration from the stripper, he reinterpreted her grinding with a distinctly masculine edge. At least that's how he saw it at the time...

When Colin walked back out into the main room, Danny was standing on his bed, shirtless with his hair slicked back. He was dancing sexy, totally unselfconscious, watching his own reflection in the window with rapt attention. Colin just stared, first shocked that his friend could move so well, and then surprised that he found it so entertaining. He realized that Danny must have opened the curtains to see himself in the window, possibly even aware that doing so would have also allowed anyone outside to see *him*. Colin felt his neck go thick as some new energy flared up in his chest. It wasn't confrontational. It wasn't judgmental. It was something else...

He didn't notice his feet carry him over to Danny's bed, but when he found himself face to face with the fuzzy small of Danny's writhing back, he knew it was up to him to decide how to proceed. (Those technicians were temperamental.) He kicked off his shoes and stepped onto the bed, directly behind Danny. Watching their reflections through the interstice between Danny's neck and shimmying shoulders, he bobbed his head and wiggled his hips like a cube of Jell-O. His movements were more reserved--stiff next to Danny, who was twisting and flailing like an Alvin Ailey dancer by that point, but together, they seemed to work. Colin's bounce complimented Danny's sway and their bodies created a bizarre symmetry.

Colin peeled off his shirt and ran his hands along the side of Danny's oozing torso. *His skin is so smooth!* With the sexual rush of touching warm flesh surging through his tingling fingers, Colin pulled Danny's body closer. Danny turned around to face him with his eyes closed and his lips pouted with intense focus. Colin gripped the back of Danny's head, massaging his neck and grinding against his hips.

Danny lowered his arms and rested them on Colin's shoulders, crossing them at the wrists behind his neck. His mind flashed back to some childhood family gathering and the day he saw his parents slow dance for the first time. His hands were relaxed at the wrists like his mother's had been when she'd draped her arms over his father's shoulders. It was the only time he could remember seeing his parents look like they were truly in love. There was something magical and sexy about that slow dance and the way they kissed... Danny was so in his head about his parents that he didn't notice the song had ended and that Colin was looking around the room for where the music had been coming from...

The next song was "The Panties" and they slowed their movement to match the sensual groove. Colin, still watching their reflections in the window, wrapped his arms tightly around Danny's waist, rubbing up and down his backside. Danny threw his head back and pressed his naked torso against Colin's. In that moment, something about Danny's physicality read to Colin as slightly effeminate.

It occurred to him that anyone watching them through the window would have thought they were boyfriends, totally hot for each other...and something about that turned him on. It wasn't about Danny, who--apart from all the jacking off--was basically asexual. It was about the random person outside getting turned on by watching them...or watching *him.* It was about Colin's own irrefutable sex appeal. His dick got hard right away, but it took him a moment to figure out it probably wasn't cool to be pressing his hard-on into Danny, even though he appeared completely oblivious.

Colin stopped dancing and stepped back off the bed. He watched Danny's nubile twisting subside into a nodding sway until, like someone had punctured the balloon, he slowly collapsed into a limp pile of panting, heaving limbs on the bed. Colin fell backwards onto his own bed, staring up at the ceiling, catching his breath. His sexy electric had mellowed to a quiet hum, more soothing than overbearing. He shut his eyes and absentmindedly began to knead his erection through his jeans. He smiled about how lucky they had been to lose Nando. His energy would have corrupted their brotherly connection and made something dirty out of the experience. Colin had never felt so spiritually connected to Danny before. Without even having to discuss it, they had shared in celebrating the beauty of their physical forms. Not only did Danny completely condone Colin's seeking emotional gratification by showing off his body--*he did it too!* There were no secrets between them.

He felt the mattress shift beneath him. He opened his eyes and Danny was looking down at him, his knees straddling his waist, his naked chest hovering inches above his own. His arms appeared to be growing out from the sides of Colin's shoulders. His hair was still damp, falling forward over his eyes. Colin smiled up at him, imagining he was pretending to be a cat or something. Danny's groin lowered and pressed against his and Colin realized it had been his own hand squeezing on his dick that whole time. Danny's face sunk closer, his lips inching toward Colin's. Danny began to grind against his hard-on and Colin, intending only to think it, said outloud, "Okay, now *this* is gay."

Danny froze...and then burst out laughing so hard, he fell over onto the bed. Colin chuckled, but he was more confused than amused. He sat up and turned to Danny, who was still rolling with laughter beside him. "What the hell was that?"

Danny finally caught his breath. "I thought that's what you wanted...dancing all close and rubbing all over me. I thought you wanted me to fuck you or something. I was..." His voice trailed off. He'd been laughing so hard, tears streamed down his face.

Colin realized that the 'moment' he thought they had been sharing was really just a drug-induced muddle of misperceptions. He knew that if they were ever going to be on the same page again, he had to tell him the truth right away.

"Danny?" He sat up and cleared his throat, peering straight out toward the window. "I didn't come down here to do fitness modeling. I came to jack off for a gay porn site. So I could put money down on a new car."

All the air flew out of the room. Danny didn't make a sound. Colin's heart was beating so hard it felt like it might break through his chest. He suddenly felt gravely sober. He prayed for the moment to pass or for someone to say something or for his ecstasy to kick back in. Thirty-seconds passed like days. He looked over at the ashy pipe on the night stand...and then back at Danny, who was staring down at his own lap, his eyes moving ever so subtly...thoughtful...confused maybe, but not angry.

Colin began to breathe a bit, but the relief he'd been anticipating about finally speaking the words had immediately dissipated after the silence that followed them. The music was still playing but the room felt eerily quiet around it. He felt compelled to speak, to fill the vacuum with something he could control, so that nothing worse could come of the situation. "It was a lot of money. But...you know. Sorry I lied about it. It's no big deal. I just didn't want you to think I was a douche for doing it."

Danny sat up, still looking forward. "What was it like?"

Colin hadn't prepared for that question. He took a deep breath and just let the words fall. "The room was really bright. There were big lights everywhere. The guy kind of went through all the positions he wanted me to hit before we started. It was just the one guy and three cameras, two on stands, one in his hand. He directed me the whole time and there was a porno playing on the television behind him. Hot Asian girl. At first, he just asked me questions. I still had all my clothes on. Shoes and socks off. I told him my age and how much I work out and that I have a best friend who I do everything with and then he told me to--"

"Not everything." Danny stood up, walked over to his own bed and laid sideways facing him.

Colin heard the quiver in Danny's voice that he had been dreading all night. Danny was too sensitive for this real life shit. He never should have told him--shouldn't have let him come down at all. He'd pretended that the only reason he'd let Danny drive was the extra three hundred dollars he'd make for not having the studio pay for a flight, but really, he needed him close in case something went wrong. Now Colin's heart was breaking over his best friend's disappointment.

Shaking, Danny leaned up against the bed post and exhaled before he spoke. "Show me. Show me what you did."

Colin nodded. *Yes, that's exactly what I have to do.*

It made perfect sense. The only way Danny would ever get over feeling betrayed, the only way they'd ever share that trust again, was if Colin recreated the scene for him exactly as it happened at the studio. There would be no secrets and no resentment because Danny would be 'with him' every step of the way. The truth was the truth, no matter when or where. All they needed for things to go back to normal between them was to finally share in experiencing that particular truth.

Colin clicked on the bedpost lamp and slipped off his socks. He got up to find his black tank top and slid it on. He wanted to recreate the scene as truthfully as he could.

"Sex, Love and Money" grumbled from the iPod with sinister irony.

Danny shifted uncomfortably, moving pillows around in his bed as Colin prepared for the scene, lumbering over to turn off the music and then collapsing into the armchair in the corner. His face went slack, like he was in a trance, trying to remember every moment of the scene he was about to recreate. Then, as if prompted by a voice in his head, he nodded and started speaking.

"Name's Bailey... I'm eighteen. Uh... Yeah, I work out. Usually, like, five days a week, probably two hours a day... Other than that, I just like to kick it. Like, me and my best friend just basically hang out and you know, party or whatever... No, no girlfriend right now. Just livin' life." A sad smile brushed across his face...and then his eyes went dead like the girl's looking out from the mirrored stage.

Breathless, Danny clutched a pillow to his chest. He was completely unsettled by Colin's commitment to seamlessly reenacting it all, rather than recounting the scene as a narrative. He'd sort of expected a graphic story with a few dirty words and maybe a few hand gestures--but not a full-out replay. *Couldn't 'show me' just mean tell the story?*

Wait. Had Colin agreed to *show him* because he had noticed Danny looking at his body earlier and he was exploiting that to make amends for lying? Was his body becoming a commodity to trade for whatever he needed? What if Danny had asked Colin to show him because he'd been subconsciously attracted to him ever since seeing him naked? Danny felt his back get hot as his heart accelerated in a panic.

Shit. The ecstasy. We're totally high! Danny opened his mouth to remind Colin that they were out of their minds...that their brains were playing tricks on them and they only needed to ride it out... But then Colin was standing up, pulling off his shirt and Danny closed his mouth...

Colin began flexing his biceps and posing like one of those 1950s bodybuilders in the black and white postcards at the movie theater. Pretty tame, considering the kind of stuff girls have to do in porn... It was harmless, really. Cheesy even. Fitness modeling was exactly right... Danny exhaled, relieved that he must have misunderstood. There wasn't anything necessarily gay about a guy, by himself, showing off his body for a camera. Had anyone even mentioned jacking off?

Then Colin unbuttoned his pants. He never looked at Danny; Danny wasn't even in the room. A phantom Anderson was floating around aiming cameras... He slid his jeans down his beefy legs and clumsily stepped out of them while he fondled himself through his FTL boxer briefs. Then he began to caress his pecs and rub circles around his nipples, a move Anderson had encouraged that afternoon. Noting he was already markedly more comfortable putting on a show since the first time, Colin pulled his shorts halfway down his bulging thighs and his clean-shaven dick sprung forward like a diving board.

Danny averted his eyes. Everything had officially gone too far. What happened to his goofy, insecure friend? Why was anybody's dick hard? Danny slid the pillow from his chest down into his tensing lap...

Colin stood there stroking his dick with a macho swagger that even he understood was totally incongruous with his personality, virtually antagonistic to his self-image. But he was finally getting it: It was all performance. He really *wasn't* Colin. He was Bailey and Bailey liked to jack off for gay guys. He cupped his hand below his dick and let a trail of spit fall past his heaving chest and chiseled abs into his palm. He sat back on the chair and stroked his dick into a bludgeon.

Danny's breath got shallow...his heart was beating so hard it was almost painful. The tingling in his lungs had all slithered south and his sexy electric had gathered into an obelisk in his lap... When he looked down at his own erection, an invisible wall flew up between him and Colin. Unable to process the situation in any terms that made sense in real life, he just checked out. If Colin had figured out a way to no longer be Colin, then Danny got to be someone else too. He wiggled his jeans down, just below his lap and quietly spit into his hand.

Colin, his eyes closed in manufactured rapture, stood and slowly turned around. With his back to camera, he placed one of his knees in the seat of the chair and rubbed his ass cheeks with both his hands. He ran his middle finger from his lower back down the crack and tapped against his fuzzy hole. Earlier, Anderson had invited him to pull his ass cheeks apart when he'd gotten into that position, to 'really share with the viewers.' Colin aimed his ass at the camera, he touched it, but he didn't cross the threshold, so to speak.

Danny's jacking was slow and methodical. He played his instrument with quiet expertise as he eyed the shadows cast across the smooth meaty crevice. When the model pressed his erection down between his legs, he arched his back just enough so that the light glimmered across the pink slit of his hole. Droplets of clear nectar oozed out of the tip of Danny's erection and he accelerated his stroke...

Colin stepped up onto the cushion, turned and sat on top of the chair's back, his feet arched against the arm rests. Flexing his calf muscles, he spread his legs wide, spit into his cupped hand and rubbed the tip of his dick in a circular motion. He groaned, remembering Anderson had directed him to 'make some noise' around that time. When he started throbbing wet against his sticky hand, he knew he was already getting close... He had two more positions to hit before he finished, but he slid down into the seat of the chair and really got to jacking. No one would mind if he rushed the last couple setups...

Danny's jacking was getting quick and squishy behind the pillow and his feet were starting to point and flex...

Colin sat back, his feet flat on the floor and his body almost completely horizontal in the chair. He jacked faster and his toes started to curl under. He snarled and looked up with a nod to let Anderson know he was close.

Danny's eyes locked on Colin's and both their faces started to contort in anticipation of the final release...

Colin's first squirt was accompanied by a gnarled *stank-face* and a guttural growl that sounded almost identical to the noise he made when dead lifting the four hundred pound barbells, and the resulting ivory puddle gathered in the ridges of his eight-pack...

Danny whimpered with a breathy shudder and pouty lips as he shot his mess up onto his shoulder, leaving a jagged sticky trail along his shivering chest.

Then...*silence.*

Colin exhaled and collapsed loudly back into the armchair. He didn't clean up right away so the camera could get a good shot of the mess...

Danny, slowing his breath, wiped everything away immediately with the pillow, not making a sound.

Colin reached over and clicked off the lamp on the table.

Danny clicked off the light on the nightstand.

The only light in the room was the beam glowing from the ajar bathroom door.

Danny pulled his pants up and sunk into a heap under his scattered sheets and blankets, tossing the suspect pillow to the floor on the far side of the bed.

Colin stood up carefully and walked naked with wide, awkward steps into the bathroom to clean himself up. He didn't close the door. He just picked a towel up off the floor, wiped himself clean and tossed it back onto the floor. He walked back to the chair and stepped into his Fruit of the Looms, and then fell backwards onto his own bed, staring up at the ceiling with a sigh.

Silence.

"So...you know. *That's* what happened." Colin's voice wheezed with a defeated humility that made it clear his alter-ego was no longer in the room.

Danny, calm in his post-orgasmic haze, breathed easy with his face pressed against a pillow wet with his own back sweat. Whatever had just happened was over. They had survived the moment. Everything was fine. Now he'd seen everything and there were no secrets between them. He glanced over and watched Colin's body curl into a sinewy golden ball. There really was a sweetness about the whole thing. Even an 'objective pornography viewer' couldn't deny the generosity of Colin's gesture. He had done everything in his power to make right a situation and save his friend from feeling left in the dark. Danny chuckled, "You're pretty good at it. I mean, you put on a good show."

Colin lay silent. The weight had officially been lifted. He didn't care who else found out now. No one else mattered the way Danny did. Fuck everybody else.

Danny sat up. "Can you hook me up with the guy? I wanna do it too."

Colin exhaled softly and closed his eyes, picturing the single tear running along the side of his own face, disappearing against the starched hotel sheet. He wasn't sure if the drugs were making him emotional or if something inside him was actually stirred by Danny's wanting to get involved. So he said nothing.

Somber silence rolled in like fog, rendering them both motionless until Colin finally stood up to click off the bathroom light... Then, they disappeared under their respective bed spreads and waited anxiously for sleep.

4

o o o

They both slept in the next morning. They'd drifted in and out of frenetic dreams, gnashing their teeth and twisting in their sheets while traces of the drug buzzed around the corners of their consciousnesses, burning holes through the fabric of the night. Neither of them had been able to fall asleep until six a.m. or so, after Danny had lumbered out from behind his pillow fort to close the curtains and block out the puffy pink dawn.

Colin was first in the shower. At twelve something in the afternoon, the previous night's bizarre events were still fresh in his mind, but he saw no point in making excuses for anything that happened while they were high. Whatever they'd shared that night would only be confusing if they pretended it meant something that it didn't. He had cleared up a lie, nothing more. The universe had brought Nando and his ecstasy into their lives to provide Colin an opportunity to clear up any confusion/ misunderstanding/lies between him and Danny, so that's exactly what he did. No one would need to bring up Anderson or Nando...or *Bailey* ever again.

They'd already smoked all the weed, but Colin figured they would spend Saturday afternoon on the beach, maybe come back to the hotel to wash up and then drive home that night. He stepped out of the shower, dried off with the three mid-sized towels left on the rack and pulled on board shorts, a tank top and flip flops.

Danny was still asleep, so Colin went downstairs to ask the front desk for a few big towels--one for Danny's shower and two for the beach. The guy at the desk was the same one who had nodded goodbye the day before--a tall, chiseled Aryan looking dude with short blond hair. He smiled reflexively at him approaching, but when he recognized Colin, his eyes popped open and his smile twisted into more of a smirk.

"Good afternoon, sir. What can I do for you?" His tone was flirtatious and condescending all at once, like he knew a secret that could reverse their roles at any moment. Colin's chest inflated instinctively when he asked for the towels, figuring the guy was friends with Sky and knew why Colin was staying in the hotel. *But so what?*

What had he ever accomplished by worrying what people who had no bearing on his livelihood thought of him? He'd always been able to grasp the benefit of 'not giving a shit' in theory, but he'd never quite figured out its practical application before then. Always so concerned with not being invisible, he'd never learned the art of manipulating people's impressions or disregarding negative opinions fueled by insecurity. But that morning, he couldn't care less...and realizing that was even an option felt like a profound victory to him.

The clerk picked up the phone with a shit eating grin and dialed Housekeeping. Colin smiled back, taking note of the scuffed name tag on the polyester jacket, and reminded himself that Zack wouldn't make as much money standing behind that desk for a whole week as he had just made jacking off for twenty minutes.

Danny woke up with a start. He'd been dreaming of flying men who looked like geese chasing him through the wooded thicket in his father's backyard. They were snapping at his legs with their beaks, trying to turn him into a goose. He'd been running for his life and slipped in a patch of ivy when the geese men pounced on him and he jerked awake, covered in sweat.

The room was still and quiet and the sliver of daylight seeping in from between the curtains didn't illuminate much. Colin was definitely not in the room but he could smell steam and soap from the open bathroom door and knew that he'd been in the shower not long before.

Eager to wash away the lingering paranoia of the nightmare, Danny hopped up, shocked at how quickly his body had responded to the idea of moving, and stepped into the shower.

Standing under the gush of steaming water, he was soothed by a new sense of hope. He finally had a way out of his father's house. He also got to blame that bitch Maggie for pushing the issue. She'd tricked Dan Senior into forcing his only son into porn.

Porn.

Danny acknowledged to himself, if only for a moment, that he was deliberately thinking about it as 'porn' and not 'gay porn.' He'd almost convinced himself over the course of the sleepless night that sexual orientation wasn't an issue. It never had been. Sex was sex, plain and simple. Getting turned on watching a guy jack off didn't necessarily make you gay. Not so long as you understood that sexuality was fluid and attraction was subjective and based on energy, not organs.

Colin could hear the shower running when he walked back into the room. He pushed open the bathroom door and placed a fluffy new white towel on the sink for Danny without announcing himself or walking inside.

He pulled open the curtains and let the sunshine fill the room. Aside from the beds, the room was in pretty good shape. Danny must have cleaned up at some point the night before. Standing there, surveying the room bathed in crisp white light, he couldn't help imagine how easy it would be for the two of them to live together. They were close enough to know when the other needed space, they were both pretty clean (for straight guys) and they were obviously both 4:20 friendly... It was the clear choice: he would use the money to get them an apartment. Then he would come back down, after giving Danny enough time to come to his senses about wanting to get involved, do a couple more shoots and put a down payment on a car.

But why didn't he want Danny to get involved? If there were really to be no secrets between them, Danny *should* start modeling. Only then would he really understand what it felt like to share every inch of his body with the entire world. Danny could do it. Anybody could do it. That was the funny thing--it didn't require any talent or anything special at all. Any asshole with a dick could jack off in front of a camera. All it required was the willingness to do it. So what was he really trying to protect Danny from?

Was it that Danny was too naive to really understand the way the world would look at him after the fact? (As if Colin had any idea.) Was it that there was something--a softness about Danny that Colin recognized as *too easily mistakable for gay* and he wanted to keep him out of that light altogether? Or...was it that modeling was the one thing Colin could really call his own? The one thing that made him distinct from his best friend... Maybe he had made a mistake in sharing any of it with him. Maybe having a few secrets was the key to their bond. Maybe they didn't need to know everything about one another.

The secret code knock tapped out against the door.

Colin stared at the door from across the room. The shower shut off and Danny was singing some faggy college rock song. Another knock. Danny stuck his head out the bathroom door and called out, "Thanks for the towel, dude!" as Colin stood there, shaking his head, finger to his lips.

Nando called out, "Bailey? Danny? It's me!"

Danny heard Nando and saw the panic on Colin's face, but didn't understand what the problem was. "You don't wanna let him in?" Even as Colin stood there, shaking his head no, Danny didn't bother lowering his voice. "Okay." He shrugged and disappeared back into the bathroom.

"You guys...? It's me, Nando!"

The childlike innocence of his voice made Colin feel like he was overreacting. It's not like he was still a risk for letting the cat out of the bag and as far as Colin knew, Nando had honored his request to keep quiet.

Despite his occasionally odd energy, he was an okay guy. Cringing at the prospect of not being in complete control of the situation, Colin walked slowly over and opened the door.

Nando was wearing the same clothes from the night before and looked like he hadn't showered or slept. His eyes were dark and dilated and he lumbered in agitated and distracted. Colin watched him collapse into the armchair in the corner...

Danny bounced out of the bathroom wrapped in his towel. "Oh, I didn't think he was gonna let you in. What's up, dude?" He rushed over to his bag next to find clothes, not even looking at Nando.

"You smell good, yo." Nando scrutinized Danny's wet back in a way Colin found curious. *Is he checking him out?* If there was any weird sexual energy about the guy, it was in his hustler spirit--that energy that communicated his willingness to do whatever it took to get what he needed. But he didn't seem like he was into dudes...at all.

Danny glanced up at Nando when he turned to go back to the bathroom and did a double take. A weighted beat of them looking directly at one another passed without either of them saying a word. Then Danny disappeared with his clothes back to the bathroom.

When the door closed behind him, Nando looked up at Colin, his brow furrowed with desperation. "Okay, what had happened was... I need you to drive me back to the house. I think I left some money over there and I've been calling and calling but those fuckers won't call me back!"

Colin immediately recognized his unsettling tone as a symptom of doing too many of the wrong drugs. He had never come across that energy in real life, but he'd seen enough of it in movies and on TV to know what it looked like. Considering Nando's appearance, it didn't take a CSI forensic expert to put it together. "You can't get them to call you back?" Colin's brain was racing to work out a plan to get Nando back to his own room to put him to sleep or at least, in the shower. "When did you call them?"

Nando shook his head sadly, telegraphing that the answer wasn't likely to be credible. "Like four or five this morning...and since then...you know, all day." His face shifted to a less frantic expression, as if hearing his own insanity spoken out loud somehow made his conundrum less daunting. "I just need to get...back to the house."

Colin looked over his shoulder at the bathroom door, hoping that Danny wasn't hearing all the talk about 'the house,' waiting to pop out and use the conversation as a segue into the topic of modeling. "We're going to the beach today. How about you get some sleep and then we check in later and see if they've called you back." Colin stood up and started drifting backwards toward the hall door. None of this was his problem.

Nando stood up, more lost than upset, walked over and gave Colin a 'pound' on his way out. "I'm a call you in a few hours. I gotta get over there and..." He shook his head, defeated. "But y'all have your day at the beach. Then maybe we can stop by my boy's spot and cop some trees."

Colin's ears pricked up. *Trees? We have a local weed connection?* Getting stoned at the beach had been the plan all along. Maybe they could pick up the weed before Nando's nap, drop him back off and then go to beach. "Unless...unless you wanted to pick up trees first, which might help you get some rest. Then we meet up later and talk about getting your stuff from the house."

Nando stood outside the doorway, his eyes darting back and forth between his Adidas sneakers and Colin's flip flop sandals. "I'm a go take a shower, call my boy and see if he's around and then we can hit his spot and head out to the beach." He slowly wandered away down the hall.

Colin shut the door and turned to find Danny fully dressed and sitting on his bed with a concerned grimace. "Is he okay?"

Having not met one another's gaze directly since the night before, a soft jolt of recognition, the flurry of an unspoken secret shared, charged the air between them. They both rushed to pretend it had passed...

"I guess he's been up all night partying, throwing his money at drug dealers and strippers and then hallucinating about someone ripping him off. He probably just needs some sleep." Colin's voice came out in a whisper, like an introspective aside.

"But you're picking up some herb before we head to the beach? That's what's up!" Danny started rubbing sunblock on his face in tiny circles and Colin noticed for the first time, with genuine surprise, how girly his best friend was.

o o o

Getting to the beach had officially become a pipe dream. By the time Nando made it back to their room, it was almost three in the afternoon. He looked better after his shower, but he still moved like the weight of the underworld was slung on his slender shoulders.

Danny started feeling anxious in the car about going the whole day without herb. He'd been working hard to convince himself that what happened with Colin the night before hadn't had such a profound impact on him. He tried to make sense of his feelings by putting it all in the context of finding the job intriguing or being a general porn aficionado, but he couldn't deny there was more to it than that. He just didn't understand what any of it meant. Was he bisexual? Could he even make that distinction if his only questionable experience was during an ecstasy trip? And did that mean Colin was bisexual too? A little weed was just what he needed to calm himself down...

He glanced up at the rearview mirror and Nando was looking back at him from the backseat with sad eyes. Danny quickly looked away. Was Nando asking himself the same questions? Had something happened between him and Colin too? Danny glanced over at Colin staring out the window, bobbing his head to Andre Nickatina's "Conversation With a Devil."

They pulled up in front of the run down apartment building and Colin handed Nando some folded cash as he lurched out of the backseat like a Sean John zombie.

Danny and Colin sat in the car and waited with the engine and the stereo off. Considering how many times they'd sat stoned stupid, quietly staring at walls together, the silence shouldn't have been awkward...but it was. So awkward that they were both afraid to speak for fear it would read as a clear admission of the awkwardness. They silently agreed to ride it out.

Two curvy Latina girls rounded the corner, carrying oversized bags, wearing bikini tops and shorts, on their way home from the beach. Colin grunted reflexively and his hand reached out and tapped Danny's leg. Danny's eye flew to the fuzzy skin on his knee that had just been touched and then up to see Colin's gaze glued to the two girls. He glimpsed the moment like a snap shot: one boy only saw the two approaching girls; the other only saw the spot where the other boy had touched him. Something had definitely shifted. *Exhale*. He turned the key so the stereo could drown out the doubts that had begun scratching at his wounded psyche.

Nando was only halfway through his secret knock when the door to unit six flew open. Eric was on the phone and held a stern finger up to his mouth instructing him not to speak. Nando stepped in quietly and stood near the door while Eric, in UCSD boxers and a sleeveless *Velvet Rope* T-shirt with his wild curly hair pulled back into two afro-like pigtails, argued with some chick on the phone. It sounded like the girl's roommate had some issue with Eric sleeping over... *Roommate drama... Typical.*

Nando thought of his best friend Paul. They had hardly spoken since Nando's last trip to California, when they'd wound up drunk at the beach and the day ended with Nando having sex with Paul's roommate Lena. That had been over a year...

Eric wandered back toward the hall, leaving Nando alone in the living room. When he was there two days prior, the place had been completely furnished. The big brown leather sofa was still set next to the cool 70s lamp with the curved stand and chrome spherical light fixture, but there had also been a coffee table and a couple chairs before. This time, the windows were all covered with heavy dark brown curtains where he'd distinctly remembered white gauzy ones. There was a small flat screen television on the floor and some magazines and DVD cases next to one of those chintzy thirty dollar DVD players. The red cover artwork for a movie called *The Dreamers* caught his eye...

Eric walked back in, still on the phone, and tossed two baggies stuffed with bud onto the couch. Nando walked over to get a look and Eric collapsed onto the couch with his legs spread wide. At that point, Nando thought he'd caught Eric eyeing the bump in the front of his shorts. Only then did it occur to him that Eric might have been into dudes. A hot girl had introduced them at that hip-hop club, but that didn't necessarily mean that Eric had sex with women. Sometimes black gay guys don't make it so obvious... Even with pig tails and Janet Jackson T-shirts.

Nando perked up. Could he get more drugs if he offered some kind of sexual favor? If he let the dude suck his dick, would he throw in some more ecstasy or maybe some coke? *That stripper chick Cristål went crazy for coke!* What if he wanted Nando to suck *his* dick? That would be too much. But...depending on what he had to offer, Nando wasn't ruling anything out yet.

Eric cooed, "I miss you too, baby," hung up his phone and looked up at Nando with a nod. "'Sup, kid? Sorry 'bout all that. Bitch drama. Anyway, you said you wanted an eighth, right? It's sixty. Or...quarter ounce is a hundred." Eric lifted one of his legs onto the couch, wrapping an arm around his knee.

Nando stepped closer, looking down toward the baggies but working hard to decipher the energy Eric was offering up. Answering the door in boxer shorts was bold enough, but lifting his leg onto the couch so that something might slip through a slit was laying all his shit out. Nando made very deliberate eye contact with him to confirm that they were on the same page.

Eric raised his eyebrows.

Tricky move. The gesture could have been read as, "Okay, so how much weed do you want?" *or* "So are you gonna suck my dick now or what?" Nando couldn't be sure what to do, so he squatted down in front of the couch and grabbed one of the baggies. He opened it and held it to his face, breathing deep. *Sticky!* Eric ran his hand up and down his shin from his knee to his ankle.

Nando closed the bag and tossed it back onto the couch. "You running any deals on E? That shit you got me before was the business."

"Any deals?" Eric's face went completely neutral. *He's too good at this!* Nando was at a loss. He'd never bartered sex for drugs. Who was supposed to make the first move? He plopped all the way down on the floor while Eric just sat there, looking back at him.

"Yeah. You know. *Deals.*" Nando attempted a sexy smile, but his face was too tired to cooperate. He could feel it play strained across his face. He glanced down at Eric's crotch instead.

Eric shook his head, "Nope. No deals. Same price as before." He got up and walked to the kitchen. "I'm about to head out, so did you want the eighth or what?" He came back with a small bottle of water and a paper towel and handed them to Nando. "Is it hot in here?"

Nando wiped the sweat from his forehead, embarrassed. He'd made a fool of himself. He stood up, pulled a wad of money out of his pocket. "I'll just take the eighth and...however many pills this will get me."

Eric, eyeing the crumpled money, slipped the hair ties out of his hair, ran his hands through his big curly fro, pulled it all back into one puffy ponytail on the back of his head and wrapped the extra tie around his wrist with a sigh. "I can give you six pills and both eighths for two hundred."

Nando extended the bills toward Eric and stuffed the bags of weed into the pockets of his baggy shorts. Eric nodded and disappeared toward the hall. Nando felt so humiliated, he thought he might throw up. He wiped his forehead and drank down the bottle of water, coughing up the last gulp back into his hand. Eric came back and handed him a small baggie with the pills.

"Thanks, man." Nando handed him the empty water bottle, turned and walked out the front door.

Eric closed the door behind him, shaking his head and mumbling something about "exactly why I need to get out of San Diego..."

Nando slipped into the backseat and Colin looked back at him, anxious. "Dude, what the hell were you doing up there? You were gone so long I thought something bad happened. Like, the cops busted in on you or the guy tied you up or something."

"Yeah, I figured he was running a train on you with all his gangster friends. Ten black guys all lined up with hard dicks--" Danny bit his lower lip and started the car...

"He was on the phone with his girlfriend." Nando handed Colin his bag of weed and leaned back with a whimper, staring out the window, suddenly missing his friend Paul and how simple his life had been before. *Before...*

o o o

The three of them sat in the car parked at the edge of a remote cliff facing the Pacific Ocean and passed around Colin's pipe. *At last.* It was already too cool outside to walk down to the water without sweatshirts, but sitting there high, watching the sun set over the beach, gave them each some sense of a mission accomplished.

Reaching the beach also symbolized a turning point that required action of each of them. Colin had to decide if they were going to drive home that night or stay in town, leaving open the possibility of returning to Anderson's. Danny had to decide if he was going to broach the subject of his own modeling career, thereby acknowledging that he and Colin had indeed exchanged the entire breadth of that...*information*. And Nando, looking at the ocean again for the first time since that night with Paul and Lena, wrestled with his compulsion to call Paul and finally talk through all their miscommunication.

Fortunately, the weed softened the edges on all those points...and the three of them managed to get high enough to independently choose to save all those decisions for some other time.

After sunset and the slow, cautious drive back to the hotel, they all agreed that naps were in order. Nando, at the end of his third or fourth wind, floated quietly up to his room. When Colin muttered, "Thank God," Danny wasn't sure if he was relieved to see Nando go or just happy that Housekeeping had made their beds and brought them fresh towels. He disappeared into the bathroom as Danny noticed the flashing light on the hotel phone and dialed the voicemail.

He didn't recognize the voice, but it was definitely a white guy. "Hello, Mr. Phillips. This is the front desk. Um... You and your...guest are invited to a party tonight. The address is..." Then, muffled, he heard him ask someone in the room for the street number. "2410 Florida Street. Should be wild." Danny wrote down the address and hung up the phone. He had no idea who the dude was, but he was intrigued.

He lay back and closed his eyes but soon realized he would need to play his iPod to drown out the sounds coming from the bathroom. He had, on earlier occasions, contemplated telling Colin that he was pushing too hard for his BMs--that if he was making that much noise, he was straining his body when he really needed to just sit there and relax until things were ready to fall on their own. But the two or three times it had come up before, he'd been so stoned that he worried he would come off like a nagging wife or doting mother for noticing. (It's not like he had a cup to the door.) Colin treated most things in his life like his weightlifting: force what doesn't fit and push through anything uncomfortable with brute muscle.

Danny paused. *Is that really fair?* Was he now painting Colin as some monster because he wasn't strong enough to bring up a subject that challenged his own sense of self? Colin had done everything from his side to make sense of a situation that clearly wasn't easy for either of them... Had Colin's forthright disclosure fostered some resentment in Danny because he wasn't as comfortable sharing the complicated details of his own truth?

The toilet flushed at the very moment Danny had settled on The Sundays' cover of "White Horses." He rolled over to face the far wall and closed his eyes just as the bathroom door clicked open. He could hear Colin step out of his shorts, pull back the blanket and slide into his bed. Danny waited for some comment on the 'faggy college rock' but it never came. He wondered whether that was a good thing or a bad thing...

The hotel phone startled Colin out of a dream that had him waiting with Danny in his brand new candy apple red Cadillac Escalade at the drive-thru window at Rally's. It took him a couple seconds to figure out where he was. He reached over for the phone in the dark and before he picked it up, he heard Danny snort from four feet away.

"Hello?"

"Hey, it's Nando. Y'all up yet?"

Danny, half awake, mumbled something about missing a party...

Colin turned the alarm clock around: 9:36. "Yeah, we're up. I mean...we're getting up now."

"I'm a jump in the shower and roll through in like twenty." Nando hung up the phone. Colin sat there in the dark with the phone still pressed to his face for a good ten-seconds before the dial tone let him know the call had ended. Then he clicked on the nightstand lamp to see Danny swing his legs over the side of his bed and shake his hair out. Neither of them spoke.

Danny casually adjusted himself and pulled his T-shirt over his boner as he got up to walk clumsily across the room. He nodded 'what's up' as he passed Colin and closed the bathroom door behind him.

Colin laid his head back against the pillow and waited for his turn in the shower...

"Okay, *I'll* get it!" Danny bursting out of the bathroom dripping wet in a towel to answer the door startled Colin out of another dream. He was sleeping so hard he hadn't even heard the secret knock.

Nando strolled in looking rested and almost respectable. He was wearing a brand new T-shirt with a giant silver graphic across the chest and he had shaved his grizzly seven o'clock shadow into a faint mustache and goatee combo. He strolled right over and plopped down on the foot of the bed. Colin sat up and watched Danny bustle back into the bathroom.

"Looks like you got some sleep, playa. Good for you." Nando grinned with what appeared to be genuine affection and then leaned in, squinting his eyes with a question. "Does Danny know yet? Cuz there might be a couple cats from the house at this party. Just so he doesn't hear it from someone else..."

Colin rubbed his face awake. "I told him last night... Wait. What party?"

Danny popped out of the bathroom, fully dressed after what seemed like hardly enough time to unwrap the towel, and bounced over to his bed. "You should jump in the shower so we can head out. It's like ten fifteen."

"Head out where? What party?" Colin stared agog at Nando and Danny, who looked to one another, expectant, but neither of them answered the question. Colin hopped out of the bed and closed the bathroom door enough to undress and still hear the plans.

Danny finally spoke up. "Some dude at the desk invited us to a big party. It was on the voicemail. Said it should be crazy." Danny nodded at Nando to confirm that they were talking about the same thing.

Nando added, "Gonna be a bunch of hot SDSU bitches is what I heard."

"Oh, word? That's what's up!" Colin cut on the shower...

Danny felt something in his chest harden and go heavy. He didn't even know what he was feeling at the time, but his eyes glassed over at the prospect of another night cluttered with unapproachable girls and more unspoken sexual frustration with Colin. He pulled on his socks with an exhausted sigh.

At that, Nando turned to Danny and whispered, "Don't worry. There should be a few dudes there too."

5

o o o

When they finally found the house on Florida Street, there was nowhere to park for five blocks in either direction. Danny, normally totally composed and the picture of patience, was ready to give up and go back to the hotel until Colin suggested trying to find something down one of the side streets.

When they found the spot, marked by the ethereal beam of a street lamp, between two SUVs and just small enough that any car larger than a Sentra wouldn't fit, Nando called it a sign from God; they were destined to be at that party. Never mind the twenty minutes of driving in circles or the four blocks they would have to trek to get there. Happening upon that parking spot was 'divine intervention.' So of course, they honored the blessing by passing around Colin's sacred pipe.

The weed and the warm summer night put the trio in good spirits for their hike up to the house. They were walking into a place where nobody knew them, where whatever unfortunate reputations they'd been assigned in the past would have no bearing on the relationships they were bound to forge...

Even in the dark, Danny noticed a vibrancy to Colin's step that he hadn't seen for almost a year. The promise of potential pussy always played an interesting trick on Colin. He'd get so excited, he'd start psyching himself up with little chants about how hot the girls were gonna be and how hot they were going to think he was. But by the time he actually got in front of one, he'd already started talking too fast and bobbing his head and rubbing his body inappropriately. Before the girl could decide if she thought he was cute, he would spaz out and she would wander away with conflicting feelings of sympathy and disgust.

Just before senior year, he had managed to fumble through a few weeks of intimacy with some girl he'd met at the mall. Danny had only seen the girl once, pumping lemonade at Hot Dog on a Stick, and he didn't think she was much to look at. Plus, her name was Gismonda. But to hear Colin tell it, she held the secret to every boy's manhood. She was Gismonda the Good Witch, carrying around a magic wand with the world's most amazing pussy stuck at the end of it.

Then, out of nowhere, the affair was over. Danny had always assumed that Amber Dorsey had something to do with it. When she came back after summer vacation, looking like a Pussycat Doll and dating that douche-bag Josh, Colin lost his shit. Seemed like, to Colin, whatever he'd been doing with Gismonda was preparation for what he would eventually get to do with Amber. When she hooked up with Josh, Colin regressed back to that goofy, no-game kid. The good witch was gone and his senior year was wasted as an overeager virgin.

Danny had been with three girls; two freshman girls during his sophomore year and an exchange student from Spain who pretty much threw herself at him the beginning of senior year. She was done with him by the end of the second week of class and quickly went on to become that semester's 'Heidi' (ho). But he'd had more sex in those eight days than he'd managed in eighteen years. He always figured he would find sex more enjoyable when he got older, when there wasn't so much pressure to have it just for the sake of having it...when there was more to intercourse than just buckling to social expectations.

Despite Nando's comment about 'guys at the party,' which they both laughed off at the time, Danny said a silent prayer for a girl, any girl, to rescue him that night...

The house was already packed with people, most of whom appeared to be college age. There was one woman, over-tanned with fried blond hair and a hot pink Bebe tank top, who appeared to be in her thirties and she was probably more drunk than anyone. Colin spotted her dancing slutty by herself just outside the kitchen, holding a red plastic cup above her head. He'd been considering making a move until she stumbled back into the florescent light and he saw that she was probably older than his mother.

There was a distinctly So Cal beach vibe to most of the revelers, which Nando picked up on right away. Everyone was sunburned and in surf gear, but affecting this obnoxious frat boy hip-hop energy. At first he found it amusing, if a little pathetic, that shirtless white dudes were imitating Busta Rhymes, wagging their necks, shaking their heads and poppin' nonexistent collars. Then he started to get offended. "These muthafuckas would get shot doing this shit in Philly."

They made their way through the crowded kitchen out to the backyard looking for something to drink. Two overweight guys in white ball caps were doing keg stands in the driveway. The fatter one was holding the uglier one's legs up as they pumped beer directly from the keg into his upside down, pimply mouth. At that point, Nando suggested that they go back to the car and smoke more weed, just to deal with 'these drunk-ass white people.' But Colin had noticed a trio of girls near the bar and decided to go get a drink instead. Danny and Nando watched him walk over, slowing his stroll and puffing his chest out as he got closer... Then he just stood there, waiting for any one of the girls to turn around and notice him. The girls continued to chatter away as Colin stood there bobbing his head, chanting to himself. Danny couldn't bear to watch so he nodded to Nando and they walked up the driveway back out to the street.

When they got to the sidewalk, someone called out, "You kids aren't leaving already, are you? The party's just getting started."

Fearing he might have recognized the voice, Danny glanced back. A tall, chiseled blond dude flanked by two brown haired pretty boys--both in puka shell chokers, stood basking in the amber porch light, poised to knock the party's decidedly heterosexual vibe awry. Danny opted not to respond. He turned back to Nando, expecting him to echo his earlier comment about the party being 'mixed.' Instead, Nando called back, "We're just running back to the car for a sec. We be back." Then he turned and headed down the street toward the car. Danny followed him into the quiet without a word.

The girl Colin was least interested in finally turned and introduced herself through a grating giggle and silver wires. Samantha's two friends, Cuter and Much Cuter, were wrapped up in some argument about Project Runway and couldn't be bothered. So Colin, looking his gift horse straight in the mouth, immediately launched into a conversation about Samantha's braces. He went on and on about how he'd thought Invisalign had made traditional braces obsolete and how surprised he was "to see metal in someone's mouth in this day and age."

Samantha, apparently finding his off-color curiosity charming, giggled in spite of herself. As much as he couldn't stand the laugh, he latched on to her smile and kept talking, because...*a mouth that stays open long enough to smile is likely to stay open long enough to do other things.*

Before he'd even had time to catch his breath, he heard himself asking her what he could get her to drink and was at the bar emptying a can of Red Bull into red plastic cups he'd already filled with ice and vodka.

The two of them eventually drifted away from Kinda Cute and A Lil' Cuter and sat down together on a low brick wall beneath a tree littered with red party lanterns. The glowing orbs gave Samantha's bulbous cheeks a sexy rosiness and he found himself transfixed by the way her lip gloss glimmered as it reflected the lights from the house. They were talking incessantly about such banal shit that he could hardly make sense of any of it. It was like they were locked in a race to keep the conversation going, so at the slightest sign of a lull, one or both of them would jump in with a new completely pointless subject. "Parking in this neighborhood sucks!"

He was so oblivious to what the girl was talking about that he had time to think to himself, while both their mouths were moving, that he was impressed with how smooth he was being. *I figured out how to talk to girls!* The trick was feigning interest in whatever they were saying long enough for them to get a good look at you. By the time you had their full attention, they were most likely going to be able to find something cute enough about you to keep them engrossed. Girls made it harder at the beginning--but once you got them, they were all yours. He noted an inquisitive shift in her intonation. *Is she asking me something?* He stared at her lip gloss and just waited for her to ask again.

"So, like, did you? Like, want my number or whatever?" Colin looked up and saw that she was looking over his shoulder at her friends. Not So Cute Anymore and Really Not Cute Either were looking back at her impatiently. Colin pulled his phone out and handed it to her. She punched in her digits as the blond one, Actually Kind of Hideous, sucked her teeth from just inches behind him. Colin just sipped his drink, smiled at Samantha and watched her dial her own number from his phone right before she handed it back to him.

Then, all three of them were gone. Like a surprise, Colin found himself sitting alone under a tree, wondering where his friends were...

They had just finished smoking the bowl when Danny adjusted the drivers seat to lay flat back. "Aaaaaaaahhhhhhh." Nando looked down at him, shook his head with a sigh and then turned to stare out the passenger side window.

Until that point, they had managed to maintain a comfortable, friendly distance. Neither of them seemed to be putting any real work into winning the other's approval, which watered down their interaction to an easy, pleasant indifference. But Danny was fairly sure he was sensing some disapproval from Nando in that moment and he was just stoned and paranoid enough to call him on it.

"Something wrong?"

Nando reached down, still looking out the window, and laid his own seat flat back. "Naw, homie. It's just... You remind me so much of somebody. My best friend. Y'all are so similar." Nando turned and looked at Danny, his eyes glassy under the street light.

Something in Nando's face made Danny feel suddenly compelled to change the subject. "Is Nando short for Fernando or is your name really Nando? Because I have a cousin whose name I think might be Fernando, but we all call him Chachi."

"See? That's just like some shit Paul would say. I think y'all would seriously get along, real talk. I called him today, but he ain't call me back. Still mad at me, I guess." Nando glanced back out the window.

Danny fought hard against the urge to suggest they just go back to the party and find Colin and stop having real conversations, but the ensuing silence was too obvious... It was inescapable. "So... Why is he mad at you?"

"I don't know. I guess because I'm not... I'm not like y'all. You're stronger than me. And...'cause I had sex with his roommate." Nando's face was suddenly wet with tears that Danny couldn't see from where he was sitting.

Danny felt his stomach churning with some psychological nausea. The conversation was treading on themes he knew he was uncomfortable with, without even necessarily knowing why. He closed his eyes and focused on disappearing...

Nando sniffled and wiped his face dry. "It's like, some people can pretend to be something they're not... They can lie their whole lives just so the people they love don't feel threatened or uncomfortable. I can't do that. I am who I am. But when he finally decided to be honest about who he was, after lyin' for so long, I didn't have it in me to lie about who I am just to make him feel better. I wasn't strong enough to fake it. I ain't who he needs me to be. So he ain't talkin' to me anymore." Then he laughed, embarrassed at his inappropriate display.

Danny was confused. There were too many details. The layers were too delicate and intricate to peel any one piece away without the whole thing falling apart. He knew he couldn't take the whole thing, whatever it was. He was really stoned and he just wanted to get back to the party. He just didn't know how to get out of the car without it looking dramatic or frantic. He seriously considered sneaking out while Nando's head was turned and tiptoeing up the street...

Nando sat up with a gruff whimper. "We need to get out this car. I am fucked up!" He pulled the seat up, pushed open the door and stepped out of the car.

Danny sat there stunned, amazed that Nando could make getting out of the car look so easy, particularly after making everything else so fucking complicated. He pulled up his seat, rolled up the windows and got out of the car.

Nando was halfway up the street when he called back, "I need a fucking *drink!*"

Colin saw Zack step out the back door looking like Alexander Skarsgård's character on *True Blood* and immediately decided he needed more vodka in his cup. He turned and walked quickly back toward the driveway. While he was standing in line at the bar, he overheard the fat guys in white ball caps remark on Zack's entrance.

"Fuckin' sausage patrol showed up early. Dude, isn't that why they have fag bars? So they don't have to drag their cock-gobbling asses through our parties, waiting around for some munch to get too drunk?"

The other one snorted, "Dude, if none of these bitches act right, I might just let one of them suck my dick. I am *that* fucked up!" The two of them laughed and stumbled away, spilling drinks, bumping into people.

Colin looked back over at Zack and his twinkie tag team. Zack was really tall and his haughty posture gave the impression that he was gliding above the crowd, scouting the masses, set to snatch up whoever he wanted to take home. He was almost godlike when he wasn't wearing that cheesy hotel uniform, but he carried himself with such blatant arrogance that he came off like a total douche. Colin wondered if the sloppy frat guys really took issue with gay dudes or if they just felt threatened by Zack's looks. Any girl in her right mind would pick Zack over either of them, even if Zack did prefer cock gobbling.

When Colin's phone buzzed, he instinctively scoured the yard for his friends, figuring it was Danny calling. Instead, he found a text from Samantha. "Line 4 bathroom is like 40 deep. This party blows!!!" As excited as he had been to try tricking some other girl at the party into finding him cute by pretending to find her interesting, he felt his heart flutter at learning Samantha hadn't left. He knew at that point that it was ridiculous to even be thinking, but he considered the possibility that Samantha might be *The One*.

He glanced up at the house for a window near the bathroom, thinking maybe she was watching him, trying to catch his eye. But the lanterns and torches were reflecting against the glass, making it impossible to make out clear faces inside from where he was standing. Then he noticed Nando's hair. He was standing next to Danny talking to Zack. Zack nodded over at Colin and Danny and Nando turned in unison to find him.

Colin glanced over his shoulder for the white ball cap guys, hoping that they weren't seeing Zack fraternizing with his friends. Then he felt like an asshole for caring. Those dick heads were just like the people who'd always made him feel like shit for never fitting in as a kid. Growing up a skinny, fair-skinned black kid with freckles and curly hair that was strawberry blond until he was six or seven, Colin liked to believe he had given up on trying to appeal to the vacillating victimizing of morons like them.

But every now and then, he felt that tug from the other side, that desire to be part of the pack.

Danny and Nando were walking up just as Colin was getting to the front of the line and he could see from thirty feet away that they were BLAZED. Their bloodshot eyes were tight and swollen and they stepped with that slow caution of people who weren't convinced the ground was going to be where it was supposed to be. Colin tossed back his drink and poured three fresh ones. Nando's voice squawked out louder than the T.I. and Rihanna anthem throbbing from the big speakers.

"That was the dude from the hotel! The one who didn't understand why I needed to be in 420." Nando looked like he might have been on the verge of a nervous breakdown. His face was flushed and sweaty and he didn't seem capable of focusing his eyes. Colin hoped that if he'd ever been high enough to look that crazy, he'd had the sense to stay at home.

Danny didn't look quite so bad, but he was frazzled enough to appear on the verge of something himself. "What are you drinking? Is that Red Bull?" Danny took the red plastic cup from Colin without even waiting for the answer. He winced at the taste, but drank the whole thing down in three or four gulps. Colin was fully aware of Danny's trepidation around alcohol, but he refilled the cup anyway and nodded for them to get out of the way, as the growing line had started grumbling behind them.

They stepped into the driveway and stared out towards the clusters of people on the lawn. There were a lot more guys than girls outside, so it was fairly easy to discern that Samantha wasn't back from the bathroom yet. Colin turned and looked back toward the house and Danny, on his right, was looking back at him with a question in his eyes.

"So how did you do?" A sad smile crept across Danny's face, like he already knew the answer wasn't going to be good.

Colin beamed back at him with a grin that bordered on bumptious. He nodded, "Really good."

Danny nudged him playfully, happy for his friend, and Colin stumbled back into Nando. Barely conscious, Nando bumped into one of the white cap dudes without even noticing him until the guy turned around with his arms spread wide, a tiny wet spot on his oversized Ed Hardy T-shirt and a stupefied expression on his already unattractive face. Then the guy tossed his cup to the ground toward Nando's feet. "What the fuck dude? You can't watch where you're going?"

Nando turned around, confused, his brow furrowed like he was watching a foreign film with no subtitles. Danny stepped in between Ball Cap and Nando, his hands raised. "Hey man, that was an accident. Sorry about that. We don't want any trouble."

Ball Cap looked Danny up and down. "Nobody was talking to your faggot ass. Why don't you and your retarded friend here just get the fuck out--"...but before he could finish his sentence, Nando's arm flew out of nowhere like an explosion and punched the guy square in the face. It happened so fast, it didn't look real. It was like a special effect, some CGI apparition, had been flung across the screen they were all watching. Until the dude stumbled backwards, Danny wasn't even sure the punch had landed.

Colin yelped in disbelief, "Whoa, shit!"

Then Ball Cap twisted around, his face contorting like a werewolf under a full moon, and swung his right arm in slow motion at Danny, apparently confused about where the punch had come from. Before his fist could reach Danny, Nando had pounced on him and was pounding his fists into him like snares on the Jefferson High Drum Corps. It was strangely amusing and horrifyingly violent all at once. Danny watched the beating in shock, while Colin kept his eye on Ball Cap's buddy, who stood there with his cup in his hand and watched the whole thing, frozen with a dull smirk.

When he noticed blood spilling, Danny knew he had to save the guy, so he pulled Nando off and yanked him out of the way. Colin stood there, watching to make sure the dude wasn't dead or waiting to spring back to life like a Chuckie doll and start more shit. He finally sat up, his eye swelling orange with blood running down his forehead and gushing from his lip. He looked more discombobulated than angry. So Colin turned and followed his friends through the gathering crowd out toward the street.

He caught up with Danny, half pushing, half carrying Nando up the driveway. For an instant, from Colin's point of view, it looked like Danny was hugging Nando and that their faces were pressed together. Maybe it was just the way Nando was clutching Danny's back, but something about the apparent intimacy of the gesture gave Colin pause...

While they were all walking down the middle of the street toward the car, Nando's wheezing the only sound between them, Colin's phone buzzed again. He stopped and read the text.

"She's still there. She wants to know where I went." Colin was standing between street lamps that cut hard shadows across his face and obscured the details of his expression. Danny could hear the excitement in his voice about going back. He had a hard time admitting to himself that he didn't want him to leave...but insisting he go after the girl seemed like the easiest way to simplify everything that had grown complicated between them in the last two days. "You should go. Me and Nando probably can't walk back in there, but you should totally head back."

They both glanced to Nando, whose silhouette was nodding in agreement.

"You're cool with that?" Colin's voice went up an octave to accommodate the smile on his face.

Danny, suddenly very at peace about the reality of what was happening, added, "Yeah, call me if you need me to pick you up." Then he considered that maybe he had come off like a doting mother again. Do guys offer to pick their friends up after they hook up at parties? Danny and

Colin didn't have enough experience with all that for him to even know. He glanced over at Nando, whose face was also blanketed in shadows.

"Yeah and if any of them punks start some more shit, call me." Nando growled like Christian Bale's Batman.

Colin chuckled, "Cool. Thanks, y'all." He patted Danny on the shoulder and jogged back up the street toward the party. Danny and Nando turned and walked back to the car.

As they were getting into the car, Nando proposed they head back to the beach to do some ecstasy. Danny was just fucked up enough that he agreed without a second thought. Somehow his concern about how they would get back to the hotel and who was going to be sober enough to pick up Colin crumbled once his vodka drunk had time to catch up with his marijuana high. He just wasn't worried about any of it...and not worrying felt good.

Lost without the GPS on Colin's phone, Danny drove in the direction he believed was west, hoping they would eventually run into the beach. Fifteen minutes later, they found themselves driving down the middle of some downtown area. When Danny noticed the red and white neon archway above the street that read, 'Hillcrest,' the name didn't ring a bell. Then he remembered passing through the same part of town when Colin got called 'Sweetie' by the doorman on the way to the strip club. "I think this is where we got lost last night."

Nando nodded, preoccupied. "Yo, that car is pullin' out. Back up and park so we could get some water to take these."

Danny stopped and backed up into the spot, acknowledging for the first time Nando's strange power over him. Nando strolled through life as the authority on everything, carrying himself with a categorical clarity of intention that forestalled any doubt or impulse to question him. He had a swagger, particularly that night, that compelled Danny to relinquish his will to Nando's word. Even though he found the ferocity of his assault at the party disturbing, there was something assuring in the gesture. He had come to his defense in a way no one ever had before. Even 'built-like-a-brick-shit-house' Colin had never kicked anybody's ass for him. He felt safe with Nando.

They walked down the street, scouring the mostly dim storefronts for a convenience store, eventually coming upon the crowded sidewalk patio of a restaurant called Globe. Nando walked up to the front door and stepped in without even acknowledging the fat black guy on the stool in the 'Security' T-shirt. Danny followed him in, holding his breath, expecting to be snatched backwards and tossed onto the sidewalk...but he floated right past the host stand and into the dining room.

Nando went straight for the shimmering black and gold bar. Wandering in behind him, Danny noticed immediately that most of the people in the upscale restaurant were male. There were enough women sprinkled throughout that someone might not catch it right away, but Danny was looking for it. All the well-dressed men were slick and lithe and they all stood too close to one another and threw their heads back when they laughed. Not to mention that the disco-tinged house music gave the room an ambience of stylish sophistication that straight men wouldn't put up with. It seemed like a classier crowd than what one might expect in a surf town gay bar, but it was definitely gay. He and Nando, in their slacker hip-hop gear with their scruffy faces and apparent lack of hair product, stood out, if nothing else, as underdressed.

Danny pondered ways of bringing up the incongruity of their surroundings with their stated plans for the evening, but then considered that bringing it up might make it look like he took issue with it. After the conversation in the car about Nando's friend and their 'feelings,' just mentioning the word gay seemed like it might invite more discussion on the topic... He wasn't in the mood.

Nando turned around and handed him a bottle of water. "Tongue."

"Huh?" Danny was confused, but already ready to be receptive to whatever he was suggesting. Nando hadn't steered him wrong yet.

"Let me see your tongue."

Danny stuck out his tongue and Nando placed a pill on the tip. "Now drink up." Nando popped his own pill and they stood there, in the middle of the room, facing one another until Danny caught himself smiling into Nando's eyes. Then, as if he had caught himself in the same moment, Nando turned and looked out at the room and muttered, "Hot bitches in here."

Danny noted three beautiful dark-haired women seated nearby. They were probably in their early 30s, with enough make-up and exposed skin to make it clear that if sex was on the menu, it wasn't coming cheap. One of them had her hand rested in the lap of the woman next to her. The one who wasn't paired off stood up to leave and the couple picked up their tiny purses and followed her out. Nando slid right in and sat down at the table. Danny watched the women walk out, totally captivated. The couple, with their sexy lower backs switching in tandem under their revealing silk tops, walked out holding hands. He was floored. He thought for sure lesbians like that only existed on Showtime.

He glanced back at the table and Nando had his arms spread wide across the right side of the booth with a big grin on his face. He was obviously pleased with himself. Danny chuckled and sat down on the other side.

Before he'd decided what he was going to say, Danny's mouth had started moving and sounds were falling out. The earnestness of his tone immediately made him self-conscious, but he couldn't stop once he'd started. "Look, I just wanted to thank you for...you know, what you did at the party. It was cool that you had my back like that, you know, considering we just met and all. And you know... That's all. Just wanted to say thanks." He felt his face crumble inward during the silence that followed...

Nando leaned in, resting his elbows on the edge of the table. "Yeah, homie. That's how real niggas roll. You were lookin' out for me, too. It's all good... You want a drink?" Nando leaned back and pulled a wad of money out of his pocket.

"Let me get it. You've been such a...gracious host." Danny pulled out his wallet and handed Nando his last twenty dollar bill. Nando looked down at the money for a thoughtful moment, then grabbed it and wadded it with the rest.

"What you drinkin'?" Nando stood up and started bobbing his head to the house music with a 'Damn-this-shit-is-so-funky-I can't-even-help-myself!' grimace.

Danny laughed. "I'll just have what you're having. Or...I guess something like whatever we were drinking before." Nando strolled to the bar, stepping in time with the beat, wiggling his fingers like a DJ scratching records.

Danny looked around the room. It wasn't too crowded, but everyone appeared to share a glamour and an ease that he found fascinating. They billowed about like they didn't have a care in the world and just *happened* to be so fabulous. Then, as he looked closer, there seemed to be something forced and affected about it all. Did anyone *need* to be that plucked and coifed? Was that a natural slouch or was he affecting his standard 'bored on Saturday night' stance? Did his skin really beam with that preternatural glow or had he slathered something shiny onto his face?

Danny wondered if he might fall victim to the same self-aggrandizing masquerade if he spent too much time around gay men. Was there something organic and specific to this particular group that gravitated toward posh affectation or did all gay men end up adopting some version of this sparkling artifice?

He didn't believe working so hard to blend in was intrinsic to his personality, but he had seen the way others--people who for some reason were acutely concerned with running with the herd--would struggle to mask all the things that were *real* about them, only to replace it all with strained imitations of the banal qualities everyone around them had chosen to appropriate. It was a sad game that he honestly believed he was above stooping to. *But what if...*

What if his staunch resolve about remaining an individual turned out to be rooted in the security he felt from his bond with Colin? What if they did end up drifting apart? Would he have the strength of character to face the world alone or would he have to resort to trying to fit in with people like these to avoid loneliness?

He glanced up to find Nando carrying drinks and pimp strolling towards the booth, followed by Zack and his two friends. "Yo, look who showed up!" Nando's smile was affable and innocent, but Zack's smile sparkled with something sinister. Nando sat next to Danny, Zack and Matthew sat across the booth and the other Matt pulled up a chair.

Right away, Zack started in about "how lame that party ended up being" and "sorry about dragging you guys all the way out there" and "the guy who was throwing the party was all cracked out anyway" and "did you guys wanna do some coke?" Nando nodded that yes, he would, but decided to hold off after he turned to Danny, whose face had contorted with disapproval. The Matts quickly disappeared to 'the powder room' but Zack stayed behind, his interest piqued by whatever dynamic had allowed Danny to derail Nando's impulse to take his party to the next level.

"So what's up with you two? I know you're here for work, but what's *your* deal?" He nodded at Danny with a cocky pout.

"My deal? I don't have a deal. I just came down with my friend and now I'm hanging out with my buddy Nando, here." Then he added, more as punctuation or a way to deflect than an expression of real interest, "You?"

Zack, with a self-satisfied smirk about the conversation being turned back to him, paused for some dramatic effect that didn't quite pay off. Then he cleared his throat. "Well, people around here call me 'the Three Pounder.'"

Danny narrowed his eyes at Zack, noticing for the first time that his shoulders were kind of narrow for his neck. "I don't get it. Are you cheesy, like a Quarter Pounder?"

Nando burst out laughing and playfully punched Danny's shoulder. "Nigga, you crazy!" Danny got that it was a reference to the size of his meat, but he couldn't give Zack the satisfaction of having a viable nick-name based on his dick.

From a strictly physical perspective, Zack was handsome enough. His off-putting arrogance was just further proof to Danny that sexuality was about energy, not organs. He wondered if maybe he was a porn model too, considering he was probably much less off-putting in photographs or in any context where his mouth wasn't being used for talking... And Nando was definitely a model! It might contradict the full disclosure clause that he and Colin had just implemented, but going through Nando or Zack would be less complicated.

He decided he'd bring it up later. If Zack was a porn model who felt the need to brag about his dick-size within the first five minutes of meeting somebody, he would rather not be associated with him at all. At least Nando was a classy enough model to not drag his dick into civilized conversation.

Nando turned to Zack with a smug grin. "I bet I could give your three-pounder a run for its money." Certain he hadn't heard what he'd just heard, Danny glanced back and forth from Zack to Nando. They each leaned back against their respective banquettes, facing off with shit-eating grins. Danny was immediately embarrassed about the company he was keeping.

"You're serious," Zack scoffed, already pitying his would-be con-tender. "We can go back to my place right now." He arched an eyebrow to underline all the implications of the invitation.

Nando laughed. "Naw, homie, I don't get down like that. We can whip it out right here. Let the world see!" The Matts wandered back to the table, eyes glassy and bulbous.

"How's my dick gonna get hard at the table?"

Matthew's mouth popped open, regretting having missed so much of the conversation.

"That's on you, son." Nando reached down and groped his dick through his baggy jeans.

A fey cocktail waiter with a tiny apron slung low on his skinny hips, stepped up to the booth and flipped his bangs out of his face. "Hey. Get you guys anything?" His lisp droned with the monotone of a petulant child forced to attend to his parents' party guests. He'd started rolling his eyes before anyone even had time to respond.

Danny, ever courteous, spoke up. "We'll just take five waters for now. Thanks."

The waiter looked down and noticed that everyone at the table already had cocktails. He turned to Zack, probably assuming he was the one with the money. "Flat or sparkling?"

Without looking away from Nando, Zack hissed back, "Iced will be fine." The waiter shuffled away, offended. Zack continued, "Who's gonna judge?" Matt in the chair was grinning like he'd already swallowed the canary.

Nando looked at Matt and then back to Danny. Then everyone turned to Danny.

With a faint tingle fluttering against his chest, he shook his head, "Hell no. And if either of you take your dicks out at this table, I swear to God, I'm walkin' out this bitch."

Matthew turned to Danny with new interest. "Wait. You're not gay?"

Feeling Nando shift in the booth with the impact of the question's directness, Danny looked up at Matthew without flinching and said, "Is that a problem?"

Matthew, his head wobbling with the hint of a neck roll, spat back, "You're sitting in a gay club in the middle of the gay part of town. I just assumed, between the two of you, there must be *something* gay. Otherwise, why not find somewhere else to hang out?"

Nando sat up, looking back and forth from Zack to Matthew, but avoiding Danny. "We ain't from here. We didn't know what kinda club it was when we walked in. But we're cool, we can kick it anywhere. It's all love, homie." Matthew sat back, unconvinced.

Zack stared at Danny, a cloying facsimile of interest plastered onto his face. "So where are you guys from?"

"I'm from Philly. Danny is from..." Nando turned to Danny, having no idea...

"Sylmar. It's up past L.A., in San Fernando Valley." Danny sighed and sipped his drink, eager to change the scenery, or at least the company.

"What do you guys think of San Diego?" Zack's bleached teeth glowed almost lavender under the nightclub lighting. He drank down the rest of his cocktail and aimed his reapplied grin directly at Danny. "Pretty cool, eh?"

Danny just nodded at the question, politely apathetic and sipped his drink.

Nando opened his mouth to offer his opinion, but then he felt Danny's knee knock against his. He casually turned and glimpsed some low-grade panic in Danny's eyes. Nando muttered, "Let me see your phone for a sec."

Danny reached into his pocket and handed Nando his phone. The Matts paired off for some inane coke-rambling, but Zack kept his eyes fixed on Danny. Nando typed in a phone number, hit dial and then handed back the phone. He turned to Zack. "San Diego's all right. We haven't seen much of it, but the beach is nice. It's all white folks and Mexicans, but it's cool."

Matt turned, mid-sentence, to Nando, "What, you have a problem with Mexicans?" His eyes shot to Danny and then back to Nando. He nodded, " What are you? Dominican?"

Nando pulled out his own phone, looking directly at Matt's face and noticing that his name was probably Mateo. "Puerto Rican. But naw, I ain't got a problem with Mexicans, long as they ain't got a problem with me." Nando started typing on his phone.

Zack caught on right away. "If you guys want to talk privately, we can find another table. No need to go to all the trouble of texting over lil' old us. I do understand, though. I would want to send him sweet nothings and secret messages too." Zack's impish smile and glossy lips twisted something in the pit of Danny's stomach...

Nando pocketed his phone and glanced back up at Zack. "I think we're probably gonna head out anyway. No offense...but it might be a little too gay in here." He laughed heartily and smacked his hand against the table, feeling the first tingle of his ecstasy with the rush of blood to the palm of his hand. Right away he realized what Danny's look of panic was probably about: he was rolling...

Zack insisted, "Stay for one more round. On me. To make up for that lame party. I'd hate to think we ruined your night in SD. This place'll be packed in twenty minutes and this table is perfect for checking out all the boys and girls."

Matthew giggled, "And the girrrrrrrrrrrrrls!"

Danny, swaying with the sudden onset of his sexy electric, looked over at Nando, noting his vaguely Roman profile and his soft pink lips... It occurred to him that he might be just a little attracted to Nando. They were already too fucked up to drive, so if they left the club, they would probably end up sitting in the car, staring at each other while the drug made their bodies ache for things their minds knew weren't real. *What was I thinking, doing more ecstasy, after the crazy shit that went down last night?* "Another round sounds great! I'll have a vodka with Red Bull."

Nando turned to Danny with raised eyebrows. "Word?" He nodded at Zack with a wink, "Let's go get more drinks, then." He jumped up, eager for a pit-stop in the powder room...

o o o

Samantha twisted the lock on the bedroom door while Colin stumbled backwards onto the tiny bed against the hot pink wall cluttered with magazine cutouts of Demi Lovato and the Jonas Brothers. Noting the girly adolescent decor through his tottering drunkenness, he wondered if that drunk blonde lady in the pink really *was* someone's mom.

After they'd tossed back a few more cocktails outside, Samantha had dragged Colin through the crowded hallway and up the stairs, more eager to 'get to the good part' than he was. Her friends had ditched her at some point and being on her own seemed to be all it took to unleash her freak. Or maybe she had downed a couple more drinks and dropped whatever semblance of chastity she had on her way from the bathroom. Whatever, the girl was on a mission...and Colin was thrown by the clumsiness of her aggression. It was one thing to be wrapped up and mutually aroused, but she was moving so fast and with so little grace, he couldn't keep up. In his boozy state, her sloppy kissing and groping was blurring into something entirely unsexy. He was relieved when she finally clicked off the light.

That Asher Roth college song was playing downstairs. He mumbled along, "I wish we taped it," as he sat up and tried to focus his eyes on the oblong box of light on the wall, shining in through the opposite window. She was shimmying in front of him, trying to slide her skirt down over her pale fleshy thighs. He could see her tits jiggling down the front of her top as she reached for her thick ankles. By the time she managed to step out of her skirt and started peeling her top off, he was burping up traces of stomach acid. He quickly glanced around the dark room for a trash can, just in case he needed to hurl. But before he managed to find one, she had leapt into the air, plunged across the room and knocked him backwards. His head slammed against the wall with enough force that he blacked out immediately.

When he came to, the back of his head was throbbing. with so much pain he thought he was seeing the red globes from the tree in the backyard flashing in front of him. Kid Cudi's "Day N Night" was playing downstairs. It took him a few seconds to even realize that his pants were off...and that Samantha's head was bouncing up and down in his lap. His dick sprang to life and she gurgled out a muffled exclamation.

He closed his eyes and imagined watching her giving him head from some remote location, with cameras catching the scene from every angle. She wasn't nearly as physically fit as he was, but she made up for what she lacked in looks with tenacity and enthusiasm. She was working hard and his dick was showing all kinds of appreciation. He snatched off his T-shirt, sat up on his elbows and flexed his abs. She reached up and ran her fingers along his eight pack. He felt himself get harder in her mouth. That itchy tingle pulsed through his dick and he knew he was already getting close.

He couldn't see low enough to get a look at her lap because she was kneeling on the floor at the edge of the bed, but he knew he wanted to see it all before they were done. He reached for the hand that was jacking the base while she knocked the tip against the back of her throat. *She is good!* He pulled her up and she let his throbbing monster, slick with fluids, slip out of her mouth. He grabbed her face with rigid fingers and kissed her lips, tasting his own sticky on her tongue, her braces grating against his teeth. Then he reached down and pressed his finger against her bush. She had more pubic hair than he thought tasteful, but that didn't stop him. Her jiggly tits had him on a mission too.

As he fingered her, she started whimpering dirty talk...but he didn't want her to play the porn star. He was the star. She just needed to play the lucky girl he was giving the honor. He put his other hand against her mouth and then slid a finger inside, figuring that keeping her tongue busy would shut her up. He pressed a second finger inside her bush, damp and quivering with excitement. She had her hands against the wall, ripping the posters as she started bucking her hips against his hand, sucking his middle finger like a Fun Dip candy stick.

Colin started shivering. He pulled her undulating hips into his lap and hooked a third finger into her cozy box. She looked down at him with an expression that may have been lust but looked like disgust from his angle below. He was suddenly self-conscious. Tense. The back of his head started throbbing again and he realized how much he despised her. She was the physical manifestation of everything that was wrong with the world. Flabby and thoughtless. Loveless and promiscuous. He grunge-fucked her with his fingers, her moistening slit inches away from his raging hard on.

Then, like it was the most natural thing, he pulled his fingers out, grabbed his dick and slid it inside her. He pulled his finger out of her mouth and grabbed her hips with both hands and started slamming his dick into her slipperiness.

For a second, he thought he might have heard her say something, "Wait, hold on baby...is that...do you have a...?" By that point, he'd already mastered tuning out her voice. All he was hearing was his own grunting and the squishing sound his dick was making, digging up inside her. He felt that itchy tingle again, pulsing in time with his thrusts. Before he even noticed that she was slapping against his chest, yelling obscenities--obviously in ecstasy, he was growling and grunting and gushing, thrusting his load deep inside her.

He shuddered one last time as she quickly slid off of him, scrambling, slapping, screaming. "Tell me you did not just come inside me! Are you fucking crazy!?! What the fuck is wrong with you?" She was upset about something, but he was too exhausted to look up at her. She wasn't sexy anymore. Her hair had flattened out and her lips had lost their color and gloss. She was all sweaty and her face just looked unhappy.

She started snatching up clothes and squeezing her back into her ugly outfit. He closed his eyes and imagined her blonde friend--the one in the cream colored blouse who had big eyes like Amber. She was in much better shape and probably would have stayed hot the whole night. A few seconds after the door slammed behind Samantha, he dozed off.

o o o

Danny could feel himself emulating the male runway contestants on *Make Me a Supermodel* as he strutted across the crowded floor to the men's room. He didn't think anyone would notice him 'smizing' and swinging his shoulders because he was so accustomed to being invisible. He was completely oblivious to the covert glances chronicling every detail of his physical form. The ecstasy had imbued him with a sly new sense of how sexy he could be, but somehow it hadn't tarnished his innate modesty. And in a crowd of people predisposed to gleaming pretense, his earthy humility made him that much prettier. A rare bird...

There was a line out the door for the two stalls, but Danny bounced right up to a urinal without waiting at all. Even as he began to feel bystanders' slimy eyeballs slithering along his neck, he wasn't self-conscious about the attention. He glanced back at a few of the more blatant spectators, noting that the light in the men's room was less forgiving and that some of the beautiful people were scary up close. Most of them seemed to be less sure of themselves than he was, nervously averting their eyes, all the while making a very obvious show of being too cool to care.

Then, just as he was finishing, a guy stepped up to the urinal next to him. Danny's ecstasy was playing roguish tricks on him and without meaning to, he glanced down at the guy's hands unbuckling his 'GG' belt. The dude turned and watched him shake himself dry. When their eyes met, Danny smiled in spite of himself and the dude nodded with the word 'yes' flickering in his eyes. He was older, probably thirty or so, handsome with a manicured five o'clock shadow and a square jaw. He had thick, dark hair and light eyes with full pink lips. Danny caught himself drifting closer to him, mesmerized by his lips, longing to touch him...so he tucked himself back into his pants and bustled away, agitated.

He whipped around and found himself facing a mirror. The lighting at the sink gave everything a bluish tint and when Danny saw himself, with his upturned collar, his first thought was that he looked like a villainess from a Disney movie (it seemed like most of them had blue or lavender faces). He leaned up against the sink and got a good look at himself. He looked pretty. *Pretty?* He'd never thought of himself that way before, but his hair was falling perfectly, his eyes were shining bright and the shadows cast by his cheekbones swooped dramatically down to the upturned corners of his mouth. His lips, still moist with Nando's Lip Medex, glistened like a woman's. *Malecifent...*

The dude from the urinal stepped up and nodded at him again, locking his predatory eyes on Danny's in the mirror. They stared at one another so intently that everything else went blurry and all Danny could see was the man's hungry face. He felt like he was in a trance...and when the guy slid up behind him, pressing his leg against the back of Danny's, all he could do was swoon at the physical contact... The guy leaned in and brushed his lips against his neck and Danny's dick got rock hard. Shocked at how good it felt, Danny spun around and noticed two slope-shouldered boys with over-styled hair staring at them from an open stall. Danny carefully slipped out from under the guy's lips and disappeared out into the dining room...

Nando was a few feet away from their table, dancing energetically with a petite, boyish looking Latin girl. She had short curly hair, a shirt and necktie and she twisted with tiny steps like she was doing some sped up version of the samba. The smiles on their faces made Danny think that maybe they were old friends...but when he got closer and heard the girl calling out, "Boricua!", he figured they were both just happy to see another Puerto Rican so close to the Mexican border.

The room seemed to have gotten much more raucous while Danny was in the bathroom. The disco-flavored house music had turned into sexed-up electro and the crowd was embracing the new raunchiness. The Matts had both gone MIA, but Zack was sitting in the booth talking to an Asian dude with Zac Efron hair. As Danny approached the table, he saw Zack nod in his direction and watched the other guy turn and look up at him, size him up and then shrug, unimpressed. Danny wasn't in the head-space to deal with whatever was happening there, so he changed course just before he reached the table and went back to the bar.

The line for the bar was four or five deep. The only two black girls in the room were standing right in front of him. They had their hair tied back and they were fanning and dabbing at themselves with bar napkins. They were both beautiful, but one of them had dark, smooth skin and full lips and the graceful bone structure of a supermodel. Her long neck was damp and he could smell rose oil commingled with her sweat. He stared at her longingly, recalling the amazing feeling of soft lips on his own neck just moments before... His sexy electric had him hungry.

The back of his head sizzled with diverging currents of titillation that wriggled forward through his hair and along his cheeks, meeting in the middle of his face, taking the form of a crazed smile. The drug wasn't knocking into him with heavy waves as it had the night before. It was more like a constant stream of sexiness. That smile was stuck on his mug like the *Alien* 'facehugger,' clinging on to the very end.

Suddenly, the other girl heard the beat of a song she liked and raised an arm above her head, shouting out, "Music is the answer...to your problem...keep on movin'...then you will solve them! Heeeeeeeeey!" She dropped into full-tilt boogie-mode right there in line. The supermodel bobbed her head with a beaming smile and before he knew it, Danny's hips were popping from side to side, his head was rocking to the left on the two and the four and then, out of nowhere, the three of them were dancing wildly.

The girls were essentially a self-contained unit, with the supermodel being the more lithe, controlled half of the duo and the party girl spinning and flailing around her. Danny was close enough to feel like he was dancing with them, even though they hadn't officially acknowledged him. He raised his arms above his head and swirled his hips in big stripper-like circles; he was feeling himself something fierce.

Finally, the supermodel turned around grinning to get a look at him. It was like she looked through to the depths of his soul and she loved everything she saw. There was none of that skeevy sexual aggression, like the guy in the bathroom, and none of that creepy desperation, like Colin at the party. They danced and shared smiles that radiated love and nothing else. Danny kicked up a knee and slid out behind her, basking in the beam of joyousness that surrounded them...but his eyes stayed fixed on the supermodel. He twisted and twirled around her, while in his mind, they were standing perfectly still in an embrace. Nothing gross. Just sweetness. Simplicity. Love.

Then he realized they were at the front of the line and the bartender was waving to get their attention. They all stopped dancing. Party girl turned and ordered two drinks. Danny slowed to a sway and caught his breath while the girls' faces disappeared in the direction of the bartender. He lifted his shirt to wipe his forehead and when he opened his eyes again, the two girls were wandering away and the bartender was asking him what he wanted to drink.

"Uh... Red Bull Vodka?" The bartender paused for a moment, like he was about to ask Danny for some ID, or maybe what kind of vodka he preferred, but then he just went ahead and mixed the drink. He placed the cocktail on the bar and told him with two hands it was ten bucks.

Danny pulled out his wallet and remembered just as he was opening it that he had given Nando his last twenty dollars. *SHIT!* He looked up at the bartender, terrified that admitting he had no money was a sure way to get him kicked out. He thought of handing over his debit card, knowing it would most likely get declined. Then the dude from the urinal slid up next to him. "That one's on me." He ordered himself a Stoli tonic and turned to Danny with a smile.

Danny, relieved and unnerved, formally extended his hand. "Thanks, man."

The dude shook his hand firmly, but then spoke in a hushed murmur. "My pleasure. Sadly."

"Huh?" Danny shook his head, noting that his hand was tingling fuzzy against the guy's tightening grip.

The guy leaned in close to Danny's ear and said, "I''m Sandy."

"Oh. Hey. I'm Danny. Thanks again." The guy was still holding his hand, leaning into his ear and Danny nodded, secretly hoping his lips would touch his neck again.

The guy leaned closer. "You ever consider modeling, Danny?"

Danny pulled back, got a good look at Sandy and took a large gulp from his Vodka Red Bull as lightning-charged feathers tickled his ears and ran down the back of his neck...

o o o

When Colin came to again, he was flat on his back with slime crusting on his thighs. Lil Wayne's "Lollipop" had suddenly been turned way up and was bashing against his skull. He lifted his throbbing head and glanced around to find that he was completely naked except for his holey socks...and the bedroom door was open. Two guys were framed in yellow light from the hallway, staring at him with dropped jaws. They burst out laughing right before a third guy poked his head in between theirs with a flashing camera phone. The door slammed shut, the music went faint again and they were gone.

Colin rolled off the bed and onto the floor and started feeling around for his clothes. He heard his phone vibrating a few inches under the bed and reached down to get it, knocking his forehead against the aluminum bed frame. "Oww, fuck!"

He grabbed his underwear and his pants and pulled his body up to standing clutching the side of the bed. While facing the wall and sliding into his jeans, he noticed that the Jonas Brother with straight hair looked a little like Danny, which reminded him that his phone had been buzzing. He'd expected to find a message from Samantha because he couldn't, for the life of him, remember where she'd gone. It was a text from Nando: "Is Danny with u?"

Why the hell would he be with me? He braced himself against the dizziness and pulled on his shirt, suddenly in a panic about what might have happened to Danny. He stepped into his shoes and yanked open the door, stumbling into the hallway just as the older lady in the pink tank top rushed past him into what looked like the bathroom...

Once outside the house, which had only gotten more crowded since he and Samantha had rushed upstairs, he dialed Danny's number. Waiting for the call to connect, his mind flashed to Samantha's twisting shadow shouting down at him and smacking wildly at his chest. He couldn't remember what exactly had happened, but chills ran up his neck as her scream echoed in his mind. Danny's voicemail prompt--*did the phone even ring?*--snatched him out of the flashback.

He was walking in the dark back to where they had parked the car earlier when he realized he had no idea where he was or how he was going to get back to civilization. He dialed Danny again, hints of stomach acid flushing through his saliva, and it went straight to voicemail. He stopped walking and sat on the curb to let his stomach settle...

After a few seconds, he called Nando, hoping as the phone rang that he would be able to talk without going off on him...even though there was no denying that if anything had happened to Danny, it would be his own fault for bringing him down and abandoning him for Samantha. His throat tightened like he might vomit...

Nando answered the phone. "'Sup playa? Where you at?" Colin could hear some party in the background and a stupid smile on Nando's face.

"Where's Danny? Why isn't he answering his phone?" Colin felt himself fighting the sudden urge to cry and held his breath for a moment to shut it down.

"He ain't with you? I thought maybe he left to pick you up. Where you at?"

"I'm outside the party. Where ever the hell this is."

"Shit, nigga. It's a wrap on ol' girl *already?*" Nando was back to his 'thug life' act.

Colin's mind flashed to a blurry vision of Samantha standing in that bedroom, struggling to pull on her skirt and cursing at him. "Yeah, we're done."

"All right. Hold tight, homie. We 'bout to come get you." Nando hung up. Colin pulled himself up to standing as he heard rustling in the bush behind him. He twisted around in the dark, unsteady, and stumbled back toward the lamp light across the street. Just as he found his bearing, he watched a large raccoon waddle out of the thicket, into the street, headed directly for him. He turned and ran back toward the party house, not even looking back to see if the animal was chasing him. When he had run as far as he could, he leaned over, his hands braced against his knees, and threw up. The vomit was completely clear. He probably hadn't eaten anything all day. He felt like shit.

Dizzy and exhausted, he collapsed onto his back, clutching his stomach with one hand and his head with the other. Smashed between the night sky and someone's manicured lawn, he blinked up at the twinkling stars...down for the count.

o o o

Danny sat rigidly in the passenger seat of the parked pearl white BMW X5, his knee bouncing involuntarily as Sandy snorted another bump of cocaine off the top of his hand. The valet had given him his car key so he could 'find that business card,' but all they'd done so far was sit in the lot behind the restaurant, while Sandy did what seemed like too much blow.

He tapped out more cocaine onto his hand and held it in front of Danny's face. "Sure you wouldn't like some?" Danny had never seen cocaine before. He looked closely at the crystalline powder. The hand just hovered there, directly in front of his face. It was like someone pointing a finger at him inches from his eyes--technically not a physical violation, but an undeniable assault to his mental fortitude. He thought back to Nando wanting to sneak off to do cocaine with the Matts. *What's the big fucking deal, anyway?* He grabbed Sandy's wrist, pulled the hand up to his face, put a finger to his nostril like he'd seen in the movies and snorted...

The air buzzed around his head for a second and then went dead. Quiet. Clear. Sandy's wrist dropped into his lap and the amber light from the parking lot lamps flashed bright white for an instant.

Danny's eyes went wide, revitalized and hyperaware. Just then, Sandy's fingers pulsated and sprung to life, slithering down around Danny's leg toward his crotch. When he looked over to let him know he'd crossed a line, Sandy's eyes were closed and his face was careening toward him, lips extended. He held his breath and let Sandy's mouth press against his, let his facial hair scrape against his cheeks and let his burly tongue force his lips apart. He closed his eyes, waiting for the ecstasy to return, while Sandy groped his stiffening dick and mauled his waning indifference with resolute aggression. Danny resigned himself to the gruff sexuality being thrust upon him and settled back as velvet swirled out of his mouth and sparkled against Sandy's undulating face. His sexy electric was fighting to keep up, but something was off.

He stopped kissing. The magical fluidity of his ecstasy had been compromised, hardened by the cocaine. He was too aware. Too awake. The kissing was harsh and disagreeable. His face froze and his body went limp.

Sandy stopped kissing when he felt Danny's lips go slack and pulled back to check his face. Danny looked back at him with wide eyes, thankful that the siege on his face had abated, but even more relieved that--contrary to what his hard-on would have one believe, he wasn't turned on at all. His lack of desire was just as surprising to him as it seemed to be for Sandy.

Danny had given himself permission to experience whatever presented itself that night. Nando, his wily tour guide, had set him up with enough exhaustible options that Danny could potentially answer any question he had about sexuality over the course of the evening. He'd expected to be back in Sylmar with Colin the following day and was confident that whatever happened in San Diego would only live on as a cloudy memory of 'that wild weekend.' But ever since things had gotten *cloudy* with Colin, Danny had been hoping that nothing would confirm for him what he'd been fearing for the last two days: that he was indeed gay.

He thought back to being bullied in elementary school for being effeminate. His mother had let him grow his hair long, cooing, "Puro Aztlan!" from across the kitchen table with his baby sister in one hand and a bottle of Corona in the other. When the other boys grew hostile, threatened by how pretty he was, he asked to cut it, but she refused. "You just need to toughen up. Never dim your light for small minds." Even as a child, Danny felt conflicted about changing who he was from the inside to cope with the way people responded to what they saw on the outside. But he toughened up anyway. He stopped being sensitive. He shoved his feelings deep inside and made himself invisible to avoid having to face their disapproval.

That weekend, however, he'd seen sides of himself that he couldn't make sense of...and he felt like he was on the verge of an identity crisis. So having no real attraction to the rugged, sexually imposing man at his left--even if only as a result of the wrong combination of drugs--was a profound relief. He smiled and shook his head, "Sorry, I'm just not... I shouldn't."

Sandy shuddered with embarrassment, sat back and stared out the windshield. A pallor of shame and self-pity washed over his face. Danny looked straight ahead too, biting his lip, trying to hide how giddy he was about the increasing flaccidity of his dick. The silence between them drained the car's interior of all oxygen and the tension quickly became unbearable.

"So should I just call tomorrow about the modeling thing?"

Sandy reached into the center console, pulled out a business card and handed it to Danny, avoiding his eyes.

"AndroFiles dot com? What's Andro...?" Danny ran his tongue along the front of his top teeth.

"Androphilia is sexual love of men." Sandy finally turned to him. "You probably shouldn't mention that you were in his car or that we kissed. Anderson prefers his models straight."

o o o

Zack's Bronco pulled up in front of the house on Florida Street just as Colin stepped out of the dark onto the driveway. He didn't recognize the truck, but there was no mistaking Nando waving moronically from the passenger seat or Zack's crooked smile glowing in the dark just beyond him.

The Matts introduced themselves as he climbed unsteadily into the backseat. Their faces were twitchy and animated, but Colin was too annoyed to question it. Zack peeled out down the street and turned up Lady Gaga as they sped through the quiet, dark neighborhood back toward civilization.

They careened around a corner and Colin lurched into Matthew, who made an obvious show of enjoying the physical contact, giggling in Matt's ear and fanning himself like Scarlett O'Hara with a club flier. Nando turned around with a maniacal smile and offered him a bottle of water. Colin leaned forward to yell over the music. "What happened to Danny?"

Nando shook his head, clueless, but didn't change his goofy facial expression. He finally yelled back, "You know Matt and Matt were both in the Marines? You'd never know from looking at them, huh..." Nando glanced over and nodded at the Matts with a vaguely sexual smirk. Colin turned to check out the Matts, who were both looking back at Nando with hungry eyes.

Clearly out of the loop regarding the evening's sexual pairings and hardly interested at the moment, Colin sat back and pulled out his phone to text Danny again. "WHERE THE HELL ARE YOU?"

Zack screeched to a stop at an intersection and turned the music down, making eye contact with Colin in the rearview mirror before twisting towards Nando. "So do you wanna go back to Globe? Because that crowd dies down around one o' clock. We could throw a little impromptu get-together at my place... Go as late as you guys want." Zack looked back at Colin with more lascivious contempt.

"I need to find Danny. You guys can do whatever you want. Just drop me off at the hotel, please...and thank you." Matthew sucked his teeth and rolled his eyes, pettish. Nando turned around to try to persuade Colin to just go with the flow, but he found his eyes weary and red with concern. Only then did he realize how worried Colin was.

In an attempt to lighten the mood, he cleared his throat to speak. "Dude, Danny's fine. He was rolling in the middle of a gay club. I'm sure he just found somebody he liked and hit it."

"Rolling in the...? What...*gay bar*? What the hell does that mean?" Colin's voice made no secret of his fear of Danny being left alone with gay men. His fragility and sensitivity, combined with his agreeable smile, could be too easily misread in the wrong setting.

"We did some E and had a few drinks. He's fine, yo." Nando, noting that Colin was even more unsettled at that news, began to worry about the missing teenager himself. It hadn't even occurred to him that some people couldn't be counted on to handle their own drugs. He'd assumed anyone old enough to partake in the partying didn't need babysitting.

"Last I saw him, he was dancing with two black girls at the bar. She was tipping and twisting like Beyoncé. I was like, okaaaaaaaay?" To illustrate his point, Matt threw his arms out in front of him, mocking choreography from the "Single Ladies" video. Matthew tossed the flier he was holding aside to join in the routine and it landed right in Colin's lap. Colin picked it up and saw the face of the straight haired Jonas Brother looking back at him with a girlish pout and the words, "After Hours Bitch" stamped across his forehead. He flashed back to them dancing on the hotel bed.

After the topic of faggy dancing, Colin attempted to conceal his distress with collected, measured speech. "Maybe he went to this after hours."

"I don't think so, dude. It was like midnight when he disappeared. That after hours doesn't even open until two. He went home with somebody." Zack's bitterness about not being the chosen chaperon was probably lost on everyone except Nando, who caught the hissing and neck rolling clearly from the front seat.

Colin shook his head and stared out the window. Zack glanced back at Colin in the rearview as he peeled out toward the hotel.

o o o

When Danny got back around to the front of Globe, the doorman asked him for ID. "I was just in there, like, ten minutes ago! I went to get something out of my friend's car."

"Well, unless you can go back to your friend's car and get some ID, you ain't walkin' up in here." The doorman's gaze lingered on Danny's eyeballs just long enough for him to figure his dilated pupils had been clocked. He turned around quickly and pulled his phone out of his pocket. The battery was totally dead; wouldn't turn on at all. He had no idea for how long. With no charger, no money and no phone numbers, he had no way of reaching Nando. Or anyone. *Shit!*

He walked back around to the front patio to see if he could get a glimpse of the booth where they'd been seated. The room had emptied out considerably, but he still couldn't see their table. He had no idea what to do. He paced the sidewalk for a few minutes, the fuzzy warmth of his ecstasy waning against the chilly night. Then the doorman grunted something about, "No soliciting" and told him to beat it.

Danny walked past an alley and noticed the effete cocktail waiter smoking a cigarette alone outside the kitchen door. "Hey, you were our waiter. We were sitting at that booth in the middle of the room, by the dance floor area? Tall blond guy and Latin guy with wavy hair. Did you happen to see if they left?"

"I'm off the clock." The waiter hardly even bothered to look up at him, ashing his cigarette, annoyed.

Finally at the end of his rope, with tears welling in his eyes, Danny's frustration just spewed out... "Well, fucking FUCK YOU THEN!" It didn't even sound like his voice. It was as if Miss Piggy had rammed her hand up his backside and was moving his puppet mouth and screaming for him. He'd almost choked on one of the "fucks."

The waiter looked up, shocked. Danny could see he might have been fighting the urge to laugh, but something must have made him think twice. "They left about twenty minutes ago."

"Thanks." Danny walked away, his fists shaking at his sides. He was unraveling. He just wanted to be out of the cold, asleep at home and done with all this insanity.

He stepped up to his car and found a note under his windshield wiper. It was a flier for an after hours. Not noticing that every other car parked on that street had the same flier on the window, he plopped into the driver seat with a sigh, assuming the note had been left by Nando, a clue to where to find them. The clock read twenty after one and the club opened at two. But how the hell was he going to find Hancock Street? And how was he going to come up with the ten dollars to get in?

He started the engine. Dizzee Rascal's "Fix Up, Look Sharp" was playing. One of Colin's mix CDs. *Colin.* He pulled the business card out of his pocket and noticed Sandy's cell number and email scribbled on the back. He carefully backed out of the parking spot and drove slowly, cautiously into the night...

o o o

Colin walked out of the bathroom to find Nando standing frozen in the middle of the room, probably deliberating over whether to sit on Danny's bed or to try getting comfortable in the arm chair in the corner. Eventually, he opted for the bed, but he sat upright and kept his shoes on. Colin stepped into a pair of gym shorts, while Nando, his jaw gnashing, busied himself with the remote control.

"You mind turning that down?" Colin's voice crackled with a chilling contempt. His panic had shifted to an eerie calm. He was bracing himself for bad news, imagining how he was going to tell Dan Senior that he'd lost his son somewhere in San Diego. *"We were only down there so I could do jack-off porn, but when I met a girl, I ditched him with this drug addict friend of ours, who last saw him dancing high on ecstasy in a gay bar."*

He rolled over, facing away from Nando and the television and closed his eyes. He imagined Danny walking through the door, oblivious. Stoned. Carrying a bag of Sun Chips and an Arizona Plum Iced Green Tea...

Fragments of a dream... Nando and Danny whispering in bed, under a sheet lit up like a tent by cell phone. Giddy schoolboys at a sleepover. The sound of stubble scratching against stubble. Candy wrappers crinkling. A raccoon's screeching hiss! Uncontrollable sobbing...and then silence.

Colin woke up early that morning to find Danny four feet away, passed out next to Nando, who was facing the opposite wall. The pang of guilt he felt for falling asleep before knowing Danny was safely home immediately faded when he noticed Danny's naked knee poking out from under the blanket. He could have easily been wearing shorts under there, but seeing the two of them in bed together, with Danny's legs exposed, stirred something in Colin's stomach. He didn't trust Nando...and Danny getting too close to him was like a bad dream...

He sat up and glanced around the room. In his mind, he'd already started packing to head back to Sylmar. The San Diego porno-drug insanity could not be over soon enough. He turned back towards the other bed and Danny was looking back at him, tired, sad. Colin nodded 'what's up.'
"What happened to you?"

"Phone died. Got separated from everybody. Nando said you guys were worried. Sorry 'bout that." Danny's voice quivered with shame.

Colin felt emotion well up in his neck and he shoved it back down, shaking his head. "All good, dude. You ready to head home?"

Danny sat up, his wide eyes betraying his reticence. "Yeah. Well. Actually... I set up a meeting, er...a shoot. With Anderson."

Colin nodded dryly, *of course you did*. "Cool. When is that happening?"

Danny looked away. "This afternoon. One o'clock. I gotta make some money and get out of my dad's house." He glanced down at Nando, snoring next to him. "Would you... Can you come with me? Just so..you know...I know somebody there?"

For a moment, Colin thought Danny was talking to Nando, who was clearly still asleep. Then it all clicked. Danny was his best friend. He wasn't doing any of this to usurp Colin's glory. The only reason he was even in San Diego was because of his commitment to their friendship. The fact that he wanted Colin there with him just proved that whole thing was a gesture of solidarity, further confirmation of their irrefutable bond. "Yeah. Of course I'll go with you... But let's go to the beach and smoke some herb, first. You'll be more relaxed when you get under all them lights."

Danny nodded with a bright smile. "That's what's up!" He threw the cover off, hopped up in just tighty-whities and a T-shirt, carelessly and ineffectively adjusting his erection out of sight, and disappeared into the bathroom.

6

o o o

Nando bailed on the beach plans. He said he couldn't wake up in time, but he was up watching TV in bed when Danny and Colin left. He hadn't mentioned that his hotel room was only paid for through that morning and that he'd already missed his plane back to Philadelphia after sleeping in. Once they were out of the room, he propped open the door with a shoe, ran up to get his things before the twelve o'clock check-out, then crawled back into Danny's bed to call the airline.

He was hoping to get another flight out, but wasn't sure if his ticket was still any good or if he'd needed to call *before* the flight to make adjustments. Logistics were slipping through gaping cracks in his wavering attention span, but he refused to acknowledge that his partying was compromising his functionality. As far as he was concerned, none of the things that were falling apart were his fault.

Then, while he was on hold with American Airlines, he got a text. It was Paul responding to his call from the day before. "Grabbing drinks with friends tonight in Culver City. Be good to see you. P." The woman was still checking on a flight for him for that afternoon. Nando hung up and responded to the text. "I'll be there."

When they got back to the hotel room, there was no sign of Nando except for the Adidas duffle bag tucked under the table in the corner.

Sky picked them up promptly at two-forty. He was much chattier that day and once they got in the car, he mentioned seeing Danny with Nando at Globe the night before. Colin noted something in his tone, an intimation that Danny and Nando had appeared to be a couple, and he felt his neck go thick. If Danny was being mistaken for anybody's boyfriend, it should have been his, not Nando's. *Wait. What?* He sat back and chuckled at his own twisted contention. Despite having slept in the same bed, Danny and Nando were not boyfriends. They weren't even gay. *It's just that queer projection, 'everybody is secretly a homo' game that bitter gay dudes like to play.*

Sky reached over and turned up the stereo--it was the same Lady Gaga song from Zack's truck. It was like she was following him around. Colin didn't like Lady Gaga, but from the backseat he could see Sky and Danny's heads bobbing in tandem to the beat.

When they walked into the kitchen, the model release forms were waiting, just like before. Sky asked them to keep their voices down because a scene was being shot in one of the bedrooms. "They should have been done twenty minutes ago, but there was some 'Viagra crisis.'" Sky shrugged at Danny with a smirk, "Straight guys."

After Sky disappeared down the hall, Colin went straight for the breakfast nook and snatched up some strawberries and a blueberry muffin. "You want some orange juice?" Danny nodded yes, but his eyes were fixed on something outside the window above the sink. Colin stepped up behind him and saw a man sunbathing by the pool. He was laying face-down, naked, on a chaise...which wouldn't have been odd at that house, except there were no cameras around and the sun wasn't shining where he was laying.

"Looks like Sandy. That dude's a mess." Danny explained that he'd met Sandy, the model scout, at the bar the night before. Why the dude was laying naked in the shade in his boss's backyard and why they were both standing there looking at him was still unclear. Colin set the glass of orange juice on the kitchen island next to the paper work and opened the refrigerator to pull out two bottles of Smart Water, unscrewing the top on Danny's before drinking from his own.

When Danny opened the folder and started reading through the contracts, Colin watched his face closely for a response to all the legal jargon. He noticed the rosy blotches of a sunburn on his cheeks, but nothing that revealed confusion or a sense of being overwhelmed. He just started filling it all out. Colin conceded in that moment that Danny was probably a little smarter than he. It wasn't something Danny ever held over him; it was more like an unspoken truth, so obvious that nobody would bother mentioning. Then, to cut himself a little slack, he recalled that when he'd initially read the contracts, he'd been in the room alone, terrified and unsure about what was about to happen. Danny had the benefit of having his best friend there with him, plus a first hand account of what to expect.

Just then, a door opened and some ruckus erupted down the hall. They looked up at one another and then toward the hallway. At first it sounded like men in some heated argument, but then boisterous laughter broke out, making it clear that the yelling was just loud men talking. A stocky guy with vibrant tattoos along his muscled arms and a buzz cut strolled into the kitchen, totally naked, covered in sweat with a fully erect dick.

"Shit! Excuse me, dudes. Er, excuse *us!*" He was talking too loudly and referring to his erection in third person. His cocksure strut only made his legs look shorter. "New recruits! Hey, I'd shake your hands, but you don't wanna know where this hand's been." He burst out laughing again, grabbed two waters from the fridge and disappeared back down the hall.

Danny and Colin stood there staring at each other in silent shock as the guy recounted the story of the terrified teenagers in the kitchen to whoever was in the room with him, again too loud and with that brash laugh. The door slammed shut and the voices became muffled again. Danny chortled, "This is some crazy shit you got us doing." Colin nodded, yeah, it really was.

Sky appeared in the doorway with a completely deadpan expression, as if sent to put the kibosh on the mirth. "I need to get your drivers license to photocopy." Danny pulled out his wallet and Sky turned to Colin. "Are you working today too? I have a copy of your license, but I need to print out your paperwork."

"Naw, I'm just here for moral support." Colin playfully shook Danny by his shoulders.

Sky didn't speak for a moment. "How sweet." Then he took the license out of Danny's hand and disappeared back down the hallway.

Danny looked up and noticed Sandy was walking toward the house in slinky black swim trunks with his towel draped over his shoulder and flashy sunglasses riding low on his nose. His mind flashed to that chiseled face tinted orange under the amber light of the parking lot, and that brawny hand rubbing hard against his dick. What if Sandy walked into the kitchen and started talking about everything that had gone down in the truck the night before? Even after the awkward ending, Danny wanted to keep it all under wraps...particularly since Colin had instated the full-disclosure clause *and*, despite obvious ambivalence about Danny's involvement, agreed to come back to the house with him. Danny's knee started trembling as Sandy stepped out of sight. He heard the dining room patio door slide open. He turned to Colin, who was back at the table, staring at the muffins, deep in thought about something. The patio door slid closed.

Silence.

When Sandy never walked into the kitchen, Danny exhaled, stepped up to the island, drank down his orange juice and picked up the pen to finish filling out his paperwork. Colin cleared his throat from the breakfast nook. "I think I'm gonna do another scene today. He told me I could make some more money if I was willing to step it up. Might as well, right?"

"Yeah. Totally. What does 'step it up' mean?" Danny's rushed amenability was more a preemptive tactic for any impending confrontation about Sandy than a response to what had been said.

Colin shrugged, his stare stuck on the fruit bowl. Finally, he shook his head and let the words fall out. "Just gotta let some guy give me a blow job. Or jack off next to me or something."

Danny burped up orange juice with some stomach acid. "Wait, like, what guy? Like the little dude with the tattoos and the Viagra?"

"I don't know which guy. Whoever is around to do it, I guess. I mean, I don't even know if they have someone on hand or if Anderson does it or what. I'll ask Sky when he comes back. If jacking off with another guy is an option, maybe you and me could do it. That way it's not weird, since we already--we could just make an extra couple thou and split."

Danny shook his head, no, that would not be a good idea. Nobody should be doing anything on film that could in any way be construed as gay. Jacking off alone was fine because everybody does that. Side by side shit and blow jobs were gay. *No. Bad. Delete.* Instead of saying any of that, he just shook his head.

As if on cue, Sky walked in and handed Danny his license back. "You all done with these?" He checked for all the signatures while Colin wiggled out of the banquette to talk to him. Danny was still shaking his head...

"So if I did wanna do a shoot today, could me and Danny just jack off together? Anderson said something about a side by side thing instead of the full contact stuff." Colin's head cocked to the side, as if inquiring about the due date on a library book.

Sky glanced over at Danny--who was screaming, waving his arms and shaking his head 'NO!', *but on the inside*--and then back to Colin. "Generally, Anderson likes pushing the models' comfort limits. So a 'side by side' usually entails a bit more than jacking off. And since you guys are friends in real life, he'd probably want to see you touch each other. Probably nothing more involved than hands to lap, but you should talk to him about that. We're supposed to wrap at five today, and Danny's the last scene on the books, so maybe he'd be open to squeezing you in." He pivoted and carried the folder back out into the hallway, calling out over his shoulder, "I'll print out paperwork for you, just in case."

Danny wandered back toward the breakfast nook, so flustered and infuriated he was unable to speak. Colin trotted up behind him and punched him playfully on the shoulder. Danny picked up a bagel and quickly put it back down. *This is bad.* How could he explain why it was such a bad idea without revealing his fear of knowing himself? The fact that he was uncomfortable about the whole thing and Colin was clearly *not* only confirmed that something was wrong with him. Of course, jacking off with your homeboy for money shouldn't be that big a deal. Or should it? *Do straight guys jack off together and not trip about it?* It was yet another question that nobody seemed ready to answer for him. *Is masturbating three times a day too much? Does jacking off repeatedly with your best friend make you kind of gay? Does making out with and being groped by some dude in his car while you're high on ecstasy qualify as a sexual experience if you didn't enjoy it?*

He exhaled sharply and plastered a calm expression onto his face. The only thing left to do was play it cool. He turned around to find Colin looking back at him concerned. "You okay, dude? You got quiet for a minute there."

"Yeah. Was just thinking about stuff. Moving out of my dad's. Making adult decisions. Gonna have to get a real job soon." Danny's smile clearly read as forced, but fortunately, his emotional alibi justified internal discord. He decided in that moment that whatever happened, he was going to step it up. He would perform and behave with just the right amount of detachment and amusement. Nothing would make him uncomfortable. He was just as much a man as anybody. If Colin wasn't bothered, neither was he. *Fuck it. Bring it on.*

o o o

Nando sat alone in the truck sweating, waiting while Zack procured more cocaine. Just from the neighborhood, it was clear that Zack's dealer was living more comfortably than Nando's dealer, Eric. *Maybe coke just brings in more cash.* Pot-heads were probably less reliable than coke-fiends.

He hadn't worked up the nerve to ask Zack for a ride up to Culver City yet. He'd hoped to have heard back from Colin, but the three texts he'd sent hadn't been returned. No surprise. Those two, *Danny especially*, would have made better company for seeing Paul again, but Colin had made no secret of his disenchantment with him after losing Danny. Even though he had taken off on his own accord and never bothered to explain where he'd gone, somehow in Colin's eyes, it was still Nando's fault. The bond between those two defied logic, the way his own relationship with Paul once did. Nothing and nobody could come between them. Colin and Danny had disappeared back into their little bubble, alone together, so they would only need to worry about keeping their secrets from one another. Third parties tend to complicate friendships like that, the way Lena did with him and Paul...

Zack climbed back into the truck with his crooked smile and a noticeable edginess, looking like he'd been sampling his purchase inside. Nando cleared his throat, "Yo, so what you got goin' on for tonight?"

Zack started up the truck and looked over at Nando with wide eyes. "Sundays and Mondays are my days off. Figured I'd do some blow and suck some cock." He glanced down at Nando's lap.

"Oh, 'cause buddy of mine up in LA wanted to hang tonight. Thought I might try and head up there. Just seein' if you wanted to roll out." Nando smiled with as much charm as he could muster.

Zack pulled out onto the street and started lip-syncing along with the Pussycat Dolls without responding. *"I hate this part right here. I hate this part right here..."*

Nando's phone buzzed with a new text from Paul: "I'll get you the address when my roommate gets home. Should be fun. P." Seemed like it took an hour or so for Paul to respond to each text. Nando imagined him toiling over the right words, taking his time to be sure not to come off too invested. Paul was always over-thinking things...

Zack finally muttered, "Sure, we can go to LA. Be cute to see some new faces... New ass." Nando's pulse started racing. He was going to see his friend again. He immediately regretted asking Zack, knowing he would give Paul and his friends the wrong impression. Not to mention he'd be high on coke and trying to fuck everything in sight.

"Cool." Nando bobbed his head to the beat of the girly pop music and watched San Diego zip past. In the side mirror, he saw his hair flapping back in the wind. He was reminded of a photo of him with short hair from his high school yearbook, before his face had grown gaunt and sallow... He ran his hand against his cheekbone, hoping the infirmity he was seeing around his sunken eyes was a trick of the light or a weird mirror angle. It wasn't. He laid back against the headrest and shut his eyes...

o o o

Just before the guys wrapped the Viagra scene, Sky sat Danny down in the kitchen and patted his face with pressed powder. Then Sky helped Anderson move all the equipment out of the 'red bedroom' into a small room with a big sofa and an ottoman.

Danny sat behind the light fixtures and tripods watching Anderson set up the cameras. His Polo shirt was riding up in the back and each time he bent over to pick up something, a hint of the indentation disappearing down the firm seat of his jeans had Danny wondering what he'd look like naked.

Anderson was older, but there was something charming about his All-American dad vibe. When he'd introduced himself in the kitchen, his smile had seemed so genuine and sweet... Danny had attributed his own nervousness then to the job he was preparing for, but as he sat alone in the room with him, he couldn't help but acknowledge that there was something about Anderson's energy that made him a little shy.

After he'd finished aiming all the cameras, Anderson excused himself. Alone in the room, Danny practiced saying his stage name out loud. *Tony*. 'Tony' gave him an ethnic edge without being too specific and paid homage to his mother's brother-in-law, Antonio. Tony was a womanizing brute of a man, so macho and sexy that the men in the family found him difficult to talk to, while all the women came to his defense every time Aunt Alma caught him making eyes at someone else. Danny had always admired his uncle. His cocky strut and his complete disregard for the opinions of others made him a personal icon. *Tony* would make Danny feel like a *real man*.

Anderson walked back in and shut the door. "Ready to get started?" Danny nodded yes, his eyes twinkling against his will. Anderson hit the switch for the bright lights and clicked on the camera in the middle. Danny's heart started pounding so hard he could see his T-shirt shuddering. It was as if that tiny red light on the side of the camera was the smiling eye of God. Suddenly he was alive--a living, breathing human, whose actions would finally be acknowledged by the world around him. That red light was a portal out of his father's house and the sad little existence he had been born into...

"So tell us your name." Anderson was nodding his head as if he could see Danny's spirit awakening behind his eyes.

"Tony." Danny nodded 'what's up' with his best impression of Uncle Antonio's cocky snarl.

"And how old are you?"

"I'll be nineteen in March." He'd only been eighteen for three months, but he felt like rounding up made sense in the moment...

"And what do you like to do for fun?"

"Well, I watch a lot of porn." Danny's eyes smirked. "But when I'm not doing that, ya' know, I'm just hangin' with my friends. Chillin', goin' to clubs, havin' a good time, whatever." For a moment, he considered clarifying that until that weekend, 'friends' really just meant Colin. *Er, Bailey.* But he didn't think that Tony would have found the point worth qualifying.

"And isn't one of our other models, Bailey, a good friend of yours?" Anderson seemed to be reading his mind. Danny didn't flinch.

"He's my best friend." *Where is he going with this?*

"The two of you are planning on doing a scene together, right? Have you guys ever done anything like that before?"

Danny's mouth went dry. "Well, this is my first time doing anything like this. I watch porn, but I've never been in one before."

"Yeah, but have you guys ever done anything sexual together before this? Like, have you ever jacked off to porn together or...?" Danny's face went pale and Anderson started moving his pointer fingers in circles as if to say, 'move it along, roll with it.'

Silence.

He opened his mouth to change the subject, but then Danny spoke.

"Yeah, once. We went to a strip club... Got fucked up. And when he got home, we were still a little wired, so we jacked off, just so we could get to sleep." Danny exhaled relieved at how tidily he'd painted the picture.

"Hot. Well, I don't expect anyone will be falling asleep today. So let's get you up and out of those clothes and get started." Anderson clicked on the other two cameras and took the one on the left off the tripod and stepped closer to Danny.

Danny stood up, lifting his T-shirt carefully, slowly over his head, telling himself he was laying on the sexy, but really, he was trying not to muss his hair. After the shirt passed over his eyes, things got blurry...

He remembered Anderson asking him to flex his biceps. He remembered that by the time he pulled down his pants, his dick was already hard and there was a tiny wet spot on the front of his Hanes briefs. He remembered that once it all got going, he was more turned on by the fact that he was going through all the same positions that Colin had showed him than he was by the porn playing on the flat screen. And that Anderson had gotten so close to him, squatting below the sofa to shoot the camera up at his asshole, then holding the camera right in front of Danny's face to capture his POV of his dick... And that at one point, Anderson's crotch brushed against his shoulder and Danny turned to confirm that he'd just been jabbed by a very large erection. And then...

He had to believe that what followed was the result of a natural progression of circumstances, because he couldn't recall making the decision to do it... Suddenly he was looking up from the floor at Anderson--still holding the camera, jacking Anderson's dick right in front of his face and jacking his own dick at the same time. He remembered Anderson's dick seeming much bigger before it came out of the pants. He remembered sticking his tongue out to touch the tip and that the clear fluid that stuck to his end of his tongue was sweeter than he thought it would be. Then, he remembered letting go of Anderson, leaning back on his haunches, puckering his lips...and coming. *Buckets*. Anderson jumped down with the agility of someone half his apparent age to catch a clear shot of Danny's fountain of jelly cream shooting up to his chest and neck. Then a few seconds of a close-up on the mess... Then it was over.

Anderson clicked off the camera in his hand, stuffed his hard dick back into his jeans and got up to shut off the other cameras. He came back and handed Danny a fluffy white towel, smiling with a hint of shock in his eyes. "Okay, *that* was fucking hot."

Danny stood up, wiping himself clean, trying to recall what had just happened. Had he really unbuttoned Anderson's pants and pulled it out? Had anyone said anything while it was happening? He knew he hadn't put it all the way into his mouth...but he had touched it with his tongue. Did that make it official? Was that the defining moment? Dazed, he began picking up his clothes and dabbing at his gooey neck with the towel...

"So...you just blew a massive load. Are you gonna be able to come again if we shoot that scene with Colin today?" Anderson was watching him closely.

Stepping into his white briefs, Danny nodded, distracted. "I can come like that three or four times a day." *Colin...* He was going to have to explain to him what had just happened when he didn't quite understand it himself...

"Great. I'm going to go make sure Sky has the blue bedroom set up for you guys. You can shower, grab a fresh pair of undies and another T-shirt in the big bathroom just past the living room. It's only gonna take us about half an hour to set up. Great work, today." Anderson nodded and swung open the door, like he'd just commented on the receptionist's expertise at answering phones, and he was gone.

The cool air from the hallway carried with it faint sounds and smells from outside the tiny room which helped drag Danny out of his trance. The stink of his own body immediately became more apparent and he realized how hungry he was. He was already in his jeans and pulling on his T-shirt when Colin poked his head in.

"How'd it go?" His face was lit up like a Christmas tree. His goofy smile was so childlike, Danny got a little emotional. They'd come so far since Mrs. Osbourne's eighth grade English class...

"Went great. Easy, just like you said."

"Smells like sperm in here." Colin trotted in and punched his shoulder.

Danny chuckled, unamused by Colin's attempt at humor, but happy to see him in such good spirits. "I'd shake your hand, but you don't wanna know where this hand's been."

"Well, considering where it's about to be, I don't think it matters too much!" Colin laughed so loud, so brazenly, Danny wasn't sure if they were still making fun of the little guy with the Viagra cock or if he was really that comfortable with the situation...

"I touched Anderson's dick."

Silence.

"Did you get more money?" Colin's concern wasn't about questions of sexuality. He was wondering if he had overlooked ways of increasing his own pay rate.

"Maybe. I don't think so, but it was real quick..." Danny considered that maybe he should have insisted on more money.

"Well, you should ask him. Plus, Sky just told me that models who get a good response from viewers, you know, from member comments and more hits and shit, get brought back in and paid more money. Apparently, Anderson's trying to create, like, a stable of his own stars or whatever. It's probably smart to play it up right away..." Colin had become a shrewd business man in the twenty or so minutes that Danny had been locked away in that room.

"That's what's up. I'm gonna jump in the shower."

"Cool. Oh, your boy Sandy is making crepes. They're pretty good. You should grab one while they're hot if you're hungry."

My boy? Danny searched Colin's face for any clue that Sandy had told him about the kissing in the car. His expression didn't reveal he had any new information...so Danny strolled out to the kitchen. Sandy, in an unbuttoned guayabera and baggy linen shorts, nodded hello with a shy smirk and kept cooking.

Colin pimp-strolled in and grabbed the plate he'd left by the sink. "Try the Nutella, son. That shit is good, yo." He hadn't even realized he'd swiped Nando's thug-life act until Danny and Sandy both turned sideways to look at him. "I mean...it *is,* though." Grasping at stereotypes of masculinity while waiting for crepes in the kitchen of a house built on the lust of gay men seemed like it should have been too obvious a trap, but Colin walked right into it anyway.

o o o

By the time they got to the beach, Nando had already done so much of Zack's cocaine, he could not be convinced that *giant squid* wasn't just another colloquialism for the 'three pounder.' That is, until he saw the giant squids. There had been an earthquake centered deep in the ocean that morning which had scared a school of giant squid off their course, causing them to wash up onto La Jolla Beach that afternoon. The Matts had called Zack, promising the spectacle would be worth the drive.

Nando stood overlooking the shore from a giant rock, astounded. The creatures were much larger than anything he'd expected to see. He honestly hadn't known that giant squids even existed. Their huge sad, bulbous eyes made him even more self-conscious about not having worn sunglasses.

Matthew was standing right over one of them taking photos with his phone. "Before we enlisted, he wanted to be a marine biologist. He was obsessed with dolphins and whales and shit." Matt kept his distance, just a few feet from Nando, but he was clearly fascinated with the whole scene. He explained that the news vans had just left and that there had been at least fifty more stupefied people on the beach ten minutes before.

Zack, who seemed excited to see the monsters while they were driving over, had gotten distracted right away by a tall green-eyed dude with Shiva tattooed on his back. With no regard for his friends or the sea creatures, Zack slid out of his truck and immediately glommed onto the guy and his surfer-skate crew in the parking area. Nando only glanced back at them a couple times, but he saw enough to be impressed with how easily Zack integrated himself into the ranks of a bunch of straight dudes who seemed oblivious to his intentions. *That nigga got game!*

Matthew finally strolled back toward the rocks where Matt and Nando were standing. He looked as if he'd been crying and suddenly, Nando's heart hurt a little for the sea monsters. They were beastly, ugly animals that probably should have gone extinct with the other dinosaurs, but these beings had lives and histories and families and spirits too. One wrong turn and they'd all found themselves washed up, most of them dead, on the beach for the world to see.

When Matthew got close enough to get a good look at Nando's face, he winced. "Are you high? Girl, the sun is still out!" Nando stammered in protest, instinctively lying because of the way Matthew's face recoiled.

"What do you expect? She's been with Zack all day." Matt shook his head, jumping on the bandwagon, casting judgment on activity in which they'd all been fiercely engrossed *together* only a few hours before. Time of day apparently made a difference in qualifying the hazardousness of the bad habits they shared.

The Matts wandered off together, mumbling about how 'people need to keep their drugs in check...' In spite of being completely aware of their hypocrisy, Nando stood alone on the big rock, ashamed. Maybe seeing Paul that night wasn't the best idea. Maybe he should wait until he'd gone a couple of days without partying. *How long has it been since I've gone a full day without...?*

A few minutes had passed when Nando stepped down off the rock and looked around to find most of the people had lost interest in the creatures and wandered away...

o o o

Sky was editing copy for the site (he'd just changed Nando's 'Escobar' to 'Esteban') when Danny stepped into the office and cleared his throat. Colin lingered just outside the door like he was on watch.

"Yes?" Sky had a way of coming off completely condescending and annoyed, even when he was in perfectly good spirits. When he turned to Danny, he was actually smiling with his eyes, but nobody noticed.

"Yeah, about this release, we just had a question. Shouldn't there be a section in the contract that breaks down how much money we make based on how far we go? Like, if we're being paid X amount to jack off next to each other, shouldn't there be a sliding scale if we end up doing more?" Danny exhaled like he'd barely passed a geometry quiz.

Sky nodded and smiled with his mouth. "Well, Anderson will go through and figure out what you're comfortable doing beforehand. But I think in a situation like yours, where there is an implicit comfort level that may lead to surprises, being specific about the figures with regard to exactly what you end up doing is...wise."

Colin furrowed his brow, not sure he was understanding everything from the hallway, but encouraged enough that they were still talking.

Danny gave a weak smile, nervous about having to talk to Anderson about compensation, especially in front of Colin. Would discussing the details of how his fingers ended up wrapped around Anderson's dick be required to determine the retroactive rate for a hand job?

He didn't even notice Colin the watchman grunting and clicking his tongue from the hallway until Anderson stepped in past him. "We're all set, gentlemen. Everybody ready to work?" Danny turned with dread in his eyes. Sky could see that the kid was too nervous to handle the business on his own.

"The boys wanted to talk to you about the specifics of their compensation with regard to exactly what they will be expected to do." Sky smirked, clearly tickled about Anderson being put on the spot about money.

"Okay. So, exactly how far did you guys plan on going?" Anderson may have intended for his befuddled grin to make him seem guileless and oblivious to the need for discussions on such matters, but he just came across perturbed.

Danny turned to Colin, who shook his head, hoping the ball wouldn't get passed to him, but then he caught it anyway. "Like...we're just here to make money. I mean, like, we're best friends. Neither of us is interested in seeing or doing more than we have to. But if we can make more money...?"

Anderson exhaled, again appearing exasperated with the tedium of details. "Right. So how about this...?" He turned around and scribbled a list of terms and figures on a post-it on Sky's desk. Then he handed the paper to Danny.

"'What's 'BB Fuck' mean?" Danny's voice cracked...

Sky chimed in, "Bareback fuck means anal with no condoms." He smiled with his eyes again. "And 'cream-pie' denotes ejaculating in and on the orifice."

Colin stepped up and looked at the paper in Danny's hand. "Whoa, that's a lot of money." He looked at Danny with wide eyes.

Danny said, "You didn't write a number for fuck with a condom."

Anderson mumbled by rote, "We have onsite rapid HIV testing, which is required for all our models. We're known for hardcore bareback at AndroFiles." He stared at Danny.

"I don't know..." It was certainly enough money to get him out of his father's house, but was any of this even about money anymore? Danny just stood there shaking his head, suddenly sensing that all the eyes in the room were on him, eagerly waiting for him to offer up his ass.

Rather than pressure him into making him concede to the role he seemed born to play, Anderson broke the awkward silence with diplomacy. "How about we have Sky add these rates to your contracts and at the end of the shoot, we'll base your pay on how far you manage to go. That way, you can be spontaneous in the moment and not feel pressured to do anything you don't want to do."

Danny nodded, already anxious about the horrible things that were to become of him.

o o o

The sunset faded from an almost neon orange with swirling purple clouds into a pale yellow smudged with hot pink and powder blue. Nando stood up with a shiver and dusted the sand off his shorts. He'd expected Zack to come back for him. He truly believed that their proposed trip to Culver City would trump whatever adventures might have arisen with the Lords of Dogtown, that their day-and-a-half-long bond went deeper than the appeal of hypothetical sexual exploits with just any unwitting strangers.

He looked at his phone. No new messages. He nodded goodbye to the few sad sea monsters who had yet to be pulled back out by the tide. Then, glumly, he walked away from the water, hoping that putting more distance between himself and the frothing waves would warm his lonesome chill...

The lights were so bright in the blue bedroom that Colin was in a dazed stupor. Danny had been in and out of the room, on and off the couch, for the last ten minutes. If he'd allowed Danny's apparent nerves about it all to seep into his consciousness, he probably would have fallen apart. So he stayed focused on the money and the ego-trip and completely blocked out any concern over the fragility of the dynamics of their friendship or his own life. He was temporarily compartmentalizing his humanity in the interest of maximizing his future capital. The rest would work itself out. Everything would be fine. Getting through the day, finishing the scene and getting paid, was all he could see.

Sky had pulled Danny aside after their rapid tests and asked him if he had 'prepared.' Danny had no idea what he was talking about, so Sky ushered him into the bathroom and handed him a small soft plastic bottle of water with a green cap over the pointed tip. "Just in case." Danny looked back at him confused. Sky continued, "Oh. You should sit on the toilet, stick this you-know-where and squeeze until all the water is gone. Then wait for it to all come back out. That way, there won't be any surprises in that department...in heat of the moment."

Danny's mouth went dry, mortified. He started to ask if Colin had also been told to 'prepare,' but he knew he hadn't. Somehow it was already common knowledge that he would be the only one having anything stuck up his ass. All he could do was nod his head, humiliated, as he uncapped the small bottle.

Sky's eyes lit up. "Oh! And if you *really* want to be prepared, I can go grab you a couple butt plugs so you can stretch out. I don't remember how big your friend is, but we have an assortment of sizes. That way, when he starts--"

"NO! I mean, I'm fine, thanks." Danny's face turned bright red as he clumsily ushered him to the door.

Sky turned just before he stepped out and looked back at him, concern emanating from under his choppy bangs. "Listen... I don't know anything about you personally. I mean, you seem like a sweet guy. I just hope, if this line of work is something you continue to pursue, that you don't beat yourself up too much, you know, if you end up enjoying it. Even if this isn't how you see yourself, in the grand scheme of things... Just, you know, give yourself a break." With that, Sky stepped out and closed the bathroom door behind him.

Danny tottered backwards and landed on the toilet seat. He sat there stunned for a few seconds and then he just started crying. The gesture of a relative stranger glimpsing something broken inside him and reaching out to mend it--or at the very least, *acknowledge* it--was something he'd never experienced. Suddenly, he could see that the world was not all bad; that a lifetime of invisibility and silence was not his only option. Someday, someone out there might actually understand him...

Walking alone down the side of the parkway at dusk provided Nando with more time for self-reflection than he knew what to do with. The bleak reality of his life caving in around him was too glaring to ignore in the stretches of silence between passing cars. He had missed his flight home, already spent a good chunk of his money on drugs and he'd managed to surround himself with 'friends' who were either too pissed off to talk to him or too busy to answer their phones. How had he managed to fuck up everything so quickly?

He was suddenly overwhelmed by a sense of needing to set things right. It seemed he could trace everything that had gone wrong in his life back to that night with Paul and Lena. If he could just talk to Paul and clear up all the mistakes he had made by him, then logically, everything else would fall back into place. He would be able to start over, from the point back when the world around him still made sense...

Then, as he was walking alongside the highway, the street lights clicked on above a neighborhood at the bottom of a grassy hill on his right. He hopped over the railing and trotted down... Every street sign he'd come across said something about Torrey Pines, which didn't sound familiar. But when he reached the foot of the hill, he immediately recognized Eric's neighborhood.

He was fairly sure that Eric wouldn't appreciate him just showing up unannounced, but maybe the element of surprise would help defuse the awkwardness of their last interaction. Maybe he could just apologize for being a freak before. Maybe God had put Eric in his path at that very moment to prove that there was no time like the present to begin repairing the damage he had done. Maybe it was a test. Maybe he was on his way to deliverance.

7

o o o

Danny and Colin sat next to each other on the nautically striped bedspread, fully clothed with the bottoms of their bare feet facing the camera. Anderson seemed to be keeping his questions simple so as not to scare them; even his most probing were fairly banal...

"Have you ever seen each other naked?"

Colin answered abruptly, "Yeah, like once or twice," not bothering to include details. He had no idea Danny had already spilled the beans about their night together after the strip club.

"Have the two of you ever tag-teamed a girl? Like a full-blown three way?"

The childlike giggle that erupted from Danny before he shook his head 'no' hinted that perhaps the idea wasn't altogether unappealing to him, but he quickly cleaned up his response. "A full-blown three way...as opposed to a *half-assed one?*"

Colin burst out laughing. "Smart ass!" And just like that, they transformed from terrified boys into best friends, tickled by the ridiculousness of the situation... Their faces opened up with bright smiles and they managed to shock each other with a level of comfort neither of them had thought possible in front of another person. They were being their silly selves with a man and three cameras in the room to document it!

"Yeah, I don't know so much about a three-way. This one likes big girls. Like what's her name, Gizmo? Gordita? From the food court..."

"Fuck you, dude. Just because you're built like a Girl Scout..."

Once they'd loosened up enough to start in with the jokes, Anderson invited them to get undressed. They looked at each other for an awkward beat and then started laughing again. By the time their clothes were off and they were side by side, back on the bed, things started moving quickly.

Colin's dick seemed to have sprung to life at the mere mention of getting naked because he was ready to go the moment he stepped out of his drawers. Danny got his up once the porno started playing behind Anderson. There was a brushed steel lube dispenser on the nightstand next to Colin, which Anderson pointed out, but they both spit into their hands instead...

After a few moments of focused silence, save for the squishy sound of rapid jacking, Colin chuckled ironically, "Yeah, this isn't awkward at all."

"Whose stupid idea was it to do this sober?" Danny was wishing they could take the porno off mute, realizing he enjoyed the sound of sex as much as the view...

When Anderson directed him to reach over and 'give Danny a hand,' Colin winced and stalled for a moment, chortling through a bratty, "Aaaw, maaaaaaan!" At the very last moment, he pulled his gaze from the porno and turned to Danny, silently assuring him with a nod that read, 'Okay brother, here we go.' He grabbed Danny and started jacking, unable to conceal how fascinated he was with the experience of touching an erection that wasn't his own. He even whispered something that Danny couldn't quite make out about how completely different it felt with foreskin.

Without being directed, Danny reached over and gripped Colin's dick, which immediately got harder in his hand. Colin's wasn't as long as Danny's, but anything it lacked in length, it more than made up for in girth. Danny commented on it right away. "Damn, dude, it's like a Coke can!"

Colin came back with, "What's with all this crazy extra skin..." There was a juvenile fascination to their tone, a childlike surprise with a twinge of disgust that seemed to put them both at ease. That they kept talking about how weird it was made it less weird. They spoke under their breath, keeping most of their conversation to themselves...

"You might need to put some lube on that, dude." Colin chuckled as Anderson moved in closer with the camera. Danny leaned over, his mouth inches above Colin's dick and dropped a line of spit onto the tip and rubbed the palm of his hand over the head just as he had seen Colin do to himself two nights before.

Colin closed his eyes, savoring the sensation, and his mind flashed to the hot pink bedroom walls and the ominous shadow of Samantha's naked body writhing above him. He opened his eyes quickly, as if racing to escape a nightmare... He tightened his grip on Danny and accelerated his jacking, causing Danny's dick to twitch and ooze clear stickiness at the tip. Right away, he muttered, "Ooh, you better slow down," and Colin released his grip.

Danny leaned over, lowering his head even closer to Colin's lap and spit onto the tip of his dick again. Then, like it was the obvious, natural thing to do, with his eyes shut tight, he closed his mouth around the head. He just held it there for a moment, savoring the salty taste and the fleshy feel of it against his lips. Then he began running his tongue in circles along the lower ridge. Colin's entire body went rigid and he sat back against the headboard. He placed his slimy hand on the back of Danny's neck and moaned. Danny's mouth slid lower, swallowing more than half of his thickness, running his tongue along the bottom of the shaft while his hand continued jacking at the base.

Anderson's camera moved in closer, zooming in and around, but Danny had no idea as his eyes were closed. He started jacking his own dick with his other hand while he continued to choke down the Coke can.

Shocked at Danny's technique, Colin opened his eyes, noticing how close the camera was, and only then did he remember to flex his abs and rub his nipples. 'Bailey,' with all his overt sexuality and showmanship, hadn't even made it into the room yet... Colin was determined to put on a good show and when his vocalizing got louder and more graphic, Danny adjusted his position to display more of his own body. He slid up onto his knees with his ass in the air and continued slurping in Colin's lap.

Colin reached across and slapped Danny's ass and rubbed circles over the red hand print. Anderson ran around to the other side of the bed to catch a shot of Danny's raised backside. When Danny arched his back toward the camera, Colin leaned over to squirt lube onto his fingers and reached back across to slather the slickness along the crack of Danny's fuzzy ass. He saw Anderson zoom in on Danny's crack and knew exactly what he was supposed to do. He really didn't want to. He tried to talk himself out of it. But he was in performance-mode and he knew what Anderson and the viewers would want him to do... He ran his pointer finger along the slit of Danny's sparkling asshole and then...holding his breath...he slid the finger inside.

Danny froze, wide eyed, with a barely audible yelp. With his jaw locked open in shock, Colin's dick slipped right out of his mouth and slapped against his flexed abs. Danny had no idea how to respond. Yes, he had just used Sky's enema to prep his insides for manhandling and yes, he had been attempting to mentally prepare for the very real possibility of receptive anal sex for the last hour or so... But the finger caught him completely by surprise. Somehow it felt more intimate to have Colin's finger, the finger on the hand that he saw everyday, inside him than it would have been to have his dick, which he would probably never see again anyway...

Once some of the emotional shock had subsided, he was left to discern the physical sensation itself. It didn't exactly hurt. It was more irritating than painful. It definitely didn't feel good or even sexual. It felt more like a school boy prank taken into really intimate territory. *Like the ultimate wet willy...* He couldn't help but start giggling. He was kneeled over Colin's lap with his ass up, buckled over with laughter.

Colin saw his back shaking, but he didn't realize he was laughing--and not quivering in ecstasy--until he heard him snort. For that few seconds, he had been impressed by Danny's porno showmanship. Of course, once he realized he was just giggling, he started laughing too and then everything fell apart. Danny toppled over and the two of them were rolling around with their legs in the air, howling. Their erections had both deflated and any sexuality they had mustered up for one another completely dissipated. It had officially gone from hot porno to bad sketch comedy.

Anderson couldn't help but chuckle when the boys finally sighed in unison at the end of their giggle fit. "Okay, let's get focused, guys. We're almost done."

Colin sat up, apologizing to no one in particular, and got back into position for their side by side setup. Danny took a little longer to collect himself. His mind was racing. He hadn't hated Colin's dick in his mouth, but he definitely hadn't enjoyed his finger in his ass. *Oral but not anal? Dicks not fingers? Halfway homosexual? Inconclusive.* He needed a break. He asked if he could go get some water.

"Of course. Grab two, but when you get back, let's get through this. We've already got some hot footage. You're really beautiful when you're in the moment..." Anderson flashed a secret smile at Danny that made him feel like a little pig staring into the mouth of a big bad wolf. He was suddenly very self-conscious about his nudity, so he stepped into his briefs and ducked out into the hallway without looking back to see if Colin had noticed the exchange.

The air in the hallway was cool and quiet. The drone of the lights and the cameras in the bedroom only registered once he'd closed the door behind him. He stepped slowly, milking the plush silence for any revelation or wisdom it could provide...but nothing came but more silence. No understanding. No answer. Just the deafening absence thereof.

In the kitchen, Sandy was wiping down the counter and jiggling his hips to something on his iPod. He quickly plucked out his earbuds when he saw Danny. "Oh hey, is this your phone? I think you left it in the office." He'd almost played off his embarrassment about being caught dancing...*almost.* Danny graciously ignored the moment and trotted over to look at the phone plugged in above the sink.

"Yeah! Did you find a charger?"

"Yeah, well, it's one of those universal chargers from Sharper Image. I bought a five-pack and just put them all over the house." Sandy glanced down at Danny's underwear, up over his shoulder toward the hallway and then lowered his voice, "I figured you probably wouldn't want your phone left unattended. Never know where your number might end up." Sandy beamed at Danny with an oddly ingratiating grin. His aloof charm and seductive dexterity from the night before had shriveled into something desperate and clumsy in the daylight.

"Thanks, dude." Danny turned, popped into the refrigerator for two bottles of water, and trotted back into the hallway without so much as a smile over his shoulder. Sandy's cloying further cluttered his mind when all he wanted was clarity.

Who would *Danny* be at the end of all this?

He stood in the hallway just outside the bedroom door for a couple moments...just to catch his breath and relax his face. He took a long sip of water and then he stepped inside.

Colin was at the edge of the bed, stroking his dick, with Anderson squatted on the floor in front of him, aiming the camera up at the action. Danny slipped in, shut the door and stepped out of his underwear. He crawled onto the bed behind Colin, sat with his back against the headboard and started stroking his own growing erection. Anderson stood up to get a shot of the two of them on the bed and then clicked on the other two cameras, which had been moved to new places in the room.

Once he knew all the cameras were on, Colin glanced back at Danny and crawled up on the bed toward him with a calculatedly sexy snarl. Danny recognized 'Bailey' right away and inhaled through his mouth in hopes of summoning 'Tony' from somewhere inside...but Tony wasn't coming. Bailey started rubbing his upper thigh, in full performance mode, but Danny hadn't had enough time to focus on checking out. He was stuck in his head, trapped in his body.

Bailey, kneeling in between his extended legs, grabbed Danny's dick. His hand already had lube on it, but for the sake of the show, he dropped a trail of spit onto the tip and started jacking. He switched hands to open up to Anderson's camera and pressed his slippery fingers down against the ridge of fuzzy flesh below Danny's balls, massaging the outer edge of his asshole without slipping inside. Danny, slightly panicked, raised his knees as if he was going to scoot away from the fingers, but his back was already pressed against the headboard. With nowhere to go, the gesture read as an invitation to probe deeper. Bailey's massaging got more aggressive and Danny's dick got harder in his hand... Neither of them made a sound.

Anderson swooped in closer with the camera to get a clear shot of Bailey's fingers against Danny's quivering slit. For the first time, Danny felt like he had officially lost control of his body. His friend was so focused on the show, his face had changed. Danny was trying to make eye-contact with him to get him to slow down, but he never looked up. He closed his eyes tight and prayed for Tony to take over.

Suddenly, the jacking and the ass probing stopped. When he felt his weight shifting above him, Danny opened his eyes to find Bailey standing on the bed directly in front of him, pressing his slimy, semi-erect dick into his face. Danny reached up and took hold of it, clearly uncomfortable. He shook it from side to side to get the blood rushing. When it started growing, he rubbed the palm of his other hand over the head, already adroit in getting his best friend's dick hard. Within seconds, Bailey was at full mast and shoving his hips towards Danny's face, pushing his hand away, forcing his dick into his mouth.

Reluctantly, Danny opened his mouth and immediately gagged on the synthetic tang of the lube. That didn't stop Bailey. He grabbed the back of Danny's head with one hand and began skull-fucking him, grunting with each violent plunge. Danny's eyes watered as he choked...but when he saw Anderson move in for a close-up of his face, he reached up to grab the dick again, using his hand to buffer Bailey's thrusting (instead of knocking him off the bed, like he wanted to). Once he had his hand wrapped around the dick, he squeezed down on it hard enough to let Colin know that Bailey had gone too far.

Danny marveled at how he was able to distinguish the two personalities in his mind. His friend Colin would never treat someone like that, least of all Danny. But Bailey was a twisted motherfucker, bent on sexual domination. Once Bailey had taken over, reasoning with Colin was next to impossible...

Colin eventually stopped thrusting and released his grip on the back of Danny's head. Danny wiped the tears and the lube off the side of his face with the back of his free hand, still holding the dick at a safe distance with the other.

Colin knelt down in front of him. Danny let go of the still throbbing erection only when it had drifted beyond his arm's reach. Colin placed his hand on Danny's face, wiping tears away with his thumb...and then he kissed Danny softly on the lips. The moment seemed to happen in slow motion. When Danny saw Colin's face floating towards his, he closed his eyes--not in preparation for the kiss, but in the hope of becoming invisible. He needed to disappear. Kissing Colin was absolutely not supposed to happen. Kissing wasn't even on the contract. They had nothing to gain...

But Colin, who was either taking his performance to the next level or genuinely repentant about his brutality, was tenderly kissing Danny's lips. While apparently trying to assuage his own guilt, Colin was compounding Danny's...because Danny liked the kiss. He believed the gesture came from a place of love. Sure, it was unhealthy, abusive love, but that very brutality infused the kiss with a profound sweetness.

He kissed Colin back, reciprocating his gentle trepidation, intent on granting absolution. Then the kiss took on a life of its own. The intensity swelled and their lips swirled into each other with such a distinct rhythm that one could assume their mouths had been rehearsing the dance for weeks. Danny's hand reached up to rub Colin's chest and Colin pulled out of the kiss for a moment to spit onto his fingers. He pressed his mouth back onto Danny's just as his wet fingers pressed against Danny's asshole. He inched toward Colin's hand, locking his knees against Colin's beefy thighs and pulling him closer.

They both had their eyes closed, but they could feel Anderson's camera floating over every inch of their trembling bodies. The camera happened to be focused on Colin's fingers massaging the flesh around Danny's hole when Colin sat up and thrust his hips forward, locking his arms under Danny's knees so that Danny reclined flat onto his back with his legs raised. Colin pressed his oozing rigidity against the fuzzy slope below Danny's balls, sliding up and down just above his slit. Colin opened his eyes to look down at Danny--whose eyes were still closed--just as Danny reached down to grab Colin's dick and rest it against his crack. Colin didn't move at all, but Danny inched his body closer, slowly wrapping the moist flesh of his hole around the head of Colin's slippery erection. They stayed frozen in that position for what seemed like a long time, until Danny opened his eyes, looked up at Colin and nodded his head. At that, Colin contracted his lower back, carefully sliding himself deeper inside...and then slipping back out just as carefully. He slid back in, a little deeper, and then his legs started shivering violently. Grimacing in pain, Danny reached up to cup Colin's beefy butt cheeks in his hands, and pulled Colin in deeper, whimpering quietly as Colin accelerated his pumping.

Colin shifted his focus down to his own body--specifically, the place where his body was conjoined with Danny's. The image of his flesh disappearing into someone else's was fascinating to him. The fact that it was his best friend's flesh was bizarre, but didn't diminish the beauty of it. He concentrated on the splendor of their skin and the corporeality of the action. Without giving in to his brain's instinct to check-out completely, without surrendering to Bailey's detachment, he pumped his body into Danny's. Anderson's camera floated in and out of view, but Colin stayed focused on the sound of his grunting and on the view of his own chest heaving and his abs flexing with every thrust forward. He stayed focused on Danny's hand jacking his own dick and the growing intensity of his writhing and whimpering. He stayed focused on the performance until that itchy tingling started and his dick started twitching...and like a surprise, he yanked it out just in time to shoot his thick puddle of sperm onto Danny's stomach, shuddering with the guttural groans of a gladiator. Within seconds, Danny was jacking a shower of semen onto his own chest and neck...

It was done.

Colin fell back beside Danny on to the bed, his eyes opened but seeing nothing. The ceiling was a distant blur...

Danny's eyes were closed, but he had laid his forearm over his face anyway. He couldn't catch his breath. His heart was beating too hard, too fast...

After some close-ups on the slippery aftermath, Anderson placed the camera back on the tripod and mumbled, "Nice work, guys." He tossed fluffy, fabric-softener fragrant towels onto the bed and he stepped out of the room, leaving the two boys alone to flounder in the wake of their shattered realities...

8

o o o

Nando gently pushed open the door to apartment 6 and the hinges squeaked like the wail of a hungry baby. "Hello? Eric?" He didn't want to just walk inside. Maybe Eric had gone to the laundry room or to get something out of his car. The front door wasn't just unlocked--it was half open...and all the lights were out. There was a sliver of pale light coming from the open refrigerator, but it wasn't illuminating much. Nando could see that the couch and the cool lamp were gone and that the living room was completely cleared out, save for a few scraps of trash and an empty water bottle. If Eric was gone, it looked like he had left in a hurry.

Nando stepped inside. "Eric? It's Nando. You here?" He ran his hand along the wall beside the door, hoping to find a light switch. Nothing...

He stepped past the empty dining room area into the kitchen and saw that the contents of the refrigerator had been tossed onto the floor. There was a carton of 'Karamel Sutra' ice cream that was perspiring, but didn't appear to have melted yet. Whatever had gone down hadn't happened too long before. Maybe he'd been robbed? Maybe the robber was still in the apartment...

Nando quietly backed into the living room and noticed that the light was on in one of the rooms down the hall. He crept toward the light, his fingers wriggling and ready to be balled into fists. He pushed open the door to the bedroom, which had been ransacked. There were clothes and sheets and papers all over the floor. Then he noticed the trail of what looked like blood on the carpet next to his feet. *SHIT!*

The dark red stains ran under his shoes and continued across the hall onto the linoleum floor of the bathroom. He reached his arm out slowly and nudged open the door... He reached in to turn on the light and saw a strip of red ran that up over the side of the tub and disappeared behind the New York subway map shower curtain. He pulled his phone out of his pocket and dialed 911...

"Hello?" His voice echoed against the tile... "Yeah, I just walked into my friend's place and there's blood all over the floor and in the bathroom... No. Well, I thought he'd been robbed 'cuz the place is trashed but then there's all this blood in here too. Naw, nobody's here." Nando reached for the shower curtain and pulled it back to find Eric's bloody dead body clutching a duffle bag. "OH SHIT!" Nando screamed and stumbled backwards into the hallway, dropping his phone when he slammed against the cupboard. He grabbed the phone and scurried on all fours into the living room. "He's here! I think he's dead! He's in the bathtub! Holy shit, oh shit, fuck!"

When the woman told him to find a safe place to wait for the police and then asked him his name, he realized calling the police had been a rash decision. *I got no business being involved in this shit!* He whispered, "Fernando Cruz" and carefully stood up. She kept asking him questions, but all he could manage to mutter in response was "Uh huh." Before he knew what he was doing, he was back in the bathroom, standing over the bathtub. He hung up the phone as the woman was asking, "Are you still there?" and slipped it back into his pocket.

His mind was racing. He had to act quickly. He reached down and carefully slid the duffle bag out of Eric's hands. Blood splattered against the side of the tub when his limp arm fell back against his body. Nando thought about rinsing the blood off the bag in the sink, but there wasn't time. He snatched a towel off the rod, laid it across toilet seat and set the bag on the towel. He unzipped the bag and found exactly what he was looking for: a huge drug stash. He zipped up the bag, wrapped it in the towel and ran out the front door of the apartment, clutching the bundle to his chest.

He leapt down the stairs and dashed out the front gate. When he got to the street and heard sirens already approaching in the distance, he slowed down. He shoved the bundle up under the front of his baggy shirt. Walking as normally and looking as casual as he could, he strolled down the sidewalk with wild eyes, scanning the street for bystanders and nosy neighbors. His racing heartbeat made it difficult to keep his pace leisurely and he tripped over his feet a few times. He told himself that, should some neighbor mention that they'd seen him moving hurriedly or looking suspicious, he had the very real excuse of just having seen a dead body. He would work the walk up the street into his story...

When he felt confident that he was being blocked from most of the street by an old Volkswagen bus, he ducked and shoved the bundle behind an overgrown hedge in front of a run down house about a block down from Eric's building. He stuck his arms up under his shirt, feigning a nervous gesture of wringing his hands against the fabric, just in case someone had seen him with 'something under his shirt.'

He was already covered in sweat when he started walking back toward the building and he considered going back to the hedge to get the towel and wipe down his face, but there wasn't time. Completely winded, he continued to the front of the building and sat on the curb, wiping his face with his shirt. He waited for the police, his heart beating harder than it ever had in his life, and scoured his clothes for spattered blood under the light of the street lamp...

An hour later, he stood on that sidewalk, streaming tears shining against the flashing blue and red lights. He watched them carry the black bag of Eric's remains out on a stretcher. He had already been fingerprinted and spoken to two officers about what he had seen and his 'relationship' to Eric. Ironically, he managed to keep drugs out of the story by concocting a gay subplot. He wasn't sure if adding the gay stuff was necessary, but he felt like it would help throw the cops off any drug trail. Particularly if they found Nando's phone number in Eric's phone. Nando was determined to keep himself out of any ensuing drug investigation if he could...

He told the cops that he'd met Eric at a club with some girls three days before--which was true. They'd all gone back to Eric's to party afterwards, also true. But in this version, Eric had hit on Nando. Nando said he had been too self-conscious around the girls to try anything sexual with him that night, but after being abandoned by his other friends at 'the giant squid beach,' he just happened to pass through Eric's neighborhood. He'd decided, in a moment of 'curiosity,' to drop by and see if the vibe was different without the girls. (Not calling beforehand turned out to be a blessing, because it didn't connect him with Eric any earlier in the day than his 911 call.)

The 'might be bi-curious' ruse also gave him an excuse for being nervous while trying to 'recount' what had happened. The cops found his story about being in town to make rent money modeling for a gay porn site so pathetic, they probably cut him some slack. They seemed even more dismissive of the whole thing once he mentioned that Eric had hit on him. A dead black man in San Diego is probably even less pressing if he's gay.

Then they were done with him. They took down his information and told him to call the precinct if he remembered any other details. Two of the three police cars drove away after the ambulance. The remaining two cops disappeared into the building to interview neighbors. The six or seven people who had come out of their homes to see what all the sirens were about had all returned to their Sunday night television shows. Nando just wandered away.

He strolled past the bush, looked back over his shoulder to confirm that no one was around and he reached in for the bundle. He carried it like a baby this time, cradling it against his chest as he continued down the street and around the corner, disappearing into the night...

o o o

Once the checks were cut and they saw how much money they'd made, Colin arranged to stay in San Diego to do more work. Anderson had been so pleased with the shoot, he had Sky extend the reservation on their hotel room before they left the studio.

Danny was ready to go home. He and Colin had decided beforehand to do the stills photo shoot after the scene so they wouldn't have to suffer the awkwardness of those sexual poses *before*, but doing the shoot afterwards was even more uncomfortable. They hadn't spoken a word to each other since the scene, which confirmed for Danny that they were out of their depth. They had no business blurring those lines, dismantling their understanding. Now there was no way to be sure they'd ever get it back. Five pivotal years as one another's everything, possibly wiped to nothing with the stroke of one ballpoint pen to a gay-for-pay-check.

After sacrificing all that, he didn't *feel* any more resolved about his sexuality. Sure, the circumstances and inherent intimacy between them had facilitated a revelatory exploration. He realized that aggressive domination coupled with tenderness and affection turned him on. He found that he liked having someone dear to him *inside* him; he appreciated that the physical act signified--practically functioned as a metaphor for the emotional closeness and trust that it required. However, the idea of hypothetical sex with any other man didn't appeal to him at all. Colin was his best friend. He had given him access to something special because he knew Colin loved him...and... *And?*

And he loved Colin. *I do love Colin.* Even as the words tiptoed through his mind, he knew in his heart that they didn't carry the significance he'd been fearing they might. He wasn't in love with Colin...and if Colin was going to get weird and distant because of something they did together for money--at his prompting, no less--it wasn't Danny's problem. How could he fight for their friendship if Colin didn't care enough to talk to him? How could their relationship--their life together amount to anything without a shared interest in understanding one another? If shutting down was the only solution Colin could be bothered to come up with, so be it. Shut it down. Shut it all down. Danny was going home.

They were dropped off at the hotel together, but when the elevator door opened in the lobby, Colin turned without a word and walked back toward the front desk. Danny didn't hold the elevator. He didn't even turn back to see where Colin had gone. It was as if, after the most intimate thing they could experience together, they had been rendered complete strangers.

Colin was afraid to be alone with Danny in that hotel room. He was afraid that what he had done to Danny, what he had allowed to happen to him, was irreparable. He was afraid that once they were alone together, the truth of what had been broken would spill out in front of them and they would be forced to scramble through trying to put it back together...or watch it die.

It was just sex. A physical deed. An exchange of bodily functions. It didn't have to mean anything. It shouldn't mean anything. So why did it? Why did Colin feel like he'd taken something away that he had no means of giving back, even if he wanted to?

It was getting cold, but he couldn't go upstairs and get his jacket until Danny was gone. He stepped out onto the sidewalk in front of the hotel, scanning the block for some place he could buy a sweatshirt... He remembered Sky pointing out 'the UTC' to Danny when they had been picked up that afternoon. University Town Center was a big outdoor mall about ten blocks away. If it was still open, maybe he could find an Old Navy or something and hide out at the food court for an hour or so.

He did his damnedest to focus on his surroundings--cracks in the sidewalk, billboards with hot girls, tall buildings, songs from passing cars--anything but Danny. So of course, his head was awash with the sounds of squishing and grunting and the memory of Danny wiping tears away from his face. Then...Samantha. Again. As soon as he would wipe Danny's face out of his mind, he saw her very clearly, slapping at his chest, screaming down at him. Had he violated her in some way too? Is that why she had disappeared so suddenly? His eyes welled with tears at the prospect.

What the fuck is wrong with me? The notion that his sexuality seemed predisposed to manifest in violence chilled him to the bone. Then, to make matters worse, his dick got hard.

Danny had sent Colin a text telling him he was headed back to Sylmar, but hadn't gotten a response. As he was pulling out of the parking garage, his phone buzzed from the cup holder. It was Nando. "Hello?"

"Danny? Where y'all at?" He sounded out of breath.

"Just leaving the hotel." Danny spotted the back of Colin's striped shirt strolling on the sidewalk ahead. "Where are you?" He didn't slow down or even glance over at Colin as he passed...

"I'm down near Eric's. Can you come get me?" *Eric...the drug dealer?* Danny assumed Nando was on another bender, tweaking and twisted out of his brain.

"I'm on my way back to Sylmar." His voice was crisp with a tone of finality that he hoped would end the discussion.

"That's perfect, yo. Culver City is on the way to Sylmar, right? I'm trying to get out of San Diego. Shit is fucked up out here!" Danny shook his head. Nando was simple like a child. At first, it was endearing the way he said whatever was on his mind and made no apologies for being true to himself. But once you got to know him, his cavalier approach to life came off more reckless than charming. He used his seductive swagger to do whatever he wanted with no concern for the possible repercussions. It was edgy and cool from a distance, but close up, it was just dangerous and stupid. Danny was certain he didn't want any more of that in his life. He wanted things to go back to being simple...but as Colin's stripes disappeared in his rearview mirror, so did the likelihood of things ever being simple again.

"Where are you exactly? I can be there in fifteen minutes." Danny slowed down and turned in the direction of the highway, his heart heavy with the sense that he was willingly walking right into his own undoing.

Colin stepped into the entrance of the UTC with swollen eyes and a pimp stroll. He could feel his upper lip snarled with machismo as he passed a gaggle of high school girls who weren't even paying him any mind. It was instinctual. His mind couldn't process what had just happened, so his body--*Bailey*--took over to spare him the guilt and shame... In that moment, he simply was not himself.

He glanced into American Eagle Outfitters and noticed a scrawny blond boy with a headset checking him out from behind the girls shirt display. He nodded sexy at the gawking twink, further fueled by the confirmation of his rampant sex appeal.

He looked up and noticed a middle aged woman standing against the second floor railing, scanning the ground floor for someone. She didn't seem to be looking at him, but he imagined what she would have seen if she had: his golden sculpted body stalking through the open air mall with the menacing grace of a jungle cat. He was sex. Sex was his business. It was his talent. His calling. No one could cast judgment upon a man who had simply answered his calling. He was doing exactly what the universe had wanted him to do. Nobody could deny that. He hadn't done anything wrong...

He strutted into the Gap and walked straight to the front, scanning the store for any girls to notice him checking out the sweaters and button-down shirts in the full-priced section. He picked up a navy blue sweatshirt and held it up in front of him as he turned toward a full-length mirror...and then he saw it. It was all over his face; the undeniable remorse that had paled his skin and reddened his eyes was right in front of him, plain as day.

The truth jolted through him like an electric shock. He had just ruined the only relationship that meant anything to him for a few thousand dollars. Worse, he had been *filmed* violating Danny, so the moment everything had fallen apart was documented and would exist forever. Perverted men who didn't care about him or have any idea how much Danny meant to him would be getting off on the violence he had just inflicted on his best friend. And there was no way to take any of it back. It was done.

He dropped the sweatshirt on the floor and ran out of the store. As he was rushing through the mall, fighting back tears on his way back to the hotel, he kept telling himself that the universe would make everything okay...

Danny pulled up to the intersection Nando had texted him, but there was no sign of him. He turned down the Janelle Monae CD that Colin used to give him shit about. ("What is this, gay surf music?") He rolled down the window, scanning the residential neighborhood for any sign of life. Just as he reached for his phone, Nando jumped into the passenger seat. Danny yelped like a Chihuahua.

"It's me, yo. Let's go!" Nando reached over, turned off the music and rolled up his window. Danny glanced down at the stereo knob, seething with residual resentment about Colin's disrespect for his musical taste. His impulse was to turn it back on and play it loud as a way of refusing to allow his music or his self-worth to ever be stifled again. But he didn't. He just drove.

It wasn't until Danny rolled up his window and caught a whiff of Nando that he remembered seeing his bag in Colin's hotel room. "What about your stuff? Wasn't that your bag in the corner?"

Nando didn't answer. Danny looked over at him, clutching the towel, his face sweaty and dazed. Danny clicked on the air conditioning, aiming the vents at the passenger seat and then he switched the music back on. Janelle sang out, "You're free, but in your mind, your freedom's in a bind..." He glanced back over at Nando, shiny and paranoid, looking like a slave on the run from the shackles of his own insanity.

Danny turned onto the 805 and they drove through the dark for two hours without a single word. Danny didn't even mind the quiet. He got to play whatever music he wanted. Every time he reached for a CD that had Colin's handwriting on it, he tossed it into the backseat. The days of compromising his sense of self to appease small minds were officially over. *You don't like it, you can get the fuck out.*

o o o

By the time Nando's phone chirped with the address to the bar where he was supposed to meet his friends, Danny had already stopped to get gas, parked at Jack N the Box for a bacon sourdough burger (making a mess of ketchup and mayonnaise down the front of his shirt) and driven aimlessly around Culver City for forty minutes. He was dizzy from mental exhaustion and all he wanted was Nando out of his car so he could get home and go to sleep.

"Shadowbox on Venice Boulevard."

Danny made a quick U-turn and drove back toward Venice. "You still don't have a street number or a cross street?"

Nando started shaking his head, nervous-breakdown style, and finally mumbled, "Fuck it. Just take me to LAX." Then quietly, an afterthought, "Please."

Danny pulled over and parked. He was at his wit's end. "What the hell, Nando? We've been driving around, waiting to hear from your friend, and now you're bailing on him to go to the airport? What's going on?" Danny unclipped his seat belt and turned to look at him. He was still clutching the towel.

Nando eventually looked over with forced a smile, like he was expecting they could throw a few pleasantries across the car and be back on their way. But Danny was pissed and he could see it. Nando unclipped his seat belt and climbed out of the car.

Danny watched him slam the door shut and walk away. That was the second time in three hours he'd watched someone he thought was a friend disappear from view through his mucky rear window. He got out and followed Nando down the street.

He caught up with him, staring up at the sign of a Holiday Inn Express, nodding like a dashboard bobble-head. He approached slowly, as he would a dog he expected might turn on him with teeth. "Nando, get back in the car. I'll take you to the airport."

"Can't go to the airport. Can't go anywhere. Shit is fucked up." Nando never turned to address him directly; he looked like he was talking to the illuminated sign.

"You need help, man. Like, your family can take care of you back in Philly, right? You can't just... You need help." Danny's throat tightened, getting choked up about his new friend crumbling in front of him on the sidewalk. He felt hopeless. He already missed Colin...

"You don't know what you're talking about, Danny. I'm fine. I'm not the one who needs help. Nando clutched the towel closer to his chest. "Thanks for the ride. I'm fine."

There was nothing left to say, but Danny wasn't satisfied. Everything around him was falling apart and he felt like he couldn't do anything to salvage it. Exhausted, he started huffing and swearing under his breath, pacing behind Nando on the sidewalk. He was *so fucking tired of this shit* and *why can't people just get their shit together* and *why is everybody turning into a bunch of assholes?* He was determined not to walk away from Nando without some indication that he was going to be okay. The hotel's automatic door slid open as Nando drifted away from his hissy fit.

"And what's with the fucking towel, Nando?!?" Danny didn't even realize he was yelling until he glanced in at a black woman sitting alone in the cramped hotel lobby looking out, uneasy. Nando stepped back toward the street and the door closed.

"Get in the car, Danny. Go home. Go back to your normal life and just be happy. Be happy you're not wrapped up in any of the bullshit the rest of us are stuck in. Just...go home." Nando finally turned to him, his eyes wet with emotion.

The tear running down Nando's face knocked the wind out of Danny. He finally understood: we really are all alone in the world. With his friends and his family life all falling apart, he couldn't count on anyone but himself. As sobering and lonely as that seemed at first, the notion that there was no one left for him to answer to was also empowering. He didn't know what his future held, but being *sane* and open to the possibilities put him in a better position than his cohorts. He just had to get out of his father's house. He'd wasted so much time being miserable, stuck in that chronic cloud because he hadn't wanted to face the reality that he needed to take responsibility for his own life. Every step he took from then on was up to him...and it was fucking scary. But it was time to pull it together and get a move on.

He looked up and Nando nodded back at him with a sad smile just before he turned and walked away. "Later Nando. Take care of yourself, man."

Nando called back over his shoulder, "You too, Danny."

Danny brushed his hair out of his eyes and bounced back down the street toward his car. He couldn't feel it yet but he was already stepping differently, with his shoulders pressed back and his arms swinging freely.

Right before he reached his car, he slipped off the edge of the curb and stumbled into the street. He collected himself, glanced back to see if anyone had noticed--even though, in the moment, he really didn't care--and kept walking.

PART TWO

9

o o o

Leslie was sitting alone in the tiny lobby of the Holiday Inn Express sipping on Red Bull Lite, watching two young men who appeared to be homeless argue on the sidewalk outside. Each time one of them would stumble toward the hotel's automatic door, it would whoosh open, making the traffic noise and the details of their drunken altercation too loud to ignore. She kept glancing back and forth from the door to the front desk, which was about the size of a voting booth, expecting that the commotion would galvanize the missing desk clerk to reclaim his post. She soon realized she would be left to fend for herself should the street urchins decide to drag their foolishness inside. Considering she'd just spent four hours on a plane, after coaching the high school girls' basketball team that weekend and working the desk at the Fed Ex office all week, she was in no mood for mess. Of course she could always throw down, St. Lunatic-style, if she needed to.

Thirty-seconds after the junior drunks agreed to just wander off in opposite directions, Leslie's 'funky chicken' ringtone clucked with a text letting her know that Tanya and her friends were about to reach the hotel. She hadn't seen her daughter since early June, when Tanya moved to California to find a job before starting her first quarter at UCLA. The two of them had always been very close, but since Leslie and Tanya's father had separated in January, Leslie found herself even more dependent on her daughter's companionship. They got on one another's nerves every now and then, talking on the phone every day, but their bond was stronger than ever. They were really growing into best friends.

Leslie had never met Tanya's roommates, but she felt she already knew them, just based on the many phone conversations about them. Max and Paul were both gay, but Max was the more flamboyant, 'free-spirited' of the two. Paul was about to begin his final year as an undergraduate, but he was semi-closeted and depressed half the time. Max, who was starting his second year, had a 'part-time boyfriend' who lived in San Diego, but slept at their Westwood apartment every other weekend. Leslie knew that because it had become a point of contention with Paul. Tanya's theory was that Paul didn't like seeing the young lovebirds all shacked up because he didn't have a love of his own. Max's boyfriend thought Paul was just in love with Max, but Tanya wasn't buying that. "Paul is way too closeted to be attracted to such a girly boy."

Whoosh!

Leslie glanced up and a rail thin boy with dirty blond hair, skintight jeans, 80s ankle boots and a leather cord tied as a headband strutted through the automatic door. *That has to be him.* "Max...?"

"Yeah! Hey, Ms. Leslie. Tanya asked me to jump out and grab you 'cause they're trying to make her pay to park in that little lot." Max's thick North Carolina drawl caught Leslie off guard. His 'high fashion' sense of style seemed contrary to anything she imagined acceptable in the South. His smile sparkled like his entire face had been dipped in shimmering gold.

"Whose car she drivin'?" Leslie stood up to shake Max's hand and in one swift movement, he hugged her and whisked her out onto the sidewalk. He was probably only two-thirds her body weight, but the child was strong!

"We borrowed my friend Shae's car, but I don't have my license yet and Paul doesn't want to be held accountable, so he refuses to drive." They were standing in the driveway when a little green Toyota Echo skidded around from the back of the parking lot.

"Heeeeeey Mamaaaaaa!!!" Tanya, her hair braided up into a fro'd mohawk, screamed from the driver seat, startling Leslie, who reached back to make sure her wig was still in place. "Get in, get in, get in!" Max scurried around to the passenger side and crawled into the backseat with Paul and Leslie squeezed into the front seat. Tanya threw her arms around her and squealed so loud that Leslie could only give into the giddiness with a high-pitched giggle of her own. She hadn't been able to admit to herself how much she missed her daughter until she had her face buried in her neck, until she could smell her TCB hair lotion, feel her heartbeat close to hers. She held her breath to keep herself from crying. They had barely been apart a month and a half.

Paul cleared his voice from the backseat to introduce himself while they were still hugging. "...You two look so much alike. Tanya, you are definitely your mother's daughter. Practically a spitting image." Leslie noted right away that there was a squareness to his voice. He hardly sounded black at all, even though she could see from where she was sitting, he was clearly a black man. A square-jawed handsome black man at that--even with the big, dark mole just under his nose.

"Not to break up the reunion, y'all, but Luis started spinning at nine. Let's get to the bar and *then* hug all night long, 'kay?" Max was so cute, he could tell you your ass was flat and your teeth were green and it would still sound sweet. Leslie pulled back from the hug and patted under her eyes, trying to catch any mascara on the run, while Tanya swerved out onto busy Hawthorne Boulevard.

Right away, Max and Paul began chattering in the backseat...something about a flaky friend of Paul's meeting them at the bar. Paul wanted to text the friend the bar's address but Max's phone wasn't pulling up a listing for 'Shadowbox on Venice Boulevard.' "You've been there before! It's the one with the Medieval black wrought-iron smoking patio out front."

"Max, I need an actual address, not a design motif."

"*Design motif?* You always gotta get all bourgie in front of company!"

Tanya, apparently accustomed to their bickering, reflexively extended a glittery purple fingernail to click on the CD player. New wave synthesizers squirming over vaguely hip-hop beats shuddered out of the little car's surprisingly loud sound system and Max stopped mid-sentence to sing along with the wailing white girl, completely off-key. Leslie glanced over at Tanya, whose head was bobbing to noise that sounded totally foreign to the Top 40 R&B she had raised her on...or even the hip-hop all the kids gravitated to in high school. *She likes this music?* At that moment, revelation hit Leslie square in the face: Tanya was already growing up and living her own life, *without her mother*. What other new and exotic experiences had her daughter managed to get into since moving out of the house six weeks ago?

Tanya was living with two gay men, about to go to college on full scholarship in Los Angeles and driving a borrowed car to a bar that must not have a problem with fake IDs. Clearly, she wasn't afraid to grab life by the balls. Up to that point, Leslie had more or less lived her life by the rules her mother had set for her: marry and stay married to the father of your children, even when you stop loving him; find a job and a home that allows you to stay close to your extended family, whether or not you have any interest in seeing them; be a good wife and a good mother, live your entire life in deference to your parents and the man who chooses you and impart those same values to your children, regardless of your own feelings on the matter.

But it was Tanya's decision to go away to school that had made it clear to Leslie that she didn't have to stay stuck in the life she was in. Tanya got out--so why couldn't she? Leslie sat back and watched a neon-lit Los Angeles zoom past until the voice screaming out over the electro beats started to sound familiar. "Is that Beyoncé?"

Max leaned in from the backseat smelling like cinnamon gum. "Yes! Isn't this song fierce, Ms. Leslie? *Sasha* Fierce!"

Leslie looked back at Max with a smile. "I do kinda like it." Max sat back and started singing along again, still off-key, "I think I'm in love with my radio!" Leslie felt her own head start bobbing...

Shadowbox was dark and crowded. Most of the patrons appeared to be in their twenties or early thirties and caught up in some glam-rock fashion movement. Lots of shaggy hair, tight distressed denim, sparkling gauzy scarves and vintage rock concert T-shirts. The music was kind of funky, too; more like Chicago house than whatever they had been listening to in the car. It seemed inconsistent with the apparent vibe of the (mostly white) clientele, but they all seemed to be enjoying it. Or maybe everyone was just really drunk.

Tanya walked Leslie straight to a booth towards the back of the bar. Max ran up to say hello to his DJ friend and Paul went to the bar to order drinks. As they were sitting down, Leslie noticed for the first time that Tanya was wearing studded belts and boots very similar to Max's. She started to comment on it--*and the fro-hawk*, but thought better of it. She didn't even bother asking how she and Max were able to get in, considering they were both underage. (Paul was very manly and looked old for his twenty-one years.) She was really just happy to be able to spend time with her daughter and get a glimpse of the life she was making for herself away from home. *Home*...the definition of that word was quickly shifting all around her...

Paul sat down with a Corona, a bottle of water and two pinkish cocktails, one of which he slid toward Leslie. Leslie sniffed her drink like she thought it might have passed gas. "What's this?"

Tanya chimed in this time, shouting over the music. "It's a Mandarin cosmo. It tastes like a Jolly Rancher, mama. You'll like it!" Leslie looked up at Tanya, incredulous for a moment about her cocktail savvy. Then she resigned to just go with the flow. She sipped the drink, Tanya and Paul watching her intently, and decided that it did indeed taste like candy and that she did indeed like it. Tanya clapped and cackled and Paul pulled out his cell phone and started texting.

When Max sat down, he slid the bottle of water toward Tanya and snatched up the other cosmo. "There are some cuties in here tonight! Luis said the place is crawling with baby daddies." Then, sipping on his drink, Max turned and looked at Leslie like he was seeing her for the first time. "Ms. Leslie, is that... Is that from the Raquel Welch collection? 'Cuz my best friend Devon back home, his mom has a wig that looks just like that. She lives for that wig, honey. Loves it!"

Paul, horrified, snatched Max by his arm to shut him up. Max's eyes popped open, immediately panicked about possibly hurting someone's feelings, with his free arm bobbing and wiggling so as not to spill the cocktail. Leslie, who until that moment had never even bothered to get offended about someone noticing her wig, was suddenly self-conscious. Unsure how to respond, she turned to her daughter and Tanya smiled back at her, completely poised and assured. Fortified by Tanya's calm, Leslie turned to Max and Paul and said, "No baby, all my wigs are from the Patti Labelle collection."

Tanya laughed and called out with her water bottle up to her mouth like a microphone, "Ooh-ooh, ooh-ooh, oooooh--She got a new attitude!" Everyone laughed but Paul, who for some reason was clutching to his anxiety around the mention of the wig. Leslie looked right at him and in that moment saw clearly how this young man had been incapacitated, probably most of his life, by fear. There was such a profound sadness to him. He was so serious, so devoted to his misery, that her heart ached for him. She wondered what his mother must be like. What inner turmoil and private shame had that woman projected onto this poor child? *Why doesn't he know how beautiful he is?*

When Leslie realized she had been staring at Paul for some time, she turned to find a really tall man standing at their table. Leslie immediately guessed that Max and Tanya were about to be thrown out for being underage, but then she noticed the smile on Tanya's face. Was she flirting with this giant white man? The house music was so loud, she couldn't quite make out what they were saying, but the man seemed to be sizing up Paul and Max with some surprise. He shook his head and pointed to Paul and

Leslie could hear him say, "This one's gay too?" Paul shook his head, annoyed with the conversation, but Tanya nodded 'yes' and then pointed to Leslie.

"And this is my mom, Leslie."

Max screamed out over the music, "That's Ms. Leslie to you, bloke!"

The tall man reached over to shake Leslie's hand as he sat down next to Tanya. Leslie was fairly sure she'd heard an accent, but she couldn't quite make sense of anything he was saying. About thirty-seconds later, Tanya turned away from him, her eyes rolling and her face puckered with the sour taste of whatever had just fallen from his mouth. Without making enough of a fuss to alert Paul and Max she told her mother, "This British buffoon just asked if we were fag hags."

Leslie glanced at cute little Max, who was scanning the dimly lit crowd for cute boys. She nudged Tanya and said, "Tell him we ain't fag hags. We are *alternative life-style companions*." Tanya nodded with a smile, impressed that her mother was already so on the ball, and then turned and just shoved the tall man out of the booth. Leslie squealed, delighted.

"Look at that one at the bar! The redbone brotha with curly hair, giving you fashion? Ooooh, that is so my stee-lo." Max was chomping at the bits about someone across the room. Leslie, who couldn't see the man in question from her side of the booth, just shook her head in disbelief about this white boy talking about some 'redbone brotha.'

"Ooh, he *is* cute! Mama, let's go get another round of drinks and see if he plays for Maxxie's team." Tanya hopped out of the booth, grabbed Max and the two of them went bouncing up to the bar.

Paul, who was texting again, looked up from his phone and said dryly to Leslie, "If they order any alcohol, the bartender is probably going to card them and kick them out. Max gets a little vodka in him and starts acting like he has no sense."

Leslie, who was already so tired of the music she was hoping someone *would* kick them out, just looked back at him and asked, "Who is that you keep textin'?"

"Uh... A friend of mine is down in San Diego this weekend. He... He was supposed to drive up and hang out, but..." Paul shook his head, disappointed. Leslie remembered that Max's 'part-time boyfriend,' who didn't get along with Paul, also lived in San Diego... *Obviously not the same person.*

She had already noticed that Paul's handsome mug was getting gloomier and gloomier every time he picked up his phone. While she didn't know him well enough to try to get him to open up about his friend, she still managed to take his sadness personally. She stood up and gently stroked his hand, motherly. "I'm sorry, baby. Most men can't do nothin' *but* disappoint. They don't even mean to be useless, they just can't help themselves." Paul flashed her a weak smile and stuffed his phone back into his pocket. She narrowed her eyes and then snatched her wig off and threw it on the table in front of him. "You can try it on if you want. I'm a get you another Corona!" She smiled, patted her short natural down against her head, turned and sashayed up to the bar. Paul was so shocked, he laughed in spite of himself. He laughed so hard that he cried a little...and it looked like a little cry was just what he needed.

At the bar, Tanya was standing right next to a lean, well-dressed black man with curly reddish brown hair who smelled like...grapefruit. Max was nowhere to be found. Leslie walked right up in between them (he was clearly too old for Tanya) and introduced herself. The music seemed to be even louder at the bar, but she was almost sure she heard the man say his name was Jamie. He had soft brown eyes and he smiled as he spoke. Leslie was immediately intrigued by how pretty the man was. Like, really pretty. She turned and said to Tanya, "He has to be gay because straight men don't sparkle like that."

Tanya nodded, "Or smell that good." She patted down a tuft of hair on the back of Leslie's head. "You lost your wig?"

"It's at the table. What happened to Max?" Leslie nodded hello to some drunk boy with long black hair and catlike green eyes who walked in and sat down on the other side of Jamie.

"We followed cutie pie out to the smoking patio...and then he turned around and came right back in. Maxxie bummed a cigarette and stayed out there, but I was cold so I followed ol' boy back inside. He reminds me of that singer... Can't think of his name." Tanya tried to sneak another glimpse of Jamie as she spoke, but he was talking to the shaggy haired boy. She turned and gazed at herself in the mirror behind the bar, pumping up the front of her fro-hawk. Leslie just stared at her, so gorgeous in that light, so grown up in that room...and she actually got choked up.

She started to ask about the mohawk again (sensing in that moment that Tanya probably *wanted* to talk about it), but she was too overwhelmed by the significance of the moment to speak. She was standing in a bar in L.A. with her only child. Her daughter was growing up for the both of them. Tanya was turning into a beautiful, independent woman, doing exactly what she wanted to do with her life. Thanks to her daughter's bold example, Leslie was finally taking the first steps toward her own independence...and she was utterly terrified.

The bartender stepped up in front of them. Tanya smiled and ordered the drinks with confidence and the bar man didn't flinch. Jamie turned with a slick hand gesture and a nod to let the guy know to put the drinks on his tab. Tanya smiled flirty and kissed Jamie on the cheek with an effusive thank you. Then she turned with a cool nod to Leslie and said, "You know I learned that from you. Everything good I got, I got from you!" Leslie choked on that for a moment and then followed her beautiful daughter through the crowded room.

Back at the booth, they found a totally straight-faced Paul...wearing the wig, seated next to a giddy Max, who was teasing out the bangs and flipping out the back. Tanya laughed so hard when she saw them she almost toppled over and spilled the two drinks she was carrying. At that moment, Leslie decided she was going to find some gay friends of her own. Sure, she had a couple of good girlfriends back in St. Louis, but they all had husbands and children. Leslie was evolving and outgrowing them with every passing day. She needed some friends who were fabulous enough to keep up. There was so much life and love and energy derived from being an 'alternative-lifestyle companion,' she was determined to get her own gays as soon as she got home! *Home...* There was that word again...

On the ride back, Max snuggled up to Leslie in the backseat and Paul, still wearing the wig, guided Tanya back to the hotel. The new-wave 'white girl' music was still pumping but Leslie was hearing it differently... There was an honesty to it, a realness outside of what she knew--beyond what she had learned to consider safe, that excited her. The music was a symbol of the world she had yet to explore. There was so much to see!

When they pulled up to the Holiday Inn Express, Paul handed Leslie her wig. Tanya asked her again if she was sure she didn't just want to just stay at their place, but Leslie was looking forward to the peace and quiet of her own hotel room. Plus, she was too aware of how annoyed Paul got with overnight guests to walk into any mess. She squeezed out of the backseat and stood outside on the driver side. "I'm good, baby. What we doin' tomorrow?"

Tanya smiled like the Cheshire Cat. "Well, we're picking you up to have brunch at the Waffle in Hollywood. Then we're going shopping on Melrose. And then, we're going to cook you dinner and then...go to another bar."

"Which bar?" Leslie noticed when Paul turned to ask that his face wasn't gloomy anymore.

"Joy Division at Clutch." Tanya winked at Max in the rearview mirror and Max popped his head up into the front seat.

"Oh, hell yes. LESBIANS!" Max laughed and screamed out the window, "Nighty night, Ms. Leslie. Sleep tight!" Leslie, not even sure how she felt about lesbians yet, waved goodbye and walked back into the hotel, shaking her head.

A thick Latina girl with dark lipstick, tight eyes and long, wavy, cherry red hair nodded hello from behind the desk when she walked inside. *So the desk clerk finally decided to show up.* As she stood waiting for the elevator, stealing glances at the girl behind the desk, Leslie whispered, "Lesbians, huh? Why the hell not?"

PART THREE

10

o o o

Rafael had put on a little weight. He wasn't fat, by any means. His waif-like rocker edge had just softened into a thicker swagger that required a slightly looser pair of skinny jeans. Since his breakup with Eve, he really hadn't been himself. When he used to occasionally drink because he *enjoyed* being drunk, he had recently made an everyday habit of blurring out the world from the dimly lit din of his favorite dive bar with no joy at all.

The music there (usually alternative rock or grinding electro) was so loud that it was impossible to hold a real conversation. Shadowbox wasn't the bar you frequented for deep philosophical discussions, but hiding in the dark and hooking up with other drunks were always viable options. As Rafael was still wildly sexy with his creamy skin, his catlike green eyes and his jagged black mane of loose curls, he did quite a bit of hooking up in that first month or so of being single. The girl only had to be 'cute enough' and so desperate/lonely/horny that she wasn't put off by his blatant disinterest in seducing her. There would be no courtship from his side. She would smile, he would nod--or maybe he wouldn't, they would get bored sitting next to each other, she would offer to drive him home and they would go through the motions in his twin sized bed. There would be no pretense of interest beyond the sex that was to take place that night. No phone numbers. No emails. No Facebook friend requests. Rafael hadn't expressed interest in a real human connection for weeks...

As much as he would tell himself that he enjoyed *fucking to forget,* his sadness had started to seep into his muscles and on a few occasions, the important muscle had been too upset to rise to the occasion. He'd called it 'whiskey dick,' poor blood circulation caused by the alcohol. But it was really depression. He wanted to be in love.

At some point, he got honest with himself and acknowledged that all the empty sex wasn't doing anything for his self-esteem. Once he'd stopped bedding girls he didn't care about, something in his consciousness shifted. For one thing, he was more intoxicated more frequently from spending more time alone in the bar. (Getting driven home before last call had been an effective way of limiting his alcohol consumption.) But as he was becoming more of an alcoholic, he was also getting more in touch with what he liked to believe was his 'higher self.'

He found he had grown very sensitive to people's energy. If someone going through an emotionally trying time sat down next to him, Rafael would get a chill. He would literally shiver. If someone was lying or had some malicious intent, he would get pangs in his stomach. And if someone was just happy to be there, he would sense that too, but that had only happened once or twice. He'd become this raw emotional nerve tapped into some higher plane of consciousness. He wasn't always clear-headed enough to offer worthwhile counsel, but usually, particularly with people he sensed needed guidance or something in the way of spiritual love, he would turn to them and strike up conversation. Sometimes they would discuss whatever the issue happened to be, but more often they'd talk about *anything but*, just to facilitate the necessary distraction. Rafael, with his newfound purpose, began to consider himself sort of an angel--a spiritual superhero. Over time, he stopped being sad about Eve and he started to feel good about himself again. Of course, he was still an alcoholic and still slightly overweight. And...he was still lonely.

One Sunday evening in July, while staring at himself in the 70s style gold-veined tiled mirrors behind the bar, Raphael glimpsed this cool breeze black guy approaching him from behind. The guy walked in and stood directly beside him and when he noticed Rafael watching him in the mirror, he smiled. Rafael nodded and glanced down at his drink. He wasn't drunk yet, so he couldn't pick up on the guy's energy. Was he an actor? He looked vaguely familiar, but his stylishly subdued fashion and the faint hint of citrus in his cologne didn't seem consistent with the bar's regulars. Still, something about his smile was very warm. *Kind...* Rafael tossed back the rest of his drink and the guy asked if he could get him another. Rafael nodded, "Dirty Ketel martini. Thanks."

The guy's name was Jamie. Rafael introduced himself and started to mention that his father's name was Diego, the Spanish version of James, when he noticed that Jamie was still smiling at him. Not a forced grin, but a genuine smile. Without even meaning to, Rafael smiled too.

Jamie had to yell over the music to explain that it was his first time at Shadowbox and that he had come to support his DJ friend Luis' new night. Rafael hadn't noticed, but the DJ's set had transitioned from gloomy ambient to upbeat, funky dance music. Normally, he didn't care for house, but something about this particular day and possibly the company of this particular person, made the music sound sort of cool. Edgy and alive. He didn't bother mentioning to Jamie that he could be found sitting on that barstool at least five nights a week.

Jamie kept ordering them drinks. While their conversation couldn't get too involved because of the thumping bass, they checked in with each other every few minutes with friendly glances and running commentary on the parade of revelers. The bar was getting crowded with people Rafael had never seen before. Jamie continued to socialize while Rafael drank quietly and waited for his higher consciousness to kick in.

At one point, a tall white guy nudged his way in between their barstools and bumped Jamie's shoulder, trying get the bartender's attention. Jamie turned around and the dude started gushing, in his marbly cockney accent, about how good-looking Jamie was. "I'm totally straight, but if I ever go gay, I'd have to come find you. You're so bloody pretty!" He turned to Rafael and said, "Isn't he bloody pretty?" Jamie threw his arm around the dude's waist, joking, laughing. Rafael bristled for an instant. He didn't know what to call the feeling at first, but he could only liken it to jealousy.

He looked over at Jamie and thought, *He really is pretty. Got full, shapely lips and his almond eyes are soft like a girl's... Beautiful, clear skin...* He laughed out loud when he realized what he was thinking. He turned back to his blurry martini. Then, the dude walked away and Jamie placed his hand on Rafael's arm. "Totally not my type." He just looked at Jamie, dumbstruck by the comment and overwhelmed by feeling taken care of by this man he had just met. Jamie nodded, blatantly flirtatious and Rafael smiled back, just as sexy.

Rafael kept drinking, but his higher consciousness never surfaced. He floated outside to bum a cigarette from a girl whose name he could never remember, even though he'd spoken to her many times. She was looking haggard around the eyes and Rafael considered that maybe he should quit smoking. *Again*. After about two minutes, Jamie came out after him, tapped his shoulder and said, "Don't leave." The girl was still standing there and she glanced at Jamie in a way that Rafael couldn't read. Feeling embarrassed and smothered, Rafael shook his head and jerked away, a drunken attempt at feigned disgust. Jamie turned to the girl unfazed, smiled and walked back inside. The girl started talking to someone else and Rafael realized he'd overreacted. Of course, he'd had no intention of leaving.

When he got back inside, there was a fresh martini covered by a cocktail napkin waiting for him. Jamie was talking to a woman who appeared to be the mother of the girl next to her. Jamie turned to introduce the two women to him, but Rafael couldn't hear their names. He downed his martini and called the bartender over to order another round while Jamie wasn't paying attention. He was all for getting drunk, but he was starting to feel weird about Jamie paying for all the drinks. Was there some scheme behind his generosity? Men pay for drinks when they're trying to get someone into bed. Rafael wasn't stupid. But he *was* enjoying Jamie's company...

Jamie had gone to the bathroom when Rafael looked up and noticed the DJ staring at him. It wasn't a confrontational stare; it was more like he was sizing him up. Rafael brushed his shaggy tresses away from his eyes and licked his lips, suddenly overcome by some urge to impress the dude, even though the DJ wasn't nearly as attractive as Jamie...and even though Rafael had no business caring either way. *What...the fuck?*

He sat there, not touching his martini--as he was clearly already too drunk--and closed his eyes. He had to focus from the inside. He was losing sight of himself. Two months ago, he was crying into his vodka about Eve, that cheating, drug-addict bitch...and then, out of nowhere, he was moistening his lips for some troll DJ and wondering who Jamie might be talking to in the bathroom. Maybe he was depressed and just needed the attention from wherever he could get it. Maybe he was really...*at-tracted to him?*

With his eyes still closed, Rafael was suddenly overcome by a sensation of warmth, joy--*laughter*. The freedom of a genuine belly laugh, that openness, that sense of abandon, warmed his core. He opened his eyes and Jamie was standing next to him, signing the credit card receipt. Jamie closed the check holder and turned to Rafael with that smile. "I'm hungry. Wanna grab something to eat?" Rafael downed his martini, slid on his jacket and followed Jamie out into the cool night.

Jamie parked in front of Rafael's apartment building and they chatted over burritos in the car. In the shadows of the street lights glowing through the knobbed branches of the jacarandas above, Rafael stole glances of Jamie eating, noting the way his lips moved as he chewed and the strong angle of his jaw line. When Jamie's lips parted to slowly lick away a dollop of sour cream from the corner of his mouth, Rafael got flustered and quickly took a bite of his burrito. A saucy glob of refried beans dripped past his chin onto the seatbelt strewn across his lap. Jamie laughed.

Panicked, Rafael rummaged through the bag in front of him for a napkin and Jamie handed him his. He apologized profusely, noting that Jamie's car was obviously expensive, if not brand new. Jamie shook his head and told him not to worry about it. Rafael wiped as much as he could off of the seat belt and dabbed at some that had fallen on his shirt. Jamie offered him another napkin, but Rafael was overwhelmed with the drippy burrito and the first napkin so Jamie just reached down and helped to dab away the beans on his shirt. Rafael, suddenly very conscious of his soft stomach and the way it didn't hold firmly to Jamie's touch, yanked away. Jamie, his eyes glistening in the shadows, pulled the napkin back and Rafael just sat there, feeling ridiculous. *None of this is about how soft my stomach is. This is something else.*

They sat staring at each other for a few more moments before Jamie leaned in and kissed him softly on the lips. Rafael reached past Jamie for his Coke to wash down the rest of the burrito in his mouth. Then he clumsily leaned over and kissed Jamie back. They kissed passionately, holding their burritos and groping one another with their free hands... Rafael was not suffering from whiskey dick that night.

"Can I come over?" Rafael's whisper barely masked the urgency in his voice.

"Of course, but we're already at your place. Do you wanna just go inside?"

"I'd rather go to your place."

"Okay. Let's go." Jamie's smile radiated sex. Rafael's heart pounded like the beat of DJ Luis' house music as they both tossed what was left of their burritos into the bag on the floor and drove away...

o o o

Jamie woke up to Rafael kissing the nape of his neck and mashing his sex aggressively against the small of his back. They'd spent those first two days in Jamie's bed, watching music videos on his laptop, ordering take-out from Joey's Cafe down the street, exhausting Jamie's wine reserve and having lots and lots of sex. While Rafael sounded totally convincing that first night when he insisted he had never even imagined himself sexually with a man before, Jamie was not entirely shocked at the way Rafael had plunged headfirst into the lovemaking.

There had been a number of occasions in those forty-eight hours during which Jamie had looked down, impressed by the young man's technique and flexibility and even astonished by his shameless show of carnal voracity. But somehow, he was never surprised by any of it.

Rafael's desire to kiss, fondle, stroke, 'give' and 'take,' seemed boundless. If they were in the same room and not physically connected, Rafael's body seemed to seek out Jamie's touch like water seeking its own level. Their physical heat was a force of nature. At the same time, there was a coolness to their interaction, a vague detachment when they weren't naked and interlaced, that put Jamie on edge. Jamie found his undeniable familiarity *with that sense of mutual isolation, of emotional disconnectedness with yet another one of his lovers, more disturbing than the detachment itself.*

Jamie turned around to press his lips against Rafael's. They kissed hard and deep with no regard for morning breath or supposed sexual orientations. Rafael pulled his face away to smile into his eyes and for the first time, Jamie noticed--with a twinge of disgust--Rafael's striking resemblance to his first real lover. The curve of his dark lashes against his sexy light eyes, the pink softness of his full lips, the wavy hair framing his sweet aloofness.... And when he glimpsed the top of Rafael's dark mop drifting down along his chest and on to his stomach, Jamie shut his eyes tight and shook his head no, racing to block out the bitter sting of his first heartbreak...

11

o o o

They'd been hanging out for almost three weeks before Rafael had any clue that Jamie was 'famous.' They were making a quick run to Trader Joe's for frozen lime bars and a bottle of Sauvignon Blanc. Since they were rushing to get there before the store closed, Jamie hadn't bothered to pull on a hat or sunglasses, like he normally would--something Rafael had never even noticed. On their way out of the store, two teenage boys were waiting for them at the door. One was a slim Filipino boy with a fluffy faux hawk and the other, a beefy white boy with choppy skater bangs.

"Hey SugarTaaaaank!" The slim one started hopping up and down, waving his bangles in the air. The other boy just smiled, staring closely at Jamie's face.

"Hi. I'm Jamie." He extended his hand formally with a smile. The kid ignored the hand and threw his arms around Jamie, hugging him tight.

"Oh my God, you are so cunt, I liiiiive! When you gonna come out with another CD? The first two were sick'ning!" Jamie, gracious if unfazed, glanced over at a wide-eyed Rafael, who had no idea what was happening.

The other boy extended his hand toward Rafael. "Hey, I'm Benji. PK's a huge SugarTank fan. I am too, I'm just playing it cool." Rafael shook his hand with a vague nod, unable to take his eyes off Jamie and the squealing, squirming 'SugarTank fan.'

When Jamie was finally released from the hug, he turned to greet to Benji and introduce Rafael. Without officially being invited, PK launched into the story of them taking their first road trip together as a couple, driving down from San Francisco to see Benji's father. Benji interjected that his dad had been diagnosed with lung cancer and even though they didn't get along, PK had persuaded him to make his peace with him before it was too late. Jamie listened patiently, politely, eventually inviting them to sit down at one of the café tables across the courtyard and Rafael watched, stupefied, as the young lovers shared the story of the day they met...

PK was sauntering down Divisadero Street, swinging his imaginary Naomi-tail to the Quentin Harris remix of SugarTank's "Fancy You," pumping from his iPod. When he reached the Java Hut, he pretended to check his hair in the reflection of the storefront window, when really, he was breaking his neck to see if the foxy new barista was behind the counter.

His plan had been to stroll inside pretending to read a text on his Instinct phone, strike up conversation with the boy...and then record his lips moving up close with the phone's video camera. It occurred to him that the new boy might not be working and the whole ruse would be wasted on that tattooed 'otter' with the full beard and gauged ears. He had to make sure the target was in place before he even stepped inside.

He was working so hard to get a clear glimpse of the register, he didn't notice the object of his obsession skateboarding toward him on the sidewalk. When Benji skidded to a stop and kicked his skateboard up into his hand, PK was so startled that he squealed, threw his arms in front of his face and almost fell backwards. Benji suppressed a guffaw at the dramatic display and then stood there, giving PK an opportunity to pull himself together before he spoke.

"You all right? My bad, dude." Then, noting his tight sparkly eyes and full glossy lips, he glanced down past PK's sand storm scarf and cardigan sweater at his American Apparel tank top to make sure he wasn't smuggling tiny breasts. He was *all boy*--his build was slim but tight. Benji could tell from the way the skinny jeans fit from the front that they were sagging snugly over an amazing ass...and all of it was right up his alley.

"Oh no, that was totally my fault. Wasn't watchin' where I was walkin'." PK plucked out his ear buds, thrilled at this serendipitous albeit embarrassing opportunity to introduce himself to the foxy new barista. He extended his hand with a shy smile. "I'm PK, by the way."

Benji took the hand and held it firmly in his own while he stared into PK's eyes. "Benji. I think I've seen you around. I work here." He rested one of his meaty shoulders against the brick wall, smiling sexy and still holding PK's hand.

He was so flustered about the immediacy of Benji's touch, PK spilled his tea. "I know. I was just looking for you inside right now." Then, realizing he had probably over-shared, he glanced down at Benji's Air Force Ones. *Silence.* They were still holding hands.

"Oh, word?" PK could *hear* the smile on Benji's lips but he was still working up the nerve to pull his eyes off the Nikes. More silence and PK's vanilla scent wafting in the air between them... A car drove past blasting hood-rat hip-hop and a surge of self-consciousness pulsed through each of them, but neither one turned toward the car or pulled back his hand.

PK finally looked back up at him just in time to see him toss his bangs away from his eyes with a jerk of his head. He smiled with a sly twinkle in his eye and let his hand slip just enough to lock his pointer finger around PK's, gently tugging him closer. Melting over the heat of the situation with his eyes locked on Benji's, PK tottered toward him. "Uh huh."

"Well, I'm off today--just came by to pick up my paycheck. I was headed down to the Haight to check for some vinyl at Amoeba. Wanna cruise out?" Benji flashed the cutest smile ever.

PK could barely nod his head 'yes,' as he was no longer in his body. He was floating above the "OBAMA: HOPE" mural across the street watching the hottest boy in San Francisco holding his hand right in front of the Java Hut. *Gag!*

"Cool. Be right back. Don't go anywhere." Benji squeezed PK's finger one last time before he disappeared into the clamor of the coffee shop. PK exhaled with an irrepressible giggle and wandered over to a parked Prius to check his 'daytime beat' in the window.

Two college-aged girls exited the café behind him and when he turned around to face them, he could swear they were sizing him up with some contempt. "Shit, I would hate me too," he murmured under his breath with an ever so slight roll of his neck. *Those pasty SF State skanks just can't take my Filipino fierceness...*

Seconds later, Benji stepped out, waving his paycheck in the air. PK was almost surprised at the gesture, vaguely girly on such a strapping hunk of teenage manliness, but he wasn't bothered one bit. Benji's black and gold T-shirt hugged his broad shoulders like a body glove, his big beautiful hands were carved for Michaelangelo's David and his sweet, toothy grin was set inside the juiciest pink lips PK had ever seen up close...

"Let's hit it." Benji dropped his skateboard onto the sidewalk and coasted slowly beside PK, who was grinning and gliding like he was wearing glass slippers.

When they reached Fulton Street, they had to wait for the light to change. They stood on the corner in an adorably awkward silence. They were both grinning, giddy and charmed out of their minds, but neither of them knew what to say. Benji looked over and nodded what's up, all sexy, just before PK finally decided to break the silence. "You are so cute to me. I can't even believe we're really hanging out."

Benji leaned in and kissed PK softly on the lips, right there on the street! PK stepped back out of the kiss with his eyes still closed and fanned himself with his hand. Benji snorted out a childlike giggle and playfully punched PK's chest. "Likewise, homie."

They inched down the street, smiling wide and talking softly. Benji told PK that he'd just moved to the city from Orange County to live with his older sister after his father kicked him out of the house for being gay. PK (whose dad had been gone for years) told Benji that his mother was his biggest fan and never had a single negative thing to say about his sexuality or his bold self-expression, but that other people in the family weren't always so kind. Benji told PK that when he was in middle school he 'used to be all

Emo' and had dyed his hair black and wore eyeliner, but that when he started playing soccer in high school, he got all beefy and the punk thing didn't quite work anymore. PK admitted to still wearing eyeliner on occasion and told Benji that his lifelong dream was to be a back-up dancer for Beyoncé and that whenever she released a dance video, he would watch it over and over until he had mastered the choreography. Benji said he liked Beyoncé's 'more ghetto' hip-hop songs, but hated "Irreplaceable" and "If I Were a Boy." PK stopped in his tracks, his mouth agape, and glared at him as if he had uttered something blasphemous.

Benji did a bunny-hop over a crack in the sidewalk and slipped off the board when he landed. PK laughed that he 'deserved that' and ran after the board to catch it before it flew into traffic. When he looked back, he noticed the huge crowd of people a few blocks away walking down Fulton, carrying signs and banners: 'MARRIAGE EQUALITY NOW!!!' 'LOVE IS LOVE.' 'DEFEND EQUALITY: LOVE UNITES.' 'STR8 AGAINST H8!'

Benji noted the quizzical look on PK's face just before he heard the approaching chant, "Gay, straight, black, white; marriage is a civil right!" He turned around to see the wall of people round the corner heading toward them. The crowd seemed to go on and on: young and old people, gay and straight people, families, couples, friends... It looked like someone from every segment of the city had stepped forward to stand up for the right to love. PK walked over to Benji and handed him his skateboard. "You thinkin' what I'm thinkin'?"

Benji gazed at PK, who was smiling wide at the approaching crowd. "We don't even know where they're headed."

PK reached for Benji's hand, "Do we care? We know what they stand for. Anyways, if we get married, we can tell people that on the day we met, we marched through the city with a crowd of people standing up together for the right to love. Which is totally hot."

Benji snorted out that childlike giggle and was surprised when he felt emotion well up in his chest. "That *would* be totally hot." He squeezed PK's hand, kicked the skateboard up into his other hand and they walked together toward the crowd and the lavender twilight settling over the city...

When the kid said the words, 'lavender twilight,' Rafael rolled his eyes and reached into the bag to pull out a lime bar. He took a bite and without even thinking, extended the popsicle toward Jamie, who held Rafael's hand steady with his own as he took a bite.

At that moment, the boys paused with their story and turned in unison to Rafael. The apparent intimacy of the gesture hadn't even occurred to him because he and Jamie shared popsicles all the time. But the boys, who had probably taken Rafael for a musician friend (he still looked more like a rock-fan than a cock-fan) were suddenly seeing him in a whole new light.

Rafael licked his lips and tossed his hair out of his eyes, barely conscious of how hard he was working to appear worthy of the company it was now clear he was keeping. Jamie reached into the bag, pulled out a popsicle and handed it to PK. "For you guys to share. We'd better get home so the rest don't melt."

"Home." In that context, in that moment, the word struck Rafael as stifling. Sure, he had probably only slept in his own bed three or four days out of the last few weeks, preferring the soft sheets and air conditioning of Jamie's West Hollywood condo to his own Sepulveda Boulevard roommate situation. And yes, he had developed feelings for Jamie he hadn't known he was capable of having and done things in bed he'd never even heard of. But using the word 'home' in front of these gay dudes who were all giddy about planning their gay wedding under 'a lavender twilight' made it sound like he and Jamie shared a dwelling--like they were a couple. A gay unit. Rafael wasn't sure how he felt about that.

On one hand, the idea of being in a committed same-sex relationship struck him as more advanced, more definitive than he was ready to be. Bisexuality was a much easier concept for people in his scene to swallow.

While he wasn't close to any of the people he used to see regularly, many of those straight 'alternative' guys at Shadowbox had gay friends. Just by constant proximity to the possibility of gay stuff (like Rafael's drunken goodnight kiss with Gay Tommy in the middle of the Venice Boulevard), many of them tossed around the word bisexual. His contemporaries considered it hip to *not be homophobic*. Only a homophobe would be completely opposed to the idea of hooking up with a dude. So yes, being young and single and open to all the world's possibilities was consistent with the devil-may-care air they were all co-opting. But a boyfriend? A shared domicile? That all sounded pretty fucking gay. He wasn't quite ready to become 'Gay Rafa.'

Yet, he had never been with anyone--boy or girl--who treated him as well. Jamie was kind and generous and gave him space to be exactly who he was. None of that nagging or emotionally needy shit he had grown to expect from girls. He'd been so shut down around the notion of what women *needed from him* that he'd started ignoring them altogether. He and Jamie maintained a comfortable distance that was just easy. Relaxed. Cozy, even. He liked the way Jamie was able to pay attention to him without hanging on his every word. Jamie noticed details, acknowledged them, but didn't make an ordeal out of every little thing. They just enjoyed spending time together. And...if Rafael was being completely honest with himself, Jamie wasn't the first guy he'd found attractive. But he was by far the prettiest thing he'd ever seen up close...

Walking *home*, Rafael waited a few minutes for Jamie to explain what had just happened, but after all the goodbye hugs and the vows to connect on Facebook, Jamie walked away uncharacteristically quiet. So Rafael asked, "Um...what the hell was that?" Jamie turned to him, almost defensive.

"What? They're sweet kids."

"But...he called you a cunt and then you sat down with him?"

"Not *a* cunt. *So* cunt. For gay boys, cunt in that context means...fabulous. They just like my music." *Music?* Rafael had seen musical equipment--a keyboard, an acoustic guitar, a microphone and a big computer with what was probably a mixing board--in the office, once, when they first started hanging out. The door to that room was usually closed but every now and then, Jamie would disappear in there, early in the morning while Rafael was still in bed. Jamie had mentioned 'conference calls with The Label,' but somehow *record label* never came up. He had probably even mentioned in the bar the night they met that he 'did music,' but Rafael had assumed that he licensed songs to score movies or did radio promotion or something. Just then, he remembered Jamie playing something for him on his laptop while they were drunk in bed that first weekend. It was kind of dance music, R&B-infused electronica with a raspy male vocal. It wasn't really Rafael's kind of music. *Was that him?*

"But SugarTank? You didn't tell me you were famous." Rafael felt guilty for not having expressed more interest in Jamie's professional life. There was such a pleasant, informal dynamic to their interaction that details like 'what they did at work' seemed beneath them. Trite. Plus, Rafael hated his job--manning the grill station at Tender Greens in Culver City--so much that he went out of his way to never talk about work.

"If I have to tell you I'm famous, then I'm not famous." Jamie's grin seemed to be masking some discomfiture. Rafael remembered thinking that night in the bar that he knew Jamie from somewhere...that he looked vaguely familiar.

"But those dudes just went ape shit. I've never seen anything like that before. You're like the gay Beatles, man. That was crazy." Jamie chuckled with a shrug and Rafael smiled back, even though he was feeling that tinge of inadequacy that crept up every now and then. Like when Jamie would hop out of bed and strut across the room naked and flawless before giving him a chance to suck in his tummy. Or when he would insist on driving without bothering to mention that no one would want to be seen in Rafael's piece of shit car. Or when he would drop bills into the café tip jar without even knowing that Rafael had pulled out his last few dollars when he'd offered to pay for coffee.

Completely innocent things he did could put Rafael on edge. He would get quiet and introspective for a while, creating and recreating all the scenarios in his mind where he believed he fell short. Eventually, after a glass of wine or a couple beers, he would mellow out. In his 'open state,' he could *feel* that Jamie's intentions were pure and that any problem between them was something he was creating. Then he would snuggle up against Jamie on the couch or lay his head on his chest while they watched TV in bed and forget all the things he was insecure about... Usually, it was that easy.

But this was different. Rafael saw the way those kids looked at him the moment they realized he was more than a friend. The nesting phase they had been enjoying wasn't going to last forever and they'd already started spending more time in public. People were going to be looking at him all the time and measuring him up against Jamie, which was daunting enough *before* he knew he was famous.

Jamie disappeared into the kitchen to put the rest of the lime bars into the freezer and chill the wine. Rafael sat on the couch to cue up *True Blood* on the Tivo and he glanced down at his fleshy midsection spilling over the top of his jeans. He had no idea how to go about getting into better shape, but it was time to figure it out. Even if he and Jamie weren't technically boyfriends, even if they didn't officially share the condo, the likelihood that they were going to be seen as a couple in public meant that he had to get it together...

o o o

Jamie was woken up from his afternoon nap by a loud snort. He turned to find Rafael purring naked beside him, flat on his back, with his mouth agape and his soft member nestled in a dense patch of black hair. Jamie contemplated waking him up and introducing him to his clippers (now used exclusively for manscaping--he hadn't cut own his hair since the year he finished his first album) but thought better of it. He was already too aware of all the possible and undeniably familiar *endings to their story. Jamie knew too well that repeating the same action and expecting a different outcome was on par with insanity. So he just closed his eyes, relinquished his fear of heartbreak and resolved to enjoy each moment as it came. Rather than try to imagine a future unfettered by past mistakes, he ventured instead to dream of a fully realized love informed by each of those invaluable lessons.*

Later that night, when they were in the shower together and Rafael knelt down to gently scrub the bottoms of Jamie's feet with the loofa sponge, Jamie made a point of relishing the immediacy of the gesture rather than placing any undue expectation on his young lover to wash away the missteps of his past...

12

o o o

Rafael's Kia Sephia died in the Crossroads Trading Company parking lot. After making excuses for weeks about why he wasn't fastening the top button on his favorite pair of skinny jeans, he'd finally gone looking for a pair with a thirty-three inch waist. However, the car breaking down seemed too obvious a sign to ignore.

Jamie used his Triple A card to get the car towed back to the Sepulveda apartment. The moment had been so humiliating, Rafael walked downtown to buy new inner tubes for his bicycle right away. It was like a direct message from God: *Instead of driving around looking for ways to be more comfortable while your ass gets fat, get your bike out of storage and lose some weight.*

He started riding everywhere he went. He stuck to side streets to avoid being stopped about not wearing a helmet. With it, his wavy mane would end up flat on top and flipped back on the bottom--very Charlie's Angels...instead of jagged and bouncy, the way he liked it. He wore it in a ponytail and under a cap at work anyway, so it really shouldn't have mattered. But the helmet was just too uncool.

A few weeks later, Jamie walked into the bathroom just as Rafael was stepping out of the shower. He stopped and did a double take. "Whoa! Your body looks amazing." Jamie had never offered an opinion one way or the other on Rafael's physique. Not talking about one another in physical terms, even in private, somehow kept them in collusion with maintaining Rafael's closet. But that day, Jamie seemed beside himself. "Has all that muscle been there the whole time?"

Rafael wasn't sure how to respond. "You mean underneath all the fat? Yeah, I guess." He narrowed his eyes at Jamie, trying to discern if the reason he suddenly felt so compelled to talk about muscles was because he'd been so disgusted by the flab before. Jamie nodded and raised his eyebrows, impressed, and walked over to the toilet to pee. Just as Rafael was gearing up to get offended, Jamie turned his back, unzipped his pants and the subject was dropped.

Rafael stepped in front of the door mirror to dry off. At first glance, he didn't even think his body looked that different. Then he tightened his stomach and noted the indentations below his midsection, the 'cum-gutters', and he realized that he probably hadn't taken a good look at his own body in a long time. Ever since things had gotten miserable with Eve, he had felt disconnected from his physical self. That was probably when he began to let his body fall apart. He'd been stuck in that cloud of self-pity and on that bar stool for so long, he'd hardly noticed himself going soft...

The toilet flushed. Jamie washed his hands and then strolled behind Rafael into the bedroom, smacking his bare ass on the way out. Rafael flinched and Jamie looked back over his shoulder with a sexy grin. That moment marked a shift in their relationship.

There had always been an ease to their interaction and the sex had always been hot, but they found a new flirtatiousness, a playful physical dynamic that spilled over into their public life. After that day, Jamie wouldn't think twice before looping a finger through the back belt loop of Rafael's jeans while they were walking out of the movie theater. He would rest his arm on the center console and lay his hand in Rafael's lap while he drove. He'd even sneak a peck on the cheek in the freezer aisle while they argued about which ice cream to buy.

Rafael finally felt like Jamie was really claiming him--marking his territory and letting the world see. He felt special, like he didn't have to worry about what people thought when they saw them together because Jamie was making it clear that Rafael was good enough for him.

Inspired by the changes, he started doing push-ups and sit-ups every morning before his shower. He'd even started trimming his pubic hair with Jamie's clippers and using an expensive leave-in conditioner because Jamie liked the way it smelled. He began focusing on his physical existence again, being mindful of what he was eating and drinking less. He'd completely lost interest in unearthing the miseries of alcoholism and hadn't been back to Shadowbox since the night they met.

They were always together and if they ever went to a bar, it was either as a favor to a DJ friend or for Jamie to DJ his own set as SugarTank--more of an 'appearance' than a night out. If Jamie wasn't spinning, they rarely stayed long enough to do much more than one or two laps, just walking around being seen together. Jamie would usher him past the nodding door man with his hand pressed to Rafael's lower back and sometimes they would even walk through the club holding hands. Jamie would drape an arm across Rafael's shoulder while drunk fans gushed about how good-looking SugarTank was in person. With each of those public gestures of affection, Rafael felt more secure. He *was* worthy of Jamie and he was at home by his side.

o o o

George's late-night busboy shift at Jerry's Deli practically guaranteed that he was never awake before noon, so Rafael figured nine a.m. was early enough to sneak into their apartment without running into him. When he walked in and heard the shower running, his first thought was that George had moved someone in...but the place was undisturbed.

Just as he was emptying his hamper onto the floor of his cramped, dusty bedroom, determined to find the dark gray WESC jeans he hadn't fit into for months, the shower stopped. He heard someone walking around just outside his closed bedroom door... The door swung open. George was standing in the hall, naked, wet and wide-eyed, in a fight stance.

"Dude! You scared the shit outta me!" He shuffled back into the bathroom and seconds later, was back in the doorway, wrapped in a towel, jabbing a Q-Tip into his ear. "Where the hell you been? Feel like I ain't seen you for mad long." Rafael looked up at his fuzzy, flabby stomach and sagging man-breasts. It occurred to him that if he'd kept surrounding himself with guys who looked like George, he may never have known how much he enjoyed the touch of a man.

"I've been around. Just crashing at a friend's place." Rafael continued rummaging through his dirty clothes, expecting that would be the end of the conversation and George would close the door and be gone. They were roommates, not homeboys.

"Oh. So like, a girl?" George rested his arm against the door frame, revealing his bushy armpit, lousy with water globules.

Rafael started to say, 'Yeah, a girl,' just to get him out of his room. But the idea of lying, like he gave a shit what George thought, just didn't sit right. Jamie was hotter than any girl Rafael had been with, and much hotter than any girl George could ever get, so why lie? If he was so interested in Rafael's sex life, why not give him some news that was worth the fuss?

"Actually, a guy. You can Google image him or just look him up on iTunes. He goes by SugarTank." Rafael swallowed the lump that had mysteriously formed in his throat and looked up. George was just nodding his head, staring at something that wasn't in front of him. He turned to walk away, but then doubled back.

"You're crashing at his place or...you're, like, *sleeping* with him?"

"I'm sleeping with him." Rafael was surprised at hearing the words come out of his mouth. George just stood there, nodding, processing.

"So...what's *that* like?" The look on his face wasn't disgust or shock at all. It was genuine curiosity. Like someone had suggested something that had never occurred to him...like a peanut butter and honey sandwich.

"It's cool. He's a great guy."

"But. Like. What about the sex?" At the mention of sex, Rafael watched George's face twist into a mystified grin. Rafael was getting a kick out of shocking him.

"The sex is hot. *Really* hot."

"Huh." George shook his head with a befuddled shrug and walked away. Rafael spotted the jeans in question balled up in the corner of his closet, stuffed behind where the hamper had been. He grabbed them, along with a couple of clean pairs of underwear and threw the rest of his clothes back into the closet.

A minute or so later, just as he was zipping his backpack to go, George called out from his own room, "This is him, in the sparkly pants? He's black?"

"Uh huh." Rafael braced himself for some frat boy joke about big black dicks. After a few more clicks across his laptop keyboard, George just chuckled.

"He's actually good-lookin'. How the hell did you score this guy?"

Rafael froze, the wind knocked out of him. How the hell did George have the nerve to ask how anyone had scored anything? George, who looked like a short, fat marsupial. Rafael didn't respond. *Fuck you, douche bag.*

He closed the door to his bedroom and walked into the living room to leave. George bustled out just before he could reach the front door, still in his towel, with his hands on his hips. "So have you always been into dudes?"

Rafael looked back at George with a wry smile. "I've never been into you, if that's what you're worried about."

George shook his head. "Naw, seriously."

"I'm not into dudes. I'm into *this* dude." Rafael nodded goodbye as he walked his bicycle out the front door, barely hearing George's muffled, "No shit," as he pulled the door closed behind him.

Gay Rafa has left the building.

Rafael woke up thinking about George in that towel. With wires in his nose, gauze bandaged around his throbbing head and machines beeping on his right, all his mind could see was George's incredulous face and sloppy body with his hands at his hips.

Like an angel, Jamie appeared, rising from the lower periphery of the globe of light expanding in front of him as he opened his eyes and tried to focus on the details around the drab hospital room.

"Hey, baby. How're you feeling?" Jamie's face was swollen with exhaustion.

"What happened?" Rafael's voice wheezed...

"You were in an accident. You got hit by a car." He remembered the car. Black Passat station wagon. Blond woman on her cell phone. Left turn into an intersection...

"Was it bad?" Rafael wriggled his toes and his fingers. Aside from his head, which was throbbing with pain, he felt fine...just tired and stiff.

"You're okay. You...you fell on... You landed on your face." Rafael could see in Jamie's eyes that he was struggling not to say too much. That there was more to the story and it wasn't good. Something had happened to his face. He remembered flying through the air after his body and the bike had smacked against the hood of the car. He could recall thinking in that moment that he should have been wearing a helmet. Then, with wind whistling through his lustrous hair, he had been asked by God if he would rather be hideously disfigured or rendered brain-dead for his insolence. Rafael specifically recalled choosing the coma.

He'd never thought of himself as particularly brilliant and he had basically forsaken his own life to bask in Jamie's light anyway. Jamie was sweet and genuine and lovely, but he didn't seem like the type who would wake up kissing on someone with a fucked up face. Now that he was no longer offering spiritual counsel to the sad drunks at Shadowbox, what did Rafael have to offer the world beyond his beauty? What else could he claim beyond his relationship with Jamie?

It occurred to him that he had made a habit of relinquishing his social life to whatever relationship he was in. Eve, being far more manipulative and much more of a climber than he, took their mutual friends with her when they broke up. One of the reasons he found himself so depressed at the end of that two and a half year debacle was that she had ripped his entire life out from under him. He eventually found that losing all his *so-called* friends had been a blessing, because it allowed him to explore new things without fear of familiar reproach. However, it didn't change the fact that his whole life was based around the life of his lover.

What the hell had happened to his face anyway? He couldn't bring himself to ask. His face. It was the one thing he'd had going for him all along. That and his hair. Now that he'd gotten his body up to snuff, God had taken away his face? He closed his eyes and concentrated on not crying. Jamie had obviously been crying, but Rafael had to hold it together for both of them. *Be a MAN!* His drunk father's threats of giving him something to cry about echoed against his aching skull.

Eleven weeks. That's how long he and Jamie had known each other. Could he really expect Jamie to stick around? *Do men like him even make commitments?* When you're beautiful and talented and financially stable, is there any reason to tie yourself down to one person? With a deep breath to brace himself against the bad news he knew was coming, Rafael opened his eyes. Jamie was still standing there. His eyes were shiny and tight but he was looking directly at him with such warm affection that Rafael immediately got emotional.

"I look like shit, huh?" Rafael laughed at how pathetic he sounded as tears welled in his eyes.

Jamie leaned in and kissed him softly on the lips. "You look beautiful. Just a little banged up." He dabbed at Rafael's face with a tissue. Just then, a guy in nurse scrubs stepped in behind Jamie.

"Look who decided to wake up." Rafael didn't bother looking at the guy until he heard the gay lilt to his Spanish accent. He was a sturdy, handsome Latino man in his thirties. While he was checking the pouch of clear liquid by the bed, he smiled down at him with that *familiarity* that

Rafael had only just started getting used to. Men who had been clued into his relationship with Jamie would look at him with a smirk, a metaphorical nudge that was meant to convey some queer camaraderie. For a long time, Rafael mistook the looks for disrespect. He thought they were making passes at him. Eventually, he realized that there was a whole language of glances and signals that gay men use to communicate with one another without revealing to the world around them what is happening. Sometimes the covert gestures were intended to be sexual. Sometimes they were just meant to say hello. Rafael had trouble reading the nurse's smile one way or the other.

"Rafa, this is Guillermo. Memo."

Memo? Rafael watched something pass through Jamie's eyes as he nodded toward the nurse and then he turned to watch Memo sneak a glance at Jamie. *What the fuck was that?* Jamie sat down as Memo fluttered around the bed, checking charts and machines. Rafael watched him carefully. His hair was buzzed close to his head and his little mustache was shaved into a sliver. When he started checking off things on his clip board with his ball point pen, the cheesy tribal tattoos on his huge biceps peeked out from under the short-sleeves of his blue scrubs. Having seen enough, Rafael closed his eyes again...

A cold puddle splashed in his stomach...and he knew right away that he was feeling the nurse's spirit oozing toward him with malice. He could feel his intent to conspire, to trick Jamie into abandoning him, seeping into the air around them like a noxious gas. The nurse's intentions were not based in any need to assuage his own loneliness--but rather, a game. He was one of those sick people who dismantled the happiness of others for sport.

Just as he opened his eyes, Memo asked how he was feeling. Without even meaning to, Rafael licked his lips. He had no idea what his face looked like, but he knew he had to prove in his weakened state that he was still good-looking enough to deserve Jamie...and that Memo shouldn't get any ideas just because he was confined to that bed. "I feel good. How soon can we go home?"

Memo glanced over at Jamie for more eye-talking, and then back to Rafael. "Looks like you're in pretty good shape. We're going to run one more test this afternoon, just to make sure there's no internal bleeding, but everything looks good so far. Dr. Harper has prescribed an ointment for you to put on your forehead and your cheek, but Jamie can help you do that from...*home*. Probably as soon as tonight. But let's get Dr. Harper to confirm that first, okay?" Memo patted Rafael's shoulder gently with another sweet smile before he nodded to Jamie, a tiny conspiracy flaring in his nostrils, and disappeared out into the squeaky hallway.

Jamie stood up next to Rafael and caressed his arm. "You're lucky, you know. The doctor said that if you had landed differently..." Jamie's eyes welled-up and his chin started trembling.

Rafael closed his eyes so he wouldn't have to watch him fall apart. He felt Jamie's warmth surround him. He imagined for a moment that his time as an angel to the alcoholics had earned him a free pass. Some angel had been watching over him the way he had been watching over the drunks. Maybe Jamie was the angel? Maybe the angel was love. *Love*. He suddenly felt compelled to honor his guardian angel.

"Thank you for being here. I love you." He hadn't opened his eyes and he hadn't necessarily addressed anyone in particular, but it was the first time the words had been spoken in front of his present company. He heard Jamie choke back tears in the air just above him.

"I love you, too."

13

o o o

It wasn't long before Rafael was back on his feet. He had sprained his wrist, but the damage to his face wasn't quite as dramatic as he'd imagined. There was a good-sized gash, where his face had probably dragged a small rock along the asphalt, that left a shiny scar just above his right eyebrow. Most of his *hideous disfigurement* amounted to a few purplish abrasions that, when treated regularly with Dr. Harper's ointment, faded with surprising speed. His new fear of losing his looks, however, didn't manage to vanish quite so easily. He was haunted with a new awareness of his own mortality and the fleeting condition of his youthful beauty.

He'd been prescribed an ample supply of painkillers after the accident. So many, he no longer needed to be drunk in the dark din of Shadowbox to pick up on people's energy. The pills were his new shield against his own feelings, against fears he wasn't sure how to process, and his all-access pass into the anxieties and ill-intentions of others. They didn't read so much as pangs to his stomach anymore--more like colors washing over him, saturating his being with emotional imagery. He stayed so perpetually doped up that he lived as a relentless raw nerve to the emotional lives of everyone around him.

He managed to get time off work; the grill at Tender Greens was visible to the dining area and his scraped up face wasn't terribly appetizing. His bike had also been totaled in the accident, so he needed to find a job closer to where he was sleeping... In the meantime, he stayed at Jamie's, popping pills and sleeping half the day away.

One afternoon, wandering down Hayworth Avenue, Rafael came across Bernetta's Soul Food. The shiny red sign out front and the fresh, vibrant exterior paint were deceptive, as once he stepped inside, the narrow shop space was hardly put together at all. There were just six small tables and a counter with a couple stools and that was it. The plain white walls and cheap light fixtures made it clear the place was new and unfinished...but the smell was amazing!

A black woman, probably just shy of thirty, was behind the counter at the far end of the empty room. She had her shapely back to the door, talking through the kitchen window to someone Rafael couldn't see.

He stepped up to the counter, looking around for a take-out menu or something that would clue him in to what smelled so good, and she turned around. Her face lit up when she saw him standing there. "Heeey, honey! How you doin'?"

Startled by her assumed familiarity, Rafael smiled at her, and tried to gather enough of his wits to remember if they'd met before. She was lovely; her caramel colored hair was slicked back into a bouncy ponytail and her soft cheeks were dewy with a pristine modesty rarely seen on women in Los Angeles. She was beautiful--but beautiful in a way that Rafael probably wouldn't have noticed before Jamie: *she had kind eyes.* He quieted his mind and tried to read her. Her energy was warm but sullied with something. She'd been hurt recently--but she was too bright and too strong to carry the weight of that pain anywhere prominently. She refused to play damaged. Rafael liked that about her. He even envied her for it...

"What can I get you, sweetie?" He realized with a start that he'd been standing there smiling at her for too long.

"Yeah, sorry. Do you have a menu I can look at?" As he was speaking, he noticed the stack of paper menus on the counter in front of him. "Oh." He was in a daze.

"What do you like?" She leaned forward with a smile, resting her elbows on the counter. She cocked her head to the side and squinted her eyes slightly, like she was trying to guess the answer. *What do I like?* He shocked himself when his brain flashed to the image of his body twisted and grunting under the pounding thrusts of his sweaty boyfriend. *What do I like?* For a moment, Rafael toyed with the idea of telling her that he was seeing somebody but that he was flattered and that maybe if she was still interested when and if things didn't work out...but the longer the joke got in his mind, the more clear it became that it wasn't actually funny and that he was probably a little too stoned from his pain medication.

"Well, what's good?" He grinned at her with glassy eyes.

"You ever had soul food before?" She grinned... For a moment, Rafael was almost certain that she was using some playful doublespeak--like 'soul food' was a metaphor for black love. He was so tempted to come back with, 'I get soul food every night...and most mornings,' and then somehow drop the name SugarTank, just to see how much she *really* knew about black love...but he didn't.

"I'm not sure. I like macaroni and cheese. Oh and my cousin Chachi's wife used to bring sweet potatoes with marshmallows to Thanksgiving. Does that count?"

"I don't know your cousin Chachi's wife, so I really couldn't say. Are you vegetarian?"

"No, I love meat. Big meat eater!" He chuckled, nervous that he was slipping back into his stupid joke without even meaning to. "I mean...I like *everything.*"

Something flashed in her eyes and Rafael felt a ripple of dark red through his stomach. Then she smiled again. "I'm a hook you up. Have a seat." Rafael slid his ass up onto the stool at the counter and folded his hands in front of him, like a good student, waiting to be schooled.

She stepped back to the kitchen window and said something about a 'works platter.' Apparently the cook didn't understand because she shook her head and disappeared through the swinging door. Rafael's phone buzzed with Jamie's ring, Mark Ronson and Daniel Merriweather's soulful remake of The Smiths', "Stop Me If You Think That You've Heard This One Before." Rafael spun around in his stool to face the front of the shop and give himself some privacy.

"Hey baby... Around the corner. You home? Want me to bring you some soul food? What do you mean, 'What do I know about soul food?' I know where to *buy* it. What do you know about it?" He giggled and spun back around to face the counter, his dangling feet swinging in the wind of that sweetness, his whole body melting into the coy curve of that boyish affection. He glanced up and the woman was standing there, smiling back at him. He covered the phone to tell her something, but she already knew.

"Make it two, right?"

Rafael nodded and mouthed, "To go," with a smile and spun back around in his stool...

He'd probably made four or five trips back to the restaurant before Rafael learned that the woman's name was Kelly and not Bernetta. After finally reading the menu, he learned that Bernetta was her great-grandmother. She had owned a number of restaurants and bars in the South back when a black woman owning her own business was unheard of. Kelly named the restaurant to honor her great-grandmother's legacy...and because she didn't think the name 'Kelly' would sell much soul food.

Sometimes when Rafael would stop by, Kelly's friend Mike would be there, sitting at the counter, drinking beer out of a paper cup. Mike was tall, chatty and baby-faced with an infectious laugh and fluffy brown hair that he kept stuffed under a ball cap. Rafael hadn't assumed he was gay because there hadn't been any of that weird eye contact when they met and he never picked up on any sexual energy from him. Kelly clarified things one day after Mike left to buy beer.

"He thinks you're cute. Loves your green eyes. I told him I thought you were seeing someone..." Kelly raised her eyebrows in anticipation of a story she was obviously eager to hear. Rafael slid bashfully up onto the stool.

"I am seeing someone, yes." The twinkle in his eye said far more than his mouth was prepared to. Kelly wasn't satisfied.

"You ever going to bring that someone by so we can meet *them?"* Rafael noted her gender neutral pronouns and felt his heart accelerate. Kelly was his only real friend since his new relationship. He had been very deliberate about not bringing Jamie in or even bringing him up in conversation before he was confident he could call Kelly a true friend. Jamie was more charming, a bigger personality than he was, and Rafael worried sometimes that he faded into the background when Jamie was in the room. Rafael and Kelly shared an undeniable rapport, but until she had mentioned that her best male friend thought he was cute, he wasn't sure how she would respond to the news that he was dating a guy.

Once he knew she was okay with the gays--as if opening a restaurant in the heart of West Hollywood hadn't made that clear enough--he found he was still having trouble saying it. Telling someone like George or the sexually inappropriate homeless lady in front of 7-11 that he was dating a dude didn't really require anything of him. He didn't care if they didn't approve. But he genuinely liked Kelly...and he wasn't entirely sure that their bond wasn't based in an unspoken sexual attraction. Was clarifying that one point about his personal life worth the risk of losing their friendship?

Before Rafael could attempt to explain his home life, Mike ran back in with a plastic bag, out of breath. "Did he come in here?"

Kelly's face dropped. "Who?"

"I just saw his truck parked around the corner." Mike collapsed dramatically onto the stool beside Rafael.

"Oh hell no! Did he see you?" Mike shrugged and glanced over at Rafael with nervous eyes.

"Who's *he?"*

Kelly shook her head with a dramatic sigh. Then, with no regard for the two girls finishing their lunch at the front table, she hissed, "My asshole ex-boyfriend, Travis. We were together five years and then..." She smiled to herself, sadly, and then just stopped talking.

Mike picked up where she left off. "This was last year, back when she was waiting tables with me at Mexicali in the valley. Before her dad left her all that money." He paused and looked over at Kelly. "I found out that Travis had been involved in...some really foul shit. So I told her."

"Mike was shaking, *crying* he was so upset." Kelly glanced over at Mike with undeniable affection.

"Well, that was also the day I came out to you. I was kind of a wreck. I mean, come on!" Mike scoffed at the implication that he might be seen as emotional or anything less than masculine.

In the weighted silence that followed, Kelly's eyes glistened and her jaw tightened at the memory. She was still devastated. *What the hell did Travis do?*

She took a deep breath and continued. 'What he did,' whatever it was, had been a huge wake-up call for her. After spending six months depressed and isolated, she found herself forced to examine all the ways she'd been settling... She'd had to look at the damage that had been done to her self-esteem over the course of their relationship and why she stayed. She'd known for at least two years before *what he did* that he wasn't 'the one,' but she stuck around. When they finally broke up, she still couldn't see living without him.

Her father passing a few months later helped her put things in perspective, with a real sense of how important it was to have her own life, independent of any man.

Rafael watched something blaze in her eyes when she said, "I don't need a man for shit!" He thought of Jamie. Rafael had moved in with no job, no car, and no life and Jamie had essentially adopted him. What would happen if Jamie lost interest or changed his mind or had to leave town or something? Rafael felt his chest tighten and he immediately thought of going home to get a pain killer. *Home...*

How long had it been since he'd given over to the idea that he belonged to this one man? Was he seriously considering never having sex with women again? Had he slipped into a pitfall of convenience that was more about the ease of a routine than true compatibility? Was he really in love with Jamie or was he just addicted to the simplicity of their life together? And if he was sleeping with Jamie--*having sex* just to secure a comfortable living situation, what did that say about him?

That grim sense of inadequacy washed over him again, compounded with the new fear that Jamie would eventually get bored and abandon him. He started chewing on his thumb nail, his mind flooding with all the ways he was unworthy...

Kelly watched the girls at the front of the restaurant stand up and leave and she strutted up and locked the front door, flipping the sign around to read, 'Closed/Cerrado.' "That muthafucka is not walking up in here."

Mike glanced over at Rafael again, who was sweating and shrinking under the revelation of his own pathetic dependency on another man. "You want a beer?" Mike pulled three bottles of Negra Modelo out of his plastic bag and placed them on the counter. Kelly, still worked up, popped her head into the kitchen to ask the cook Rogelio if he wanted a beer. He waddled out with a grin and asked Rafael in Spanish if it was someone's birthday.

Rafael answered in Spanish that no, they were not celebrating a birthday. They were drinking to mark a new day: *The day of waking the fuck up.*

o o o

Jamie was the first to point out to Rafael that he'd been losing too much weight. It was around the time that his last refill on his painkiller prescription was about to run out. He'd already started rationing pills, taking one a day instead of one every few hours, so he could wean himself off them. He hadn't realized how much they'd been suppressing his appetite or even that he had been sleeping so much until he started waking up early in the morning to hunger pains.

Jamie happened to mention 'the gauntness' the morning after a gay charity dinner where Rafael had gotten too drunk and 'caught' Jamie making eyes at the cute, young cater-waiter. Then, some guy Jamie knew from college had walked up to their table, all nervous, to say hello. Rafael picked up right away that the energy between them was complicated. He hadn't been able to discern specifics on their relationship, but he was certain they shared a secret. He'd *felt* them both racing to appear less familiar than they actually were. It was similar to the vibe he'd picked up on with the nurse and a few others since, but more intense...

Oversensitive after the night of sneaky eyes, he took the critique of his appearance as an indication of disdain. It never occurred to him that the comment had been made out of genuine concern. In his mind, Jamie was no longer attracted to him because he had found someone younger, cuter, more helpless... *Definitely the cater-waiter.*

He decided to get serious about finding another job. Tender Greens had let him go after he missed his third week of work. Unemployment Insurance would never cover his cost of living if things with his boyfriend fell apart. He needed a backup plan.

Jamie had been collaborating with some lesbian producer friends on scoring a new television show, so he was out of the house most afternoons. Rafael opened Jamie's laptop and found the Hipstamatic photo of their hands clasped as the desktop background. A jolt of giddiness passed through him, followed immediately by a cold surge of disappointment. The playful intimacy of their first few months had been smothered by some new unspoken tension. He had started to see every awkward silence, every lull in their interaction as confirmation of whatever was broken. They had both grown withdrawn and Jamie's *blatant* criticism of his appearance signified for Rafael that the end was imminent.

He did a CraigsList job search and found that every posting required some skill he didn't have. No one was looking for amateur grill cooks or vodka drinkers. Thinking he might get part-time work doing construction or house painting, he scrolled down to 'gigs-labor,' but clicked on the link to 'gigs-talent' by accident. The first posting in that section read "MALE MODELS WANTED." It continued: "Seeking confident, attractive, fit males for professional website. Nudity required." *Nudity?* He glanced up at the floor length mirror next to the bed. He tossed his hair out of his eyes with a sexy pout. He slid off his T-shirt and tightened his abs. As far as he was concerned, he was in the best shape of his life. If Jamie didn't want him anymore, would anyone...*ever?*

Maybe seeing sexy photos of him would show Jamie how good he had it and he'd change his mind about leaving him for the cater-waiter. Maybe seeing himself through a pornographer's gaze would help Rafael finally claim his sexuality. He looked back at the posting. *Hmmm...*

At that moment, his phone buzzed with a text from Jamie: "Hey baby, Wendy baked cupcakes! Help yourself. Kitchen table. XO." Rafael closed the laptop with a sigh of relief. All was not lost. *Not yet, anyway...*

When he finally told Kelly and Mike about Jamie, they had no idea they could have Googled him from their smartphones. Jamie lived in their imaginations as some antisocial blur of a ball and chain who simply couldn't be bothered to stop by to meet them. The truth was that Rafael was keeping him tucked away.

At first, segregating his worlds felt like an assertion of his independence--a way of proving to himself that he could move in and out of each world without the burden of expectation from either. But as his bond with Kelly and Mike grew stronger and Jamie seemed to get more distant, the introduction felt less and less pressing.

Mike's crush on Rafael hadn't exactly relented, but he did manage to find some consolation in their budding friendship. The two of them spent hours on those stools, sipping beer, keeping Kelly company. The fact that Rafael was more reticent about his crumbling home life just had Mike rushing to fill those silences with elaborately romanticized tales from his own life. One story, in particular, resonated with Rafael...

Mike had been a runt all the way through middle school, but the summer between eighth and ninth grade, he had grown six inches *and* had his braces taken off. So he showed up that first day of freshman year looking like a new man, ready to prove gawky Lil' Mikey was gone for good.

Two years his senior, Stacy was gorgeous and popular and everything he could have asked for in an older cousin. She introduced him to all of Pasadena High's cool kids and for the most part, they welcomed him into the fold. He wasn't particularly close with any of them--or with anyone, for that matter--but the majority of what he considered his social circle was made up of her friends. The day Stacy graduated, Mike knew that, come fall, he'd have to find some casual acquaintances his own age. But it was the *night* of Stacy's graduation when he made his first real friend...

It was just after eight o'clock and there was already nowhere to park on Woodlyn Road. Mike pulled up to the front of the house to let Stacy out. She sat there for a second, looking at her cell phone, then turned to him. "What are we doing?"

"I was gonna go look for a parking spot." Mike was so grateful about being invited to the graduation party--even if only as Stacy's designated driver--that he eagerly adopted the role of chauffeur.

"I can walk, Mike. I'm not gonna have you strolling into Greg Spencer's party alone. How lame would that be."

"Greg knows me. I was on the swim team with him last year, remember?"

She looked over at him with an expression that, without a word, very clearly communicated, *You poor, delusional boy. Greg Spencer is the district's only All-American qualified swim champion. He's training to be on the U.S. team for next year's Olympics. He has no clue who you are.* She smiled sweetly. "No, hon. I'll totally ride with you. I don't think Ryan's here yet anyway."

Just then, a car parked two houses down pulled away and Mike slid right into the spot. He checked his trucker cap in the rearview, then hopped out of the car and checked it again in the window's reflection. Stacy gave his 'hip' little outfit a once over with a smirk and shrugged her approval. "Cute." Then her phone rang. "Yeah, we just got here. Where are you guys?" She wandered away from the car. Mike followed her, bracing himself for what would be his last hurrah with the class of 2003.

Stacy's boyfriend Ryan was waiting for her on the front lawn with Jason and Doug. Once Stacy showed up, the friends disappeared inside. Ryan gave Mike a high five and a 'Sup bro' and then dove straight into Stacy's face. He was going away to Penn State in the fall and Stacy was going to UC Santa Barbara, so they were in the throes of that, 'oh-my-god-we're-going-away-to-different-colleges' insanity, kissing and cuddling every chance they got. It was almost sweet...but not quite. Somehow, Mike knew they were just horny teenagers fixated on the sex they were no longer going to be having with each other. He shook his head and strolled into Greg Spencer's party. *Alone.*

The house was fairly large, but there didn't seem to be quite as many people inside as the parking situation had implied. The energy was also notably low for what was typical of that crowd. People were probably exhausted from the afternoon's pomp and circumstance and from dealing with their families all day. The stereo was turned up loud and the wide-screen TV was playing a slideshow of photos from the yearbook archives, but it felt more like a casual get-together than a blowout graduation party.

Mike drifted quietly though clusters of familiar faces, arranged by cliques and often, he noted, by skin color. Adrian Johns, Trey McBride and a couple of the other basketball players were all parked on the couch in the front room, talking loudly and bobbing their heads inattentively to Jay-Z's

"Excuse Me Miss," while Angela Stewart and Shawna Pitts chatted and nursed their red plastic cups nearby. In the opposite corner of the room, Jason and Doug were working hard to get friendly with three unfamiliar girls in short skirts. In the next room, which was probably the dining room when all the furniture wasn't cleared out, Stacy's good friends, Lucy Padilla and Kris Kantrowitz were already drunk and dancing too close to Ron Bergen, who was clearly stoned and bobbing his Jew-fro with his arms raised like Snoop Dogg. Just beyond them, Gabi Marquez was standing alone with a can of Diet Pepsi.

Gabi was Mike's year. She sat in front of him in Mr. Prud'homme's ninth grade English class. She was one of the few people Mike's age who didn't seem completely immune to his charm. Her older brother Jerome had been a senior their freshman year. He'd played Varsity football and was on the Homecoming court. Mike remembered him being really friendly...one of those guys who would bounce in and hug all the girls and give all the dudes dap. Jerome had joined the Marines right after he graduated and less than a year later, was one of the first American casualties of 'Iraqi Freedom.' Gabi had probably gained twenty pounds in the three months since his death. Mike tentatively walked over.

"Hey Gabi. How's it going?"

She looked up at him with bright eyes, working hard to convince everyone that she was ready to be back in the social saddle. "Wassup Mikey! Like the trucker cap. Cute look for you... Anyways, how are you?" She tugged on the bottom of her stretchy magenta blouse.

"Not bad. Kind of bummed all these guys are leaving. But you know, summer time...should be fun." Mike found himself concentrating on not saying anything that could be related to death or brothers or football. "Uh...I'm still working at Souplantation down on Lake. Hey, where'd you get the soda?"

"Oh, all the drinks are out back. There's an ice chest right by the keg. Here, I'll go with you." She tugged on her shirt again and waited for him to lead the way. They walked through the kitchen, past an ethnically mixed cadre of girls from the pep squad, half of them in their red and white skirts, and assorted athletes who appeared to be trying to recreate a pose from one of the slideshow photos.

Outside, steam was rising off the pool which was lit up and emanating shimmering ripples along the back fence. The Delgado twins, Paolo and Carlo, were sitting on the lawn right at the edge of the pool deck, chain smoking and twirling their curly hair with their spider-like fingers. The mousy white girl who was dating one (or both) of them was laid flat on her back in front of them wiggling her arms in the air above her like a hula dancer. None of them were wearing shoes. Gabi glanced over at Mike and rolled her eyes...

Mike could remember back when the twins would never have been invited to a cool kids' party. Paolo and Carlo had always been outsiders--far too satisfied with one another's company to bother vying for the fickle favor of the in-crowd. With their tight black jeans and bushy dark hair, the twins seemed completely content as the Class of '03's black sheep. But at some point during their senior year, their classmates started to recognize the allure of autonomy. The fact that the Delgados couldn't care less about being involved seemed to make people all the more interested in having them around. Soon, they were being invited everywhere. While they did show up to most of the parties, they would only speak to one another. (They even seemed to ignore the girlfriend.) The enigmatic duo had gone from outcasts to The Must-Have Party Guests of the season. It wasn't just about the novelty of their being identical twins, either. It was their utter nonchalance that the cool kids coveted. Mike wondered if his classmates would ever learn to appreciate *his* 'otherness' and start inviting him to their get-togethers. Of course, as far as Mike knew, the reason behind his outsider status was still unknown, or at least *unconfirmed*, to the students at Pasadena High...

He stepped around the cluster of people huddled around the keg and was reaching around in the ice chest for a soda when he heard Robyn Potter's shrill cackle echo from across the yard. He looked up to see the back of Robyn's short 'Halle Berry-do' and Greg Spencer seated in front of her on the chaise on the far side of the pool deck. The light from the pool gave Greg's angular face a golden tint that made him look even more superhuman. His wavy hair was tousled and much longer without all that product shellacking it back. He'd let it grow out quite a bit since the year Mike was on swim team. He could still remember the first time he saw Greg, in his little black speedos and red swim cap, fly off the starting platform into the pool. He looked like a real-life superhero. His lean, caramel brown body plunged through the air with his muscular legs kicking out behind him like he was already under water...

"Oooh, is there another Grape Crush in there?" Gabi's voice snatched Mike out of his trance. He handed her the Grape Crush and reached in to find another one. He pulled out a can of Cactus Cooler instead. Just then, Lucy came barreling down the back steps toward the keg holding two plastic cups. As Mike was sliding out of her way, Lucy changed directions last minute and slammed into him, causing him to drop his Cactus Cooler and tumble into Gabi, whose Grape Crush exploded all over the front of his shirt...his light blue shirt.

Lucy didn't bother to turn around when she mumbled, "Oops sorry," and continued to push her way through to the keg. If she had, she would have seen Mike, standing in Greg Spencer's backyard with a giant purple stain down the center of his Alternative Apparel T-shirt, horrified. He looked over at Gabi, who was covering her face in shock, shaking her head, trying not to laugh. "Sorry Mikey!"

Devastated, he floated into the house, holding the front of his shirt out, away from his body. The kitchen sink was still being blocked by the pep squad and the bathroom in the hallway had a line out into the dining room. He walked around the line, up the empty staircase.

The upstairs hall was deserted and the bathroom was the only open door. He stepped inside and started running cold water. He wet a frilly hand towel, lathered it with liquid hand soap and started scrubbing. It didn't take long to see the purple wasn't going anywhere. He shut the water off and stood there for a second, staring at the big purple wet stain in the mirror...and then he fixed his hat, cocking it just so. *Just...make it work.* He'd clicked off the light and was stepping out when Greg came leaping up the stairs, racing toward the bathroom.

"Mikey! Wassup, dude?" Greg burst past him and disappeared inside. He was already peeing when he called out, "Hey, could you hit the light for me?" Still reeling from the fact that Greg Spencer had just called him 'Mikey,' he reached inside without looking, running his hand against the wall until he flipped the switch.

"Thanks, bruh."

"No problem..." He was still standing there outside the door when the toilet flushed. Greg was already at the sink washing his hands when Mike realized he probably ought to not be just *lingering* outside the bathroom door. He started for the stairs, but Greg was moving too fast. The bathroom light had clicked back off before Mike had reached the top step.

"So what's been up, dude? I haven't seen you in minute! When did you get all Ashton Kutcher on me?" Greg threw a jovial arm around Mike's neck as they started down the stairs. "Oh shit! What happened to your shirt?" Greg laughed so hard that Mike couldn't help but smile. *Someone's a little drunk...*

"Lucy Padilla and some Grape Crush. Not a good look, right?" Mike was grasping for words that sounded relaxed, while his brain was exploding with excitement.

Finally, Greg stopped giggling enough to catch his breath... "Yo... We cannot have you walking around like that. People are gonna start calling you 'Grape Ape' or 'Out Damn Spot' or some shit. Here, come grab a shirt." Greg doubled back toward the end of the upstairs hall. Mike followed him, but very slowly...as if any sudden movements might shatter the moment. Greg got to the door on the far left and tried to turn the knob, but it wouldn't budge.

"What the--" He put his ear to the door... "Ryan? Is that--"

"Yeah? Don't come in." Ryan's voice was muffled and out of breath, but it was him.

Greg turned around to find Mike staring back at him, aghast. Greg shrugged. "Looks like Ry and Stace are using my room." He glanced down at Mike's shirt and started giggling again. "Here, just take this one." He lifted the shirt he was wearing up over his head and handed it to Mike. "And stay away from Grape Crush." He glanced at Mike with a sparkling smile, "Little Ashton," then he turned and trotted down the stairs.

Mike stood there holding the T-shirt in shock for a few moments. Then he stepped back into the bathroom and closed the door. He pressed the T-shirt to his face and breathed in deep. *Greg Spencer smells like peach cobbler and fabric softener and Right Guard and sex...*

He took off his hat, set it on the sink and slid out of his own shirt. He held up Greg's T-shirt in front of him. It was just a faded red J.Crew V-neck, but it was unbelievably soft and it looked perfect pressed against the front of Mike's slender torso. He pressed the shirt to his face again and closed his eyes... *Pull it together!* He slowly slid the red shirt on over his head and looked up at himself in the mirror. It was a little baggy but it looked good on him. He pulled on the hat, cocked it to the side just so, tucked his grape-stained shirt into his back pocket and clicked off the light.

Whatever was left of the party seemed to have moved out into the backyard. The dining room was empty and someone had turned off the music, but left the TV on in the living room, with just a blue screen as the DVD had apparently ended. On his way to the kitchen, Mike heard Lucy's shrieking laughter ring out from the other side of the living room wall. He doubled back and slowly rounded the corner to find Greg, still shirtless, sitting alone with Lucy on the couch. She noticed Mike right away.

"Hey, *he* stole your shirt!" Her head flew back in more piercing laughter.

Greg, his tawny complexion beaming, turned around to see Mike frozen under the archway. "See? Mikey's turning into a little Ashton Kutcher. Minus the annoying."

Lucy looked back over Greg's shoulder at Mike with a smirk. "Yeah, he *is* a cutie." Then to Mike, "Come sit down!"

Mike's mind began racing with the fantasy that Greg had been talking to Lucy about him being cute. He approached the couch slowly, but mustered every ounce of swagger left in his body to move casually enough to not look terrified.

He sat on the other side of Lucy and right away she handed him her iced beverage. "Here! Apparently, I'm cut off." Mike could immediately see--and smell--that she was quite drunk. "Sorry about your shirt. Greg's shirt looks good on you, though and Greg looks good without it, so.... Win-win!" She sat back against the sofa, gazing at the two of them expectantly.

Mike glanced at Greg, who was looking back at him, and then they both quickly looked to Lucy.

"You guys are so cute. How hot would it be...?" She burped up the stench of cheap beer. "Ew. Give me that back so I can wash down the...taste of..." Greg shook his head no and handed her the water bottle that was sitting on the couch between them instead. Apparently, he'd been working on sobering her up for a while.

"How hot would what be, Lucy?" Greg pulled a knee up and folded his body back into the corner of the sofa, watching her, amused. She turned to him with the water bottle still pressed to her mouth. Mike looked down at the cocktail in his hand and then lifted it to his nose to smell it. Greg nodded for him to try it when Lucy started talking.

"If you two were, you know... If he wasn't wearing your shirt and you weren't wearing your jeans and he wasn't wearing your jeans and if everybody was naked." Mike raised the cup to hide his mortified expression and sipped the fruity drink. It was a little watered down and kind of sweet but it was clearly loaded with alcohol.

"He's not wearing my jeans. He's wearing *his* jeans. Whose jeans are you wearing, Lucy?" Egging her on, Greg smiled at Mike conspiratorially. Mike just sat there, bewildered about what they might be conspiring.

Noting Greg's sly little smile, she continued. "My jeans are Juicy Couture. Juicy Lucy... You two should kiss." She turned to Mike, who was taking another sip of the drink. Greg chuckled, peering at Lucy. Mike was still holding the cup in front of his face, but he wasn't drinking.

"Why would Mike and I kiss?" Still focused on Lucy, Greg pointed at the cocktail and held his hand out towards Mike. Mike handed it across Lucy, shaking, as she squinted, trying to keep track of what was happening in front of her. Greg took two large gulps and handed it back to Mike, who took another sip and watched Lucy, careful not to make eye contact with Greg again until the question about kissing got answered.

"Why not? It would be fucking hot. Plus, what else do either of you have going on right now...?" She looked to Greg with an expression that seemed intended to make a point of how long it had been since he'd broken up with Julie Kim.

Just then, some commotion from the backyard came rushing towards them. Shawna stomped in from the dining room, soaking wet and cursing up a storm. She was immediately followed by Angela, who was overplaying how upset she was and repeating over and over, "And she *just* got her hair done, too!"

Within seconds, half the party had come bustling through the living room and out the front door. Adrian and Trey were laughing loudly, cruelly, leading one to assume they had played some part in Shawna's misfortune.

The three short skirt girls walked out with Doug and Jason.

Carlo stopped to thank Greg for the invite and Paolo nodded that he liked Mike's new shirt. "Good color on you." Mike sat there speechless, in awe about being directly addressed by one of the twins.

Kris staggered in with some older sunburned guy with bleached hair and grabbed Lucy's arm. "Come on, chica! Keg's tapped and Kyle's got a hot tub!" Lucy stood up on wobbly legs, turned around and clumsily kissed Greg on the forehead, then kissed the top of Mike's trucker cap...and then stumbled out the front door.

The living room was suddenly packed with people piling out into the front yard. A couple of them mentioned another bash brewing at Shannon Evans' house. Mike and Greg drifted over to the door to watch their friends meander rowdily into the street.

"Nothing like messing up a black girl's hair to clear out a party!" Robyn came trotting through, announcing that she and Gabi were the last ones. With downcast eyes, Gabi stopped at the door and hugged Mike a little too tight for a little too long. Robyn and Greg exchanged concerned looks behind her. Then Gabi hurried out into the front yard, dabbing at her makeup with her sleeve. Greg offered to walk them to their cars.

Robyn shook her head. "Naw, boo. I'm giving her a ride and I'm right across the street." She glanced out at Gabi and lowered her voice. "Poor thing." Then she turned to Mike, "You gon' have to look after her next year." Mike nodded his head, but he was too choked up to speak. She hugged him and turned on her toes to squeeze Greg tight. "Thanks for the party," and she stepped out onto the porch and smiled sadly at him. It was one of those 'this-is-really-the-end-of-an-era' smiles. Rather than dwell on the melancholy of the moment, she spun around with a giggle, trotted down the walkway, threw her arm around Gabi and they walked across the street.

Someone shouted, "Bye Greg!" and drove off blasting Missy Elliott's "Work It." He waved with a tired smile before he closed the door, mumbling, "Drive safe," under his breath. He clicked on the light and they turned in unison to survey the damage. Besides Shawna's water trail, the discarded cups and cans and some dirty footprints across the hardwood floor, the place was in fairly good shape. "Jeez. What a day..."

Mike was still pretending to size up the mess when Greg stepped up, took the cup out of his hand and drank it down. With him standing so close, Mike couldn't help but stare at his smooth caramel chest and the tiny curly hairs around his milk chocolate nipples. Greg offered him the last of the cocktail and Mike slurped it down just to distract himself. When he lowered the cup, Greg was still standing there, staring at him.

"You know, I like the Ashton hat..." He reached up and slipped off Mike's hat.

"...but it's really nice being able to see your face. It's a sweet face." Greg placed a hand against his cheek. Mike closed his eyes, like he was leaping from a plane, leaned in and kissed him tentatively on the lips. Greg gently pulled out of the kiss and gripped Mike's shoulder, their foreheads barely touching.

He whispered, "You're shaking."

Mike tried to stop his teeth from chattering before he whispered back, "I'm nervous."

"Me too." Greg leaned in and softly kissed him again.

Mike swooned, reeling at the possibility of opening himself up to another person. The intimacy of really trusting someone was something he had never experienced.

Greg reached back to turn off the light, then lead Mike over to the couch and lifted off his shirt. "Oh, did you want your shirt back?" Greg chuckled, pulled him closer and ran his hand over Mike's trembling naked torso from behind. It was an insane moment. Both their hearts were beating so hard, their entire bodies were throbbing.

From the couch, Mike looked up at Greg's silhouette against the blue light from the TV, breathless. "Lucy Padilla totally called it." Greg kissed him again...

They were slipping out of their jeans and Greg was nibbling on Mike's neck when his cell phone chirped. It was a text from Stacy: "Ready when U R. ;)" Greg, hearing the floor creak above them, mumbled that he'd figured as much.

He got up and turned on the light as Mike pulled his jeans back on. He'd just pulled his stained shirt out of his back pocket, when Greg swiped the red shirt off the couch and handed it to him. "So...why don't you give me a call tomorrow so we can trade. Your hat for my shirt." Greg slipped the cap on backwards, leaned in and kissed Mike one more time before he pulled on his jeans--

Mike's story was interrupted by Kelly snatching their beer cups off the counter. Business was picking up and she needed the stools for actual paying customers. Mike and Rafael made plans to hang out that night to finish the story...

o o o

Mike tried to talk him into going to one of the many bars on the WeHo strip, but Rafael wasn't having it. He never felt comfortable in gay bars; the monotonous dance music, the stuck-up men, the overt-sexualization of EVERYTHING--it all just made him uncomfortable. If he was avoiding going home to his boyfriend, avoiding suffering the barbed pangs of apathy and laying side by side in that cold king-sized bed, the frivolity of a gay bar was the last thing he wanted for distraction. He preferred a gloomier backdrop for his moping.

Shadowbox hadn't changed at all in the four months of his absence. Same rude bartender, same dismal DJs, same strong drinks. A few familiar faces nodded hello, but Rafael maneuvered his reentry without much fanfare. Back on the same stool where it all started, a cold, dirty martini perspiring in front of him, he glanced at himself in the mirror behind the bar and caught a glimpse of what the regulars were seeing of his return: his face, supermodel skinny with black smudged faintly along the edges of his eyes; his hair, longer and less unruly, coiffed so carefully he almost looked dandy; and Mike smiling goofily at his side.

Mike stood out like a glaring mistake next to all the alterna-hipsters leaning sleazily into the dark corners. Rafael's skintight rocker chic only highlighted the contrast between Mike--with his clean-shaven face, his side-cocked ball cap and his mall fashion--and everyone else in the bar. They appeared an unlikely pair, but Mike was such easy company. His puppy-dog affability was a welcome and necessary distraction from Rafael's looming depression. He'd been on the verge of losing sense of his physical-self again, wandering aimlessly through the labyrinth of yet another lost love. But Mike was too intent on having a good time to let that happen...

The screeching electro was too loud for them to do much talking, so they spent most of the night signaling to the bartender to refresh their drinks and scoping the room as unremarkable faces found charm and finesse behind the haze of alcohol fumes. Rafael picked up on a couple people's broken auras, but he couldn't be bothered with trying to talk them off of their psychological ledges. He was off duty for the evening.

There were a few moments he felt giddy about being back in the company of all those drunks. He was surprised how much he had missed communing with his raucous little congregation. But as the wall clock ticked closer to twelve and more giggling girls found themselves pressed into the laps and faces of bleary-eyed boys, he couldn't deny how much he missed Jamie. They should have been snuggling on the couch, watching 'Biggest Loser' and then sharing the bathroom sink to brush and floss their teeth. Their life together was so simple. He contemplated rushing home and begging to be forgiven for whatever he had done wrong. But somehow, the drinks kept coming and his ass stayed firmly planted on that stool.

At eleven minutes after one, Mike nodded at him in the mirror, directing his attention to someone standing to his right. Rafael turned to find a slender Latino boy with floppy bangs covering half his face, leaning against the bar. He looked too young to drink legally--probably why he was facing away from the bartender--but his eyes betrayed some world-weariness, even set against the taut-skin of his baby face.

Rafael turned back to Mike, who was practically drooling over the boy from two stools away. "You wanna trade seats?" Rafael tilted his head to the side, realizing with a smile that he had just experienced his first moment as a gay wing-man.

Mike leaned in and shouted over the music, "Offer to buy him a drink." Mike never took his eyes off the boy, who was making a show of scanning the room for someone. Rafael thought back to that night, when Jamie was sitting in Mike's seat, buying all those drinks, until Rafael finally went home with him...and never left.

"You like him, you buy him a drink." He could feel the boy's attention homing in on their conversation, his eagerness fluttering like butterfly wings against the lining of Rafael's stomach.

Mike, who had been maintaining his cool until that moment, leaned across Rafael--elbows on the bar, ass in the air--and tugged on the boy's sweater sleeve. "Hey, what're you drinkin'?" The boy turned calmly, glanced at Mike and then Rafael, and mumbled that he didn't drink. Mike looked at Rafael confused. "What did she say?"

Rafael laughed at how quickly Mike's boozing had transformed him from goofy frat boy to bitchy sorority girl. "He doesn't drink." He patted Mike on the back, encouraging him to sit down so he didn't slip off the bar and really make an ass of himself. "Maybe you're not his type, Mike. We're not at Mother Lode."

Mike sat down slowly and then hissed, "Ask him his fucking name!" Rafael suddenly felt a surge of sadness from him, some sorrow twisted with resentment. He turned to see Mike glaring back at him, agitated. "Just ask him!"

Rafael exhaled and leaned toward the boy. "My buddy here wants to know your name...and maybe buy you a nice nonalcoholic beverage." The boy didn't turn to respond, but grinned with an affected cockiness. He was play-acting, putting on a 'hot-boy' facade. He was new to the game, but he had every intention of mastering it, and he was clearly prepared to fake it in the meantime.

"I'm Danny." He turned with an expression that might have read as sexually brazen to an untrained eye, but Rafael could feel the boy's nerves trembling in his own stomach. He felt sorry for him for thinking he needed to work so hard.

"I'm Rafael and this is Mike." Mike stood up and reached across Rafael to shake Danny's hand, remarking that it was like holding the giant paw of a puppy who hadn't quite grown into his appendages yet. Rafael chuckled at Mike's flirting, but he was still curious about the sadness that had seeped out for that brief moment before.

The three of them continued shouting over the music and the kid quickly realized he was out of his depth with Mike's honey-dipped seduction. Rafael didn't contribute much to the conversation but he could feel the kid's warmth wafting toward him and away from Mike. He pulled Mike in to tell him to slow his roll, that he was scaring the kid off, but he could see in his bloodshot eyes that he was not to be deterred. Then, like divine intervention, the music faded and the lights came up.

"Shit. Quarter to two already." With the lights on, Rafael quickly confirmed that Mike, the one with the car keys, was in no shape to drive. He waved at the bartender to close their tab while Mike continued blowing gin-soaked exhaust across his face at the kid, who looked even more childlike and terrified under the bright lights.

A few minutes later, the crowd had carried the three of them outside, where their faces were jaundiced by the dingy street lamps as they meandered down the sidewalk. Most of the people leaving at that hour were the guys with no game, who had either gotten too drunk or not quite drunk enough to score...just like it had always been. Rafael had been one of those unhappy hipsters with nowhere to go, too drunk to safely stumble home. Now it was up to him to make sure that his plastered sidekick got home unharmed before he crawled into bed with his man.

He pulled out his phone to find he had missed a text from Jamie: "Going to bed. Nite baby. Xo." His heart sank. He hadn't told Jamie he was going out. He knew the message was him checking in, wondering where he was at twelve-thirty a.m. There was no precedent for this situation. It was the first time he had been to a bar without Jamie since they'd met. He was suddenly wrought with regret. He needed to get home.

"Hey Mike, let's get going." Mike twisted around and glared at him like he'd said something in Cantonese. Rafael didn't flinch. "Yeah, man, time to get home."

Danny cleared his throat, "Hey, do either of you know a guy named Paul? Hangs out at this bar?" Mike twisted back around to face him. "He's friend with a guy named Nando. Nando's like my height, about a buck forty, Puerto Rican dude with wavy hair?"

"Puerto Rican? Whatever!" Mike wasn't following the plot but he was finally grasping that he wasn't likely to get much further with Danny.

"Tonight was Mike's first time and I haven't been in ages, but no, I don't remember a Nando or a Paul. What's Paul look like?" Rafael felt Mike getting woozy so he grabbed his shoulder to stabilize him.

"Never met Paul. Was just hoping to find my friend Nando. Lost track of him a few months back and he told me his friend Paul hung out at Shadowbox. It's cool. Just thought I'd ask." Danny shrugged, defeated, and began to wander away.

Mike turned to Rafael with exhaustion and humiliation reddening his eyes. The loneliness Mike had been drowning in booze suddenly became very apparent. Rafael's angel complex kicked in and he called out to Danny. "Hey, if we run into your friends, how should we get in touch with you?"

Danny bounced back over and dictated his number while Rafael typed it into his phone. He made his exit with firm handshakes, oddly formal and macho considering the coquettish energy he'd put on when they first came across him in the bar. Then he was gone. Rafael threw his arm around Mike and walked him to the car.

"Keys? I'll give you his number when you sober up. Drunk-dialing...not a good look for you." Mike pressed the keys into Rafael's hand with a squeeze. It was all he could do in his state to let him know how much he appreciated him looking out for him. Of course, Rafael already knew because he could feel it.

It was almost three in the morning when Rafael got home. Exhausted, he brushed his teeth and popped two tablets of Aleve with a large glass of water. He rinsed away the grime of the night with overpriced facial cleanser and when he looked up at himself in the mirror, he finally saw what Jamie had seen. His face did look unhealthy. Unhappy. At some point, fear had slipped in and blinded him to all the beauty he had been so blessed to find. *But when? Why?*

He thought back... Everything seemed to have fallen apart around the time he started taking the painkillers. In trying to shield himself from the pain of believing he didn't deserve love, he'd shut love out. *It's all my fault.* He opened the medicine cabinet, flushed the few remaining pills down the toilet and clicked off the light...

The bedroom was completely dark. He stripped naked and crawled in next to Jamie without a sound. It had been weeks since they'd slept together naked. Jamie often wore little shorts to bed, but Rafael had been sleeping in the nude since he was a teenager. Yet, he'd somehow convinced himself when the weather cooled down that the T-shirt and boxers were more practical. That night, however, he was certain that the pajamas were more about closing himself off than the temperature dropping in November. Denying Jamie access to his body was his attempt at gaining some control in the relationship. He had been childish, acting out of spite. He didn't even want that kind of control. He just didn't want to be left alone. There was so much loneliness in the world, so much loneliness in his own life, why would he go out of his way to close himself off from the one person who wanted him?

He slid over and snuggled up against Jamie's warm body and Jamie folded his back into his embrace. And there, under the goose down comforter, all the coldness they had been clutching to so fiercely began to melt away.

PART FOUR

15

o o o

Danny was standing by himself near the entrance to the smoking patio, pretending to text someone on his phone. Colin had decided to stay in San Diego that night to celebrate his birthday. Danny's feelings were hurt, but he never let on.

He'd been back to the bar twice since meeting Rafael and Mike with no new leads to Paul. Nando had given him an idea of what to look for: a smart, sensitive boy who was probably questioning his sexuality. Rafael was consistent with what he'd been picturing, with his shy eyes, his slight build and his slinky movements, but nobody else exhibited that softness. Just when Danny was ready to bail on the whole mission, he saw *him*.

He was rail thin with low-riding skinny jeans and cowboy boots--probably more ostentatiously gay than Danny had imagined Paul, but his smile was sweet enough that Danny wouldn't feel like an asshole for asking his name. The guy was smoking a cigarette and talking to a cute black girl who was laughing with her mouth wide open.

Danny slid over and stood behind the girl, facing away. She was talking about meeting an actress named Amber from *Glee* at the Beverly Center. He was working hard to catch any names dropped during their conversation, his ears pricked up for 'Paul' or 'Nando.' But before he could make any progress on that front, the guy in the boots turned to him and asked if he had a light.

"A light? Oh...yeah, hold on." Danny dug through his pockets. By the time he remembered that he hadn't been carrying his lighter for weeks, the girl had turned all the way around to check him out with a huge grin. That was when Danny noticed the guy's cigarette was already lit.

"You know what? I'm good on the lighter. Thought my fire had gone out, but then I found you." Danny looked up at the guy's mouth, shocked at the thickness of his southern drawl and the deepness of his voice. He didn't look old enough or bold enough to be coming on so strong in a straight bar. But there he was, staring at Danny with a wily smile and a sly twinkle in his eye.

"Okay. Well... I'm Danny." He chuckled when he heard his own voice crack.

"Good to meet ya, Danny. I'm Max, this is Tanya." Tanya was still staring up at Danny with that huge grin.

"Where you from Danny? Don't think we've seen you here before." Tanya was country too, but her accent wasn't quite as thick as her friend's. Max was smiling and puffing on his cigarette, like the hookah-smoking caterpillar in the Alice In Wonderland cartoon. Danny had seen that DVD too many times, stoned out of his mind, babysitting his little sister.

"Me and my best friend just moved not too far from here. From up in Ventura County. Sylmar?" He was nodding his head and talking too fast, the way his best friend did when he got nervous.

"Never heard of it. Smoke?" Max held out a pack of cigarettes, slinking up alongside Tanya to get a little closer.

"No thanks. Those things'll kill you, man." Danny's face flashed a moment of panic at the realization that he had possibly just offended someone.

"Suckin' the wrong dick can kill you too, but that hasn't stopped any of us yet!" Tanya burst out laughing at her own joke and Max, horrified, stepped directly in front of her to run damage control. He was clearly aware of the delicate dance that was required of seducing a boy who didn't quite know what he was looking for.

"Please ignore her. She's doin' too much right now. So...is your friend here with you?" Max's voice got progressively deeper with each phrase. He flicked his cigarette through the patio's wrought-iron railing onto the sidewalk and leaned against the wall next to Danny with his hips thrust forward. Tanya took her view of the back of Max's choppy haircut as her exit cue and wandered back inside the bar, mumbling about getting someone to buy her a drink.

"No, he's out of town... On his birthday! I mean, today's his birthday, but he's out of town on business." Danny could feel Max closing in on him, inching closer with his body, trying to lock in on his eyes. Danny thought maybe he should excuse himself and keep looking for Paul, but he didn't move. Max's blatant flirting intrigued him. *Why does he think he can be so aggressive?*

"Business? Really. What kind of business do *you* get into?" Max smiled innocently, as if his obvious come-on might be mistaken for a real question. Danny opted not to put all his *business* out on the table just yet.

"I just got a waiter job at this new restaurant. Kindle, up on Sixth? It's cool." He flashed a smug smile, as if to point out how deftly he had dodged the real question. Still, he found Max's attention charming.

There was a big guy with eyeliner and a feather earring standing a few feet behind Max who seemed keenly interested in their conversation. Max turned around to see what Danny was looking at and the guy nodded at him with thinly veiled contempt. Max returned the curt hello and turned back to Danny.

"That's just Tommy. He's harmless." Max reached into his pocket for another cigarette, but thought better of it when Danny cleared his throat. Instead, he launched into a monologue about how many times he had changed majors and why he had chosen not to go back to North Carolina for Christmas break, just to keep the conversation from dragging.

Danny could still feel Tommy glaring at them. "Your friend looks kinda mad."

Max rolled his eyes and shook his head, annoyed that Tommy was cutting in on his action...and maybe a little annoyed that Danny was allowing him to. "Okay, long story short, I'd been seeing this other dude for almost a year and then, like, a few months ago, he just dropped off the face of the earth. Stopped answering his phone. No email, no text, no IM, not even a fucking Facebook message. And I mean, I'm a good guy, you know? People don't just up and dump me without some kind of explanation. Well, so my feelings were hurt. I was pissed. Then one night I got wasted and...probably gave Tommy the wrong impression. And now he won't leave me alone." Max let out a dramatic sigh.

"So...is this place, like, a *gay* club?" Danny looked back over his shoulder cautiously, like he was expecting the patio to transform into a disco ball-littered, leopard-printed feather boa factory.

"Not really. Some of the straight boy regulars can be kinda sissified. But really, I think it's just me, Gay Tommy and...?" Max smiled at Danny, hoping he would confirm his membership to the coterie.

Danny wasn't ready to confirm or deny anything just yet. He knew staying vague about his orientation held some cachet in places like Shadowbox. He also knew he wasn't getting any closer to finding Nando by being coy. "What about that guy Paul?"

"Oh, and Paul. He doesn't come out much, though." Max did a double take. "Wait. How do you know Paul?"

"You know Paul?!" Danny was so excited, he grabbed Max's arm and shook him.

"Paul Simms? Yeah, he's my roommate. How do you know him?" Max glanced down at Danny's big hand wrapped all the way around his forearm.

"I don't know him. I mean, I've never met him. If it's the same Paul, he's friends with my friend Nando."

"Nando?" Max's voice went up an octave and Danny let go of his arm.

"Yeah. Nando's phone got turned off a while back and I've been trying to find him. Make sure he's okay."

"Oh. Right. Never met him, but I've heard." Max gave Danny another once-over. "Are you...good friends with Nando?" His energy immediately shifted from sexually intrigued to suspicious. Danny sensed that his impression of Nando, however limited, was not a good one, so he proceeded carefully.

"We just hung out a couple times, a few months back. We're not that close. But last time I saw him, he didn't seem...like he was in a great place. I knew he was kind of on his own out here. I just wanted to make sure he was, you know...okay."

Satisfied that Danny's interest in The Wayward One was respectable enough, Max relaxed his shoulder back against the wall. "Like I said, I never met him. I know that Paul tried to stage an intervention or whatever and that Nando cussed him out and physically assaulted him. They haven't spoken since. That dude's got issues."

Danny nodded his head slowly, his fears confirmed: Nando had fallen apart...

Max wriggled his nose, bewitched like Samantha. "If you want, you can come check out our place. Paul went home for break but maybe he left some clues. Maybe I can help you find what you're looking for." He shifted his hips toward Danny again.

Danny inhaled with a nervous smile. He knew with a boy like Max, anything could happen. Even though he was apprehensive about being intimate with someone new, he was excited about the possibilities. For the first time, he didn't bother considering what implications going home with a boy might have on his identity. That night, it was simply a question of whether he liked him. So far, so good. "Okay. Let's go."

16

o o o

Colin spent his nineteenth birthday in San Diego without Danny, but he wasn't alone. He'd shot four scenes for AndroFiles over five days. When he was done, rather than rush back up to their unfurnished apartment in West LA to watch Danny obsess about finding Nando, he decided to stay and party with some *new friends* from the studio.

Ted was another meathead--twenty-two years old, military background, obvious steroid abuser--whose conversational topics were limited to how much weight he was benching and how many girls he was banging.

Damon was twenty-five years old, six feet tall, one hundred forty-five pounds and nine and a half by six inches. He was paranoid about his receding hairline compromising his twink-appeal, so he always wore a Yankees cap--even while he was 'working.' Manic and mouthy, he fancied himself a smart-ass even though he wasn't very smart.

Andrew was eighteen, soft-spoken and boyish--a reticent newer model from the Midwest who had been staying in the hotel room adjacent to Colin's. He had expressed early on that he wanted to hang out for Colin's birthday, even though he was shooting a big three-way scene the following morning. When he found out that the others were also coming, he backed out last minute. Colin had assumed Andrew was gay, but it hadn't occurred to him that he might have mistaken the dinner invite for a date until he watched his face fall at the mention of Ted, Damon and...

Then there was Marcus. Marcus was twenty-one and painstakingly 'metrosexual.' He was handsome and well-spoken enough that one might assume him capable of finding more challenging work, but his muscular physique and slightly larger than average cock made gay porn an easy choice.

For Colin's birthday dinner, the guys went to Park, a Korean Benihana-style restaurant in North Park. Marcus ordered a Long Island Iced Tea for Colin when they sat down and then got up to get himself a drink from the bar. By the time the guy came up to the table to grill their food in front of them, the four of them were already tipsy.

Ted took one look at the cook, a slim, sort of effeminate guy, and shook his head with contrived contempt. One by one, Colin watched as each of the guys rolled his eyes or made some point of indicating to the other three how uncomfortable he was about the cook, this delicate Filipino guy who was just being himself. *Would they be making those faces if Danny was here?*

Once the cook ambled away and Ted launched into a crude and seemingly non sequitur story about the single young mother in his 'stable of bitches' back in Manhattan Beach, Colin understood. Insecure straight men who have gay sex for a living often feel the need to distinguish themselves from actual gay men. If the straight guy is working as a bottom, as Ted had been all week, he's likely to be even more conflicted. Was there really a difference between riding a dick for four thousand dollars and riding one because you like dick? As far as Colin could see, the only difference was four thousand dollars.

Colin had probably been more concerned about maintaining the distinction before he and Danny had had 'the talk.' It had taken them two weeks to muster the guts to discuss what happened in San Diego. Danny had called him in the middle of the night, drunk and crying. They sat on the sidewalk in front of Dan Senior's house talking until four a.m. For Colin, working in gay porn was mostly about the challenge of staying in character and appearing to enjoy himself enough to get more work. For Danny, it had been much deeper than a performance. Having sex with a man had opened a door to a side of himself he wasn't ready to see. It had been one of the most emotional experiences of his life. Colin couldn't deny that getting paid to get off was awesome, but the only thing appealing to him about gay sex was the easy paycheck.

Colin turned to Marcus, who was sipping his drink quietly as Damon and Ted cackled and cosigned on the advantages of boning MILFs. Ted, who had bottomed for everyone at the table and was called 'Teeny' behind his back, was working especially hard to convince the guys that he was just as good at giving it as he was at taking it. Colin shook his head. *Doubtful...* It was sort of ridiculous that they were all so concerned with affirming their untarnished heterosexuality, given their line of work, but Marcus was really the only one Colin found suspect.

He and Colin had worked together that last day and while the scene was billed as Marcus' first time bottoming, Colin already had enough experience fucking men to doubt the validity of the claim. He had never bottomed, but he knew from his experience as a top that when a straight guy has something rammed up his ass--especially the first time, his body is going to do everything it can to reject the intrusion. That means the muscles go tense, the asshole clenches up and the guy loses his hard-on right away. Doesn't matter how good the straight porn in the background is...put something in his butt and the dick deflates instantly. If the something is as thick as Colin's dick, there's bound to be some whimpering and complaining as well. Marcus didn't do any of that. On the outside, he may have been as macho and heterosexist as the rest of them, but he wasn't as resolved around his sexuality as he wanted people to believe.

Of course, role playing was part of the job. The two guys Colin worked with immediately after Danny left were 'playing straight' for the cameras, but clearly gay in their day to day lives.

One kid who went by Ace had come in just to give Colin a blow job. (Anderson explained that they were shooting out of sequence and that he would post that blow job scene before he released the hardcore scene with Danny, to give the viewers the impression that Colin's foray into gay sex had been more gradual.) Ace somehow lost his lisp when he explained, on camera, that he had never sucked a dick before. He stayed fully clothed the whole time, but didn't manage to conceal the raging hard-on in his skintight Diesel jeans. He even pretended to be put off by having to handle Colin's cock for the first couple of minutes. But soon enough, he was deep-throating and showboating with more cock-sucking prowess than even seemed possible for a boy of eighteen. When the scene was done, after he had swallowed most of Colin's load and the cameras had been turned off, he went all swishy again and started giggling with Sky about how much he loved straight cock.

Even gay boys knew that their appeal to gay audiences was incumbent upon a stated discomfort with gay sex. Fully functioning homosexuals were turning in Golden Globe-worthy 'straight guy' performances just to work in amateur gay porn. Marcus didn't seem quite as far gone as all that, but there was something about him...

The waiter told them as he served their third round of drinks that it would have to be their last. There was some 'three drink maximum' restaurant rule. Ted immediately suggested they take the party to a strip club. Damon asked Colin if he wanted to celebrate his birthday with male or female strippers. They all laughed it off at first, but Damon wasn't joking. The option of going to a gay bar was actually on the table.

Nobody's heterosexuality was directly called into question. There was just an understanding that now they could function in either world. Damon, who had been working in the industry for close to three and a half years already, had made 'appearances' in gay bars while working with other production companies and he said the models had been treated like royalty: VIP sections, free booze and lots of cute girls getting drunk with their gay friends. "I've gotten tons of pussy in gay clubs." Not to mention all the connections they could make for future gigs as go-go dancers...or escorts, 'if times ever get tough.'

Marcus finally spoke up. "Dude, I've already seen more than my share of dick this week. Let's just go to a regular club and get hammered. I don't feel like tipping hoes or hunting down fag hags tonight." No one could argue with that, so they decided to go a nightclub a few blocks away called the Tavern. Damon had been there a few times and Ted had heard on the radio that afternoon that it was 'the place to be.' *Perfect.*

Marcus waited with Colin, who was good and tipsy, in his new 2004 Pathfinder while Ted and Damon walked around the corner to the club. The plan was for Damon to come back out in twenty minutes with Ted's ID for Colin to use to get in. Ted was clearly from redneck stock and Colin was a light-skinned mulatto, but their thick pink faces were practically indistinguishable on a drivers license photo.

At first, Colin couldn't figure out why he was feeling so on edge, sitting with Marcus. Then he turned to him with a smug grin and Colin remembered... Their scene together had invoked something savage in Colin. He realized then that his tendency toward violence in bed was rooted in contempt for his partners and a need to punish them.

He'd only had sex with a few girls, but with all of them--except for that one hot chick from Jamba Juice--he'd felt like he'd been debasing himself by dipping into ranks that were beneath him. Even though he was getting paid well to do it, fucking men often inspired the same disdain. He'd been taking out all his personal shame around his proclivities on his sex partners--the literal personifications of his disgrace.

It was during a particularly sadistic stretch, when he was really pounding into Marcus, that it had occurred to him: he was essentially grudge-fucking his own shame. He'd forgotten about those revelations until, sitting in the car, he realized he was still harboring an impulse to do the guy some damage.

Just as Colin had decided to think only good thoughts about his innocent new friend, Marcus pulled out a small plastic baggie. "I only had enough for two of us, so don't mention it to the other guys. Those fuckers can blow through an eight ball in like ten minutes." He tapped out the powder onto an old CD case rested on the center console and chopped out two lines with his credit card. "Plus, they've both been up for like three days..." Colin was drunk and didn't say anything, but he did find it odd that a twenty-one year old internet porn model had an American Express card.

Marcus presented the first line to Colin, who burped up some Long Island Iced Tea and then shuddered with excitement about the addition of party favors. "Tony Montana in the house!" He didn't notice that the cocaine was oddly off-white until he'd already snorted up his line. His face went tingly and then it felt like a can of warm paint had been poured over his head. He had only done cocaine six or seven times, and all in the last few weeks while hanging out with guys from the studio, but it had never hit him like that before. He watched Marcus lean into the shadows and snort up his line...and then they both reclined in their seats and said nothing. Colin felt his limbs get heavy and hot. The inside of the truck seemed to get darker but the air was swirling with sparkling dust. *This coke is fucked up...*

Marcus' Blackberry chirping woke Colin up. He had no idea how long he'd been sleeping, but the inside of his chest felt like it had been scraped clean and filled with hot molasses. Marcus didn't move, but he was breathing loudly so Colin knew he wasn't dead. Colin picked up the phone from the cup holder and read the text from Damon: "Door trippin. No ins outs 4 party. Blak radio station here but hot bitchz N E way!"

Colin couldn't make sense of it so he put the phone down and leaned back in his seat. Then, like he was possessed by some slow-motion ballet dancer, he sat up and started the car so he could turn on the air conditioning. Until he felt the cool air on his face, he hadn't noticed his arms tingling or that he was sweating, even though the windows were down and it was fairly cool outside. "I am. Fucked. Up!"

Marcus turned to him slowly. "Happy birthday, bro. Now I'm fucking *you*, metaphorically speaking, of course." He leaned forward and pressed his face against the dashboard like it was a pillow. "You know...eight months ago, I was a completely different person."

Colin's head was slightly less muddled with the A/C on. "Are you in the witness protection program?"

Marcus chuckled with his eyes closed and his cheek still planted firmly to the top of the glove compartment. "No. I mean, when I first got into this shit, back in South Beach, I was absolutely not doing anything beyond the solo. No hand jobs, no blow jobs, no toys, nothing. Figured I'd jack off for a couple studios, make some quick cash and then transition into straight porn. After my first solo, the *first one*, the guy--this fat old man, offered to pay to give me a hand job. I was like, 'Fuck no. I'm not letting another dude touch me, period.' No disrespect. Like...my dad was gay."

"*Was* gay? Is he straight now?" Colin wondered if maybe Danny might change his mind... Or change it back.

"No. He's dead now. AIDS. Was closeted most of his life...but I'm just saying I don't have a problem with gays." He opened his eyes and continued in his gruff, sluggish monotone. "But I did it. I let the guy jerk me off. It was disgusting. Fucking awful. He asked to come back and shoot a blow job scene and first I said no, but I mean, by then it seemed like a random distinction to make, you know? Like, he'd already touched me. Then he offered me more money if I'd...use some dildos." Colin nodded... *Dildos, riiiight.* Marcus continued, "Dude, cash was tight. My buddies from school were all getting laid off from their legit jobs. Just felt like I couldn't say no. But that was gonna be it. After that, I was done. I fucking left Miami to start over. Put a period on it, you know?"

Colin shook his head and muttered to himself that he never would have gotten into it if he'd had to touch some gross old man. Apart from the two weeks of not speaking to Danny--which he still blamed on Nando for taking him to that gay club--Colin's gay porn experience had been relatively easy. He noticed that Marcus had started rubbing his face in circles against the dashboard and it occurred to him that his own face was itching. He pulled his knees up, curled back into his seat and started rubbing his cheek against the head rest, suddenly full of gratitude about Danny being with him for his first shoot.

"Then people started recognizing me. When you first get into it, you think nobody's gonna see that shit. But ever since Fucktube and all those free porn sites got popular, gays started coming out of the woodwork. Like, dudes I would never have guessed were winking and nodding at me at the gym, you know? My shit was everywhere."

As far as Colin knew, none of his videos had been posted yet. He had been checking the site fairly regularly after that first weekend, but when he accidentally clicked on a hi-res photo of Nando peeling his ass cheeks apart, he never went back. That had been over a month ago. He was far more concerned about people in his life finding out what he had done to Danny than he was worried about getting hit on by random gay guys anyway. That shit didn't bother him. "So...what made you get back into it?"

Marcus lay silent, thoughtful. Then, "I don't know. Just seemed like...what else was I gonna do, you know? Needed the money. Anderson pays more than most studios. He takes care of us..." He was staring at the side of the steering wheel, squinting, like he was really trying to see how he had managed to end up back in that place. "Like, I did a blow job and then I fucked a couple dudes... Didn't seem like that big a deal, you know? But Ted used to work as an exclusive top and then, he did a flip flop scene with that Brock dude and he's been bottoming ever since..."

Colin knew where Marcus' mind was going and he slowly raised a finger in protest. "But that's by choice. It's not like he couldn't go back to topping if he wanted to. Ted makes more money as a bottom." Even as he was defending the prospect of being a versatile performer, it occurred to him that getting fucked that first time could be more of a slippery slope than he wanted to admit. *What if there really is no going back once you cross that line?* Brock, the Viagra guy with the tattoos from the kitchen, had obviously gone back to topping. "And Damon does both. It doesn't mean shit."

"Yeah, that's what I thought too...before. But then...we did *our* scene and now it's like...*I let a guy fuck me.* Nothing but spit between me and some random dude. It's a trip when you think about letting a man inside your body, you know? You lose something when you let someone do that. It's like I don't own my body anymore, you know?"

Colin nodded in agreement. Pounding the ass of some dude you just met--on camera--was completely insane if you thought about it for too long. *Getting* fucked must have been a whole other level of crazy.

Their eyes glazed over as their minds wandered into dark, uncharted places. Colin didn't even want to entertain the notion that sexual experience had any direct bearing on sexual identity. Allowing a physical act to define him required that he relinquish his free will. That meant any action imposed on him would supersede his own desire and emotional consciousness.

In the three months since he'd signed as an AndroFiles exclusive, he'd already shot nine scenes. All the nerves he had suffered the first couple times were completely gone. He had gotten good at fucking men. But that didn't mean that fucking men defined who he was. The fact that he had already become proficient at cock-sucking and ass-pounding--when his prowess at cunnilingus was probably still severely lacking--was no reflection of what kind of man he was. *It's a job.*

Then, as if Marcus had been following Colin's silent conversation with himself, he said, "None of this is real if you don't let it be."

Colin's eyes met Marcus' just as sirens began howling in the distance...like an alarm to rouse them back into the material universe. Colin reached up to shut off the A/C as the dark, rippling dreamscape faded around him and the stiff gray interior of his truck reappeared in its stead.

He'd never had a conversation so intimate and honest, not even with Danny. *It's gotta be the coke....* Only drugs would permit two straight men, virtual strangers, to sit in a parked car and spill their guts like that. Of course, they had already shared a level of physical intimacy that, in most other circumstances, would grant them--at the very least--some pretense of emotional closeness. But even after ejaculating onto one another's necks, their relationship was no more profound than that of two office temps in adjacent cubicles.

Colin glanced over and for an instant, he saw Danny sitting beside him. He screwed up his eyes as Marcus lifted his head off the dashboard and picked up his phone. "What the fuck happened to those munches?"

Colin turned around to see the flashing red and blue lights of two police cars racing past them, rounding the corner. Marcus' phone chirped. He read Damon's text out loud: "Help! Cum get us!" Then the phone rang and Marcus answered.

"What the hell does that text mean?" Colin could hear Damon yelling over the phone, but couldn't make out what he was saying. Something about guns and cops...and Ted. Marcus' face dropped in shock. "Okay, we're coming!"

"What happened?" Colin had the engine on and was pulling out of the parking spot before Marcus had even managed to put down the phone.

"Not really sure. Ted was drunk and hitting on some girl and then somebody pulled out a gun...or something." Marcus was talking slowly, like he was recalling the details of a dream...like the urgency of the situation hadn't quite processed in his mind yet. "Damon's got him outside in an alley."

Colin had pulled out into the street and was making a three-point turn when a car came out of nowhere, screeching and honking and shining headlights onto their faces from just a few feet outside Marcus's door. That seemed to wake Marcus up. He sat up straight and pulled his seatbelt across his chest as Colin sped toward Tavern.

"This is so fucked up! Who does shit like this? Stupid high school fucking bullshit!" Marcus' speech was still slurred but he was getting loud.

When they turned onto Juniper Street, there were flashing cop cars blocking the front of the club from all sides. Colin slowed down and pulled over alongside a parked car.

"You gotta get out and go find them." Colin could feel his right leg getting stiff, cramping up as his foot pressed against the brake. He shifted the car into 'park' and looked over at Marcus, whose face was frozen in an expression identical to Macaulay Culkin's, minus the hands slapped against his cheeks, in the 'Home Alone' poster.

"I can't go out there. It's crawling with cops and I'm totally fucked up!" Spittle was flying from Marcus' mouth and his eyes were watering.

Colin yelled back at him, impatient, "Just go get them!"

Marcus clumsily reached for the door handle and slid out slowly. It was like watching someone trying to maneuver a body he had only recently occupied. Colin watched him pick up speed as people started milling about the sidewalk in front of the club, meandering out into the street like an angry army of mediocrity.

He didn't see Ted or Damon anywhere...and as he was scanning the crowd, he caught himself scoping for Danny's floppy skater hair and long arms. He wondered what Danny was doing. They hardly saw each other anymore. Even though he was totally cool with his choice to explore everything he was discovering about his sexuality, he felt oddly compelled to offer his support from a distance. They were both immersed in gay porn, but for different reasons. It wasn't as awkward as it could have been, but their diverging interests were definitely allowing them to drift. Danny wasn't even smoking weed anymore. It was like they suddenly had nothing to talk about. But if he could listen to Marcus ramble on about losing his sense of self by getting fucked--

Thwack! Thwack! Colin turned panicked toward the sound of slapping against glass. "OPEN THE FUCKING DOOR!" Damon was standing outside the passenger side of the truck, holding up Ted with one arm and banging on the window with the other. Colin reached back to hit the unlock switch on his door panel. Damon shoved Ted--barely conscious, his forehead gushing blood--into the backseat and then hoisted his gangly self, slamming the door behind him. "Let's go! Where the fuck is Marcus?"

"He went looking for you guys!" Colin turned around, worried that Ted was getting blood all over the upholstery.

"Fuck him, let's go. Go! GO!" Damon's eyes were crazed and he was out of breath. Something really messed up had gone down.

"I'm not just gonna leave Marcus. That's fucked up, dude." Colin was putting the car in reverse, speeding backwards and trying to come up with excuses for why they were, in fact, leaving Marcus. He backed around the corner and started driving back toward the hotel. He glanced up into the rearview mirror and saw Damon snort something from a small vial. Colin screeched, "What the hell happened to him?"

Damon shook his head and looked over at Ted, who was moaning and drooling. "He's fucked. He was trying to holler at these hoes and some gorilla nigger got up in his face, talking mad shit and started pushing him around..."

Colin hit the brake and looked back at Damon, stunned. *Did this motherfucker just say something about a gorilla nigger?* In the three days they'd known each other, the fact that Colin was half-black hadn't come up in conversation...and while he was accustomed to people assuming he was mixed with something, Colin was light-skinned and fine featured enough for someone who didn't interact with many black folks to not necessarily notice. That still didn't give anyone an excuse to say some ignorant shit like, 'gorilla nigger' in his car. He just stared at Damon, stupefied.

Damon nodded back at him, apparently mistaking his surprise for shared disgust about the audacity of the characters in question. "I know! That's why I hate being around them. Ignorant fucking animals. I hate niggers."

Colin snapped. He unbuckled his seatbelt and leapt into the backseat, pummeling Damon with the ferocity of...a *fucking animal.* Damon screamed and immediately collapsed under the impact of Colin's blurry fists. Ted woke up to Colin knocking the back of Damon's bald head against the window, but his moans of protest didn't slow Colin down...until he heard a click and felt steel pointed against the back of his head. Damon's limp body slid with a whimper down on to the floor between the passenger seat and the backseat, next to his baseball cap. Colin turned half way around to see Ted holding a gun in his blood-crusted hand.

"Get off him."

Colin carefully crawled back into the driver seat with his hands up next to his head. His heart was pounding outside his chest and he couldn't inhale deeply enough to catch his breath. The headlights were shining on Marcus in the middle of the street, walking angrily toward the car with his arms out, yelling, "Where the fuck are you going?" Colin's boiling blood was throbbing against his eardrums. Then he heard the whistle of the gun flying through the air toward the side of his head. Everything went black.

When Colin came to, he could taste blood in his mouth. He was laying face down, flat on his stomach with his legs dangling over the edge of whatever was holding him up. His feet were on the ground and his shoes were off. It was completely dark and he could feel the cold night air against his bare ass.

He felt cold steel pressed against the crack of his ass...and then the barrel of the gun shoved all the way in. A surge of excruciating pain pierced his insides. He screamed but it sounded more like a low growl with his face pressed against the carpet. *Carpet?* He was in the back of his own truck, laid out on the open tailgate.

The gun was being shoved in and out of him. He screamed again but even less sound came. Tears streamed down the side of his nose and mixed with the salty blood in his mouth. He tried to kick his feet, but his legs were too heavy to lift. He could feel dirt and twigs through his socks. He tried to lift himself up, but his arms were tied behind his back, probably with his jeans. Whoever was behind him pulled the gun all the way out and Colin sighed with relief. He heard Damon laughing...getting closer...and then...

A bell tower chimed in the distance...and it reminded Colin of Danny's annoying cell phone ring. *I wonder what Danny is doing...*

Colin's body went into shock. He felt Damon's huge erection rip into him and then he went numb. He could hear the truck shaking and squeaking in time with the sound of Damon's bony hips slapping against the back of his thighs, but he couldn't feel anything. Damon was sniffling, cursing and grunting above him. Marcus was talking somewhere nearby. His voice had slipped back into that quiet, eery monotone. "Who's the bigger bitch? Payback or that guy?" Ted never said anything. Damon howled and slapped at Colin's meaty behind...

Colin closed his eyes and thought of Samantha's soft, glossy lips spread in a sweet smile across the hard wiring of her braces, and he knew there was no escape. The universe was going to balance itself out whether he liked it or not. He blacked out again.

Colin woke up fully dressed in his hotel bed with a terrible headache. He'd been startled awake by knocking at the door, but it took him a few seconds to figure out why he was so jumpy. He threw all the blankets off of him and answered the door. Andrew stepped in slowly, sizing him up with cautious concern. "You all right, man?" Colin looked back at him blankly. He wasn't sure he understood the question...

Andrew explained that he'd seen the guys carry Colin up to his room late the night before. Marcus told Andrew they'd all just had too much to drink. "But those guys were all so cracked-out and beat up, I just wanted to make sure you were okay."

Colin glanced down at the mud stains on his jeans and his asshole throbbed in pain. "Yeah, man, I'm fine. We just got really wasted..." With that, Colin conceded to what fate had bestowed upon him, lying to himself that he had no hard feelings. *That shit wasn't personal. We just got too fucked up, is all...* They had, after all, driven him back to the hotel and put him to bed. "Naw, I'm good, man. Thanks."

It wasn't until Andrew was gone and Colin had stepped into the bathroom to undress that he realized that his brand new 2(x)ist boxer briefs were gone and that the seat of his jeans was stained with blood. *Fuck!* He closed his eyes tight, racing to erase the memory, wipe his mind clean. It didn't work. He stepped into the shower and tried to scrub it off, but it held fast, crawling through and clinging to his consciousness like body lice. Nothing was working. He had a little weed left in his bag, but he knew he was going to need something much stronger.

17

o o o

Jeff was wiping his chest clean with scratchy toilet tissue after bad sex with a GRINDR hookup. It was quarter after three in the morning when he noticed the text reminding him to be at the studio at eleven a.m. that day. That meant he had to drive home *drunk* to Riverside and then wake up and drive to San Diego to cover Sky, who was in Martha's Vineyard all week for his sister's wedding.

Jeff had been without full-time work for almost a year, so he was happy to get the gig. He'd told anyone who would listen that he'd lost his job as restaurant manager at Gameworks because of 'The Economy,' but the truth was that he'd been fired for repeatedly showing up to work drunk. Fortunately, the recruiting and occasional clerical work he did for Anderson didn't require that he *not* get plastered. So to celebrate, he had a couple coffee mugs of Scotch, right before he raced his mom's Saturn SL down the Interstate-5.

They were shooting AndroFiles' first three-way scene. The energy in the studio was especially manic that morning because everyone was so nervous and excited about the shoot. The models were far more raucous than usual, laughing loud, bouncing off the walls. Apparently, all the anxiety they suffer when just two of them are waiting to perform gets diffused by the addition of a third. Anderson's boyfriend, who never worked the shoots, was manning a brand new fourth camera. The whole house was in a twitter. It was a big deal.

Jeff surprised himself with how quickly he'd managed to get all the contracts signed and all the IDs photocopied. He was feeling so good about getting everything done while maintaining his buzz that he emptied a bottle of Smart Water into the kitchen sink and filled it with Anderson's Belvedere vodka.

The shoot was scheduled to start at one p.m. but it was already half passed noon when Anderson poked his head into the office to confirm that Jeff had run the rapid tests and that everyone was ready to work.

"...Rapid tests?"

Anderson glared at Jeff with an expression that fused pity with contempt. "The HIV rapid tests. We test all the models working hardcore scenes. You were supposed to do them before the releases were signed. Come on Jeff, you know the drill. I brought you in this weekend because I need you on your game. Run the tests!" Anderson stormed out into the living room and sent the models back into the office as Jeff rummaged through cabinets for the rapid test packets.

Brock, Damon and Carter had all mellowed out since the rowdy car ride from the hotel. Damon was all jittery with jokes, but they were falling flat as the other two had apparently started thinking about the shoot. Carter, whose real name was Andrew, was especially nervous as this was not only his first three-way scene but also his first bareback scene. He'd only been in the industry a couple months, but he'd already worked for three production companies. Intent on making as much money as possible before getting back to work on his Criminology Degree in the spring, he was having to spread himself out to stay busy. His nerves seemed to be less about the danger of bareback sex and more about the stigma it carried in the industry. He didn't want to compromise future employment opportunities by getting into so-called fetish work. Anderson assured him with a fatherly grin and a pat on the back that barebacking didn't carry the stigma it had a couple years before. "It's not even considered fetish anymore. Not like fisting or getting pissed on. Everybody's doing it."

Flustered, Jeff handed the first swab to Damon and noticed for the first time that he was wearing his ball cap extra low and to the left to cover what appeared to be a recently acquired black eye. He inattentively ran the swab along both sets of gums and handed it back to Jeff. Damon had obviously done more than his fair share of HIV tests. Jeff clumsily inserted the swab into the receptacle and sat it on the desk in front of him. He handed the next swab to Brock, who showed Carter how to do it, big brother-like... After all the tests had been administered, the models wandered back out into the living room.

Jeff sat at the desk, staring at the three tests, racking his brain to remember which swab belonged to which model. (They all went by their porn names while they were in the house. He knew *Carter's* real name was Andrew Benton, but was Travis Hartman *Brock's* or *Damon's* real name?) He was supposed to attach little numbered stickers that came with the tests to the corresponding model's contracts but he'd completely forgotten that part...and then before he could figure it out, the models were back in the living room. So he just attached the stickers at random. Then he walked out into the kitchen, where Anderson and his boyfriend were hissing at one another about someone's drug problem.

"The tests are all run. You're good to go." Anderson looked up at Jeff, annoyed, and strolled out of the kitchen.

"Let's get to work!"

When Sky came back into the office the following Monday to do paperwork for a new model named Walter, he found rapid tests still lined up on the desk and contract folders stacked haphazardly next to the desktop keyboard. He was about to clear the tests into the trash when he noticed that one of the OraQuick swabs had two reddish bands instead of one. The test read 'positive for HIV antibodies.' Sky stood staring at the vial with his mouth agape. His knee started trembling and he collapsed into the chair. He held it up to the light, trying to get a better look, trying to see it differently. He had never seen one with two bands before. The tests had always been seen as a technicality, a legal precaution. But now, someone actually had it! He looked at the corresponding stickers on the contracts. It was Carter, né Andrew Benton's test. *Shit!*

He jumped up and ran around to the other side of the desk with the editing bay. He found the file folder, 'BrockDamonCarter3way' on the computer desktop. The raw footage had been imported but none of it had been edited. He clicked on the files, his wild eyes scanning and scrutinizing all the sticky flesh flashing across the screen. *Brock and Carter sucking Damon. Brock fucking Carter. Damon fucking Carter. Damon sucking Brock and fucking Carter. Damon sucking Carter and being fucked by Brock. Damon and Brock coming on Carter's face.* Carter/Andrew never topped!

Sky ran back over to the other side of the desk and emptied the tests into the trash can and then carried the trash outside to empty into the garbage bin. He went back to Andrew's contract folder and underlined his name twice in red ink. That was the office code for 'serious drug problem or sketchy behavior,' which ensured that Andrew would not be called in for more work and no one would be held liable for using him. As long as he stuck with the standard speculation that the *inserters* could not be infected by the *insertees,* everything was fine. Problem solved. *That was too close...*

Walter poked his towhead in from the hallway with a flirty smile. He was probably the cutest AndroFiles model Sky had ever seen in person. "I'm all done filling these out."

Sky turned to him, breathless, unconsciously shaking his head 'no' ever so slightly and answered, in his sweetest voice, "Great. You're all set, then."

Walter's porn stint didn't last long. The day after his solo, he did a blow job scene with another new model. He had also been scheduled to do a hardcore scene with Brock, but on the day of the shoot, Anderson *informed him* that he would be doing the scene bareback, explaining that, "All the models are doing it now" and that, "Everybody's being tested beforehand." Walter's eyes widened, terrified. He loved sex, but he was adamant about using condoms. He'd never had unprotected sex--not even with any of his ex-boyfriends. When he refused to bottom without protection, Anderson pulled him into a corner of the hallway and tried to appeal to his business side.

"Okay, here's the deal. Our rate is higher than most other studios because we only do bareback. I've already paid Travis that rate for your scene. If you don't do it, I lose that money. I can kick in an extra couple hundred dollars for you if that's the issue. Is it just a question of money?" Anderson grinned conspiratorially, like he knew exactly what Walter was all about.

"No... It's a personal boundary. I just don't have sex without condoms...especially with someone I don't know." Walter was shaking as he was talking, shocked that he was speaking up for himself, defying the authority of this grown man.

"Well, I can't use you then, buddy. Sorry." Fury blazed in the pupils of Anderson's eyes as his lips tightened into slits....

"Okay." Walter slid past him to head back toward the office, but Anderson grabbed his arm and turned him around.

"Wait. Listen..." Walter looked up to see Anderson rubbing his face gruffly with his free hand, shaking his head. "We had a deal. You're kind of fucking me here, because now I've paid for your flight and your hotel with the understanding that you would be working all week. Travis is the only model I have on hand until Wednesday and I advanced him money so he could move out here... Anyway, point is, I'm losing money having you here, not working."

So why keep me here? Walter was so uncomfortable that all he wanted to do at that point was go home. Finally, he shook his head and whispered, as if Anderson's hands were clenching his throat, "I don't have sex without condoms."

"But...the members *expect* bareback!"

Walter didn't budge. He bit his lip and looked down at the plush beige carpet.

Anderson hissed and stormed off, leaving him alone, humiliated. Walter's first impression of Anderson--warm, generous, considerate--had crumbled under the weight of something far more real and sinister. In reality, Anderson couldn't give two shits about the models. They could all live or die as long as he was making his money.

Within minutes, Sky had called Walter into the office with his rescheduled flight back to Seattle, telling him that they needed to go back and get his things out of the hotel room before noon.

Two months later, two other popular models on the site tested positive. That time, Sky went straight to Anderson. It took Anderson all of fifteen-seconds to decide to let the models perform together as scheduled. They were both positive, so neither was in danger of being infected. Instead of telling the models about their seropositive statuses, Anderson instructed Sky to behave as if everything was fine and just let the models find out when and if they tested elsewhere. "They've both been working for other studios, so it was bound to happen eventually. We might as well get this scene. Call it their swan song..."

Sky quit AndroFiles the next day. From that point on, Anderson handled all the clerical work himself...

18

o o o

Andrew's calls to the studio weren't being returned. Anderson seemed to have been pleased with his performance in the three-way, so he couldn't, for the life of him, understand why he was being blown off. He had four more scenes scheduled for the month before classes started, but he couldn't get anyone on the phone. Contrary to Anderson's advice, other studios *did* frown on bareback film work, so he was counting on AndroFiles to fulfill their commitment. Without that money, he wouldn't be able to afford tuition and rent for the coming semester.

He slid his phone into his apron pocket and walked back into the restaurant. His ten minute break was almost over, but he slipped into the men's room, locked the door behind him and stared at his face in the mirror. His eyes betrayed his exhaustion, but his countenance still radiated kindness. He was a genuinely good guy...and it was written all over his face. He didn't understand why people kept fucking him over. *What is wrong with me? What are people seeing in me that makes them want to cast me out?*

Without thinking, he shut his eyes and said a prayer. *Please, God, just let me get through this.* Then he remembered, it had been over a year since he'd lost faith in the power of prayer...

He was sitting in his bedroom, stunned, practically paralyzed with fear, when he heard his father's truck pull into the driveway. He heard the back door creak open and shut...and then the chair slide along the kitchen floor as keys jangled against the table. He could hear his mother's quivering voice but couldn't make out what she was saying.

Of course, he knew exactly what she was saying. She was telling his father that she had walked in on Andrew with his best friend Clem that afternoon. She was no doubt sobbing and sniveling as she recounted how she'd dropped the laundry basket when she stepped in to find Andrew with his mouth full, sitting on his bed facing Clem, whose pants were around his ankles and whose hand was wrapped around the back of Andrew's neck. She was probably managing to somehow make the whole thing about *her,* asking what she had done for God to punish her so, going on about how hard the whole ordeal had been for her and how she'd never be able to forget the image that had been burned into her mind...

Then...the kitchen went silent.

Andrew said a prayer, turned around and watched his bedroom door, waiting breathlessly for whatever calamity was to come...but nothing came. He sat there staring at the door, his hair soaked with sweat, for forty-five minutes. No one ever came in. He finally stepped outside his room, the floor creaking beneath his bare feet and walked toward the top of the stair case to try to hear what was going on in the kitchen. Nothing. Silence...

So he went back into his room, lay in bed facing the wall, his tongue running back and forth against the back of his unbrushed teeth and eventually, he fell asleep.

He woke up the next morning, showered, ate breakfast and made his way to school alone. The house was as eerily silent as it had been the night before. Any other day, while he was getting dressed, he would have heard his father's work boots clomping down the stairs, the back door slamming shut and the truck backing out of the driveway. Normally, when he'd go downstairs five minutes later to eat, he would find his mother in the kitchen watching something on the 700 Club, drinking coffee and smoking a cigarette at the table. But that day, neither parent was seen or heard. Andrew ate quickly and left twenty minutes early so he could walk to school and get there before first period. He couldn't bear waiting around for his mother to offer him a ride through her gritted teeth of self-righteous disgust.

As he walked down the street, the morning sun shining in his bright blue eyes and the crisp Ohio air filling his lungs, he was warmed with a sense that everything was going to be all right. His mother was most likely too racked with Christian guilt and self-pity to go public with the information and his father obviously just didn't want to talk about it at all. Dad hadn't wanted to talk about much of anything for a long time...

For years, Andrew's father used to drag him out to baseball fields and into batting cages. Every summer would begin with everyone in the house hoping against hope that Andrew had grown out of his 'awkward phase' and that he would finally take to the sport that for some reason meant everything to his dad. But they'd all stopped hoping by the time Andrew began high school. He knew that his father had given up on him a long time ago... As it turned out, that very apathy might have been Andrew's saving grace. His father may have already been too bored with being disappointed to even bother addressing the whole blow job in the bedroom fiasco. Maybe it would all just blow over...

Andrew knew that he and Clem would just have to get through the next four months and then they would both be at University of Chicago. That's when their life together would finally begin... They'd be able to stay up late to watch their favorite Madeline Kahn movies together in bed. (Andrew was obsessed with "Clue" while Clem couldn't get enough of her Mel Brooks stuff.) They could play their R&B divas loud and proud--Jennifer Hudson, Mary J. Blige and Mariah Carey, just to start--without any sideways glares from their CMT-fixated kinsmen. And they would get to hold hands and kiss each other on the lips whenever they wanted, which would be all the time.

Andrew had been having recurring dreams of the two of them waking up in the same big bed with the sun shining in through the giant bay windows of their modest future apartment. Hardwood floors and homemade curtains, walking distance from the famous Halsted Street in Boys

Town. Just thinking about how simple and sweet it would be left him all choked up ...

Clem didn't show up at school that morning and his cell phone kept going straight to voicemail. By the time lunch rolled around, Andrew was sick to his stomach with worry. He skipped fifth and sixth period to walk to Clem's house and make sure everything was okay. He decided on the way to stop at home to drop off his book bag and brush his teeth.

When he turned the corner on to his street, he saw them right away. There were trash bags lined up along the sidewalk outside his front gate. As he got closer, he saw that the bags were filled with his clothes and all his things. His Spelling Bee trophy from fourth grade had been broken and the bottom half was poking out of a plastic bag. His personalized cover to his favorite book, *To Kill a Mockingbird,* was on the ground next to the bags but the book itself was nowhere to be found. There was a chain with a deadbolt lock around the entrance to the front gate. He dropped his book bag on the sidewalk and hopped over the fence. When he got to the front door, he found his key didn't fit in the lock. He walked around to the back door, his heart racing, terrified, and found the same thing. He banged on the door, hoping to see or hear his mother stirring inside. Nothing.

He banged and banged until the flat side of his fist was red and raw, then he slid down the door, scratching his face against the peeling paint, his body shuddering with panic. When he finally collapsed into a pile of quivering limbs on the back step, he began sobbing. He cried until his body went into convulsions because he couldn't get enough air into his lungs. Then he just whimpered and choked because his eyes had dried out.

When the sun went down, he was still laying on that back step. Nobody came home. Nobody opened the door. Nobody called. He dialed Clem again and got a recording that the phone he was using was no longer in service. It was really happening. His parents were completely cutting off their only child because he was in love with another boy.

He got up, wiped his face and walked unsteadily back toward the front gate. Mrs. Acton, the old lady next door, was watching him from her front porch, smoking a cigarette, shaking her head and sucking her teeth. *She knows...* He hopped over the fence and rifled through the trash bags for a jacket and as many clothes as he could fit into his book bag. Then he walked to Clem's house.

Clem's father answered the door, reeking of whiskey and cigarettes, and stood in the doorway with so much revulsion in his eyes that Andrew's legs began to shake uncontrollably... "Clem don't want nothin' to do with you. Don't be callin' and don't be tryin' to talk to him and you stay the fuck away from him." Then he slammed the door closed.

Andrew stood there, his eyes glazing over as locks and bolts fastened on the other side of the door. *This isn't happening. This is not happening.* When he finally walked away from the house, he saw Clem looking down from an upstairs window. His cherubic face was exhausted and a purple bruise above his left eye was barely visible behind the shadow of the lace curtain. Clem shook his head, 'No' just before he let the curtain fall in front of his face and he backed away from the window. Andrew understood. It was over. Nothing could be done.

When Andrew finally fell asleep on a bus station bench that night, he dreamt of the same future apartment with hardwood floors and homemade curtains...but instead of Clem at the kitchen table, it was his mother, chain smoking, sucking her teeth, glaring back at him with her purple, bruised eye. Sadly, her contempt felt absolutely normal to him.

How long had he known that his parents didn't like him very much? How long since he'd grown accustomed to them holding him at arm's length? How long had they been walking around him rather than looking at him and addressing him directly? How long had they been merely tolerating his existence in their house?

They seemed to have recognized something untoward in him before even he had managed to comprehend what is was that made him different. By the time he had been able to qualify his attraction to other boys as something they wouldn't approve of, their hearts had already hardened. He couldn't even remember a time when they had been openly affectionate. They didn't even seem to like *each other* very much... It was that lack of tenderness, that emotional indifference that had made him so eager to start his new life with Clem. As *normal* as his loveless home-life had become, he never stopped believing that there was more in store for him. He knew that the God he loved and honored wouldn't let him down.

Then his entire world shattered. A nightmare come to life...

The next morning, he paid forty-five of his last four-hundred and twenty dollars for a bus ticket to Chicago. As he watched Ohio's flat green landscape drift past from his window seat, he said one last prayer for his parents. He asked God to forgive them and watch over them, because he knew he would never see them again. Then he closed his eyes and imagined Clem walking into their future apartment... His curly blond hair glowing like a halo and his angelic face smiling, strong and safe. Love would prevail. Because it had to...

His manager knocked on the bathroom door. "Break's over, toots. Table eight wants their check." Andrew wiped at his tired eyes, only to realize he hadn't been crying. He hadn't cried once since he'd moved to Chicago. There was no time for feeling sorry for himself. He didn't even cry when he heard from a friend in Ohio of Clem's failed suicide attempt. He had too much to get done to waste time and energy on feelings. All he could to do was take care of himself.

He bustled out of the men's room, his eyes glued to the scuffed, checkered linoleum floor. He tried desperately to summon up a smile as he dropped the check on table eight, but when it didn't come, he kept it moving...

19

o o o

On the afternoon Rogelio found out his youngest daughter had fallen ill with H1N1 back in Oaxaca, the restaurant was completely slammed. The LA Weekly had featured Bernetta's in a tiny write-up about the resurgence of soul food and ever since then, Kelly had been busting her ass to keep up with all the business. Mike had started coming in on week-days to help take lunch orders and run the counter while Kelly helped in the tiny kitchen. The three of them managed to hold it down and she was even making enough money to keep the restaurant dark on Sundays. But on that Thursday, after Rogelio got the call and broke down crying, he walked right out the front door, never to be seen or heard from again. It was the week before Christmas.

'By the grace of God,' Kelly made it through that incredibly stress-ful afternoon. All the orders, save for two pulled pork sandwiches, made it out of the kitchen in time for the lunch rush, but she knew she wouldn't be able to handle the following day's lunch by herself. So that night, she called Rafael and asked him to come in and help her in the kitchen until she could find another permanent cook. Rafael, who just happened to have Fridays off from waiting tables at Joey's Cafe, leapt at the opportunity to learn how to cook with Kelly.

As it turned out, the lunch crowd that Friday was much smaller than expected... It was as if people had heard how busy they'd been and how dangerously close she had been to falling apart on Thursday and they decided to give her a break. Maybe fifteen orders came in all day, which gave Kelly enough time to really school Rafael on plating the dishes. He was already good on the grill, but he had officially never been much of a line-cook. Most of her dishes had been pre-prepared to some degree; sauces already in containers, meat already marinated, seasonings already concocted. So he didn't learn enough to go home that night and prepare a soul food dinner for Jamie, but he got to spend some quality time with Kelly, which had been long overdue.

Since their reconciliation, he and Jamie had been spending more time at home again. They'd embarked upon a second nesting phase, eating in every night and having sex at least once a day to really solidify their bond and reacquaint themselves as lovers. Jamie had even bought a self-help book called "Staying In Love" that he left on top of the toilet tank for casual perusing, just to help them both grasp some of the language of a functioning couple.

With all that going on at home, Rafael did manage to hang out with Mike a couple times a week but didn't get to see much of Kelly at all. The two of them had so much fun on Friday that Rafael got his shift covered the following day to help Kelly out again.

She was chopping up bacon and showing Rafael how to season the collard greens when Mike, totally panicked, poked his head into the kitchen window and stage-whispered, "Travis!"

Kelly dropped the chopping knife onto the cutting board. Then she snatched it up, her clenched fingers gripping the handle, ready to attack. Then she put it down again, calm, resolved to play it cool. She exhaled, wiped her face with her apron and stepped through the kitchen door.

Rafael glanced up through the window into the front to find a stocky white guy with a buzz cut and tattoos up and down his muscly arms standing at the counter, watching Kelly with a solemn expression. Mike ducked into the kitchen and snatched Rafael out of the window. They stumbled together into the cramped corner behind the door and Rafael whispered, "Travis is white?"

"Of course. His name is *Travis*. Nobody dates within their own race anymore if they can help it." Mike's eyes sparkled with some excitement about how close to his friend he was standing, but Rafael was facing away and didn't notice. They waited there in silence, huddled like gossipy school girls, for what seemed like a long time.

"What do you think they're talking about?" Rafael whispered, too loud.

"He's begging her to take him back, which he does every two months or so..." Mike muttered after a couple sniffs, "What's burning?"

Rafael remembered the macaroni and cheese in the broiler. He leapt out of the corner, grabbed an oven mitt and slid the platter out. He scraped the charred bread crumbs off the top and looked over at Mike. "Table three's apps are up." They laughed at the ridiculousness of what was happening in the kitchen while three chubby men in sweaters and khakis sat in the dining room waiting for their appetizers.

Kelly rushed back into the kitchen, slamming the door against Mike in the corner. Her face was shell-shocked... Her hands were shaking. She collapsed against the refrigerator door. Mike ran over to grab her as she slid down the door to the floor. Rafael stood frozen at the plating station, afraid to move.

She looked up at nothing in particular, tears streaming down her face. "He's HIV positive."

Kelly was too upset to wait to schedule an appointment with her general practitioner. She had to know right away. Mike suggested they walk down the street to Out of the Closet and all take the test together. Rafael called ahead and found out that the AIDS Healthcare Foundation's free anonymous HIV rapid testing site was 'mobile on the weekends.' They would have to go down to Boys' Town and find 'the AHF mobile home' parked near the gay bars and take the test there.

They closed the restaurant for the night and Mike drove them down Santa Monica Boulevard to find the testing trailer. It was parked right in front of the Bank of America ATMs on Santa Monica. It was only six p.m. or so, but the sidewalks were already crowded with boys underdressed for the chilly weather. While they drove around looking for parking, Kelly collected herself enough to explain to Rafael what Travis had done that was so terrible it caused Mike to burst into tears when he told her. "He had been doing bareback internet porn, having unprotected sex with men, for the whole last year of our relationship."

Rafael's throat went dry...

She went on to explain that it wasn't just about the sex...*with men*. It was his utter disregard for her. Had Travis been conflicted about his sexuality and keeping that side of his life a secret from everybody, she might have had some sympathy for how he'd been struggling. "Maybe..." But he was basically fucking men in public for money. Not only did he not have enough sense to wear a condom while having sex with men who got fucked for a living, he didn't have the common decency to warn her, for her own safety. "He was stupid enough to believe that he was going to have a porn career on the internet without anyone in our lives ever finding out."

When they'd broken up, thirteen months before, Travis had assured her that he and all the other models were routinely tested before they were allowed to work. "He was absolutely sure he was negative." She believed him...so she never got tested. After everything she'd gone through with the breakup, going down and getting an HIV test was more than she could bear. She didn't want to have to share all of her humiliation with her doctor when she asked for the test. She didn't want to know that her blind trust in love had ultimately lead to her demise. He was most likely infected sometime after they broke up, but with the six month window period, it was impossible to know for sure. Mike shook his head, disgusted, his eyes welling with tears as he drove.

In an attempt to console her, Rafael leaned up from the back seat and confessed that he had never had an HIV test. Ever. And that he and Jamie had been having sex without condoms since the weekend they met. Everybody in the car fell silent.

Mike finally found a parking spot on Melrose. As they walked in silence up San Vicente, past the splashing fountains in front of the Pacific Design Center, Rafael couldn't help notice that Mike was pissed. Fuming. His fists were clenched, his face was pinched--he was ready to fight! Rafael was completely sober so he couldn't quite tell where Mike's anger was directed, but he felt sorry for everyone involved. Even Travis.

Nobody would ever know how his lifetime of circumstances and mistakes had lead Travis to that point. Rafael's heart went heavy with the realization that people everywhere were suffering through personal traumas that were completely beyond anyone else's comprehension. Many of us turn that suffering into bad life choices without even knowing it. Travis probably never set out to hurt Kelly. He just made some bad choices based on the particular damage he had sustained. *And now...*

There was no one in line for the trailer, so Kelly walked right inside while Rafael and Mike filled out paper work on clipboards at the little table set up on the sidewalk. Overly coifed boys in short-sleeves scampered by on the sidewalk, clutching themselves for warmth, carefully averting their eyes to avoid the trailer altogether.

Rafael watched as Mike quickly checked off answers to questions that had never even occurred to him. "'How many alcoholic drinks do I consume in a week?' 'How many people have I had sex with in the last twelve months?' How the hell should I know?" Rafael was shaking his head when Mike looked up at him with so much anger in his eyes that he got chills.

"What the hell is wrong with you?" Mike's lip quivered. Rafael was so caught off-guard, he couldn't even respond. "You've been fucking some guy for five months without condoms and you've never had an HIV test? Do you realize how fucking stupid that is? Are you really *that* dumb?"

"What are you talking about? Jamie's fine."

"How do you know that? Did you ask him? How do you know you're not one of a hundred guys he's fucking without condoms? You're so fucking naive, Rafa. You..." Mike bit his lip and shook his head, at a loss.

Rafael's head began to boil. His anger at the way Mike was talking to him was immediately confounded with a sudden fear for his life and more of those nagging feelings of inadequacy. "He wouldn't do that. Jamie loves me." As he heard the words crackle in his mouth, it was impossible to deny how foolish he sounded. He had offered himself over completely, no questions asked, in the heat of a drunken moment. If they had talked about HIV that first night, Rafael couldn't remember. But five months later, there hadn't been any other discussion of safe sex. At all.

His assumption that Jamie was healthy was based completely on his appearance. He was beautiful and confident with a new car and a nice place so obviously, he was fine. Suddenly, none of that made any sense. His heart was racing and he couldn't catch his breath. The silence that had fallen around them on the sidewalk quickly became unbearable. "I'm fine..." Rafael could hear the doubt quivering in his voice and decided not to talk.

Mike switched tactics. "Rafael. Listen. I'm not trying to scare you, but you have to take care of yourself. Nobody else is going to do it. Not even someone who you think loves you. Love won't protect you! If he didn't ask you and you didn't ask him, the assumption might as well have been that you were both HIV positive. But..." He reached across the table for Rafael's trembling hand, "I'm sure you'll be fine." Then, with his eyes glued to the sidewalk, Mike opened his mouth to speak again. "I haven't told anyone... I'm positive. I'm HIV positive." He exhaled with unexpected relief.

Rafael thought he heard the earth open up behind him. His friend, his twenty-three year old friend who looked completely healthy, had it. Rafael's eyes were aimed at Mike, but he wasn't seeing anything. He couldn't feel the chair beneath him. He couldn't feel the December air chilling his face. His senses were completely shut down. Wiped clean. Empty. Nothing made sense. The truth was not the truth.

He flashed back to the night at Shadowbox with that kid Danny, when Mike got too drunk and spilled that profound sadness... When Rafael offered to text him Danny's phone number the next day, Mike wasn't interested. He loved to romanticize past relationships, but was totally guarded and defensive about meeting anyone new...as if something had rendered him unloveable...

Tap.

Tap, tap.

Tapping. Someone was tapping on Rafael's shoulder.

He turned around to find a short Latino guy with diamond studs in his ears, probably about forty, grinning at him. His Day-Glo hip-hop getup seemed especially clownish on a man his age. His face was vaguely familiar, but Rafael couldn't place him.

"You're Jamie's friend, right? SugarTank's little sidekick? I'm Luis. The DJ? I spin at Shadowbox on Sundays. 'Memba me?" His thick Brooklyn accent was further muddled by the gum he was chomping for dear life. Rafael nodded his head, remembering the DJ from that first night with Jamie at the bar. He was even creepier up-close...and in the harsh light of sobriety. Luis looked up at the 'freeHIVtest.net' sign on the side of the trailer and then glanced down at Mike's hand still rested on top of Rafael's. "Yeah, so anyways, you still see Jamie?"

Rafael slid his hand out from underneath Mike's and immediately regretted doing so. He had nothing to prove to this guy. "Of course. I see Jamie every day..." By that point, Luis had already turned to size up Mike.

"Oh, okay, cool. Well, tell him Luis says wassup. You take care, papi." Luis pivoted and pimp-switched over to his cadre of homo-thugs, posed like the original cast of Fame in front of Greenwich Pizza. Rafael turned back to Mike, whose mouth was agape.

"You're dating the SugarTank dude? Your Jamie is *that* Jamie...? You're kidding, right?" Rafael shrugged and tossed his hair out of his face and Mike sat back in his chair with a stupefied grin. "You casually neglected to mention that your boyfriend is gay-mous? And hot!?! You're such a dick weed."

Rafael picked up his clip board to finish filling out his form. "I was kind of hoping we were all too cool to be star-fuckers." He could feel himself squirming around the idea that Jamie's fame had any bearing on his own relationships, when he wished he could have just been proud of his lover's celebrity.

Mike choked on a chuckle. "You're the one fucking him, dude. I'm just surprised you wouldn't tell your best friends something so..." *Tell your best friends something so important...* Mike's voice trailed off as the weight of the pre-star-fucking conversation settled back over their rickety table.

The trailer door creaked open behind them and Kelly stepped out with her jaw tight and her eyes fixed on her shoes. Mike inhaled, bracing himself to break the news again.

Rafael stood up to give them space to talk. "Guess it's my turn." He carried his uncompleted form up the shaky steps and closed the trailer door behind him...

Twenty minutes. Twelve hundred-seconds. Two possible test results. One million ways to torture yourself about getting the wrong result...

Kelly was a complete wreck. When her test came back negative, she just stood on the sidewalk with tears streaming down her face. Mike gently insisted that she pull it together, if only for the sake of his own image in the *gay-borhood*. "Please don't have these people calling me 'that guy with the girl weeping outside the mobile HIV clinic.' I'll never get laid again." She smiled and wiped her eyes, comforted by the fact that he was able to at least fake a sense of humor. But she was still beside herself...

AIDS tests in trailers parked in front of gay bars on Saturday night in West Hollywood. None of it should have had anything to do with her life. She was a straight girl in what she thought was a monogamous long-term relationship. She only learned that HIV infection rates among heterosexual black women had been skyrocketing when she found out her *white* boyfriend had been doing bareback gay porn. She could never bring herself to get tested on her own. She wasn't brave enough to know for sure.

Then she was sitting with her best friend, who had been positive for almost a year but never told her, and her new friend, who had been having unsafe sex and had never even thought about getting tested. And they were all sharing this moment because the man she believed at one time to be the love of her life had broken her heart and with no apparent remorse, continued engaging in behavior which eventually got him infected. If God was punishing Travis for being self-absorbed, why was He punishing Mike? Mike was one the kindest, most generous souls she knew...

The trailer door swung open and Richard smiled and nodded for Rafael to enter. Rafael stood up slowly and floated up the stairs with no discernible emotion. He was in a completely different headspace than Kelly. The evening would provide no simple answers for him. Richard had explained to him before that even if his test came back negative, there was technically a six month window period, which left him another month of uncertainty. Regardless of the results, he had to go home and initiate the most uncomfortable conversation he could imagine. Not only would he have to reconcile the fact that Jamie had put him in this position of uncertainty, he was also going to have to cop to his own role in the risk they had shared. And if the results were positive, he couldn't officially be sure that he hadn't caught it from Eve, who had been cheating on him. Which meant that if Jamie also ended up positive, Rafael might have been to blame. His head was flooded with worst case scenarios, but his face betrayed no emotion at all.

The trailer door clicked shut behind him and he sat down across from Richard, who was holding of a slip of paper on the table between them. Richard was maybe fifty or so and his face was calm and kind. He had sunken cheeks and a swollen neck and his skin was shiny and pink. Without even recalling how or why he knew, Rafael recognized Richard's appearance as that of someone on HIV drugs. A lot of gay men in the 90s had that look, but most of them were gone by the time Rafael was old enough to understand what AIDS was about. The facial wasting from the harsh medications seemed to have disappeared just in time for everyone in Rafael's generation to play oblivious to any pretense of 'safe sex.' But Richard's face brought all of that reality back into vivid focus. Richard leaned in as if he was going to share a secret. "So, your test came back..."

Rafael's mind flashed back to all the moments in his life where he had been presented with a clear opportunity to do the right thing. He could distinctly see himself at eleven years old, looking around the bookstore, making the choice to steal that *Nightwing* comic book. He could see himself at sixteen standing over his passed-out drunk father, choosing to steal the keys and drive the car down to Anaheim for the Nine Inch Nails concert. He could see himself at nineteen at that lame house party deciding to try cocaine with his friend Bart. He could see himself drunk in bed underneath the guy he'd just met in a bar, making the decision to slide Jamie's dick inside him. He could see all those scenarios just as clearly as he could see his bike helmet in the corner on the shelf of his Sepulveda apartment closet... All those chances to be good when he had opted to throw caution to the wind instead. His life was a collection of bad choices. Who would he be, where would fate have taken him if he had chosen to do the right thing instead?

"...negative."

Rafael shook his head and repeated in his mind the word he'd just heard. *Negative?* It came as more of a relief than he'd expected it to. Somehow, until he sat down and Richard had started speaking, the very real possibility that the test might have come back positive hadn't quite sunken in. Richard was reiterating all the points about being safe, trying to drill into his head that he could continue to have 'an enjoyable, monogamous sex life as a gay man'--he just needed to use condoms. *Yeah, sure.*

A few minutes later, Rafael stepped out of the trailer with a big smile. The unmistakable relief on Kelly and Mike's faces warmed his heart. But when Mike suggested they all get a drink, "To celebrate," reality came crashing back. Mike still had it. Life was delicate and difficult to maneuver. One wrong turn and anyone could get lost...

As they stood in line at the bar at Here Lounge, Mike with his arm draped around Kelly's shoulder, Rafael texted Jamie and asked him if he'd like to come out to WeHo to meet him and his friends.

Seconds later, Jamie was stepping naked out of a Century City hotel suite bathroom with the stupefied grin of someone already regretting a bad decision, typing on his iPhone: "Sure baby. I'd love to."

PART FIVE

20

o o o

His first year at UC Berkeley, Jamie lived on the all boys floor of Priestly Hall. When he was filling out his dorm application, he imagined the residence hall would be crawling with lusty young men, eager to explore and experiment...something reminiscent of the dormitory in his favorite French film, *Wild Reeds*. That, however, was not the case.

The guys on the fourth floor turned out to be shockingly inept at all things homoerotic. Every Friday after class, Jamie would strip down to his underwear or a pair of gym shorts and cut his own hair under the florescent lights of the communal bathroom. The thought of catching an *as-yet-undeclared* stripling half-naked in the mirror might have incited something lascivious in Jamie's own testosterone-addled imagination, but as far as he could tell, it proved completely unremarkable to the forty or so sexually retarded teenage males with whom he shared the floor.

With his clippers in one hand and a handheld mirror in the other, he would finish his fade and step directly into the shower a few feet away without getting hair clippings on any of his school clothes. (Doing laundry in college was EXPENSIVE!) During those two semesters in the dorms, thirty or so haircuts had transpired in that bathroom without a single incident.

By the end of his uneventful first year, Jamie knew he needed to continue cultivating the momentum of his bourgeoning sexuality--and *not* at his parents' new home in Leimert Park. He opted for a summer library job, re-shelving books in the stacks and moved into the most affordable campus-adjacent housing he could find.

El Castillo was a far cry from the pristine fourth floor of Priestly Hall. The student 'co-operative' was a giant old house that had clearly fallen into disrepair some time in the 70s and by the time Jamie got there in the late 90s, was barely holding together at all. Filthy doors hung off their hinges, rotting wooden planks boarded broken windows indefinitely, old 'anarchist' graffiti showed clearly through pitiful coats of cheap, ugly paint; the place was a disaster.

Most people who lived in the house--who ranged from hippies and ravers to metal-heads and punk-rockers--would have seemed unlikely candidates to assist in Jamie's proposed period of sexual exploration. However, the cross section of outcasts did provide a comfortable environment for his preliminary attempts at adult self-expression.

His housemates, while generally hospitable, unfortunately held less stake in hygiene than Jamie would have liked. Most of them were more interested in cultivating the compost pile out back, pruning the 'crops' in their closets, drinking themselves sick and finding new ways to work tofu into *every fucking dinner recipe* than they were invested in scraping the scum off the bathroom floor. In the dorms, which had a hired-cleaning staff, Jamie and other hygienically concerned students often wore flip-flops into the shower. At Castillo, where 'work-shifts' were divided among the residents, making them responsible for maintaining the house themselves, Jamie wore closed-toed water socks.

The bathroom at the end of his floor was much smaller than the one in the dorms. It was also set up so it was impractical for him to stand at the sink in his underwear for forty minutes without being interrupted by a constant barrage of hippies who needed to stink up one of the stalls or steam up the dingy mirror. After scouting all the other bathrooms and viable spaces for haircutting, he resigned to calling his time at Castillo his 'experimental hair phase.' Rather than take the bus five miles down Telegraph Avenue to pay twelve dollars for a fade every Friday (he hadn't paid for a haircut since prom), he decided to just grow out his hair.

His initial contract only bound him to the house through summer break, but he vowed that until he could afford to move into his own apartment--where he'd only be responsible for cleaning up after *himself,* he would relinquish the close-cropped fade he'd sported since ninth grade. Maybe shacking up with hippies and party-people had inspired him to be a little less clean-cut than his normally pristine aesthetic dictated. The rumored house-wide staph infections and the scabies scare of '93 didn't encourage him to spend any extra time in the moist Petri dish called the second floor bathroom either.

By the end of that first summer, he'd made enough friends and earned enough resident points to have a room all to himself, so he extended his contract through the coming school year.

Classes resumed during one of the hottest Augusts in history. People were wearing tank tops and tiny shorts to class, looking more like beach bums than future UCB alumni. One student had even attracted national attention by strolling the campus completely naked. Two months into fall semester, temperatures hovered in the mid-nineties, which was unheard of for the Bay Area that time of year.

By October, Jamie was rocking a short natural. It looked good on him. His tight chestnut curls softened his recently angular face and gave him a funky edge he hadn't known he could pull off. Soon, though, he became convinced that all the hair was making the heat wave that much more unbearable and the hair gel-infused sweat running down his face all day was causing his forehead to break out. With the theme of the house's Halloween costume party being 'Sexual Fantasy Island,' Jamie felt he had no choice but to give in and resurrect his clippers and handheld mirror. Even in a house of outcasts, frizzy-haired and pimply was nobody's sexual fantasy.

He devised a plan: the night before the party, he would sneak into the bathroom on the basement floor (where most of the senior residents lived) because it was well-lit and clean enough that he could see his reflection in the mirror. He would strip down to a pair of gym shorts, cut his hair quickly and run back upstairs to shower in the blue bathroom before any of the territorial upperclassmen could fuss about him being in the way. Easy enough.

As luck would have it, when he went downstairs to handle his business, the basement was deserted. He yanked off his T-shirt and got to work.

His hair was freshly shampooed and watching the soft, fluffy curls fall past his shoulders onto the floor almost made him wish he had honored his original plan to grow it out...but there was no time for regret. He needed to get out of the basement.

He had finished his fade and was lining up the back with the handheld when he heard clumsy feet clomping down the staircase... Sandy staggered into the bathroom, appearing a little drunk or stoned--or maybe both. He was a former resident, a student who was taking time off from classes but not his campus-based social life. Even though he reportedly had a girlfriend with an apartment in the city, he frequently 'crashed with friends' in the house. He seemed to spend more time with Castillo's stoners than any girlfriend would be likely to put up with, but Jamie didn't spend much time with stoners so he didn't care either way...

Jamie had been facing the door when he came in and was almost sure he'd glimpsed Sandy's eyes rested on the frontal imprint of his gym shorts. By the time his bloodshot gaze worked up the naked torso to find Jamie looking back at him, a goofy smile splashed across his face. Rather than betray any embarrassment about being caught scoping Jamie's goods, Sandy's smile communicated an affable charm and an easy obliviousness. Had he even been scoping anything?

"Hey man. Look at you, all self-sufficient and proficient with the power tools...and such." Sandy smiled as he spoke, but his eyes never seemed to rest anywhere too comfortably...

Jamie nodded 'what's up,' clicked off his clippers and watched Sandy shuffle into a stall and continue talking over his shoulder with the door open. "You're James, right? I've seen you around... You hang out with Rosa and...you're in twenty-seven--my old room!"

Jamie wasn't sure whether he should try talking over the noise of Sandy's stream or wait it out. After a few seconds, when it became clear the stream wasn't about to let up, he cleared his throat to speak. "Yeah, I'm Jamie. And you're... Alessandro. You're the one who painted the walls green..."

"Sage. Green is for Celtics and jolly...giants. Please, call me Sandy. Only my father calls me Alessandro and he's a fucking...asshole." The stream paused for a beat to punctuate the word 'asshole' and then started up again.

"Sage, right." Jamie exhaled a soft chuckle about the force and duration of Sandy's piss. It was impossible not to imagine what the instrument capable of such an impressive demonstration must look like... Then it occurred to him (a surprise, given his general disdain for stoners) that Sandy was actually kind of sexy. His olive-toned complexion against his big light brown eyes; his tall, lean build slouched by the clumsy shuffle of his step; his ironic, buttoned-up sense of style set off at the top by his wild mane of shaggy dark hair... Then the toilet flushed.

Sandy shambled out of the stall tucking his shirttails into his unbuttoned pants. Jamie absentmindedly glanced down to catch a glimpse of the substantial presence being adjusted in the front of Sandy's white cotton boxer shorts with each jab of hand against fabric. He had started to button his pants, but paused when he noticed Jamie's drifting eyes... Caught, Jamie clicked on his clippers and held up the mirror, affecting preoccupied disinterest--totally unconvincing.

"You're really good with those." Sandy stepped up next to him and looked carefully at the reflection of his haircut in the wall mirror. "This is a much better look for you. I like you clean-cut." Jamie attempted a 'thank you' that got stuck in his throat when Sandy stepped even closer to inspect the work from a few inches away.

Jamie clicked the clippers back off and inhaled to collect himself. "Thanks. Had lots of practice. Been cutting it for years." He glanced down at Sandy's pants, still unbuttoned at the top. Then, as if possessed, he whispered, "You smell good."

They stood there looking at one another until Sandy flashed a smile that read distinctly different from the charming, oblivious grin from before. "Molton Brown, Warm."

Jamie shook his head, not understanding what those words meant in that order. In the silence that followed, he noticed he wasn't breathing and couldn't remember how long it had been since his last breath...

Sandy slid up to the sink, his left shoulder pressed against the left side of Jamie's naked back, and turned on the water to wash his hands. "Molton Brown is a British skin-care line. I'm wearing their scent for men called Warm. They have one called Cool that I bet would smell really good on you."

Jamie inched away from the sink, flustered. He had misread harmless conversation as flirtation before and ended up hungry and humiliated. He'd even lost a couple male friends from the ensuing confusion. Fortunately, Sandy wasn't a friend.

He met his gaze in the wall mirror and Sandy smiled again... Jamie smiled back with a shy nod. A surge of sexual energy radiated between them. *Silence...*

Then, Kurt strolled in. Kurt was a cute fifth year senior who was rumored to sell weed from his pimped-out basement single. Right before Jamie whipped around to say hello, he noticed Sandy's gaze in the mirror drop to his hands in the sink...

"Nice Caesar, dude. That whole Shaft mini-afro *was* gettin' kinda played." Then Kurt, with his cornfed, midwestern hip-hop swagger, burst into a stall to pee.

With a quick glance back at Jamie on his way out, Sandy disappeared without a word... *Gone.*

Kurt finished peeing and strolled up to the sink. "Yo, word of advice: since you're gonna end up scrubbing this sink clean and sweeping up all that hair anyway, you should just sign up for basement bathroom cleaning duty. Knock out work-shift hours and stay fly for the ladies all at the same time."

"Good thinking," Jamie grunted. Kurt--who knew very well that Jamie wasn't doing anything for the ladies--strolled out humming "Mo Money, Mo Problems." Jamie rested his lower back against the cool sink to finish lining the nape of his neck, not even realizing until a few minutes later that he had just been reprimanded for using the senior bathroom.

Freshly showered and shorn, Jamie returned to his room at almost one-thirty in the morning to find the red 'new message' light flashing. He clicked on the floor lamp, collapsed onto the full-sized mattress on the floor in the corner of the tiny *sage* room and reached back for his answering machine. Just before his finger hit the button, there was a quiet knock at the door. His heart leapt into his neck, throbbing like Kevin Aviance's house anthem, "Din Da Da." No one had ever knocked on his door at that hour.

Jamie bolted up out of the bed and checked his reflection in the five dollar full-length door mirror leaned against the wall. After almost six months, the haircut had cleaned him up nicely. Three more quiet knocks at the door. He snatched off his oversized *John Muir High Show Choir 1992* T-shirt and draped his towel around the back of his neck, opting for a 'more relaxed' look for his late-night visitor. He opened the door.

Sandy was leaned back, peering toward the staircase at the end of the hall. He quickly turned to Jamie, his pensive expression shifting reflexively back to that oblivious smile and he muttered, "Hey, I didn't wake you, did I? Mind if I come in?"

Before Jamie had finished saying, "Of course not, I was just putting on a shirt," Sandy had slid in past him. Jamie hung the towel on the door knob and closed the door slowly, taking a moment to ingest the titillating scene unfolding before him.

"Like what you've done with the place..."

Jamie turned to find Sandy standing beside the lamp with his hands in his pockets, his expression slightly expectant. "Yeah. So..." and Sandy ran a hand through his shaggy hair as he studied the thirty-six inches of floorboard spanning between his and Jamie's feet, "...did you get my message?"

Jamie glanced down at the flashing red light in the corner and then back up at Sandy, whose right leg had started to wobble just enough to betray some nervousness. "I didn't get a chance to listen to it. Should I...listen to it...now?" Jamie drifted toward the bed and sat down, slowly stretching back toward the answering machine. Sandy's awkwardness was infectious. The apparent tension between them had charged the room with an uneasy thickness that slowed their movements and left their limbs trudging through some dark molasses of longing.

Sandy twisted around, looking like a vampire with the lamp light casting jagged shadows under his eyes, and sank like a feather into a seated position on the bed beside Jamie. Like magic, he opened his hand to reveal an Altoids tin with a rolled joint and a lighter inside. "Do you mind if I...?"

Jamie sat upright, ignoring whatever was on the answering machine. Sandy had already lit the joint and was blowing on the burning end by the time Jamie had offered his permission. With a smile that seemed more polite than friendly, he handed the joint to Jamie--who had fortunately puffed enough times in the dorms to avoid making a production of it. After a couple modest coughs, Jamie handed the joint back to Sandy, who puffed it like an expert and then coughed himself. He puffed again. After Jamie declined a second toke, Sandy puffed a couple more times, licked his finger and thumb to stub out the lighted end and placed the joint back in the tin.

He stuffed the tin back into his pocket and then they sat and looked at one another with shy eyes. Sandy glanced down at Jamie's lips and he spoke in a hushed murmur.

"Actually, I just called to ask you if...if you might be able to help me out with my costume. For the party tomorrow...?" Sandy's eyes lit up, his whole face suddenly alert with a new confidence and purpose. Jamie felt himself smiling, even though he'd been trying to maintain a neutral expression until Sandy had made a clear statement of his intentions. (As far as Jamie could tell, he still hadn't.) Sandy's face softened into a smile as he spoke again, louder and more clearly than before. "It's kind of a weird request..."

Jamie glanced at the flashing red light and then back at Sandy. "Sure, what did you have in mind?" Considering the party's theme, Jamie envisioned himself yanking at chords with his foot braced against Sandy's fishnet sheathed legs, straining to lace up the back of a pleather bodice in some ill-advised Rocky Horror incarnation.

Sandy shot back, "Well, first, what's *your* costume? I'm just wondering how literally people are taking the whole 'sexual fantasy' theme, because maybe I'm over-thinking it. I tend to approach things more intellectually than the average person and then end up looking stupid in a room full of morons." Sandy shifted his seated position toward Jamie and leaned forward, suddenly chatty.

"Um... I'm gonna be..." Jamie felt his face flush as his mind raced to determine how literal his costume idea was and whether he had approached the theme intellectually enough to not be deemed a moron. "I'm uh... Well, I'm wearing a brand new white crew neck T-shirt and a new pair of white briefs. I'm going as... I'm going to be 'the perfect top *and* bottom.'" He searched Sandy's face for any indication of how well his concept had fared. Sandy's face gave nothing away until suddenly, he burst into laughter.

"That's brilliant! That's even better than my idea. I'm impressed."

Then Sandy, with his eyes locked on Jamie, leaned back onto his elbows, splaying his lean build across the lower half of the bed. He nodded his approval as he shamelessly scrutinized Jamie's naked back. "It's in the same vein as mine, but yours is a play on words where mine is more literal. Well-played."

Jamie's heart raced, giddy at the response--given that a general knowledge of the terms 'top' and 'bottom' would suggest that Sandy might be amenable to the idea of receiving or giving something of himself...

"So I was going as... I'm almost embarrassed to say now that I've heard yours." Sandy flung his hair out his eyes, smiling eagerly, milking the hushed moment for the last drop of suspense. "I'm just wearing a pair of red Speedos and flip flops and maybe a robe. I'm going to be...'swimmers' build!'" His eyebrows raised in anticipation of Jamie's endorsement. *Silence*. Jamie grinned, trying desperately to cover up that he had no clue what 'swimmer's build' had to do with sexual fantasies.

"You have no idea what that means. That's probably a good thing. I'm slightly ashamed that I do." Sandy shook his head, not certain he should keep talking. Jamie's engrossed expression encouraged him to continue. "Okay. See, it's a term men use in...um... personal ads to describe themselves, you know, 'white, twenty-five, swimmers build,' which basically means they don't go to the gym and that they're tall and skinny like me. The joke is that it's a 'sexual fantasy' for skinny men to describe themselves as having a swimmer's build, because in actuality, swimmers are in amazing shape. Really lean, but really cut." At that, Sandy sat up and started unbuttoning his shirt.

Jamie, whose head was now *swimming* with all the new information he was attempting to process, politely averted his eyes while Sandy undressed, telling himself that he still had no idea where the night was headed. The impending fornication was ostensibly still all in his head. When Sandy's nimble fingers reached the bottom button, he shrugged the shirt off his shoulders and turned his naked chest to Jamie.

"See? I have this patch of hair on my chest." Sandy ran his hand over the diamond of fuzz nestled in between his caramel-colored nipples. Jamie gazed at the slender torso and nodded, as if it was all finally starting to make sense. It wasn't. "Swimmers typically shave their bodies, because hair slows them down in the water. The hair on my legs is even worse." Sandy stood up and started to unbutton his pants.

As the garment-shedding continued, Jamie drew his knees close to his chest in an attempt to conceal the way Sandy's striptease was moving things in his gym shorts. The humiliating memory of having to strip down in front of other boys in his junior high locker room twisted something in the pit of Jamie's stomach. He exhaled sharply, resolving to just allow the future to happen. When Sandy shook off his pants, standing in the dimly lit room in just his boxers and his tan socks, Jamie could feel his face contorting into the same prepubescent love-struck expression he'd been teased for years before. Or...had he really gotten stoned off that one hit and become paranoid? Maybe his expression was more paranoid than love-struck? Maybe if he could slow his brain down and stop worrying about what his face was doing, he could figure out if he was stoned. Or maybe...

"I know, I know. I have legs like a...satyr. The half man, half goat?" Sandy pretended not to notice the dizzying effect his near-nakedness was having, but clearly enjoyed watching Jamie squirm in the wake of his brawny display. "Believe it or not, I have pretty nice legs under all this fur. When I lived in the city, I rode my bike everywhere! The *real* city, New York...not San Francisco."

Then it clicked for Jamie. Sandy wanted to be all smooth bodied for the party. *Swimmers build.* "So you...wanna use my clippers to shave the hair on your legs?"

Sandy grinned with the glint of a scheme beaming in his eyes. "Yes, well, here's the thing. I'm no good with electronic gadgets. Motorized contraptions make me nervous and my hands get all jittery. I would shave them with my straight razor, but the hair on my legs is so thick. I mean, look at it! I'm afraid I would end up slicing up my legs, which would not be sexy. So... I was hoping, since you're so good with them, maybe you wouldn't mind trimming them for me?"

Jamie glanced down at Sandy's fuzzy thighs and let his eyes wander up, over the bump in his boxers and on to the thick trail of hair leading up to his belly button. Jamie felt a knot form in his throat and a drop of perspiration run from his armpit down the side of his torso as his thickness stiffened into a weapon. Albeit visibly ample, Sandy's *bump* was clearly flaccid, making it clear that they were not having the same physical response to the proposed proceedings. Were the sexual innuendoes and lust-charged glances really all Jamie's imaginings? The physical proximity required to shave a man's legs would qualify as the most sexual intimacy he'd enjoyed since moving into the house.

Staring at the floor around Sandy's socks, Jamie tried to focus on not being stoned. If he could just stop his teeth chattering... He glanced up to find Sandy holding the clippers out toward him; the end of the coiled chord swinging back and forth like a hypnotist's watch. He hadn't even remembered agreeing to do it. Was this about to happen? His throbbing heartbeat seemed to indicate that it was. He reached up for the clippers, careful not to reveal the incriminating protrusion in his lap.

Sandy turned to adjust the lamp, directing an oblong pool of light onto the floor next to the bed. Jamie attempted to shift his stiffness out of sight while Sandy had his back turned, but quickly determined that without a shirt to conceal the waistline of his shorts, there was really nowhere to hide it. He reached for the discarded show choir T-shirt on the other side of the bed. Then he reconsidered and sat back up; putting the shirt on might read as some disapproval of Sandy's near-nudity. *But then...what if...or maybe...*

Realizing he was probably more stoned than he wanted to be, he left the shirt on the bed, shamelessly adjusted himself to the right, put on his version of a poker-face and stood up to get to work on Sandy's legs.

"Okay, you should sit on this side, so I can plug these in." Sandy bounced over to that side of the bed, suddenly energized with a goofy, childlike enthusiasm. Jamie hardly noticed. He had a job to do which required focus. He plugged in the clippers, snapped on the number one guard and readjusted the lamp to illuminate the appropriate side of the bed. Facing him, he lifted Sandy's right leg from the back of the ankle, peeled off the sock--an unexpectedly intimate gesture--and rested the foot on top of his left thigh. Sandy wriggled his toes and brushed off the lint with frantic fingers.

When Jamie clicked on the clippers, he could feel Sandy shiver at the hum of the motor drawing closer to his leg. He looked up at Sandy and found his face tensed and staring at the clippers. "It's got the guard on, it won't cut you. Watch." Jamie ran the clippers from the ankle up the side of Sandy's calf. A roll of soft, dark hair gathered like a bale of cotton at the blade and then cascaded onto the floor. Sandy looked closely at the strip of leg and his eyes tightened, skeptical.

"Can you get it any closer than that? I still see hair there."

"Well, I can take the guard off." Jamie added with an apologetic shrug, "Just wasn't sure how close you want me. To be. Going. On you." He bit his lower lip to stop muttering. Sandy chuckled, shook his head playfully and ran his hand through his shaggy hair.

Jamie, pushing through his mortification, snapped off the guard, clicked on the clippers and poured all his concentration into swiping the hair off of Sandy's leg. With a few meticulous strokes and a few twists of the ankle to reach the back of the calf, most of the hair on the lower half of the first leg was gone. Sandy's muscles did look more defined without the hair.

Just then, some commotion approached from down the hallway. Jamie glanced at the clock. People were coming home from the bars up on Shattuck Avenue. Male laughter erupted just outside his door. Sandy, panicked, yanked his foot off Jamie's thigh and scrambled on the floor towards his pants near the desk.

Jamie, suddenly agitated himself, shook his head and whispered, "The door's locked." They listened breathlessly as the bustle continued down the hall and then they sat in embarrassed silence, a pall of shame settling around them.

Sandy, eyes to the floor, forced a chuckle as he plopped back onto the bed. "Sorry about that. Not even sure what that was all about. Kind of a weird thing to do, I guess..." He exhaled and extended his half-shorn leg toward Jamie, unable to meet his gaze, still mumbling about his odd behavior. They'd both forgotten they were stoned.

Jamie lifted the right ankle and replaced it on his thigh. *Click*. The hum of the clippers helped drown out Sandy's murmuring, but didn't exactly put Jamie at ease. The grinding of the machine's tiny engine was suddenly ominous. Might some harm come of this coupling? He could have taken Sandy's obvious guilt about their new friendship as confirmation of his unsavory intentions. But the fear in Sandy's eyes for that brief moment only put Jamie on edge--and made him keenly aware of the situation's fragility.

After cleaning up the few stray hairs around the ankle and the knee, Jamie continued up onto the right thigh... He glanced up and noticed that Sandy's flat nipples had hardened into tiny knobs. Jamie's mind involuntarily flashed to the thought of his teeth grazing against those nipples and the tip of his tongue darting out to swirl around the stiffening areolae. He suddenly wanted nothing more than to be done with his task so he could find out once and for all how his night was to end.

Sandy scooted forward on the bed toward Jamie, so that the hair falling off his thigh would land on the floor rather than the ecru bedspread, and his boxers rode up a couple inches on his leg. Jamie noted that the creamy skin beneath the shorts was a slightly lighter shade and right away, his erection was back, throbbing in plain sight. Sandy titled his head back, as if averting his eyes. As the humming blades slid higher up on the thigh, Jamie noticed the muscle under Sandy's shorts was also throbbing and expanding. *Shit!*

Jamie concentrated on pacing his breath, hoping that slowing his heart rate would stop him from shaking. He cut with shorter strokes to conceal his hand's unsteadiness and curb any urge to luxuriate in the area. Unable to reach the back of the thigh because Sandy was seated, he continued over to the top of the left thigh without missing a beat, again rushing through the work to avoid the obvious trap of enjoying any of it too much. All the while, he pretended not to notice Sandy's meatiness pressing at full mast against the strained fabric--that soft cotton, the only remaining semblance of their fleeting chastity.

Jamie swapped the right leg for the left and quickly ran the clippers over the lower half of the latter, behind the knee and along the calf. When he finished buzzing the shin, he peeled Sandy's other sock off and swiftly trimmed the hair off the ankle. He was almost done... He gingerly dusted the stray hair off and placed Sandy's foot back on the floor, slyly eyeing the swelling erection.

Sandy looked down and examined his legs in the lamplight. He nodded, "I'm impressed. You definitely know what you're doing." He wouldn't look Jamie in the eye...

"Did you want me to get the back of your thighs? 'Cause I'm gonna need you to stand up." Jamie sat back on his heels, giving Sandy space to decide. Sandy leaned forward, casually placing his hands over his lap--almost concealing the evening's main attraction, but not quite. He looked at his legs again, extending each out in front of him as if deliberating whether ignoring the back of the thigh would compromise the integrity of the costume. Then, without a word, he stood and turned his back to Jamie.

When he looked up and found himself face to face with the thick patch of hair on Sandy's lower back, Jamie felt a pang of...disrespect. The fact that neither of them were talking about the obvious sexual nature of what was happening while he was essentially 'servicing' Sandy's ego and mediocre costume idea was suddenly humiliating. Was he going to finish tending to his body hair just so Sandy could put his pants back on and leave? Jamie clicked on the clippers and just held them for a moment, thinking...

He was all too familiar with this moment. Two possible paths were laid out before him and out of fear and/or some twisted respect for the hang-ups of others, he was prepared to take the path that would make things easier on everyone else; the path in direct conflict with him getting what he wanted. Learning how to stop cutting himself off from new experiences was one of the reasons he had moved into that house, so why keep choosing the path with no payoff? This was his moment of truth. It was up to him to steer the night in the right direction. Without touching the back of Sandy's leg, he clicked off the clippers.

"Maybe you should take off your shorts." Jamie spoke the words clearly and plainly, but once they were in the air, all he wanted to do was inhale deeply enough to suck them back in. The eternity of silence that followed was the very reason he never asked for what he wanted... He felt pathetic and desperate and lecherous...until Sandy carefully slid his boxers down to his knees, mindful of not pressing his fuzzy behind into Jamie's face. Jamie helped pull them down to his ankles and off his feet, tossed them onto the bed and inhaled the faint musk of Sandy's nudity. He'd never seen an ass that hairy...

He clicked on the clippers and ran them right up the back of the thigh, along the incline of his bubble butt and up to the patch of hair on his lower back. As he continued trimming, he lifted the cheek with his finger to run the clippers smoothly under the crease of skin separating the buttock from the leg. When Sandy didn't respond, Jamie didn't hesitate to finger any flesh that was required to finish the job. He crouched over, running the clippers along the top of the inner thigh near the crack and Sandy spread his legs, widening his stance, to give him all the space he needed. From the back, Jamie could see that he had swept up all the front junk into his hands to give him a smooth plane on which to operate. "Thanks."

As clinical as the process had become, Jamie's lust was still at full attention as Sandy was still a *butt-ass naked man* standing in his room at two-something in the morning. When he had trimmed as much of the backside as he could cover without peeling apart Sandy's ass cheeks, Jamie clicked off the clippers, sat back with his knees raised and his arms behind him on the floor and basked in the full glory of his handiwork. *Beautiful.* "All done."

Sandy twisted his upper body around to inspect Jamie's work in the door mirror. He stepped backwards, moving closer, still holding the majority of his manhood in his right hand, even though his lax grip made him appear far more interested in examining his own beautiful behind than concealing anything in front. He just stood there, completely naked, looking over his shoulder at himself. The deafening silence highlighted a new sense of intrigue and foreboded a dramatic shift in the evening's tone. When he reached back to run both his hands over his newly smoothed ass-cheeks, he unleashed the erstwhile contents of his right hand into the ether.

At that revelation, Jamie stood up--not even bothering to hide the wet spot at the end of his eagerness, and tapped 'play' on the cassette player on the shelf above his desk. Rosa's mix-tape was still in the deck from when he had been studying that afternoon. Suzanne Vega warbled, "You'd make a really good girl, as girls go..." as Jamie leaned against the desk and watched Sandy slowly lose interest in the novelty of his own reflection. The syrupy thump of the acoustic music shifted the mood immediately...

With cupped hands firmly planted against smooth buttocks and a warm smile settling on his face, Sandy turned around to face Jamie, free as a semi-erect bird. "This looks great. Thank you." Jamie could see the swelling in his lower periphery, but he focused his gaze on Sandy's eyes as he nodded acknowledgment of the gratitude. They quietly stared at each other for what again seemed like too long. Then, Sandy's gaze dropped down to his throbbing thunderbird and he asked, "Would you mind getting the front too?"

Jamie looked down and for the first time, took in the full splendor of Sandy's arousal. The thing itself was larger and fleshier than any Jamie had seen in person; dangerously thick at full mast and curved slightly to the left. The hair around it was dense and dark and cut a swath across his groin like a forest burnt black. The thick trail of fuzz running north on his lower torso disappeared completely when it reached his navel and then reappeared as an island on his chest. Jamie shook his head calmly; no he would not mind at all.

He bent down to pick up his clippers. When he looked back up, Sandy's countenance had softened into a cocky smirk. He shifted his stance wide enough to leave about forty inches of floor between his feet and rested the palms of his hands flat on the top of his head. Jamie lowered down onto his knee with his eyes still fixed on Sandy's.

Jamie's mind was suddenly very clear in its purpose. If Sandy wanted to make it a game, a challenge to see whose willpower was stronger, he was happy to play along. He didn't even mind losing if the forfeit would grant him access to the playing field. Jamie broke from Sandy's gaze to focus on his task and clicked on the clippers.

He slowly ran the blades along the outer edges of Sandy's inner thigh, shaping the unruly dark patch into a clean 'V' without touching the baby's arm at all. Sandy watched Jamie work, matching his tremendous focus. With such palpable concentration between them, the baby's arm abated a bit and Jamie slid in to trim away the happy trail and the northerly edge of the bush. He didn't bother addressing the surface area of the organ itself as that would have obviously been concealed by the Speedo.

When he was satisfied with the tidiness of the circumference of the suit's expected coverage, Jamie stood up and casually ran the clippers over the patch of hair on Sandy's chest, polishing off the area with two or three swipes. He reached back and grabbed the T-shirt from off the bed to dust off any remaining stray hair and glanced up to find Sandy's eyes beaming into him. Sandy's legs were still spread wide, making the two of them seem closer in height than they really were. With their faces so close together and their eyes locked, they fell into one another's mouths...kissing hungrily. The T-shirt rolled down the side of Sandy's leg and landed on the floor.

Sandy placed the palm of his hand against Jamie's quivering cheek and pressed his restored rigidity into Jamie's throbbing groin and at long last, the clarity of mutual desire suffused their bodies with a warm resonance that felt like love--even though it would have been foolish to deem it such so early in their relationship. Their kisses became slow, lush, lyrical. Sandy's hands gently caressed Jamie's face and neck while Jamie's hands kneaded the soft muscle of Sandy's newly smoothed ass and lower back.

Sandy slipped Jamie's shorts completely off without breaking away from the kiss. Once they were both naked, the heat between them escalated quickly; their kisses got more fervent and their groping got so aggressive that Jamie almost lost his balance. At that moment, Sandy in some balletic frenzy, twisted and lowered him quickly but gracefully onto the bed. By the time they were horizontal, they weren't holding anything back. That night, all the childish timidity, the affected propriety and the undeniable yearning between them found a release far beyond what Jamie imagined possible.

They made brief appearances at the Halloween party that Saturday. Both of their costume ideas turned out to be more cerebral than sexy and neither caused much of a stir on the dance floor--even when Jamie turned away from Rosa for a few seconds to gyrate against one of Sandy's smooth legs.

Wyatt's panty-less 'alter boy' was the surprise hit of the night and despite displaying little to no originality, Summer got quite a bit of attention as a 'naughty Catholic school girl.' For Jamie, it was Kurt's 'quarterback' in just a football jersey, a jockstrap (all bubble-butt) and striped athletic socks that was the costume to beat.

Even though he had spent the previous night and most of that morning naked in bed with Jamie, Sandy played coy around him for the entire forty-five minutes they bothered to spend downstairs. Of course, once the party got raucous enough that they were able to sneak back up to Jamie's room unnoticed, those costumes were never to be seen again.

The next two months were a beautiful blur. While Sandy was definitely the aggressor in the relationship, he was also very particular about keeping their romance a secret. Their flourishing friendship was the subject of a fair amount of public speculation, but Sandy went to great lengths--and insisted Jamie did as well--to never allow any of those suspicions to be confirmed as facts. They spent all seven weeks of their affair sneaking one at a time up to Jamie's room, stealing frenetic kisses in the hallway late at night, lying with straight faces to friends and housemates about how they were spending their evenings, going out of their way to keep their love a secret.

Jamie allowed himself to be dragged backwards, willingly conceding to some compulsory interpersonal regression in the name of love, when his whole reason for moving into that house was to advance his sense of self and establish his sexual identity. He even took on a passive role in their daily interactions. If Sandy wanted to eat dinner on the front porch while it was raining, they sat on the porch in the rain. If Sandy needed to sleep alone for whatever reason, he disappeared into the night with no explanation. Sandy also turned out to be limited sexually in ways that Jamie found troubling, but never challenged. And all of Jamie's sacrifice still proved insufficient in the end.

One afternoon, after sleeping apart for three consecutive nights, Sandy walked into Jamie's room and blurted out that he 'just wasn't feeling it anymore.' That was it. Whatever they had was effectively over and there was nothing else to say.

Jamie flew into a tailspin trying to make sense of it, blaming himself, assuming he had done something wrong that had caused Sandy to leave him. For several weeks, he came up with countless new theories on the mistakes he must have made which had rendered him suddenly undesirable. *I was too clingy. I was too pushy about wanting him to be more sexually flexible. I was too openly gay for him.* In the end, he could never make sense of it. It was just over.

After the brutally unceremonious breakup, after offering no explanation and no consolation, Sandy disappeared. He was rumored to have fled back to the East Coast and developed a serious cocaine habit. Wherever he went, after that Christmas break, he was never seen at El Castillo again...

Jamie, truly heartbroken for the first time in his life, eventually learned to accept and even, at times, embrace the twisted idea that his love could only be worthwhile to another man when it was effectively kept a secret. Showing his true feelings, letting his guard down, would only result in love's demise.

21

o o o

Sandy was alone at a dinner for the Board of Directors for Trevor Project Los Angeles, the nonprofit organization that works to help prevent gay teen suicides. When Jamie stepped onto the stage to introduce a speaker, Sandy all but spit up his Diet Coke.

Ever since he'd gotten sober again and seriously committed to his twelve step program, Sandy had been taking the notion of 'being of service to others' very seriously. After a childhood plagued with bullying and years of puerile lying and self-loathing, he decided to make *gay youth* the focus of his philanthropy. He would do whatever he could to help create a world where puritanically imposed shame and the so-called stigma of living honestly would no longer hinder young people from finding happiness.

So it felt all the more like divine providence when one of the most profound love affairs of his life, which happened to take place at the end of his teenage years, was rekindled that night, at that event raising awareness and money to save the lives of teenagers.

Sandy watched in awe as Jamie stepped off the stage and strutted coolly back to his table. He hadn't changed much since college. He was certainly more self-assured and debonair than the shy student Sandy had seduced twelve years before, but all the kindness and humility that had made him irresistible at nineteen seemed intact. There had been a beauty in his awkwardness back then, but he was a far more handsome man than the boy he had been in school--a fact only made more apparent by the calm composure he radiated. He seemed so comfortable with who he was that he put everyone around him at ease.

Seeing him in his tailored suit, with his beaming smile, made all the charmed innocence and juvenile trepidation of their tumultuous love affair come crashing back. Sandy couldn't have admitted it to himself back then, but the way he had seduced Jamie, only to turn around and dump him, had been incredibly cruel. He had told himself that he left to avoid being discovered by their housemates. The truth was that he was afraid of what he might discover about himself if he really opened his heart to a man. Rather than confess his fear, he fled, never looking back, never bothering to explain.

Sandy could feel his jaw clenching as he approached the table. He considered that one-hundred and eleven days before, a bump of cocaine or a shot of vodka would have calmed him down, or at least numbed his nerves long enough to get him through the moment. But those short-term solutions were no longer options in his life. He had to face each emotion, good or bad, just as it came to him. He tapped Jamie's shoulder and he looked up at him with a polite smile but no sign of recognition. When he extended his hand and said, "Hi... I'm Jamie," it was almost as if he was greeting a fan. Sandy nodded, *yes, I know who you are.*

"It's me, Sandy." He silently conceded that the years had probably not been as kind to his face as they had been to Jamie's. Plus, he'd cut his hair and put on all that muscle... Then Jamie saw him. He really *saw* him. Sandy watched the wheels turning behind his eyes as Jamie scrambled for the right response.

"My God, Sandy! How are you?" Jamie stood up poised, offered his hand again, and pulled Sandy into a firm, friendly hug. They exchanged more awkward smiles and nods and Jamie sat back down and introduced a few of the people at his table. Sandy was too beside himself to catch any of the details. He just nodded like a moron, trying not to reveal all the memories and regrets that were bashing against the inside of his skull.

When Jamie appeared to be finished talking, Sandy reached into his pocket for a business card. He sent thanks up to his Higher Power because just that week, he had stopped carrying 'AndroFiles' cards and printed up some with just his name and number.

Jamie took the card with a polite smile and then Sandy turned and walked breathlessly out of the banquet hall. His brain was so flustered, he couldn't remember where he was. By the time he got into the lobby, he was moving so quickly, everything was a blur. Somehow, the word 'Cracked' kept coming into focus. Trevor Project's gala event that weekend was to be called 'Cracked Christmas' and there were posters with Neil Patrick Harris' face plastered everywhere. He had paid five hundred dollars and driven two hours to attend the event and all Sandy could think, rushing toward the valet halfway through dinner, was that something inside him had finally *cracked.*

Standing at the curb on Wilshire Boulevard, staring at his Prada wing-tips, waiting in the cacophony of mid-city traffic for them to bring his car around, his mind raced to make excuses for all the things he'd fucked up, all the people he'd hurt in the past.

He'd always managed to blame others for his arrested emotional development. His Catholic father, staunchly homophobic and humiliated over having a *sensitive son*... The guilt-ridden priest who had fondled him as a child only to weep immediately afterwards... The skittish classmate he had seduced when he was fourteen, who later came back with his friends and beat Sandy to a bloody pulp in front of his own house... His brain was besieged with the faces and words of all the sad men in his life who'd made him believe he could never be honest with himself or anyone else about his inclinations.

After years of barely getting by while seducing and then freeloading off of unsuspecting women, he'd spent six miserable months in the Army, grasping feebly at what he imagined his last hope for stability and maturity. Following his inevitable dishonorable discharge, he got a job as a trainer at a gym where he finally met someone--a man who vowed to love and take care of him. Only then, when his sexuality had opened a door to financial security, did he manage to come out of the closet. He made himself believe he was in love.

He played the good husband for two years, transforming himself into the very image of gay affluence. He'd cut his shaggy hair when he enlisted and was encouraged by his lover to keep it short. He'd worked his slim build into the perfect gym body. He'd even stopped doing drugs and kept his drinking to a minimum because his sober lover convinced him that the drugs were only blurring out the world he was 'finally ready to embrace.' During those few months in 2008 when same-sex couples were legally allowed to marry, they had a fancy Malibu wedding at the beach, complete with gift bags for the guests and a former American Idol contestant singing, "I Was Made to Love Him." Sandy became the very thing he'd claimed to despise all those years: an archetypical, superficial gay man.

Then, like a cold sore, so-called compunction reared its ugly head...again. Rather than examine the likelihood that he had some deep-seeded issues around his homosexuality, he convinced himself that he was ashamed of the lifestyle he'd adopted. He'd been tricked by *that man* into becoming somebody he loathed. He was bored with being a househusband. He was tired of only socializing with other gay men. He wanted out, but he had nowhere to go. So he went back to cocaine...and whatever other drugs he could get his hands on.

His narcotic haze left him in constant pursuit of young 'straight' men, boys who were 'confused' in the same ways he had been. Without understanding why, he became obsessed with exploiting the curiosity and defiling the innocence of youth. It just so happened that his obsession coincided perfectly with the family business. He abandoned his role as First Lady to become the company's head talent scout. While his marriage became a farce, the business and his addictions flourished.

Sandy replaced the key in the valet's hand with a twenty dollar bill.

After everything he had done to block out the real world, after a lifetime of emotional denial, dodging attachments and disregarding the feelings of others, he had finally come to a crossroads. He knew that he needed to right wrongs and undo damage. Something had to change...and seeing Jamie that night made everything clear. He'd been desperate to recapture the magic of young love, seducing boys with drugs and money, because he'd forfeited every possibility of love in his own youth out of fear. But the moment he decided to clean up his act, love came back to find him.

Jamie called two weeks later. Sandy sat quietly for the first few seconds, reeling at the sound of Jamie's voice over the phone. His rich timbre took Sandy back twelve years to when they would call one another to set up secret rendezvouses back in their college co-op. The thrill of those stolen moments came flooding back and Sandy's heart fluttered up into his throat. Then he heard Jamie say, "Have you had lunch yet?"

Sandy was still living in San Diego and needed a couple hours to get to Los Angeles. He showered quickly, cursed himself for not working out that morning and raced the company X5 up to L.A.

Jamie picked the restaurant, a new spot called Kindle. When Sandy got there at quarter to three, the place was empty. Jamie was seated near the back, two-thirds into a glass of white wine. He explained that the kitchen was about to close and there was apparently only one server still on the clock. Sandy's eyes were so fixed on Jamie's lips that the building could have been going up in flames around them and nothing would have broken his focus. That is, until the server finally approached the table. His name was Danny. Sandy had recruited him in a San Diego night club a few months before, back when he was still using 'scouting for the site' as a ploy to pick up on young men. They had done cocaine together that night in the company X5 and Danny had come in to shoot two scenes the very next day... Sandy had purloined his number and ineffectively stalked him for weeks, just before getting sober again.

The boy's eyes practically popped out of their sockets when he glanced up from his waiter pad to find Sandy looking back at him. Jamie's face was in his menu and he missed the entire exchange. Eventually, Danny mustered the gumption to ask if he could get Sandy something to drink.

Sandy turned toward the table flustered and asked for a glass of whatever wine Jamie was having. Then he remembered... "No, make that an iced tea. Unsweetened if you have it." The waiter shuffled off.

Patting his sweaty forehead from behind his menu, Sandy told himself he was playing dumb out of respect for Danny's privacy--which was partially true. He really just wanted to make amends for the pain he had already caused *before* he invited new sources of personal shame into the conversation.

Only recently, since his sober attempts at humanitarianism, had he found himself in the company of people who were 'respectable' enough to send him scrambling to cover-up the details of his professional life. People who work in porn generally only socialize with other people who work in porn--or people who are at least cool with it. Being married to one of the biggest names in the online business had always carried bragging rights in the circles he was accustomed to running. Lately, though, he had been going to great lengths not to mention the nature of the family business...and for the purposes of this particular conversation, he hadn't planned to mention 'the family' at all.

They'd already launched into pleasantries when Jamie noticed Sandy glance back at the servers' station. Jamie smirked, "This place has only been open for a month or so and it's already renown for its delicious wait staff." Sandy shook his head and forced a chuckle.

While Jamie appeared genuinely fascinated by Sandy's transformation, casually scrutinizing his slightly weathered face, noting the ill-fit of his Hugo Boss button-down over his bulging shoulders, it wasn't long before their small talk felt forced. The tension was undeniable. Sandy decided to bite the bullet.

"Hey, I'm really glad you called. I wanted you to know that...that I know how fucked up I was in Berkeley. I was really a mess...with the drugs and everything, but my whole life back then was dictated by fear. I know we were kids, but the way I bailed and never bothered to, you know, make sure you were okay...was fucked up and I wanted to say that I'm really sorry." Before Jamie had a chance to respond, Danny had reappeared and was placing a sleek glass of iced tea on the table between them.

"Did you guys have a chance to decide what you were going to have? The kitchen is closing at three...and uh... Yeah." Jamie finally looked up at Danny and noticed how nervous he was. He smiled to himself, as if accustomed to gay boys losing their shit around him. They ordered their lunch and another glass of wine for Jamie, watched Danny hightail it back to the kitchen and then turned to one another with strained smiles.

Jamie leaned back in his chair with glassy eyes. "Thanks for that. It means a lot to hear that you're even aware. Of that stuff. It's good to see you, Sandy." With that, he stood up and tossed his napkin onto the table. "Excuse me. Restroom."

Sandy watched Jamie's perfect ass, cradled in crisp dark denim, quickly disappear around the brass and mahogany bar across the room. He drank down his iced tea, cautiously training his eyes off the sip of wine at the bottom of Jamie's glass. Jamie hadn't even officially accepted his apology before he practically sprinted away from the table.

"Hey." Sandy turned to find Danny standing beside him with a shy smile. He placed a glass of wine on the table and picked up the almost empty one.

"Hello." Panicked, Sandy glanced back toward the restroom and then looked up at Danny. "What can I do for you?"

"Yeah, I just wanted to say sorry I never called you back. It was nothing personal, really. I was kind of going through some stuff and you were...well, you were kind of aggressive. But I do think you're a nice guy, and like, if you ever wanted to grab coffee--"

Sandy squinted his eyes and shook his head before blurting out, "Shouldn't you be refilling ketchup bottles or something?" Danny stood there humiliated for a moment before he slid quietly away from the table.

Sandy dabbed at the back of his neck with his napkin. He knew he had lashed out at the boy just to feel in control of something at a moment when everything else felt hopeless and uncertain. Twelve years before, Jamie had allowed Sandy to call all the shots because Jamie was the one with feelings. Now Sandy was feeling something and Jamie had all the power. It was a shitty position to be in...

He hadn't even realized he was staring at the frosty condensation on the chilled glass of wine until Jamie sat back down. He flashed a sexy smile before he lifted the glass to his lips. Sandy inhaled, savoring the buttery pear aroma, just as Jamie's foot brushed against his leg...and stayed there. Their eyes locked...and Sandy leaned forward with a sultry snarl to grasp Jamie's hand. "You, know, you're more beautiful now than you were then. And even then, you were a real specimen."

Something fluttered behind Jamie's eyes and his lips tightened for an instant, just before he took another sip of wine. Sandy couldn't tell if he had offended him or if Jamie was simply bridling an impulse to leap across the table into his lap. He chalked it up to the latter.

Danny stepped up to the table with their plates. Sandy slid his arm back out of the way, but he did not let go of Jamie's hand. When he looked down at the Grilled Chicken Caesar Salad Danny placed in front of him, all he could see was the loogie that had probably been hawked into his romaine lettuce in the kitchen. Sandy pushed the plate away with his free hand and looked up at Jamie.

"You wanna just get out of here? Let this young man get on with his Friday afternoon?" Jamie nodded with a pensive smile. "Great. I'll take the check." Sandy pulled a Platinum card out of his Coach wallet and handed it to Danny, never taking his eyes off Jamie.

Danny took the card and returned seconds later with the bill and the credit card receipt. Sandy left a two hundred dollar tip on the sixty-two dollar check with a note that read, 'I'm an asshole. Sorry about that, S.'

Jamie finished off his glass of wine and together they stepped out into the crisp winter afternoon.

o o o

Jamie kept stealing glances at Sandy, searching for any of the mannerisms of that gangly teenager in the hard-bodied man walking a few steps ahead of him. The big, clumsy feet were unmistakably Sandy, but everything else about him seemed contrived, some facade he'd been wrapped up in for so long that there was nothing real left underneath.

Meandering down Sixth Street after the aborted lunch, they were clearly less interested in finding their cars than in prolonging their quiet time together.

When Sandy stopped in his tracks and looked back at him with those puppy dog eyes that had haunted him since Castillo, Jamie realized how easily he could fall back into the habit of letting Sandy lead the way. He had been completely acquiescent before and given everything to this man who had, in turn, abandoned and *ruined* him for every man that followed. Sandy's teenage callousness had broken something in him. Twelve years and too many lovers later, Jamie still hadn't completely gotten over it.

But he had come too far in his life to continue repeating those mistakes. He was ready to break the cycle of fear and resentment that had kept him isolated for so long. He owed it to himself...and he owed it to Rafael--sweet, unsullied Rafa, who had still only known the cool, detached version of Jamie that people were allowed to see...

Without a word, Jamie stepped past Sandy and crossed the street to get to his car. Like a puppy dog, Sandy followed him... He walked around and sat down in the passenger seat of Jamie's Audi A5...then he flicked his head to the side, as if to fling the hair he'd long since cut off out of his eyes. Jamie got antsy and twisted the key in the ignition. The stereo was on and Sy Smith's cover of Aaliyah's "If Your Girl Only Knew" thumped out of the Bose speakers. Sandy reached over to lower the volume. "Sweet car. So...what've you been doing with yourself?"

Jamie glared at him, defensive. *None of your fucking business! You forwent access to that information when you bailed...* "I do music." *Like you haven't already Googled me by now.* He considered adding, *I write songs about getting fucked over and left heartbroken by spineless men,* but decided he would play it cool for as long as he could. There didn't seem to be any point to mentioning that the only reason he'd agreed to meet was to finally get closure on their relationship and hopefully cure his writers block. It had been two years since his last album. He turned calmly, "What do you do?"

Sandy shook his head, wringing his hands anxiously, staring out the windshield. "I'm a... I am VP to an internet porn mogul. I administer in the peddling of smut and the sexual objectification of young men for a living."

Jamie snorted out a chuckle. "Seriously?"

Sandy looked over at him, sheepish. "Yeah, but that partnership is on its last leg. I'll be looking for a new line of work soon."

"Wow. How did you ever get into that?" Jamie could feel his face twist from shock to genuine concern...

"Long story..." Sandy squirmed, probably wrestling with some impulse to overplay his contrition. He changed the subject instead. "But that's old news. Let's talk about this. Us."

Old news.

Jamie's mind flashed to a few weeks before. He and Rafael had spent Sunday afternoon cuddled up together on the couch. During the opening credits for *This Week with George Stephanopoulis*, Rafael started fidgeting, bored and eager to change the channel. But as they continued to lay there, fingering the drawstrings on one another's sweatpants, vaguely focused on the television, Jamie witnessed his man-cub's petulant boredom soften into mild interest. By the time they got to the end of the show, when they listed the names and ages of soldiers who had died that week in Iraq, Jamie was watching tears run down the side of Rafael's face. "Nineteen years old? *Jesus!*" Rafael wiped at his nose and eventually disappeared to the bathroom to clean himself up.

Jamie recognized in that moment what he found so irresistible about his young lover: Rafael's delicate, inchoate ideas about sexuality and manhood and life in general were just waiting to be shaped. His sweet naiveté represented Jamie's second chance at determining hope and clarity in his own view of love. Maybe his future with Rafael would help him finally shake his unrelenting disenchantment with the trifling ways of gay men. Maybe Rafael was an angel sent to awaken him from his bitter sleep. He wanted so desperately to believe that their relationship was everything he needed...

Jamie was aware of his own tendency to seek out relationships with men who allowed him to keep his heart and his true self at bay. Rafael had started off fulfilling that archetype: seemingly unavailable, clearly confused and probably a little bent on self-destruction. However, during the few months they'd spent together, Jamie had watched all those qualities fade in him. He had transformed into a sweet, supportive, loving boyfriend. While Jamie had hoped to change, to grow along with him, he hadn't been able to. There was still something blocking his heart. That thing was sitting in the passenger seat of his car, batting its eyelashes and grinning at him like a prom date at midnight.

If there was any chance of Jamie moving on in his life, he had to take back what Sandy had stolen from him all those years ago. He had one night to make Sandy fall in love with him, to give himself over completely, so Jamie could then leave him with no explanation and go back to his own life, vindicated. He glanced over at Sandy with the faintest hint of vengefulness twinkling in his eyes. "Get your car and follow me."

The Crowne-Plaza Hotel was oddly quiet that afternoon, considering it was so close to the holidays. Sandy insisted on paying for the room. So Jamie, tipsy from the wine but too smart to be seen checking into a hotel room with some strange man, went straight to the hotel bar. He ordered two shots of Patron and had downed them both before Sandy texted him the room number.

He was resolved to turn his life around--not by turning the other cheek, but by turning back the clock and taking an eye for an eye. That had been the plan ever since seeing Sandy nervous and starstruck at the Trevor Project dinner. Yet, he still wasn't sure he was far gone enough to exact his revenge. He had a hard time seeing himself as spiteful. Even with the condom in his front pocket, he couldn't admit that any bad intentions were premeditated. He ordered a third shot and tossed it back with a shaky hand before he floated behind his sunglasses towards the elevators...

The door to suite 1007 was slightly ajar. Jamie stepped into the bedroom to find the lights dimmed and Sandy completely naked, face-down on the bed. It was like wandering into a longtime dream fulfilled... All Jamie could do was stand in the doorway, terrified. Would his plan even work if Sandy offered up the very thing he had come to steal away? It seemed too easy. How would he ever be vindicated if Sandy was still getting exactly what he wanted out of the exchange? Jamie shut the bedroom door and stepped closer to the bed. Sandy raised his muscular ass ever so slightly as he approached.

Jamie's mind flashed to Rafael pressing his naked ass into his groin while they were trying to fall asleep that first weekend. Their bodies had fused so effortlessly, so quickly, like the most natural thing ever. *What the hell am I doing here?*

Sandy swiveled his ass again, slow like caramel running along the curve of a candied apple...and Jamie's dick sprung to life. He burped and expensive tequila with the faint tang of Sauvignon Blanc singed the back of his throat. Suddenly, the plan was back on track. If Sandy wanted it, he would give it to him--*once,* and he would give it to him good. Then he would leave and never speak to him again. Done.

He fished the condom out of his pocket, stepped out of his boots and his jeans, tossed his jacket and sweater onto the chair and lifted his shirt off over his head. He spit into his hand and rubbed the crack of Sandy's hairless ass as his mind flashed back to the night he had trimmed all the hair off of that fuzzy behind... He crawled onto the foot of the bed and buried his face between the meaty mounds of flesh, slathering his tongue along the soft stubble around the crack, slobbering into his surging crevice. Sandy's whimpering was uncharacteristically girly and caught Jamie by surprise. He sat up, spit into his hand again, stroked his dick and slapped it against Sandy's wet asshole. He unwrapped the condom, put it on and then slowly, he slid inside.

Sandy groaned in pain at the entry, but then raised his ass and pushed back against Jamie's thrusting. Jamie grabbed the back of his thick neck and started pounding into him. His objective, to get Sandy to fall in love with him, had been lost in the moment. All he wanted to do was hurt him.

As his pumping got more ferocious, he could feel everything he thought he knew about Sandy crumbling underneath his body. There was no power struggle. There was no game to win or lose. Sandy was giving Jamie everything he physically could as penance for the past. But the *physical* wasn't enough. Jamie needed more. Breathless, he stopped pumping and flipped Sandy over onto his back. Sandy gazed up at him, his eyes wet with emotion...and he actually looked vulnerable. Humble. The expression gave Jamie pause. It was like seeing the *sweet nineteen year-old Sandy* that his mind had blocked out all those years to cope with all the hurt the other Sandy had caused.

Jamie leaned in and kissed his forehead sweetly, working his way down Sandy's wet cheeks to his soft pink lips. It was like a flashback happening in the flesh. All the ways Sandy had changed in those twelve years disappeared when their lips touched and all of a sudden, they were back in that tiny green room in that Berkeley co-op.

Jamie spit into his hand and slid himself back inside slowly, looking into Sandy's eyes, watching what looked like tears of relief stream down the sides of his face.

They made love for what felt like hours and afterwards, they lay in bed together, their sweaty limbs entwined, their bodily fluids commingling and crusting on one another's skin. Jamie played with Sandy's fingers rested on his chest, noting how their hands had aged, but still fit together perfectly. It occurred to him that in another life, on a different path of destiny, he could have been holding that hand for the last twelve years. Fate had failed him the first time around, but there he was, holding that hand...
Wait. No!

Jamie sprang up in a panic and began dressing to leave. Sandy pleaded for him to stay, completely unselfconscious, naked, desperate. Jamie insisted with smug resolve that he had to go. Sandy hugged him tight and told him he would wait in the hotel for him to come back that night... Then, with a hungry glimmer in his eyes, he looked up and whispered, "You'll come back...and I'll be here."

Jamie strolled out of the hotel lobby onto Century Boulevard with the swagger of the victorious, but his sneer played strained. He had accomplished exactly what he had come to do and yet, his heart was heavy.

He was telling himself, as Sandy's Gucci scent wafted around him in the night air, that the hold Sandy had on his heart was finally lifted. Now that he had seen how damaged Sandy really was, he was free. But something was still amiss...

He got into his car and glanced down, noticing one of Rafael's leather bracelets in the cup holder, and the reality of what he had just done hit him like a barrage of poison darts... As guilt washed over him, he began hastily concocting excuses for his transgression. *But I did it all to save our relationship. I did it so Rafael and I could finally move on together without the baggage of what Sandy did to me!*

He made every effort to justify his behavior to his conscience. While he was too smart for his own self-righteous bullshit, he did succeed in convincing himself for most of the ride home that having sex with Sandy wasn't as nearly as offensive an infraction as having sex with some stranger. He and Sandy had already had sex, long before Rafael had ever come into the picture. Therefore, sex with Sandy was inconsequential to his commitment to Rafael. That logic lasted him most of the way up La Cienega Boulevard, but by the time he passed the Beverly Center, he was racked with so much guilt, he felt physically ill.

Over the course of the next six or seven hours, Sandy left four voice messages and nine texts. Jamie didn't respond to any of them. He was too busy trying to avoid Rafael--ducking into the bedroom when he got home and then disappearing back into the kitchen when it was time for bed--thinking he'd just steer clear long enough for the guilt to wear off. Then he would get right to work on being the man he knew Rafael deserved, the boyfriend he'd always hoped to be...

The following morning, Saturday, Rafael woke up early to go help out some friends who were short a cook in their restaurant. Jamie had planned to spend the day working on music at home, but by noon, when he hadn't heard from Sandy--after all the messages the night before, he started to worry. The last message hadn't even sounded like Sandy; his speech was rushed, frantic. Something was wrong, but all Jamie could see was the new power he had over Sandy. Their roles had finally been reversed and Jamie was drunk on the idea of dominating his tormentor. When Sandy's attentions suddenly seemed to dissipate, Jamie worried that he was losing the advantage he had worked so hard to gain.

He drove down to the Crowne-Plaza, rushed up to room 1007 and knocked on the door. Sandy, in just boxer briefs, flung open the door and leapt into Jamie's arms, kissing him wildly and dragging him into the bedroom and onto the bed.

Jamie had wanted to hold back, torture him a little more by playing standoffish for the first few minutes, but Sandy didn't give him the chance. Within seconds, Sandy had peeled off all of Jamie's clothes and was slobbering all over his rock hard dick. The whole animalistic tone threw Jamie for a moment. He and Rafael had their fair share of passionate moments, but their sex was always bridled with a sense of sweetness and calm. They were constantly checking in with one another, making sure all the good feelings were still mutual. Jamie had hardly even seen Sandy's face. Sex without that connection was something Jamie had never found appealing. But somehow with Sandy, he managed to rise to the occasion...

They were kissing and scratching and slapping at each other with such raw passion that Jamie was sliding in and out of Sandy again before he even knew what was happening. He thought about asking about a condom, but things were already moving too fast. The lights in the bedroom were off, but the light from the suite's common area illuminated enough for Jamie to look up and see Sandy writhing on top of him like a feral cat in heat. He was in such obvious ecstasy that Jamie seriously considered flipping him onto his back and sitting on Sandy's fat cock. Close encounters with real *pig bottoms* often made Jamie rethink his preference for topping. *When does it ever really feel* that *good?* Then he realized that it was probably Sandy, who had fucked him for seven weeks and then deserted him, that had turned him against bottoming in the first place.

But if Sandy could learn to enjoy taking it like a man, why shouldn't Jamie? Together, the two of them could come to represent some new version of the modern man. Prototypes of fearless male sexuality in the age of lost love reborn. *Sandy and Jamie, together at last.* He reached down and began stroking Sandy's cock...which wobbled indifferently in his hand.

Suddenly, Sandy was sliding off of him and scrambling into the bathroom, mumbling about "just a second." Jamie assumed that he had thrust too deep and upset something and that he had gone to sit on the toilet for a second. He touched his sticky erection and sniffed his fingers for anything suspect. *Nothing...* Then he heard the flick of a lighter and the crackle of what sounded like...a bong? Within seconds, a very distinctive odor wafted out from under the bathroom door. Jamie had caught a whiff of it when he'd first come in, but he'd figured it had something to do with Sandy being locked in the suite all day. Like some odd combination of body odor, fresh paint and dirty socks. Now the smell was clearly chemical and something was definitely burning. It smelled like melting plastic...

Jamie sat up in bed. *Is he smoking something?* He walked over to the door and tried to hear what was happening inside. He heard Sandy exhale through a shuddering jaw. Jamie pushed open the door to find Sandy standing at the sink, his dick fully erect, holding a small glass pipe and staring at himself in the mirror. It was as if he hadn't even noticed the door swing open. Jamie cleared his throat. "What is that?"

"Little pick-me-up." Sandy turned to Jamie, his eyes wide but completely devoid of life, his face sweaty and pale. He snarled his lip into something that was probably supposed to look sexy, but read more as pained in the harsh bathroom lighting.

"Why are you--"

"Because it feels good." Sandy turned back to the mirror to let Jamie know the topic was no longer up for discussion.

Jamie's hands started shaking. It was happening again. Sandy was blowing him off--and this time, right in the middle of sex. Sandy was making it clear one last time that Jamie didn't mean shit to him. That no matter what Jamie sacrificed for him, no matter what Jamie put himself through, no matter how Jamie felt about him, Sandy's heart would always be somewhere else. Jamie was being left behind. Again. He had let himself *catch feelings* and Sandy was about to pick up and walk away unscathed. Again.

He stepped into the bathroom and took the pipe out of Sandy's hand. He placed it to his lips and grabbed Sandy's other hand which was holding the lighter and held it up to the bottom of the glass bowl. Sandy smiled like the Devil Himself and held the flame under the pipe. The crystal melted and sizzled against the glass. Jamie sucked in the sticky white vapor and his eyes blazed with his determination to not let Sandy win. *Not this time*. Even if it meant that they both had to lose.

22

o o o

Just a few seconds after Danny and Max slipped through the side patio door at Here Lounge, Mike twirled around and spilled his entire drink on to Max's boot... Mike was so drunk, his first response to the rolling high ball glass was to blame Max and insist he buy him another gin and tonic. Then he noticed Danny squinting at him, trying to place his face. But Mike didn't remember Danny from Shadowbox. "Hey! You're What's-His-Name... Tony with the long, uncut cock."

Tony? Danny froze, horrified. Max was completely unfazed.

"And you're What's-His-Name...Messy Queen with the drinking problem. Excuse us." Max grabbed Danny's hand and pulled him toward the bar, bumping right into Rafael and Kelly. Rafael was texting and didn't look up, but Kelly apologized for Mike.

"Sorry, you guys. Our friend might have been over-served. Please pay him no mind." She smiled, reaching for Mike's arm and turned around to Rafael. "Ra, maybe we should get him home. He's throwing drinks on people."

Rafael, also drunk, looked up and saw Danny staring back at him with terror in his eyes. Rafael slipped right into angel mode, smiling, calm. "Oh. Hey, man... Danny, right?" He reached out to shake Danny's hand. "Rafael...and you remember Mike." Rafael nodded toward Mike, who at that moment snatched Danny by the shoulder and spun him around to get another look at his face.

"Wait a minute, I actually know you. I KNOW YOU!" Mike was grinning with coy mischief, connecting the dots between the cute kid from the straight bar and the latest AndroFiles model. Kelly stepped between them, throwing her arm around Mike's waist to hold him back and diffuse what was quickly degenerating into an oddly aggressive encounter.

"Mike, you need to quit screaming and grabbing people. Someone's gon' bust your lip, boo!" Kelly turned back to Max and Danny, forcing a sweet smile. "You guys know Mike and Ra? I'm Kelly." She extended her free hand toward them.

Max turned to Danny, confused, and then his face tightened as his eyes bolted from face to face, trying to make sense of the circus unfolding around him. Rafael stood by quietly, watching as Danny's gaze sank into a blank stare and Mike's red eyes struggled to focus...

Then, like he'd just woken up, Danny grabbed Kelly's hand. "Hi Kelly. I'm Danny and this is Max." Danny turned to Max with all the composure he could muster. "Yeah, I met these guys at that Shadow bar, like, a couple weeks ago. Just before I met you."

Mike draped his arm over Kelly's shoulder, looking Max up and down, and then turned to Danny. "I thought you were somebody else before. My bad..."

Max shifted his weight backwards and smiled sheepishly, seeming to shake off his initial concern about what kind of company Danny had been keeping before him. "Well, nice to meet y'all." He turned to Rafael who was still leaning against the bar. "Would you mind grabbing a couple cocktails for us? I don't have my ID and the doorman didn't give us those little 'over twenty-one' bracelets." He pulled out his wallet and held out a twenty dollar bill for Rafael.

Rafael glanced over at Danny, looked down at the twenty and shook his head. Twenty bucks would barely cover a cocktail and a half at Here Lounge. Not to mention the tip. "It's on me. What're you guys having?"

Max arched an eyebrow, impressed, and quickly stuffed the bill back into his pocket. "Oh thanks. A bourbon soda and a mandarin cosmo on the rocks." Max smiled and turned to Kelly. "So what are y'all doing for the holidays?"

Mike opened his mouth to offer some snide commentary on people who use the word 'y'all,' but burped up some Jack and Coke instead. Kelly fanned at the stink of stomach acid and slipped her arm off of his waist to move closer and respond. "We'll be working for most of it. Bernetta's Soul Food on Hayworth, just off Santa Monica. Y'all should stop by." Mike glanced at Kelly, remembering with a smirk that she was also one of those people.

Rafael turned from the bar holding Max's drinks and stopped in his tracks, a smile spreading across his face. "That's Jamie!"

Mike whipped around. "Where?!"

"No, the song. It's a bad gay remix but that's him."

Max tilted his head back and squinted his eyes like he was trying to read the song's liner notes on the ceiling. "SugarTank, right? Do y'all know him?"

Mike slithered behind Kelly toward Rafael to bask in the glory he was set to bestow. "He's Rafa's boyfriend."

Max turned to Rafael. "Really? Hot! Is he cute? I like some of his music but I've never seen his face."

Rafael smiled and handed Max the cocktails. "He's beautiful. Prettiest man I've ever seen." As he spoke the words, Rafael felt a pang in his stomach that stung like some twist on shame. Jamie still hadn't shown up. It had been over two hours since he'd agreed to meet them at the bar but he hadn't responded to his last three texts. Something was wrong.

A sly twinkle lit up Max's eyes. "Really? The prettiest, huh? Well, I wanna see him. Is he here?" Max turned to Mike, still hovering behind Rafael's shoulder.

"Yeah, where *is* Jamie? I thought he was coming out!" Mike was yelling at Rafael but staring at Danny, who was sipping his drink and avoiding everyone's eyes.

Rafael shook his head no, letting his hair fall in front of his eyes. "I'm not sure where he is right now." He picked up his own cocktail off the bar and drank it down.

Kelly squinted at the booming speakers. "Is Jamie black? This guy sounds black." Then she turned to Rafael, who nodded back at her with a tight smile. "Well, go 'head then." Kelly's eyes softened as she stood there, looking at Rafael in a whole new light. "The song is cute, too. I can't wait to meet him.

Mike glanced over at Max and noticed that he had been watching him stare at Danny. Too drunk to play it off, he just started talking... "Danny. Uh... So did you ever find your friend?" Mike bit his lower lip when he realized that mentioning the old friend might have been bad form in front of the new friend.

"Nando? No, but Nando's friend Paul is Max's roommate. I guess Nando went home to Philly or something. Small world, right?" Danny noticed that Mike's eyes had locked on something behind Max...

"Yeah. Small world. Tiny." Mike nudged Rafael.

Just then, Jamie stepped up behind Danny and Max, with a brittle smile. Rafael exhaled, relieved, and slipped between the boys to hug and kiss him. Everyone turned around to see Jamie, freshly showered and immaculately put together. His eyes were bright and anxious and his jaw seemed tight with some distress, but he was just as pretty as Rafael had promised.

Max mumbled, " Oh my God, Redbone..." but no one responded.

Beaming with pride, Rafael turned to introduce Mike and Kelly. Jamie shook their hands perfunctorily, avoiding prolonged eye contact, but friendly enough under the circumstances. Mike studied him, suspicious.

When Rafael turned back to introduce Danny and Max, Jamie got notably jittery, his wide eyes twitching like he'd seen a ghost. That's when Rafael noticed something was off. Then, as if to highlight how ill at ease he was with the situation, Jamie barreled toward the bar to order himself a drink. When he shouted over his shoulder, "Anybody else want a drink? On me," no one responded. Rafael watched him carefully. His body language was completely tense. His shoulders were tight and hunched, his whole body braced against shuddering. Rafael glanced over at Mike who was staring back at him, confused. *What the fuck is going on...?*

Danny began slowly backing away from the group and Max, just shy of oblivious, turned to him and said, "Wait, you know him too, huh?" Everyone turned to Danny, who was shaking his head no, trying to disappear. At that moment, Jamie glanced back at them with a scowl so sinister, Rafael hardly recognized his face.

Then he felt it--like a jagged knife stabbing at his stomach. Jamie was bursting with secrets and steeped in more bad energy than he could contain. Jamie turned back to the bar just as a rush of a very different emotion pulled Rafael's attention behind him...

He looked back at Max and Danny. Danny shook his head again, trying to communicate without speaking. Rafael closed his eyes to intuit what Danny was trying to say... He could feel concern, trepidation...but no explanation. Then more stabbing at his insides. Jamie's bad energy was making him sick to his stomach. Rafael opened his eyes to find Danny looking back at him, distraught. Rafael couldn't take it anymore. "What is it? Just say it."

Danny breathed in deep as his teeth started chattering and his eyes went tight with trepidation. He spoke very quietly, as if keeping his voice down would soften the impact of what he had to say. "This guy, this model scout I met a few months back, came into my restaurant yesterday. With him." He nodded at Jamie's rigid back. "They looked to me like they were on a date, but...then Sandy, the model scout guy, was texting me at three o'clock this morning...asking me if I was into PNP."

Mike whispered from behind Kelly, "Party and play. Crystal meth and unsafe sex."

Danny continued, his voice quivering, "I didn't even know what that meant, but then he offered to pay me to come to his hotel room. I told him to go to fucking Hell." Danny glanced up to see everyone, including Jamie, watching him.

Rafael nodded, *Thank you,* and turned back around. When his eyes met Jamie's and he could feel the guilt and the cold wall of secrecy that Jamie was trying to hide behind. A tear ran down Jamie's cheek and in that instant, like a short circuit, Rafael felt nothing. His body went numb and his sensitivity to the emotional lives of the people around him completely vanished. All he could feel was his own emptiness. The vacuum of betrayal. Somber silence...

For a moment, nobody moved and nobody spoke. It was as if they were all in some emotional holding pattern. No one knew how to respond. Time stopped.

Then Mike pulled his car keys out of his pocket and handed them to Kelly. "Let's go." Kelly followed Mike, who had taken Rafael's hand and was walking him out of the bar. Danny nodded to Max and they wandered away through the crowd into the club. Jamie was left standing alone at the bar, perspiring with his overpriced drink and his gnashing jaw.

PART SIX

23

o o o

Bianca slammed her laptop computer closed and sucked hard on her cigarette. She squinted, steadying herself against the cafe table with a quivering arm, suddenly lightheaded. She had gotten a text that afternoon from a 'concerned' friend, directing her to the website where Nando's deterioration had been documented in high definition, for anyone who paid the thirty dollar monthly membership to *AndroFiles.com*. Bianca hadn't seen Nando for eight or nine months, but it was clear from the photos that he was not well. He had lost at least fifteen pounds. His face was too angular, almost skeletal, and his skin was pallid and acned. How had things gotten so bad so quickly?

She opened her laptop back up and clicked on her web browser to see the photos again. With any luck, none of her Park Slope neighbors would walk by and see her perusing gay porn on the patio of Southside Coffee. She clicked on 'Esteban' in her browser's memory. The site's tagline sizzled across the top of the screen: 'There's a first time for everything!'

Nando was clearly strung out...and someone had still paid him...*to do that?* She immediately considered that perhaps she had set a bad example, dancing in that strip club to put herself through cosmetology school years ago. Although she'd had enough sense to never do anything documented on film, maybe she had been *too effective* in justifying her sex industry work to her little brother. "It ain't nearly as humiliating as waiting tables and the pay is way better! It's just some easy money while I'm in school. No big deal!"

Now, for all she knew, her baby brother was holed up in some crack den back in Philadelphia. *Or worse...* She could feel her breath catching in her chest, as if she might hyperventilate or pass out. *Breathe...*

She pulled her phone out and dialed Nando's phone. Disconnected. *FUCK!*

Her hand started shaking and her bracelets clicked against the flimsy aluminum table like a ticking time bomb. She had to do something! She picked up her phone, sucked hard on her cigarette and dialed information. "Los Angeles? Yeah, I'm looking for a Paul Simms?"

o o o

Bianca tracked down Nando, strung out on heroin, in a seedy studio apartment in East Los Angeles. When she learned that her IATSE health insurance would cover most of his rehabilitation, she had hoped they'd be able to get him into a program back in New York. It turned out that *New Generations* in Scottsdale, Arizona was the only facility she could afford under her policy.

Life in Scottsdale wasn't nearly as miserable as she had expected. The rehab facility was nestled in the middle of a desert spa and resort Mecca, where a surprising number of intelligent, well-to-do people made a living selling and securing the wellness of others. Before spending those first couple days looking for short-term work, she'd had no idea that a fairly progressive community of freethinkers had settled among small-town Scottsdale's primarily conservative, rich, white population.

Even still, after spending three weeks and a good chunk of her savings finding him, she was ready to drop Nando off and get back to her own life. Her makeup artist gig on *CSI: New York* was fairly new and they weren't likely to hold her spot for much longer. On the day she was checking him in, he had collapsed and burst into tears and she saw under harsh florescent lights just how pathetic and broken her baby brother really was. She couldn't just leave him there and go back to the East Coast after seeing that.

Two days into his treatment, one of Nando's counselors suggested to Bianca that she get involved in a local Al-Anon program. Somehow, her sisterly devotion was seen as problematic to his recovery. She was going to 'keep being an enabler' if she continued to bail him out of every bad situation. She protested, "I haven't even seen him in a year! How could I be enabling him?"

"This isn't the first time he's been in trouble." The counselor glanced down at a folder and listed a number of previous occasions in which Bianca had come to his rescue.

She exhaled slowly, shaking her head, suddenly embarrassed. "It's not his fault our parents were fucked up. I have to be here for him. He doesn't have anybody else."

The counselor smiled and patted her hand and repeated, even more sternly, that she needed to get into an Al-Anon program. "Immediately." He handed her a small pamphlet with addresses and times. She stuffed the piece of paper into her oversized purse and strutted out of the office, pissed. As far as she was concerned, the man had just told her that it was her fault--that something about the way she loved her brother had caused him to become a drug addict. She lit a cigarette in the parking lot and broke down crying before she could even get to her rental car.

A woman who was in the lot saw her, walked over to her and put her arms around her. Bianca sobbed into the shoulder of some middle aged white woman she'd never met and for those few minutes, she thought she remembered what it was like to have a mother.

The woman's name was Alice. She worked at the rehab facility as a receptionist, but she sat down with Bianca under a tree and listened with the patience and concern of a loving family member. At the end of Bianca's story, Alice offered to take her to an Al-Anon meeting. Bianca accepted.

Standing outside the meeting hall of Bethany Lutheran Church, Alice introduced Bianca to a number of people walking in. Between forced smiles, Bianca sucked on her cigarette and shook their hands...still clutching tightly to her conviction that she had no business being there. Nando's mistakes were in spite of her, not because of her. She was only there as a favor to the woman who had allowed her to unload her stress.

When they finally went inside and sat down, Alice quietly explained that her youngest daughter, Laura, had gotten hooked on pills in the eleventh grade. Alice and her husband had been going through a complicated divorce. Their other daughter was in college when things fell apart at home, so at sixteen, Laura had been forced to bear the brunt of her mother's disillusionment alone.

Alice had blamed herself for the stress that had pushed Laura into her addiction and even though she had worked around recovery for years, she hadn't had the tools to process the difficult and delicate undertaking of supporting a loved one in their sobriety. That is, until she started going to Al-Anon meetings.

The whole time Alice was talking, Bianca couldn't help but feel like she was being recruited for a cult. There was something too preachy and self-realized about Alice's tone. She didn't even know Bianca or Nando and yet she seemed to think she knew what was best for them. Bianca wanted to leave, but she didn't. She stayed...out of respect for the woman. *One hour of this bullshit ain't gonna kill me.*

Half an hour into the meeting, another self-help obsessed middle-aged white lady stood up to share about her relationship with her alcoholic brother. Something about her face, her kind eyes and the calmness of her expression as she spoke about the ongoing process of learning to be supportive without putting up with bullshit, completely drew Bianca in. The woman loved her brother dearly and she was determined to support his wellness, even when it required her to feel like she was 'being a bitch.'

Bianca flashed back to the run-down two bedroom apartment her mother moved them into after their father disappeared. She was seventeen but Nando was only twelve or thirteen, a child barely through puberty, trying to be the man of the house. He usually slept on the couch, but when their mother started bringing men home, he would crawl into bed with Bianca, just to stay out of the way. Bianca missed the second half of her senior year of high school because she had to get a job and run things at home. She was so protective of Nando that she didn't even tested for her GED or go to junior college until he was done with junior high. But by the time he started ninth grade, she had to move out of that apartment. When her mother's boyfriends started hitting on her, Bianca knew it was just a matter of time before things got completely out of hand.

She moved in with friends nearby and visited Nando as much as she could before eventually moving to Chicago. But she had never been able to shake the feeling that if she hadn't abandoned him in that apartment, he might have been okay. Their mother eventually got a job and remarried and managed to pull it together, but Nando never seemed to recover...

Sitting in that room, looking closely at all those sad people under that unflattering lighting, Bianca's head flooded with 'what ifs' and 'should haves' and more resentment about having to cop to her own role in *somebody else's* addiction. Like she didn't have enough problems in her own life, she needed to take responsibility for someone else's. By the end of that meeting, she knew Al-Anon was not for her. She never went back.

o o o

Since completing rehab and moving with Bianca into her Brooklyn apartment, Nando had been arrested twice for heroin possession. The first time, he was so high he didn't understand what was happening. All he remembered was going to some hipster bar in Williamsburg and waking up in the jail cell. The second time, he had just copped and was on his way home to shoot-up when a plain clothes police officer pulled up and snatched him off the street. He'd been extremely paranoid ever since, assuming everyone--from the old Russian lady down the hall to the pimply faced kid working at the corner coffee shop--was undercover and on a stakeout to bust him.

When Bianca bailed him out of jail that second time, she told him in no uncertain terms, that it was her last time coming to his rescue. "If you use again, you're on your own. I can't do this shit anymore." Nando could see the sadness and exhaustion in her eyes and it broke his heart. He decided in that moment that he would never use again. He called on God to give him the strength to do right by his sister, the only person who ever stood by him. If he could make himself believe that his well-being was integral to Bianca's peace of mind, he would make it through. She deserved it. At last he was determined to do the work to save his own soul... He placed himself in God's hands.

Less than thirty-six hours later, he was sneaking out of the apartment with a wad of bills from the back of Bianca's underwear drawer, reminding himself of all the times God had let him down before. He was telling himself that God didn't care about him. God was selfish and cruel and if God had given a shit about him, He wouldn't have let his life fall apart in the first place. And if Bianca had given a shit about him, she wouldn't have left him in that apartment a decade before, helpless to watch as their mother lost her mind and her morals... Nobody gave a shit about him. Nobody understood the depth of his pain. The drugs were his only respite from the vicious world into which he had been abandoned. *Abandoned by everybody...*

As he scurried out of the subway station at Washington Square Park, looking over his shoulder every few seconds for plain clothes cops, he tried to convince himself that he didn't feel like a piece of shit for going out and looking to score drugs. He wanted to believe that it wasn't that big a deal and that everyone else was overreacting and that it was his life and his body and that he would be just fine and that this time was the last time anyway and that everyone just needed to *SHUT THE FUCK UP!* But the truth rang out too loudly, even in his jumbled head. The truth was that he hated himself for ever trying...ever wanting...ever *needing* the drugs. And the only way to quell those prickly jabs of self-hatred was to do more drugs. He was trapped and he knew it...and all he could do in the face of that helplessness was get high and hope to forget...

Having no idea how suspicious and unsavory he looked stalking about in his dark hoodie and his stained sweatpants, he crept up to the fountain in the park and waited. He hadn't copped in the park for a long time, but he knew he couldn't trust his dealer in Brooklyn anymore. Not after being arrested walking out of the dude's apartment. Of course, buying drugs in public, in plain daylight didn't make much sense either, but he wasn't thinking clearly.

He looked around for that dark-skinned dude with the gold tooth... *He used to have good stuff*...but he didn't seem to be around. A short Mexican-looking kid with sad eyes walked up and nodded at him. *Maybe?* But Nando could see, when the kid doubled back and nodded at him again, all jittery and desperate, that he was looking to cop too. They were both in need of a fix. Something about seeing that kid, sick with hunger, struck him as pathetic. *At least I don't look that bad...*

Nando stood up and walked back out onto Fourth Street. His fingers and his toes were itching like crazy and his back was cramping up into his neck. He tried to focus on the sunshine warming his face, tried to find peace in the frenetic energy of all the bodies bustling around him...but the corners of his mind were quickly growing dark with his need for sugar. He needed it right away. This wasn't a joke. He wasn't locked up in rehab where they could give him doses of methadone to wean him off slowly. No. His body was aching with a very real hunger. It was as if giant concrete blocks were stacking in his mind around the notion of getting high so that every other thought was blocked out, not accessible, not even visible. All he wanted, all he needed was a fix...badly.

Just then, he felt someone's eyes on him. He looked over his shoulder to the right and left and then straight ahead. He saw a uniformed policeman across the street, looking directly at him. Nando turned and rushed back toward the park, glancing back over his shoulder... The pig didn't seem to be looking at him anymore, but he kept walking anyway.

He was already halfway across the park when he practically walked right into a tall skinny white dude in long basketball shorts. "You all right, homie?" The guy's eyes sparkled with angel-like magnanimity. Nando shook his head, no.

"I got you, dawg." The guy smiled sweetly and nodded toward a grassy patch of shade behind a nearby tree. Nando's heart raced with his rejoicing...and his back immediately cramped up. His body's hunger was lashing out toward the promise of salvation's proximity, clutching violently at the sweet relief that was finally in sight. His legs went wobbly and his face went numb, but nothing could stop Nando from following the guy behind that tree.

Seconds later, Nando was watching the crumpled bills in his hands disappear without a trace, immediately replaced by six small packets of candy. Nando's brain was awash with the fuzzy heat of relief. He stuffed the candy down the front of his pants, into the crotch of his boxer briefs and then he turned to walk out of the park...

The sun seemed to be disappearing behind the buildings in front of him and the darkness of the city's shadow sent chills through his scrawny body. It was almost as if, even with the candy in his possession, he could feel that he was walking into the cold clutches of doom.

Shivering, he glanced back over his shoulder, ready to make a break for the C Train. When he turned back around, the uniformed policeman was headed straight for him. Nando twisted around without thinking and took off walking in the other direction...and he saw two more police officers walking towards him. *It's a setup!* They had him surrounded. He stopped where he was standing and prepped himself to take off running, but then his legs went wobbly again. He was trapped. He knew he couldn't outrun all three of them and if he was in jail, he wouldn't be able to get high. He needed it so badly, his body was giving out underneath him. He was so close, he could practically taste the warmth swimming through his veins!

The pigs were closing in. He reached into his underwear, pulled out all six baggies and popped them into his mouth. The first cop began running toward him and Nando started chewing on the baggies, trying to trick his body into believing it was eating so he could swallow. He gulped once and he could feel that most of the baggies were still stuck in his mouth. He swallowed again and that time, nothing went down. So he stuck his fingers into his mouth and pushed the remaining baggies down his throat--gagging, coughing, but swallowing. He could feel the edges of the plastic bags scrape against the lining of his esophagus, just as the officer...ran right past him to break up a fight between three kids near the dog run. He turned and watched the other cops trotting off toward the same fight. They hadn't even noticed Nando.

His rushed escape to the subway station was a blur... He remembered ducking behind some scaffolding and shoving the same dirty fingers into his mouth, trying to make himself throw up, to no avail. He remembered having a hard time summoning enough strength to push the turnstile once he was in the station. He remembered a beautiful teenage black girl with a baby in a stroller on the train looking up at his face and recoiling in horror. And then...

Nando was unconscious on the couch when Bianca found him. His clothes and his body were soaked with sweat and his face was so pale, he looked like he'd been dead for days. She could feel his heart still beating so she called 911. He woke up for a moment while they were loading him onto the ambulance and he saw Bianca crying on the sidewalk. He opened his mouth to say, "I'm sorry," but nothing came out.

A few hours later, he was in a coma. After six weeks of no brain activity, his doctors told Bianca that keeping his body alive would be solely for the benefit of his loved ones. Nando was not going to wake up. "You might let the family know it's time for them to say their goodbyes." She had called their mother and her new husband when Nando had first gone into rehab and neither of them had bothered to check up on him. Not once. So this time she didn't call anybody because as far as she was concerned, she was the only family he had left. She didn't even cry when she told the doctor to pull the plug. She just let him go. She finally let him go.

o o o

Danny continued dating Max for a couple weeks. Then, out of nowhere, Max stopped returning his calls. Even though he'd expected that the discovery of his brief modeling career might complicate things, he was really heartbroken about Max's disappearance. Danny found that he suffered from a rare disease--*rare* in that it was normally seen as limited to females of the species. Some overzealous endorphins or misfiring synapses in his mind tricked him into honestly believing that the sexual connection he and Max shared equated to a genuine *mutual* emotional attachment.

Danny's besottedness was merely a symptom of that physiological trickery designed to keep humans attracted to one another long enough to procreate. There was a time when women seemed to bear the burden of romantic devotion alone, with men only pretending to play along after the advent of the nuclear family. But somewhere in the evolution of the species, as females asserted more emotional independence, certain unfortunate males became directly afflicted with that misguided belief that sex, no matter how ephemeral or casual, amounted to love. Danny would go on to have his heart broken by a number of charming men before he finally learned that he needed to save his physical intimacy for a man who understood the gravity of his attachment.

Alcoholic mother notwithstanding, Danny opted to spend the rest of that winter alone, drunk at home. He just couldn't bear any more disappointment from loved ones.

o o o

Colin had signed a twelve month exclusive contract with Andro-Files. At the time, he took great pride in being added to Anderson's *stable*, even though the rush he'd gotten from being ogled and lusted over waned considerably once his videos had been posted. In the context of the scores of other boys also featured on the site, he realized his appeal wasn't so special anymore. He was just another cog in a larger machine.

He continued to work for a few months after his nineteenth birthday. He even shot a threesome scene with Ted and a new model--some married guy with kids and a mortgage. While Ted was fucking him, Colin kept telling himself over and over that he had no hard feelings about that night in the woods. *The universe takes care of everything...*

It was around that time that Danny moved out and into his own studio apartment because he 'wasn't comfortable' around the company Colin had started keeping. Colin tried not to take that personally either, but had a harder time reconciling that loss. It was like a piece of him had been sawed off or carved out and dragged away. He quickly began to unravel. Anytime he found himself faced with thoughts or memories too painful to process, he would just get fucked up to forget.

Weed and ecstasy worked for a while...but soon after he moved in with Ted and another model into a run-down one bedroom in San Diego, he found that rock cocaine--the medicine of choice in the house--was far more effective. Six months into his contract, he was so strung out that his file in Anderson's office was completely covered in red ink.

He started stripping in gay bars, but found it wasn't as lucrative as film work. His crack diet had slimmed him down so much that most men in bars looked at him in a way that just made him feel pathetic. He wasn't making enough money, gyrating uncomfortably to music he hated, to not take their pity personally.

San Diego was lousy with low-end porn production companies that would have been happy to hire him, but with his AndroFiles contract, he was afraid to work for any of them. When Anderson wouldn't return any of his phone calls, Colin took it personally. *What am I, disposable? That asshole can't just fuck with people's lives like this...*

Sometimes, while staring at his phone, he would flashback to that morning when Nando had walked into their hotel room, a stinking mess, complaining that Anderson wouldn't call him back. Colin vividly remembered thinking that Nando was a loser for letting things get so out of control. *And now...* It was as if the universe was taunting him. Whenever those karmic catcalls cried out, Colin would reach for his glass pipe in a rush to forget all the ways he'd let down the people who once cared for him...

o o o

The morning Danny called, Colin had been up for two days, trolling Encounters--San Diego's oldest gay hustler bar, high on crack. He almost burst into tears at the sound of his voice. It had been almost a year since Danny had moved out and they'd drifted apart. He was friendly as ever, joking and chuckling as if no time had passed at all. Colin felt his heart go weightless at the prospect of going back to the way things used to be.

"You know, I finally started working out. Joined a gym and everything. I'm not nearly as big as your X-Men Colossus-ass, but I'm not built like a girl scout anymore." Danny's smile sparkled through the phone.

Colin started to say, 'I'm not that big anymore,' but those words didn't come. Instead, he inhaled as deeply as he could. "Remember Ernie Watson? Remember how he always used to fuck with you after Mr. Shakoor's math class? Always callin' you names and shit? Well, the whole reason I... I started lifting weights so Ernie would see that your best friend was big enough to kick his ass so he'd leave you alone. And, like...he *did*." Colin's voice began to quiver. "Then when Nando beat up that dude at that party, it was like... I was your best friend. Looking after you was *my job*. I just... I felt like he ran in and took my spot, you know? Like after that night, we were never the same. I hate him for coming between us."

Danny cleared his throat, as if he'd been choking on some emotion. "...He never came between us. He died, Colin. He was in a coma for a couple months. Overdosed. I called to see if you wanted to go to his funeral in New York." *Silence...* Then, "We could hang out. I miss you, man."

Colin dropped the phone into his lap and whimpered into his hands. After all the times he'd wished Nando would *just fucking disappear,* he'd never expected that his passing would be the thing that brought Danny back into his life.

He pulled himself together and picked up the phone. "Can't go to New York... I'm like, totally broke. But maybe we can hang out when you get back?" Colin wiped the snot off the mouthpiece on his phone.

"Sounds good, man. I'll give you a call next weekend."

Colin hung up the phone and for the first time in a long time, pictured himself sober and sane and smiling side by side with his best friend. Just the thought of it gave him hope for the future...

o o o

Paul had met Danny while he and Max were dating for those few weeks. Max had been at the tail end of one of his slutty phases, bringing new guys home all the time because he was feeling so rejected after his boyfriend had 'blown him off.' He seemed to really like Danny, though. When Paul came back after Christmas and finally sat down to talk to Danny, he completely got it--from Max's side. Danny had an old soul--a wisdom that belied his youth and apparent inexperience. He came off so boyish and sexually aloof at the same time, he was really kind of irresistible.

However, he didn't quite understand what Danny saw in Max. Max was a sweetheart and certainly cute enough, but he had to be one the most shallow, superficial people Paul had ever known. Danny didn't seem at all versed in fashion or pop culture, so... *What the hell could he and Max have to talk about?* Unable to reconcile the apparent discrepancies in the pairing, Paul eventually dismissed Danny as just another trifling-twink-in-the-making.

When Max had his big breakdown and locked himself in his room for three weeks after hearing a rumor that his San Diego boyfriend had been murdered by a Mexican drug cartel, Paul assumed he'd never see Danny again...

Then, at Nando's funeral, Danny reintroduced himself. Paul had forgotten that he and Nando had been friends because at the point when he met Danny, Nando was not a welcome conversation topic. Until Nando's sister called him in a panic, Paul had gone out of his way to cut Nando completely out of his life. Months before, Paul had tried to get him help and Nando had assaulted him. Paul didn't understand the insanity of heroin withdrawals at the time and he'd made the mistake of taking Nando's very personal attacks personally. But as Danny said softly over the punch bowl at the repast following the service, "By that point, there was probably nothing left of the Nando you knew."

Paul shook his head, his dampened eyes locked on something in the distance, and quietly shared the story of the last day he spent with the 'Nando he knew...'

"Scooch over, yo," Nando mumbled half asleep from beneath the bouncing silhouette of wavy black hair standing straight up on his head. Paul quickly rolled toward the wall without a word and Nando slid under the sheets next to him. For two weeks, that had been the routine. Every morning at around a quarter to eight, the futon sofa in the living room would get flooded with so much sunlight that Nando would have to escape to Paul's bedroom and the forest green Ikea blackout curtains. Paul's full sized bed could have easily been 'too cozy' for another pair of young men, but these two didn't mind being close.

Nando's mother was single when they were kids and she 'liked her privacy,' so he ended up sleeping over at Paul's a lot. On a couple occasions, right before they started high school, late at night after Paul's parents had gone to sleep, Nando had nuzzled up against Paul and they had allowed their hands to rove... Even after those pubescent nights, flushed with racing heartbeats, sweaty necks and sticky fingers, they never had a problem falling asleep side by side.

That morning, however, Paul lay wide awake. Nando was going back to Philly on a redeye that night and it was their last day together in LA--literally the last day of summer vacation. In just over twenty-four hours, Paul would be back on the UCLA campus, dozing through his first class of the quarter and Nando would be back at his mother's house in Philly, resting for his security guard night shift. Childhood best friends thrust back into their new adult lives on opposite ends of the continent. All the secrets Paul had planned to share during Nando's two-week visit remained seared onto the roof of his mouth, while fingers frozen in fear of unrequited passion and the possibility of friendship lost clung to the top edge of the bed sheet. He knew Nando loved him. *They were boys!* To expect anything more was just inviting torture...

Nando rolled toward him onto his stomach with a grunt. Paul froze and watched Nando's nose wriggle against the cool fabric of the pillowcase in the dim light. Nando's lips were inches away from his. He was staring so closely at the neat patch of shiny black fuzz above Nando's soft pink lips that he hardly noticed his own face drifting closer, caught in the tractor beam of his manliness. Perhaps he was too aware of the blood rushing to his nether regions and the ensuing stiffness that had suddenly seized his entire being. Paul twisted is torso ever so slightly, slid his arm under the sheet and rested his wrist gently against Nando's naked knee. Then...

Lena knocked quietly on the door before slipping inside and sitting at the foot of the bed, clutching her Noah's Bagels coffee mug. Her strawberry blond hair (by L'Oréal) was pulled back in a scrunchy and her makeup had been stealthily applied to give the illusion of a clean face. Paul feigned just waking up, rubbing his eyes, stretching his arms. She smiled, shaking her head, "You guys are just too cute."

Lena was Paul's best friend in LA. She'd offered Paul the second room in her apartment before her previous roommate had even made plans to move out. They'd met the year before in a Poli-Sci discussion section and clicked right away. Their shared love of BBC America, In-N-Out Burgers, *30 Rock* and Stevie Wonder's entire 1970s songbook seemed to have bonded them for life. He got her dry sense of humor and respected her constant need to affirm her independence. She appreciated his occasionally grating fastidiousness and adored the 'Cindy Crawford mole' above his lip. And...she might have been a little in love with him.

What should have been a harmless crush may have gotten very complicated when he agreed to move in with her at the end of the last quarter. He'd been so desperate to avoid going home for the summer to witness his parents' messy divorce firsthand, he'd taken the room without considering the possible ramifications. Paul never explicitly told her that he was gay. He'd never spoken of his personal connection to the G word to anyone--not even himself. She never explicitly told anyone that she was in love with him either, but anyone outside the two of them could probably see it. Nineteen and twenty year-olds don't realize the way they wear all their emotions on their sleeves...

Paul stepped back into his room after his shower to find Nando still snoring quietly, face down in his bed. The sheets were pulled down below his frayed plaid boxers and wisps of black hair dusted the back of his thick muscular thighs. Paul sat down on the bed next to him and gently shook his shoulder. Nando breathed in deep, rolled backwards and looked up at Paul with a smile. "You smell good, yo."

Paul stood up, stuffing a clean towel into his denim tote bag. "You smell like Jack Daniels and ball sweat. Get in the shower so we can go. It's already after ten."

Nando sat up groggily and shook out his mad scientist hair. "Your bed is too comfortable, son. How do you ever get up on time?" Paul looked back over his shoulder, fixing his lips to make a joke about Nando's incessant, coma-inducing pot smoking, when Nando grabbed him by his waist and pulled him into the bed. Nando tickled him until Paul squirmed, giggling wildly, out of his arms with a thud onto the floor... Paul was still catching his breath when Nando stood up, slid out of his boxers and disappeared into the bathroom for his shower.

An hour later, the three of them lay on the beach, talking and laughing and filling the silence with loaded glances and winsome smiles. The sky was the most beautiful shade of blue that day and the blazing sun was tempered every so often by a cool, salted breeze off the ocean.

Lena, lying flat on her stomach, unfastened the back clasp of her bikini top and without a word, held up a tube of Neutrogena sun block for one of the boys to get her back. Nando obliged with a lascivious smile. Paul, knowing that the smile was solely for him, snorted uncomfortably at the display.

A Mexican family settled on the beach nearby and Lena started hissing obscenities about their wailing toddler. She reached over and turned up the volume on her iPod dock. The singer (sounded like Fink, one of Lena's favorites) kept insisting he'd be "right on the train, first one out of here, to take you out again." The song hit Paul in the put of his stomach. At that moment, he caught himself staring at he dimples in the small of Nando's back and suddenly felt suffocated by a thick sheen of shame. *What am I doing? He's my best friend!*

Paul strolled down to the water alone. Barely getting his feet wet, he walked along the shore, his eyes locked on the rippling ocean. He was imagining Nando's body rolling and crashing like a wave into his own when he heard the smack of rapid footfall against the wet sand just behind him. With one arm locked behind Paul's knees and the other around his back, Nando swept him up off the ground and ran giggling like a mad man into the water with Paul flailing in his slippery grip. Their wild laughter was so uninhibited, so REAL, that their voices squeaked with high pitched abandon and they sounded just as they did when they were teenagers... SPLASH!

Nando tossed Paul into a crashing wave and they tussled like twelve year olds in the water. Just as Paul had started to catch his breath and make his way to the shore, Nando tackled him again and they went under together, embracing like lovers falling through time...

Later, pretending to clean his sunglasses, Paul scrutinized his reflection in the lenses, trying to gauge how fuzzy his hair had gotten and wondering if it would have been too 'ghetto' to bring his wave cap to the beach. Of course, he hadn't planned on getting in the water, but when he finally dried off, it occurred to him that some cocoa butter for his legs and arms might have also been a good idea.

Lena was on her cell phone when Nando hopped up to head back towards the sandwich stand on the PCH. She didn't even notice he was gone until he came back ten minutes later and collapsed onto the blanket with a styrofoam cooler of cold Coronas. Paul noted that Nando's mocha skin had bronzed to a rich caramel since he'd been in LA. It suited him. The faint patch of black hair nestled in the middle of his firm, muscled chest was shiny with sweat. A memory of Nando's hairless, teenage chest splayed against the sheets of his childhood bed zipped across Paul's mind.

Nando held out a beer for Lena. "You do know it's illegal to have booze or bottles on the beach," she snickered and took the beer anyway.

"Well, let's see how much trouble we can get into. It's my last day here, yo!" Nando winked at Paul as he uncapped a bottle and handed it to him.

Paul took a swig and smiled at his best friend. Nando smiled back at him, but with a sadness that dampened his eyes and shortened his breath. Paul's heart started racing as an unspoken understanding passed between them. *If only...*

Lena sat up and glanced back at them smiling at each other. "You guys are just too cute." Nando shook his head and turned to stare at his toes wriggling in the sand.

The three of them sipped their beer and watched the water lap at the sand in front of them as the sun descended slowly on the last day of summer...

Nando's girlfriend Vida, who had met Paul during the failed intervention and then tracked him down when Nando later threatened to kill her, stepped up in her inappropriately revealing black dress to speak to Paul. She'd been moping around like the grieving widow, only to find that nobody had a clue who she was. Danny excused himself, dabbing at tears with his crumpled cocktail napkin.

When Paul got back to Los Angeles, he found a message from Danny on his work voicemail. Apparently Danny had found his contact information online.

He mentioned in the message that he had wanted to make sure they had an opportunity to stay in touch but feared it might have been in poor taste to ask for his number at the funeral. Paul smiled to himself as he scribbled down Danny's number. "Finally, a man with class..."

25

o o o

Sandy had just gotten sober again and moved into an apartment in West Hollywood when Anderson's house was burned to the ground. Nobody was hurt, but for a couple days, Sandy was a 'person of interest' in the investigation. He and Anderson were calling their separation temporary--mostly because Anderson hated the idea of getting a gay divorce when couples were no longer legally allowed a gay marriage. However, their separation was far from amicable. Toward the end, during his last sprint for 'rock bottom,' Sandy had gone off the grid for about ten days, getting high in a hotel room until he ran out of money. Anderson was confident that Sandy had burned the house down out of spite. Then, less than a week into the case, former AndroFiles model Marcus Ramsey (real name: Scott Greenwald) was charged with arson.

Late in the trial, Marcus explained on the stand through emotional tears that he'd become extremely depressed when he found out that he and three other AndroFiles models had turned up HIV positive from the "supposedly safe sex" they were having for the studio. He was simply "trying to stop [Anderson] from ruining anyone else's life." His testimony might have swayed the jury had the prosecution not brought to light the fact that *sex without condoms is never safe* and that Marcus was also having unprotected receptive sex with his wealthy, older, longtime 'roommate' during the time of his infection.

Anderson's very expensive insurance policy put him in escrow on a newer, bigger house in no time. However, during the few months it took to get the studio up and running again, California's Occupational Safety and Health Standards Board put into effect a law that required all adult film performers to use condoms on the job. Anderson became very vocal on the issue, claiming that his protests were based simply on principle. "Government has no business telling me or anybody how to have sex. As Americans, we pay taxes for the right to express and enjoy ourselves as we choose. FIRST AMENDMENT, people!" Of course, he was really only concerned about the money he was expecting to lose by having to play by the same rules as all the other the amateur gay porn sites.

While launching his so-called Free Speech campaign, he tracked down old site favorites and stayed busy recruiting new models; posting on Craig's List again and stationing cute girls around the University Town Center Mall to scout for hot boys. He had enough stockpiled videos that his 'three new scenes a week' schedule went uninterrupted.

Then, just two days before the first shoot in the new studio was scheduled to happen, Anderson disappeared. His housekeeper (former office assistant and talent scout) Jeff Billheimer reported him missing after going to pick up a paycheck and finding the front door unlocked with nobody home. According to Jeff, the only things missing from the house were two computer hard drives and the office HIV testing supplies.

Due to the recent arson case, police immediately suspected foul play. It wasn't until they found Anderson's 'company' pearl white BMW X5--completely intact and wiped clean of fingerprints--parked near the woods outside Balboa Park's bell tower, that the investigation really kicked into gear. Clearly, he hadn't just gone for a long walk...

Forensics found traces of blood, semen and saliva in the carpet of the X5's hatchback. The saliva had high concentrations of stomach acid, as well as traces of the chemical used on the swabs of OraQuick Rapid HIV tests, leading investigators to believe that *the victim* had been gagged with a number of the devices. The traces of semen and fecal matter in the blood all pointed to anal rape. But none of the suspects (disgruntled former AndroFiles models) or 'people of interest' (Jeff and Sandy among them) were a match for the blood samples. So while Anderson's body never turned up, it was assumed that he had been raped in the back of his own car, while gagged with a bundle of HIV tests, and that his body had been disposed of by someone who knew exactly what they were doing.

o o o

Sandy made a show of mourning for a while and then thrust himself headlong into West Hollywood's Gay Alcoholics Anonymous scene. There were hundreds of hot, upwardly mobile gay men in recovery in Los Angeles and Sandy, for the first time in his life, felt like he got to run with a pack. Part of his problem with sobriety had always been that it never *looked* quite as appealing as getting fucked up. Sober life was boring and stiff. The AA meetings in San Diego were so dismal, you were likely to be more suicidal and bent on self-destruction *after* attending. But WeHo's teetotalers had effectively twisted the tedium of recovery culture into a non-stop party. Being gay and sober did not have to mean being miserable and alone...

Within a month, he found a sponsor, got an entry level job at a PR firm and started going by Alessandro again. Changing his name back was his way of reclaiming his childhood from his father. The destructive self-loathing that had kept him emotionally withdrawn his whole life had to be traced back to someone and most of the trails he managed to unearth lead to his father. After *working the Steps*, Sandy decided he was ready to start making amends and ready to forgive his father for 'never truly accepting his son.' With each passing day, he told himself he was taking a little more of his life back and learning to be at peace with his past.

Within two months in Gay AA, Sandy started dating another 'newcomer' (one who is only recently sober), a twenty-six year old civil rights activist named Eli. Eli had flung open the closet doors early in high school. For Sandy, Eli represented a connection to the possibility of living one's life fearlessly, without the burden of society's hang ups on sex.

The reality that soon became apparent was that being out of the closet doesn't necessarily solve all of life's problems or simplify the challenges of being a gay man. While Eli certainly had his own issues to work through, he loved Sandy--flaws and all, and he was *in it* for the long haul. But before the end of the year, Sandy had 'outgrown the relationship' and decided he needed to be single again. "Sorry, I'm just not feeling it." Then, four months later, Sandy had fallen in love with somebody new. Eli was the first in a long line of young lovers who served as little more than personifications of a romantic ideal--mere props to convince Sandy that he *deserved* to be in love, despite his past.

The damage Sandy had sustained didn't heal as quickly as he'd hoped. There was something deep inside that, even after working the Steps, remained broken. He never fully got over his father's emotional abandonment. So at the first sign of a lover's waning interest, he would shut down. He would leave before they could leave him...and it all went back to his childhood and his father.

Sandy's mother died in childbirth, but Roberto never made a secret of his disinterest in his son. He even went so far as to coach a neighborhood boys' basketball team that Sandy was never invited to join. Sandy was already a teenager when Roberto remarried and started a new family, but watching his father fawn over his new children made him feel like that forsaken child all over again.

Without ever fully acknowledging that his fear of abandonment was what gave every one of his so-called love relationships a fixed shelf-life, Sandy quickly earned a reputation in Gay AA as a serial monogamist, falling in and out of love two or three times a year. His drug of choice became 'new romance,' and he was constantly chasing that incomparable rush of feeling completely loved and desired and accepted... And just like all his other distractions, it was a high that never lasted as long as he'd have liked.

26

o o o

Rafael completely lost his ability to pick up on people's energy. It was as if the heartbreak had fractured whatever part of his brain had facilitated his supernatural intuition. Without the escape of focusing all his energy on the sadness of others, he was forced to face his own very real depression.

He'd been so drunk the night he watched everything in his life fall apart that alcohol no longer offered the cleansing power it had in the past. Being inebriated had lost its appeal and for a while, he stopped drinking altogether. Consequently, he was left wide awake to confront the truth, and the truth--as he saw it--was that even the Beautiful and the Benevolent would not be spared the misery of loneliness. *Love is just the lie we all buy into to distract ourselves from the reality of how alone in the world we are.*

Rafael had been crashing at Mike's place since that night at Here Lounge. Sleeping on the ratty couch and living out of bags only compounded Rafael's deepening despondency. Having his tiny living room cluttered with Rafael's dismantled life started putting Mike on edge, too. So rather than allow the situation to put any more strain on their friendship, Mike suggested they find a new place together. By the time they had signed the lease on their new apartment, Rafael had really started seeing things in his life differently.

Moving into the two-bedroom in Silver Lake with his best friend as a sober, single man felt like a new beginning. He started his new life with a commitment to eating healthy. He cut his hair short and simplified his wardrobe. He started going to yoga classes in the mornings with Kelly. He rode his bike and wore his helmet everywhere he went. He even learned to ignore the sideways glances from his friends when he decided he would be just as open to seeing women as men when he finally started dating again. He began focusing on what it felt like to be his 'own man.'

Of course, with time, he settled back into being a twenty-seven year old. The organic diet didn't last more than a month or so and the yoga classes didn't work into his budget for much longer than that. But he kept his drinking to a minimum and he wore a helmet and a condom every time either was called for.

On those days when he missed Jamie, missed the sweetness of loving someone and feeling loved, he would snuggle up with Mike or Kelly on that ratty couch just long enough to remind himself how thankful he was and how much he loved his friends. And if he closed his eyes, sometimes he could feel the faintest swirl in his stomach that would let him know that they loved him too.

o o o

Kelly was on a date at the Grove with a man named Hakim when she ran into Jamie--about ten pounds too thin--walking out of the same movie theater, alone. He tapped her shoulder to say hello and was clearly surprised when she turned around with a bright smile, remembered his name and engaged him in pleasant small talk before he asked her to please send his best to Rafael. She could tell, just from their brief interaction, that he was still racked with guilt and regret about the way the relationship ended.

The next time she saw Rafael, she tortured herself about whether to tell him about 'the sighting.' In the end, she decided that Rafael's healing was better served without the reminders--without the temptation to look back. She knew too well that love, even bad love, could be as addictive and destructive as a drug. And who's to say any of it is ever worth the risk?

o o o

Jamie's next album was dedicated to Rafael. It was all sad love songs and apologies, acoustic and soulful. While *Missteps* didn't sell as well as his previous, more upbeat, *victim-driven* records, hardcore Sugar-Tank fans really appreciated his new emotional depth. It was like he had been reborn with a more profound sense of himself... Like the outer layers had finally been peeled away... Like he had found a new voice and was singing through all the dark complexity of heartbreak and still reaching for the light of love on the other side...

ACKNOWLEDGMENTS

A very special thanks to Mitchell Ivers for his invaluable assistance in shaping my collection of short stories into this novel. Many thanks to Sloane Hoepelman, Kevin Collins, Shay Moore, Lesley Covington and Karen Hunter for their feedback and encouragement. Big thanks to Rebecca Sanabria for the beautiful book cover. Giant thanks to Rory Arnold for all his support and business savvy. Huge thanks to my mother Janice for insisting that I speak English when all the other kids were talkin' smack. Love and thanks to all my close friends and family for keeping me sane and smiling through the madness--YOU KNOW WHO YOU ARE! Middle finger and thanks to all the ex-lovers who inspired me to examine the psychological sickness of men. And undying gratitude to all the *Noah's Arc* fans who remind me every day that life is a gift and the best gifts are those we get to share. Thank you all from the bottom of my heart.

Made in the USA
San Bernardino, CA
22 April 2013